"THRILLI
AND UTTE

[Glass] chillingly sets up the premise of a serial killer stalking Chicago women while meticulously preparing to turn the plot upside down halfway through. . . . *Eyes* recalls the early—the best— Patricia Cornwell novels. That is high praise."
—*Magazine* (Baton Rouge, LA)

"Susan Shader and David Gold are convincing sleuths, going about their grisly business with calm and logic."
—*The Orlando Sentinel*

"A vortex of heart-pounding suspense . . . It's always a special pleasure to see a new mystery writer who can combine the inventiveness of a clever plot with the grit of grisly crime. Few have done this as well lately as Joseph Glass in *Eyes*. . . . We can't wait for the next Susan Shader novel."
—*Arvada Community News*

"Susan is one of the best protagonists to surface in a long time because all of her relationships feel real and add to the humanization of the character. Especially intriguing is how her family reflects modern society as her six-year-old son lives with his father (her ex) in California."
—*The Midwest Book Review*

EYES

Joseph Glass

FAWCETT CREST • NEW YORK

This is a work of fiction. Names, characters, places, and incidents are the products of the author's imagination or are used fictitiously. Any resemblance to actual events, locales, or persons, living or dead, is entirely coincidental.

A Fawcett Crest Book
Published by The Ballantine Publishing Group
Copyright © 1997 by JSL Productions, Inc.

All rights reserved under International and Pan-American Copyright Conventions. Published in the United States by The Ballantine Publishing Group, a division of Random House, Inc., New York, and simultaneously in Canada by Random House of Canada Limited, Toronto.

Fawcett Crest and colophon are trademarks of The Ballantine Publishing Group, a division of Random House, Inc.

www.randomhouse.com/BB/

Library of Congress Catalog Card Number: 98-93420

ISBN 0-449-00512-7

This edition published by arrangement with Villard Books, a division of Random House, Inc. VILLARD BOOKS is a registered trademark of Random House, Inc.

Manufactured in the United States of America

First Ballantine Books Edition: February 1999

10 9 8 7 6 5 4 3 2 1

To the Chicago Police Department

The children left a trail of bread crumbs to help them find their way back. But the birds ate the bread crumbs while the children were deep in the forest, and so there was no trail to show them the way home.

—"Hansel and Gretel"

The killer always leaves a trail. There are two reasons for this. First, he is human and thus fallible. Second, and far more importantly, he cannot bear the thought of being completely alone.

—Sándor Ferenczi,
"The Criminal Mind"

Acknowledgments

I am indebted to David Rosenthal and Marysue Rucci of Villard Books for their invaluable editorial advice. I also owe a debt to Deborah Schneider, my agent, for expert counsel as well as belief and encouragement.

Special thanks to Donna Riddick for technical advice, and to Ernst H. Huneck, M.D., who equipped me to enter the mind of a character whose profession as a physician affects all her thoughts.

Finally, it has been said that Chicago is a state of mind as well as a place on the map. For this author, that state of mind is permanently linked with M. F. Basch (1929–1996). To his memory I and my heroine, Susan Shader, owe acknowledgment.

Prologue

CHICAGO, ILLINOIS
OCTOBER

FREEZING RAIN.

Pedestrians walking with both hands held out for balance. An old woman being helped to her feet at a bus stop after a fall. Michigan Avenue traffic moving in slow motion. A yellow cab sliding slowly sideways across a busy intersection, the driver turning the wheel madly.

Behind his window sixteen stories above the street, Peter Tomerakian laughed. He took a childish pleasure in the weather's ability to reduce busy city dwellers to silent-movie pratfalls. He also enjoyed the rain itself, dripping icily down the windows. It reminded him of his boyhood, when he and his friends used to pull icicles three feet long from the eaves of their houses and have mock sword fights with them.

Peter Tomerakian had never really grown up, though he was a consultant to the law-enforcement community on one of the biggest investigations undertaken in a generation. He still saw the world as a sort of cartoon, not to be taken seriously but rather to be enjoyed from a safe distance, with plenty of popcorn and candy at hand. Luckily for him, he had found a profession that allowed him to achieve success without having to play the adult game by the rules.

He turned back to the suite. The hotel furniture had all been removed, except for the king-sized bed, which he

1

smiled at now. There were numerous file cabinets, most of which he had not opened in weeks. PCs were on computer desks here and there, and the IBM 9200, the monster, was against the inner wall. Modems were everywhere, for information that was constantly coming in from government agencies, research foundations, and police departments. There were scanners, of course, to take in the fax pages, and one large copying machine.

Peter enjoyed being connected to so many people, serious people who were doing their jobs and depending on him. Most of all, he enjoyed the contrast between their seriousness and his own playfulness. They were bores, limited by their bourgeois mind-set as much as by their lack of intelligence. He could help them without having to be one of them. He remained as free as a bird.

On the walls were corkboards with photos of some of the targets. Caldwell, Reda, Reimann, Waxman, and of course Haze. Corporate criminals of the highest order. Just for fun Peter had drawn mustaches on some of the pictures, or added humorous sayings in cartoon bubbles. The fellows from the Justice Department thought this was childish, but Peter told them he needed a light touch to keep his concentration. After all, it was up to him to make the case against them. He could do anything he wanted.

In spite of his contempt for the prosecutors, he felt proud of his work. When this investigation was finished and the indictments went out, it would be as big as Watergate. Men worth hundreds of millions of dollars would be put behind bars. The whole world would know about Peter Tomerakian. He would be a hero.

He thought of his old friends from school, who were all mere programmers or computer salesmen now. None of them had ever dreamed of coming this far.

He stretched and yawned. He was beginning to get hungry. He had been working all morning, and had forgotten to eat anything. Come to think of it, he had been losing his appetite lately. His shirts fit more loosely, and he had had to take in his belt a notch. No doubt it was bad for his health, being cooped up here.

He picked up the phone. "Hello?"

"Yes, sir." It was Dalton, a member of the "palace guard" who had the unenviable task of guarding Peter's suite and seeing to his needs.

"Dalton, would you get me my usual?" Peter asked.

"What do you want to drink?"

"Diet Pepsi. No, wait. Diet Coke." Peter started to hang up the phone, then changed his mind. "Wait. Dalton, are you there?"

"Yes, sir." The voice was humorless, as always.

"Make that a Dr Pepper. No—a Diet Dr Pepper."

"Diet Dr Pepper. Okay, sir." With palpable impatience Dalton hung up.

Peter sat down at the PC nearest the window and opened the computer game he had invented, Dream Girls of Kuntu. It was a masterpiece of interaction, embodying rules as challenging as those of championship chess. He had done all the programming himself. The artwork was being done by an old friend from the Silicon Valley days named Jason. Peter planned to market it worldwide, but the software people complained that much of it was overtly pornographic. This did not faze Peter. There were plenty of ways to get a system out to users. The main commercial channels were basically for fools anyway.

He looked at Jason's rendering of the Queen of the Snakes. Big in the breasts, long of limb, steely-eyed, the way Peter had envisioned her from the outset. The sight of her lush body took his mind off his hunger. After a moment he turned away from the computer and looked out the window.

Cynthia would be here in an hour, as soon as the corridor watch changed for the afternoon shift. She had promised to wear nothing under her coat. Peter smiled to think of her slipping through the freezing rain, those gorgeous legs trembling as the cold air flowed along her naked thighs. He would have to warm her up. He would hold her close and rub her all over. Perhaps he would lie down with her on the bed, without even taking her coat off.

Life had become immeasurably more interesting since Cynthia came along. He had met her in a movie house where a revival of *The Lickerish Quartet* was being shown. He ran into her at the candy counter, and they struck up a conversation about filmmakers. She seemed a bit embarrassed to be caught seeing porno alone, but Peter assured her that some of the best films made in the last generation were porno. *Lickerish* was, in his opinion, a masterpiece, more profound than *Rashomon*.

It had been difficult to keep his cool, talking with her those first moments. She was incredibly attractive. Tall, with wispy hair and liquid eyes. Straight shoulders, slim arms, and long, delicate fingers. She was wearing jeans, and it was easy to see that her long legs led to a rich, sensual pelvis. She was young and innocent, but she had a dirty mind. That was a combination hard to resist.

They sat together through the movie, and by its end he was holding hands with her. He couldn't take her back to the hotel that day because he knew the guards would hassle her. She took him home with her, to a small apartment on the North Side. They made love slowly, beautifully, three times. Her naked body was everything the tight jeans had promised. She was an inventive lover, and she smelled as sweet as the spring mornings of his youth. Peter had never done terribly well with girls in the past— he was too much of a nerd to know how to charm them— but Cynthia seemed to know how to put him at his ease. Impotence, his old nemesis, was not a problem. She made him feel like a tiger.

He told her what he could about his work. He didn't get into the technical end, because she said she was a computer idiot. But he bragged a little about all the Justice Department people who were hanging on his every word, and the big shots he was going to put behind bars when the investigation was complete. Cynthia was impressed. He swore her to secrecy, of course. That seemed to excite her even more.

After that he took it as a challenge to get her into the hotel room. He got to know the guards, whom he had snubbed up to now. He joked with them about their jobs, their families. One of them, a Justice guy named Bob, was a good sport and understood about Peter's need for occasional entertainment. With Bob's help Peter found out that he could get a woman into the room at noon and keep her all afternoon. Nights were still a problem, but that could perhaps be worked out in the future.

Cynthia worked four days a week in the Loop, but Thursdays she was free all afternoon. Peter had smuggled her in for the first time last month, and they'd had an amazing time. She had brought a video of a Polish porno film about the conquistadores in Mexico. They both got off on it. He was getting used to her mind now, as well as her body. There was no limit to what they might experience together. He almost gave up working on Dream Girls of Kuntu. All his spare time he spent thinking about Cynthia.

Lunch arrived on schedule. Two Whoppers, the Dr Pepper, and a box of peanut butter cookies. Peter ate quickly. Then he went back to work for a while, just to pass the time. A lot of documentation had come in last night on the blind trust that had been set up in Geneva to launder money for some of the big shots under investigation.

It was a clever piece of work, Peter reflected. The accounting was very subtle. The drug connection was so tenuous that no one but Peter Tomerakian could have even seen it, much less proved it.

Arnold Haze was behind the scheme. Peter was sure of that. It all bore Haze's signature. The inspired mathematics, the attention to detail, the scrupulous bribes to officials who were in a position to help. Haze was a genius of sorts. His operations bore his own unique stamp, like a Capablanca chess game or a set of variations by Beethoven. Haze had an elegant mind. If he had wanted to, he could have made his fortune in computers. But he came from an earlier era. In any case, pursuing him was a privilege. Catching him would be a triumph.

Peter concentrated as long as he could, then closed up the file. He lay down on the bed and watched the freezing rain drip down the windows. The afternoon was incredibly dark, almost like dusk. That gave a romantic air to his anticipation. He had a slight stomachache, but it did not attenuate his desire.

He was half asleep, lulled by his fantasies of Cynthia, when the knock came at the door. It was her code, three short taps followed by two more.

Peter got up and opened the door. A small man stood in the corridor, smiling. He wore the uniform of a bellman.

"Mr. Tomerakian?" he said.

"Yes." Peter gave him an irritable look.

"The young lady gave me a message for you," the man said. "She asked me to wait for an answer." He handed Peter a folded piece of notepaper.

"Hang on a minute." Peter closed the door and opened the note. The darkness of the afternoon combined with his weak eyes to make it impossible to read. He took it to the desk by the window and turned on the light.

Peter, dear, I'm trying to . . .

He recognized Cynthia's handwriting easily. But the note appeared to have been written in haste. He had trouble making out the words.

His hand was trembling slightly, for he could feel her body and her smile behind the characters on the page. *Peter, dear . . .* He started over.

"Do you know who I am?" a voice asked behind him.

Peter whirled to see the bellman standing inside the room. He had taken off his cap, and his gray hair shone in the half-light above a pale face with tiny black eyes.

Peter smiled, crumpling the note in his hand. "So," he said. "The mountain comes to Mohammed. Glad to meet you, Mr. Haze."

"You're a hard man to see." The little man returned his smile. "Look at all the trouble I had to go to."

"They take good care of me here," Peter said. "To tell you the truth, they don't think I'm grown-up enough to take care of myself."

He was not afraid. He felt as though he had known Arnold Haze for years. He knew his mind, knew his inspiration. He was not really surprised that Haze had sensed the danger and come himself.

"I presume you want to talk deal," Peter said.

"Indeed," the other man said. "I didn't think it would ever come to this. I underestimated you, to be honest."

"A lot of people have done that." Peter felt he could afford a certain arrogance, under the circumstances. After all, Haze had baffled the authorities for twenty-five years. They hadn't come close to an indictment in all that time, though the extent of his criminal activities was common knowledge. It had taken Peter Tomerakian's wit and cunning to weave a web so strong that not even Haze could escape it.

"I've learned my lesson, at all events," Haze said. "By the way, I admire your methods. You're very original."

"The feeling is mutual," Peter said. "You're quite a celebrity around here, in case you didn't know it."

"Oh, I know it." Haze was looking at the photo of himself on the wall. "Where did you get that?" he asked.

Peter shrugged. "One of the prosecutors found it somewhere," he said. "Not a very good likeness, is it?"

"Still, it worries me never to have seen it before," Haze said. "I thought I knew them all." He moved closer to the corkboard and peered at the photo. "I had my other eyes in that day."

"Contacts?" Peter smiled.

Haze nodded. "I could keep them in for days at a time without discomfort. Amazing, really. They were designed for me by a man in Buenos Aires. A brilliant fellow. He later patented it, the rascal. I never saw a penny." He shrugged. "But that's how it goes."

Peter went to look at the picture. "I can see the hair isn't right either."

"Oh, hair." Haze shrugged. "That's a mediocre commodity."

A peculiar smell came to Peter's nostrils as he stood next to the little man. He sniffed at the air. "Odd . . ."

"The result of an illness," Haze said. "I'm sorry."

"Doesn't bother me," Peter said offhandedly. "They didn't put it in the file, though."

"They're not going to, either."

A hand had stolen around Peter's waist. The touch was affectionate. In that instant Peter suspected Haze wanted to embrace him. The idea wasn't entirely absurd. After all, their long cat-and-mouse game had created a bond, a sort of intimacy.

But the arm around his waist pushed him forward, against the wall. Before he could recover his balance, Haze's other hand closed around his neck.

Peter did not think to fear Haze physically. Peter was a healthy man of thirty-two, over six feet tall. Haze was tiny, sickly-looking, and well into middle age.

But the grip of the hand around his neck was extraordinary. Peter felt paralyzed by it. His face was flattened against the photograph on the wall. He felt a sharp blow to his side. He slumped toward the floor.

He groaned and reached for his cracked ribs. A noose was slipped over his head and tightened.

"You can't," he gasped, trying to turn around. "I'm the only one who can save you."

"Not true," came Haze's whisper. "You're the only one who can *catch* me."

Peter's hands flailed for the little man's face. He scratched and clawed like a child, his body jerking this way and that. He could not believe that this long, subtle contest was to end in the crudeness of physical violence. Five minutes ago he had felt invulnerable.

"I'll deal," he gasped. "I tell you, I'll deal!"

"No, thank you." Those were the last words Peter Tomerakian heard. The noose tightened suddenly. Blood inundated his eyes. The image of Cynthia rose before his mind, and he followed it into oblivion.

PART ONE

1

FIVE MONTHS LATER

IT WAS SIX A.M. Dr. Susan Shader lay in the heavy silence of her last moments of sleep. Her eyelids fluttered as dreams bore her toward awakening.

In her dream she was small again. A little boy was in the window making faces at her. He had his hands over his eyes, peeping mischievously through the gaps in his fingers. Behind him a bird flew suddenly up into the sky.

The colors around him were unnaturally bright, as though sky and trees and soaring bird were created for the first time. Too bright, Susan thought. The sun was exploding; this was the end of the world.

She tried to call out a warning to him, but her lips wouldn't move. She made a signal with her hands, but he didn't see it because he was hiding his eyes. The house was already trembling; wisps of smoke were coming from cushions and curtains and even the pillow under her head. Now a haze was outside the window, darkening the sky. There was no time left.

Susan awoke with her hand already reaching for the alarm clock. The dream flew from her mind as she saw the time. She turned off the alarm and sat up. The distant gurgle of the coffeemaker in the kitchen comforted her. She took one look at the empty bed, sighed, and got up to take a shower.

She was a morning person. The habit had begun when she was in medical school and never left her. Nowadays she found herself getting heavy-eyed by ten, and she was almost never able to sleep past six. She remembered with some nostalgia her college years as a night owl, but she enjoyed the silence of the early morning, the peace of the world poised to spring into its routines of action.

She turned the water very hot as she washed herself, then very cold for a bracing moment before she turned it off. She shivered as she brought the towel to her face. She caught a glimpse of herself in the mirror as the steam cleared. Fair skin, slim shoulders, breasts still pink from the hot shower. A woman's body that had not known the caress of a man in a long time. Sighing again, she put on her terry cloth robe and headed for the kitchen.

She was dressed for work and finishing her third cup of coffee when the phone rang.

"Hello?" She balanced the receiver against her shoulder as she turned another page of the *Chicago Tribune*.

"Susan? This is Gold. We need you this morning. Are you booked?"

"Not really. I can reschedule. What's up?"

"A girl murdered in her apartment near the Circle Campus. A coed. An athlete. I haven't been over there yet, but Garner tells me the MO matches the two girls this winter."

"I'm sorry to hear that, David."

"You want me to pick you up?"

"No. I'll meet you."

He gave her the address.

"Okay," she said. "Give me half an hour?"

"I may need more than that. Thanks."

Susan hung up the phone and sat for a moment looking out her window at the gathering winter light. If what Gold had said was true, she would not be wanting any breakfast this morning.

A FROZEN RAIN was falling when she arrived. Chicago PD black-and-whites vied with unmarked cars for space in front of the apartment building. Gold was talking to a uniformed officer and the other detectives. He turned to greet her. Then they both went upstairs.

Sirk, of the State's Attorney's Office, was stalking around with a clipboard, an unlit cigarette in his mouth.

"Where is Able Weathers?" Gold asked.

"He'll be here." Weathers was the State's Attorney.

"Tell the press to stand by," Gold said wryly.

"They already know."

Abel Weathers—the "Able" spelling was not a compliment—liked publicity even under the worst of conditions. He was up for reelection next year and would not fail to make the most of this crime scene.

Sirk nodded toward the interior of the apartment.

"In the bathroom."

The corpse was in the tub. One look at it left no doubt that it had been the same killer. The eyeless sockets gaped emptily at the bare walls. The hands were outside the tub, giving the body an uncanny, reclining look.

"Is everything the same?" Susan asked Sirk.

"Eyes gouged out."

"Postmortem?" Susan asked.

"Sure. She was strangled in the bed, to judge by the appearance of the sheets. Everything else was done in here."

Gold had taken a step toward the bathroom sink. There was a smear of blood on the medicine cabinet mirror. Blood was also on the sink and fixtures.

"Okay," Gold said. "It's our man."

Sirk nodded. "He waited two months this time." The previous two homicides had taken place within a month of each other. Until this morning the authorities had been hoping the crime spree was over. Perhaps, they thought, the killer had died, or moved away. No such luck.

Gold gestured to Susan. "Want a closer look?"

"Thanks." She stood before the mirror looking at the blood. The sameness of the MO was almost scientific, as though staged for the benefit of those who would find the body. This in itself was not unusual. Most serial killers stage part or all of their scenes. But there was a simplicity about this—the eyes missing, the blood on the sink in front of the bathroom mirror—that sent a chill down her spine.

"Was she raped?" she asked almost hopefully.

Sirk shook his head.

This was another significant point. Few serial killers can resist tampering sexually with their victims in one way or another. Susan was convinced that these killings were sexual in their motivation. But the three victims were unmolested. Except for their eyes, which were gouged out, snipped off with some sort of blade or scissors, and taken away by the killer.

"Her name is Patsy Morgenstern," Gold was saying. "She's a varsity volleyball player at the university. Athletic scholarship."

Susan was looking more closely at the body.

"She's had surgery," she said.

"Anterior cruciate ligament," Gold said. "The parents have already been notified. The father told us about the operation over the phone. It almost ended her athletic career, but she came back this year." He pursed his lips. "She must have worked very hard. A twenty-year-old girl . . ."

He gestured around the small apartment, which bore posters equally divided between rock groups and European mountain scenes. "Her roommate was away for the weekend."

"Another athlete?" Susan asked the question a bit too quickly. If the roommate was an athlete, her absence might have saved her life. This killer would hardly have shrunk from a double homicide.

Gold shook his head. "No. She's a French major. Her name is Stephanie Mertz." He glanced at the walls. "I guess she's the one who put up the European posters. She spent the weekend with her parents down in Bloomington. I have a man talking to them now. She'll talk to us this afternoon. I don't want her coming back here until we get all this cleaned up."

Susan nodded. "Does she have a boyfriend?"

"Which one? The victim?"

"Yes." Susan had meant the roommate, but the question had to be asked about the victim.

"No boyfriend."

Somehow this question made Susan look again at the corpse. The upraised knees extended well above the top of the tub.

"How tall is she?" she asked.

"Six-two in her stocking feet," Gold said, looking at his notes. "You can't tell that very well from this posture." He glanced at Susan. "Why do you ask?"

"No boyfriend," Susan said. "Tall girls sometimes have a problem attracting the opposite sex."

Again Susan's nerves tingled with sadness and outrage. A young, strong girl, strong enough to fight her way back from serious knee surgery. Strong enough to fight her way through a world where tall girls were not the first to be called for dates. But not strong enough to defend herself against a murderer.

Susan searched her memory. The first two victims had been athletes as well. Both were basketball players. But neither was anywhere near this tall.

"So it isn't tall girls he seeks out," she said.

"Nope." Gold was looking at his notes. "Cheryl Glaser, the first victim, was only five-six. Jennifer Haas, the second, was five-ten."

"Athletes," Susan murmured.

"Goddamn it," Gold said. "How did he get in here, anyway?"

Susan almost smiled. Every time Gold went to a crime scene, he expressed surprise and dismay. He behaved as though he believed in a sane world, a world where violence was a senseless exception rather than the rule. The daily routine of mayhem that made up his job never changed his attitude. It might have been an act, but he would never admit to that. This was one reason Susan liked him.

Sirk had heard Gold's question.

"Through the door. She let him in."

Susan nodded. This had been the case with the first two victims.

"Either she knew him," Gold said, "or he's a smooth talker."

This had been a point discussed after the first two killings, and now it was obviously central to the investigation. All three girls had let the killer into their apartments. It was impossible to avoid the speculation that they knew their killer.

"At least it was quick," Gold remarked.

"Hardly a struggle," Sirk said. "Fractured hyoid. The boy has strong hands. She probably lasted twenty or thirty seconds before she blacked out."

But there must have been an interval of terror as the girl realized she was in danger. And rising panic when he told her to go into the bedroom. Susan felt her heart beat faster as she thought of the girl's last moments of life.

The police photographer had finished his work, and the fingerprint and trace specialists were on their hands and knees in the bedroom, placing tags as they worked.

Gold looked at Sirk. "Okay if Susan has a look around?" he asked.

"Sure." Sirk nodded with a sour look that did not seem natural to him. "Just don't touch anything we have tagged."

Gold accompanied Susan to the bedroom. There was a bookcase along the wall, made of bricks and boards, with textbooks from various subjects, including organic chemistry, microbiology, and anatomy.

"She was majoring in sports medicine?" Susan asked.

Gold nodded. "She intended to teach PE in college and do sports medicine on the side. Her grades weren't the best, but she worked hard."

There was a scattering of romance novels and a small stack of *People* magazines. On the top shelf of the bookcase were photographs of the victim's parents, a brother, and a sister. Prominently displayed was a picture of the two sisters in matching varsity letter sweatshirts, pointing at each other mockingly.

"Twin sister?" Susan asked, reflecting grimly that she could not tell, given the corpse's lack of eyes.

"No. The one in the picture is a year younger. Patsy was the oldest child."

The victim in the picture looked tall, with curly auburn hair. There was confidence in her eyes. She was standing behind her father and mother at some sort of family gathering. One could almost guess that she was an important member of the family, a leader. She was not pretty in a feature-by-feature sense, but there was energy in her face, and youth. She was probably far more attractive than she realized.

The father was a handsome man, in a rugged, countrified way. Susan guessed from the photograph that it was he who brought the genes for tallness to the family. His wife was shorter and somewhat overweight. She looked diffident and a trifle abashed.

"How much have you told the family?" she asked Gold.

"Only that she's dead," he replied. "They're on their way up. The social worker and I will talk to them this afternoon."

Susan shook her head. Her years of experience with violent crime had not armed her against painful empathy with the families of victims. Every mother worries when she sends her daughter off to college. It is difficult to hear a phone ring when your child is out in the world on her own. Today Mrs. Morgenstern had received the nightmare call she had probably been dreading for two years.

There was a large and very old teddy bear on the bed. Underneath the pillow Susan saw something folded.

"What is that?" she asked.

"Baby blanket." Gold's face betrayed his disgust at the destruction of a creature young enough to still cling to a remnant of earliest childhood.

In the cramped closet there was a small collection of clothes. Slacks and jeans, mostly, a couple of skirts that looked like they hadn't been worn much, a few blouses. A dozen or so T-shirts were folded on the shelf, and some sweatshirts with university logos hung on hangers. Several workout suits. Running shoes and loafers sat alongside a single pair of dress shoes. Flats, Susan noticed. The victim must have shunned high-heeled shoes ever since her height became an issue in her life.

Susan ran a hand gently along several of the garments. Then she said to Gold, "Can I sit on the bed?"

"Go ahead."

Few things were more helpful than sitting on the bed of a person whose thoughts one wanted to know, Susan had found over the years. The bed was not only the scene of a person's nocturnal dreams, and of his or her sexuality. It was the place where serious problems were pondered, where anxieties bloomed in the dark of night after having lain dormant throughout the busy day.

Susan ran the back of her hand over the pillow, along the mattress to the foot of the bed. Then she touched the baby blanket. Her hand stopped. Her eyes closed.

Sleepy.

"There is a man," she said. "Older. Someone she admires. Maybe a professor. She fantasizes about him every night. It's more than—it's not just sex. She's carrying a torch for him. She once asked . . ." Susan passed a hand over her brow. "No, I've lost that."

Sleepy. Grumpy.

She kept her hand inside the baby blanket. "It's because he's so much older. That's why she chose him, and why she can't have him. He's—he's an athlete himself. Or was. There is an injury. Yes, he's injured. Not the knee, like her. The back, I think."

"Was he here?" Gold asked, looking down at her.

She shook her head. "He's never seen this apartment."

She looked at the phone by the bed. It was covered with fingerprinting dust.

"She's called his number on that phone at least a hundred times," she said. "He has an answering machine. She hangs up when it picks up. When she hears his voice." She thought for a moment. "Two, nine, something. Something with two and nine. His number."

"Who is he?" Gold asked.

Susan shook her head. "I don't know. Maybe a professor." Her brow furrowed. "And something else . . ."

Gold waited patiently.

Grumpy. Bashful. Which dwarf are you today?

Susan tried to clear her mind to give the thought entry. But it held back. Perhaps, she mused, because the girl, Patsy Morgenstern, had herself fought it, resisted it.

"She wanted to have his baby," Susan said at last. Her breath was coming short. She felt exhausted. Her mouth was dry.

"And it wasn't him who came to the door," Gold suggested.

Susan shook her head. "I don't think so. He's so important to her thoughts, I think I'd know if he was the one who came. But I can't see anything now."

"Shall we go into the other room?"

Gold helped Susan to her feet. They went into the small living room, where there was a TV and an old VCR. There was a very small collection of videotapes, most of them blanks that the two roommates had used to record Ricki Lake, Oprah, and *All My Children*. There were also a few commercial, prerecorded videos, including *Moonstruck*, *Sleepless in Seattle*, *Enchanted April*, and *A Room with a View*.

"She's a romantic," Gold said. "Those are pretty much romantic movies, aren't they?"

"Yes, they are."

Susan lightly touched the VCR with the backs of her fingers.

"Pornography," she said. "They got some tapes from an X-rated video store. They watched together. Later she looked at one of the tapes on her own. It showed—no, I can't tell. Possibly two women. I'm not sure."

Gold was nodding. "With the roommate?"

"No," Susan said. "They're straight, both of them. I feel sure of it."

She looked around the living room, the afghan on the battered couch, the prints on the walls. Then she accompanied Gold to the kitchen, where the usual collegiate disarray reigned. The cupboards were filled with canned food, and there were a few frozen dinners in the small freezer. Boxes of granola bars and other health foods testified to Patsy's concern about her weight and her desire to stay in shape. But scattered paper napkins and leftover paper cups suggested regular visits to Arby's, McDonald's, and Burger King.

"I'm not getting anything at all," Susan said. "I may be finished."

"What about the man?" Gold asked.

Susan shook her head. "She thought about him when she came into the kitchen to get food," she said. "She worried about her looks, a great deal. She felt clumsy, oversized. She didn't feel feminine. This tormented her when she thought about him. The two thoughts go hand in hand. Her desire to please him, to be pretty for him—and her conviction that she was not pretty. That she could never be pretty for anyone."

Her face fell. She touched her temples. She looked drawn. "That's all," she said. "I've got to sit down."

"Take a moment," Gold said. "I want to talk to Sirk."

She sat on one of the kitchen chairs while he stood in the foyer talking to Sirk and one of the detectives. She took deep breaths. She began to feel stronger. She opened her eyes and looked around the apartment. One thing was clear: Patsy Morgenstern was a healthy, normal girl. There was no sign here of the secret, festering anguish of mental illness, or of deep sexual disturbance. Only the painful self-doubt, the shame at one's physical blemishes, which was so normal at that age, but magnified in Patsy's case by her height and her athletic life.

"Okay," Gold said, returning. "Let's go."

Susan accompanied him downstairs.

"Thanks, Susan." He squeezed her arm lightly. Courtly as ever, Susan thought. But the look in his eyes was angry. He was personally offended by what he had seen. Three girls destroyed at the threshold of their lives. Gold had two young daughters. He avoided pontificating about the dangers girls faced in the world, but Susan knew it preyed on his mind. Before many years had passed, his daughters would be on their own in college apartments.

She turned to give him a last look. He was taking the radio from a uniformed cop standing beside his unmarked car. Gold was a tall man, over six feet. He always looked out of place among the other detectives. Susan was not sure why, though she had noticed this from her earliest times with him. It was not so much that he looked like something else—a lawyer, for instance, or a businessman— as that he did not look like what he was. Detectives have a recognizable posture, a cool and somewhat empty demeanor that reflects the contradiction between their confidence in their own skill and their hopelessness about human nature. Gold looked a bit too vulnerable, a bit too concerned. He believed in a brighter world than his colleagues, and he was disappointed when this one let him down. For this, also, Susan had always liked him.

He gave her a brief, preoccupied wave as she left the scene.

2

SUSAN'S APARTMENT WAS large and well-situated, with a fine view of the lake and of the North Loop. It was the view that had made her decide to take the place. The city's skyscrapers seemed to march in quickstep toward the shore and then to halt disappointedly at the water's edge. On fine days, which were not very frequent, the sun gleamed down on shiny buildings and blue-green water like a cymbal accenting a melody with a golden crash. It was a beautiful, dramatic view, perhaps worth most of the exorbitant rent Susan shared with her roommate.

Inside, the apartment had a schizoid look, at once comfortable and disorganized. It looked like a place where someone had come to rest in a hurry and never completely unpacked.

This was because after her divorce Susan had moved to Chicago suddenly and had to find a place in a hurry. She remembered Lincoln Park from her days as a resident at Northwestern. An energetic realtor had shown Susan the apartment the day after her arrival. Susan had signed the lease the same day she moved into her office at 30 North Michigan.

She had settled in, put a few old pictures on the walls, bought some furniture, but had done almost no decorating. As a result the place looked a bit like a warehouse. Makeshift bookcases had been stuck in unlikely places and filled hurriedly with books that had now gathered dust.

A large oak table in one corner was littered with professional journals in psychiatry, psychology, criminology, and forensic science. Cardboard boxes along the wall contained journal numbers Susan had decided to save but had not found a place for. It was safe to assume, after five years, that she would not get around to it for a long time.

The books she consulted the most often had found their way to the top shelf of the bookcase, much as root matter comes to the surface when topsoil erodes. There was the twenty-four-volume Strachey edition of Freud's complete works, and the three-volume biography of Freud by Ernest Jones. There were good selections of writings by the other pioneering analysts, like Stekel, Abraham, Ferenczi, and Sachs. Ernest Jones's collected papers were well thumbed. So was Michael Basch's first book, *Doing Psychotherapy.* Jung was represented, though his volumes were three shelves down and dustier than the others.

Pictures of Susan's six-year-old son, Michael, were everywhere. The refrigerator was covered with his drawings, fingerpaintings, and samples of his block-lettered school papers. Recent photos of Michael with Susan were in frames on two tables. A single framed picture of Susan with her ex-husband and then-infant Michael was by the bed in the extra bedroom, where Michael slept when he visited. All the other photographs from her married years were in a scrapbook that had not been opened in a long time. A couple of pictures from Susan's youth were on the wall where Michael could see them from his bed. She had put them there to amuse him when he told her he liked them.

An unopened pack of Newport cigarettes, now five years old, sat on a bookshelf under a thick layer of dust. A Tunturi exercise bicycle, dusty on all surfaces except the seat and the handles, stood by a window. A book entitled *Analysis Terminable,* by Dr. Berthe Mueller, lay on the lower shelf of an end table. On the back cover was a photograph of the author; on the flyleaf was a dedication to Susan.

Susan came in after a long afternoon of patient sessions and found the answering machine blinking with a dozen messages.

"Carolyn?" she called. There was no answer. Her room-mate was a news producer for WGN and worked even longer hours than Susan herself. It was a rare thing for Susan to cross paths with her during the day. Occasionally they drank coffee together in the morning, both sleepy-eyed and monosyllabic. Otherwise they saw each other only late in the evening.

Both had answering services, so the machine was reserved for personal calls, messages from repairmen, plumbers, and the like. The number was unlisted.

Susan frowned as she saw the light blink. The press had got hold of the number in the last few months, and they were besieging her for interviews about the murders.

Susan moved through the apartment, stripping off garments as she went. She paused in the kitchen to turn on the toaster oven and take a frozen dinner from the freezer. Carolyn's vast collection of Weight Watchers meals reared before her, alongside a tempting half-gallon tub of Ben & Jerry's ice cream.

She opened the refrigerator, noticing Michael's drawing of a brontosaurus against a background of palm trees, and opened the vegetable drawer. The lettuce, mercifully, was still fresh. She would have salad tonight.

She padded down the hall, clad only in her skirt and bra. The door to Carolyn's room was ajar. As Susan passed it she caught a glimpse of the confusion inside. Carolyn was a slob. She always went to work immaculately dressed and groomed, but she had neither the leisure nor the inclination to keep her home clean. However, out of consideration for Susan, she kept her mess to herself.

Susan threw her clothes into the hamper and put on shorts and a loose cotton top. She was feeling preoccupied. The memory of the crime scene this morning was fresh in her mind. She still had the headache that always came when she used her second sight. It started in the temples and then ensconced itself at the front of her head, just above her brow, with tendrils of pain throbbing down into her eyes every few minutes. Long ago she had learned that all medication was useless against it. Only a night's sleep could help.

She returned to the kitchen and poured a glass of white wine from the bottle in the refrigerator. She stood barefoot, her weight on one leg, twirling the glass absently.

The phone rang once and was silent. Then it rang again. Recognizing the code, Susan picked it up.

"Hello."

"This is Gold. I was hoping you'd be home."

"How are things going?"

"About what I expected," Gold said. "The press is going wild. Weathers told them the crime has certain aspects in common, but he's not confirming that it's the third in a series. I think he wants to milk it for twenty-four hours."

"And the university?"

"They're ready to split a gut. I had to drive over and see the dean of students this afternoon. He wants the lid off. They're planning a special security program for female students off-campus as well as on. I can't blame him."

"How about the crime scene?" Susan asked.

"No prints, of course. The blood is probably the victim's. They're working on that. No clues from the strangulation. But Geri at the ME's office thinks she's found a fiber to match the first two crime scenes."

"So there's not much doubt, then," Susan observed.

"You saw it yourself. It's our man, all right."

Susan had not needed the physical evidence to convince her of that.

"Have you talked to the roommate?" she asked.

"Yeah, she got back this afternoon," Gold said. "She's pretty shook up, but she told me there is no boyfriend that she knew about. Patsy's sex life was not too active. It was a sore subject with her."

Susan had had an inkling of this at the scene. Sexual insights were often the first things that came to her.

"Did the roommate say anything else that might help?" she asked.

"Not a lot, no. Patsy was a fairly gregarious girl, with a

lot of friends, most of whom were athletes. She partied a little here and there, drank her share and hid the fact from her coach. No recreational drugs, she was too straight for that. As a student she was on-again, off-again. She got depressed, the roommate said. She never showed it to the outside world, but sometimes she would stay in the apartment for days, eating junk food and watching soaps and talk shows on that little TV you saw. Looks like there was some self-destruction in it. The roommate says she would come out of it after three or four days and go back to work, bitching about the classes she had missed. It cramped her style a little bit, but she covered it well. No one else knew she was depressed."

"Interesting," Susan said.

There was a pause.

"Susan?" Gold knew her very well. "Something else?"

"Well, yes. I've had a funny feeling all day. I didn't quite realize it until now. Just a nuance, really. I can't swear to it, but something about the crime scene, or the crime, was strange."

Gold waited patiently. He knew Susan couldn't be pushed. Often her feelings were too subtle even to put into words. The clues a psychic deals with are sometimes faint shifts of focus, variations of tone. Enough to alert the psychic that something important is at hand, but not enough to convince the skeptic that the feelings aren't meaningless.

"Something there was planned," she said. "We were meant to see it. I'm not sure in what sense. There was an intention, over and above the cruelty and the destruction."

"A copycat?"

"No. I think it's the same killer. I just think a game is being played on us. I didn't see it at the first two crime scenes. I should have, if I'm right this time. I just think there's more here than meets the eye."

"Uh-huh." Gold was listening, but he also knew Susan wasn't giving him anything he could act on.

"Anyway," she said. "See you tomorrow."

"Thanks, Susan."

She hung up the phone and glanced at the *Tribune* that had been waiting outside her door.

THIRD COED VICTIM FOUND, the headline read. That meant a leak. The story was under the byline of Gates Wagner, the top crime reporter at the *Trib*. He must have got it from one of the detectives or from someone in the Medical Examiner's Office. Susan glanced through the story. The repetition of the MO was mentioned prominently, but there wasn't a word about the MO itself. Gold and the state's attorney were playing their cards close to the vest, and risking the benefits they might have gained by opening the case up more to the public.

She watched the news while eating her dinner. The story was at the top of the news, but the MO was kept out. A lot of women were going to be scared by the story. Two months had passed, and people had begun to think the first two crimes ended it. Now the specter of a serial killer was big news. It would get a lot of press.

Carolyn came in, looking rushed, as Susan was putting her dishes away.

"I hoped I'd find you home," she said. "I heard all about it at work. I've got to get back. I just wanted to see you." She threw her purse on the counter and opened the cupboard to get a glass. She stood on tiptoe, her long legs showing off their slimness and strength, the result of spending much of every day on her feet and working out on the bike at home.

"Is it the same man?" she asked over her shoulder.

"Yes." Susan knew Carolyn would never use the information professionally. Carolyn kept her friendship with Susan entirely separate from her career. They had established this ground rule from the outset, and Carolyn had never broken it, despite the fact that Susan's participation in several investigations had been explosively newsworthy.

"What does Dave Gold say?" Carolyn asked.

"He really doesn't know. There is some physical evidence

linking the three homicides, and of course the MO is the same. But nothing to lead the police to a perpetrator."

"Female athletes." Carolyn shook her head. "I should have known some nut would get around to that eventually. The girls at the university must be scared shitless."

Susan smiled faintly at her roommate's forthright use of language. "I assume so," she said. "I haven't talked to any of them yet."

"Did you notice anything at the scene?" Carolyn asked.

This question told Susan that the press knew she had been there.

"A few things." She knew what Carolyn was asking. "Mostly personal. Again, nothing that would lead to the killer. At least it didn't feel that way."

"What a mess," Carolyn said. "How are you? Are you all right?" Carolyn knew that Susan suffered physical effects whenever she used her second sight. The more painful or emotional the circumstances, the more profound were the pain and exhaustion.

"I'm fine," Susan said. "A good night's sleep will do wonders."

Carolyn looked at her watch. "Well, I have to get back down to the station for a meeting. I just wanted to touch base with you." She looked at the drawings on the refrigerator. "Have you heard from Michael?"

Susan shook her head. "Not today."

"Is he still coming?"

"Sure."

Susan's son was to arrive next week to spend his spring vacation. His visits always delighted Carolyn, who somehow managed to find time for lengthy outings with him, from shopping to movies to languid afternoons in Lincoln Park. Carolyn called Michael "my fella" and made no secret of the fact that she was crazy about him.

Like Susan, Carolyn was divorced. She had just finished her journalism degree and gone to work at WGN when Susan moved to Chicago. Susan was feeling insecure enough to want a roommate at the time, and the parallels between the two women's lives—they were just the same age, and their marriages had lasted the same number of years—gave them a lot in common. The arrangement was to be temporary. Both women were absorbed in their careers, and there was an unspoken sense that they were waiting for their personal lives to settle down before changing domiciles. But it didn't happen.

Meanwhile Carolyn, who had no children of her own and no husband on the horizon, saw the clock ticking. Emotionally she had adopted Michael, and she behaved like an impassioned aunt, sending him letters and little gifts when she wasn't preparing for his visits. She relished the opportunity to spoil him and literally glowed whenever he was here.

"If you talk to him, tell him I bought him a shirt," she said.

"Will do." Susan smiled.

Carolyn spent a quick two minutes before the bathroom mirror and swept out of the apartment in her usual hurry. Susan turned on the answering machine, standing at the kitchen counter with her pencil poised over the notepad.

As she had suspected, nearly all the messages were from journalists. An aggressive investigative reporter from the *Sun-Times* headed the list, calling back every hour on the hour all afternoon. There was a brief message from Nick, Susan's ex-husband, concerning Michael's reservations. And a message from the repair shop that had had Susan's TV and VCR for the last month.

She took a long, hot shower and sat down to work on the article she was writing for a new anthology on schizophrenia. She gave up after a few minutes. Concentration was impossible. The visit to the crime scene had hit her harder than she thought. Perhaps it was the young girl's face in the photographs. It was a strong face, attractive. A youthful face, still not completely formed by a mature personality. Now it never would be.

The thought of that face contorted in terror under the killer's assault was upsetting. Worse yet was Susan's memory of it mutilated by the gouged-out eyes.

The blood on the bathroom sink was an integral element in all three crime scenes. Its proximity to the medicine cabinet mirror was an eloquent clue to what must have happened. Everything suggested that the killer's last move after the crime was to take a long look at himself in the mirror. But not with his own eyes. He must have held up the victim's eyes in his hands, like trophies.

Exhausted, Susan returned to the living room and sat down on the couch opposite the empty TV stand. A copy of Marcia Clark's book on the Simpson case was on her living room table. Susan was on page 200.

She took the book into her bedroom and lay down to read. She could not seem to concentrate on the text, despite its sensational content. At last she sighed and turned out the light. She waited for dream images to begin eclipsing her waking thoughts, but the confusion behind her eyes seemed to throb along with her headache. She saw the furious killer bent over the helpless woman, pulling her head back to slash. And she saw the strangler throttling the young coed, his plan as coldly efficient as his mind was sick.

Susan turned on her side, hoping to bring herself a step closer to sleep.

Sleepy . . .

She saw Carolyn reaching up to get a glass from the cupboard. Another woman, shorter and less attractive, strained to get a folded sheet from the linen closet. She looked over her shoulder and smiled. She opened her mouth to speak, but her words made no sense.

Sleepy, Grumpy . . .

Susan pricked up her ears, trying to understand. But the smile had faded, and the woman was leaving the room, the sheet in her hand. Outside a siren sounded. Emergency vehicles streaked through the town streets, between the pastures. Susan kept calling out something. But no one heard her.

She fell asleep with the words of warning still on her lips.

3

THEY WERE BOTH still breathing hard. The fragrance of her perspiration joined that of her hair, and the natural spicy scent of her body. She was nestled in his arms.

"What am I going to do with you?" he whispered, holding her closer.

"You just did it."

He raised himself on an elbow to study her. She was beautiful in a thousand ways, but this way—naked, after making love—was the hardest to resist. She looked as innocent in her nudity as a small child. But her body was rich with secrets, the essence of womanhood.

It was that composite quality that had attracted him to her in the first place. Often she was girlish and callow in her conversation. Yet her eyes, deep with generations of pain, were not those of a girl. This was one reason he loved her.

He kissed her rib cage, her breasts. The afterglow of her excitement was in the fingertips that touched his hair.

"I have to get moving," he said, kissing her brow. "Meetings before dinner."

She lay back and watched him as he got up. He was slim but well-muscled. She knew he worked out in the gym when his busy schedule allowed it. He also played a lot of tennis. She wished she could join him. But they had never been seen together in public, and there was no point in starting now.

Her last glimpse of him naked was as he opened the bathroom door.

"There's an article about your dad in the *Tribune* today," he called over his shoulder. "Did you see it?"

"Not yet."

"Pretty well done, I thought. I wish I had press like that."

Your dad. Geoff was always respectful when he mentioned her father. Respectful and affectionate. They knew each other already. But of course her father knew so many people, dealt with so many people.

He would be shocked if he found out Geoff was her lover.

But he would never find out. She had made up her mind to that already, and made all the sacrifices necessary to ensure it.

She had never heard her father speak of Geoff. He was just one of a thousand people who crossed through Dad's orbit, here and in Washington. Sometimes, childishly, she wished she could hear Geoff's name on Dad's lips just once. She even had to restrain herself from asking, as though out of curiosity, "Dad, do you know Geoff MacAndrew?"

But she would never do that. Not only because it would be indiscreet and unfair to Geoff but because her father had not got where he was by being naive or unobservant. Dad would remember that she had asked the question. He would remember her tone, her eyes as she had asked. In the end, he would see through her. He knew her too well to be fooled by a lie. Especially about a man.

The *Tribune* was sitting on the chair where Geoff had left it. Still naked, she squirmed over the bed and retrieved it. Sitting with her legs crossed, she scanned the front page.

THIRD COED VICTIM FOUND. The headline was large, eye-catching. Troubled by it, she forgot her father long enough to read through the item.

A third Circle Campus coed has been found murdered.
　　Patricia Morgenstern, known to her friends as Patsy, was found strangled in her off-campus apartment early today by a neighbor.

*Morgenstern, a member of the varsity volleyball team,
was a junior at Illinois. She was scheduled to accom-
pany the volleyball team on a South American tour this
spring.*

*Police refused to speculate on the killer's identity, but
the Tribune has learned that clues inside Morgenstern's
apartment suggest the same MO as the previous two
murders.*

*University authorities are expressing outrage at the
crime and deep concern for the safety of all female
students.*

*"Emergency security measures will be put into effect as
of this morning," said Elaine Simmons, a spokesperson
for the campus police. "No female student is to go anywhere unaccompanied, and the living quarters of all female students will be monitored by our operatives in
conjunction with the Chicago Police."*

She had now forgotten all about her father. The newspaper
was still in her hands, which were trembling. The sounds
of Geoff in the bathroom seemed a thousand miles away.

There was no photograph of the victim. But she didn't
need to see one.

Hi, I'm Patsy. I'm the tall one.

She closed her eyes. It was hard to believe this was happening. Hard to believe, but not surprising. Ever since the
second victim was discovered, she had felt this coming
closer.

"Hey, you look as though you've seen a ghost."

Geoff was standing in the doorway, buttoning his shirt.

"Are you all right?"

"Sure. It's just these murders."

"Yeah. More work for the cops. Maybe you should be
grateful you're not at Illinois."

She frowned. "Maybe no one is safe anymore."

He came to her side. "You know, you're right. This is
getting out of hand. Are you sure you're safe where you
are?"

"Sure I'm safe. I've got Reta, and the dog. And we have a doorman. It's about as safe as you can get."

It was her father who had insisted she live in a building with a doorman. Reta, her roommate, had bought the dog as a lark last year, but Jaime had come to love her. They took turns taking her out for walks. Jaime did feel a new safety in walking the lovely but dangerous streets around the University of Chicago with a big dog on a leash.

"Well, I want you to take extra precautions," Geoff said. "This looks bad. Three victims." He shook his head. "Innocent girls . . . I'll bet they never thought for a minute that anything like this could happen to them."

Jaime looked away. She could not tell him what she was thinking.

He stood up to tie his tie before the mirror. "Did you see the item about your dad?"

Jaime's eyes darted quickly over the front page. She saw her father's face looking at her with the expression he reserved for the press, and sometimes for her, when, as a girl, she had been bad.

"Yes."

"You going to be all right?"

She nodded.

He came to her side and kissed the hollow of her neck. "You know what I would like more than anything else in the world?" he asked.

She shook her head.

"To walk out of this place with you on my arm. To have everyone see us. So that when all those heads turn and people think, *Who is that gorgeous girl?* I could say, 'She's mine.' That's what I would like."

Jaime frowned.

"You want what you can't have," she said.

He nodded, passing a gentle hand across her cheek.

"That doesn't stop me from wanting it," he said. "Sometimes it can feel good just to know what you want."

She was silent. This was an old bone of contention between them. He enjoyed pondering his dreams of a life with her. She had been brought up not to think about things that were impossible. There was pain enough to go around without dwelling on impossibilities.

"Sorry," he said.

"You've got nothing to be sorry for."

He gave her a last, slow smile as he let himself out. She lay alone in the room. The feel of him was in all her senses. Yet he was gone. She reflected that this was love. The presence inside you of someone who could not stay, who was as fugitive as a ghost.

"Shut up," she told herself. She stood up and took a step toward the bathroom. Her clothes were folded neatly on the chair. The reflection of a beautiful young girl glided by in the mirror.

But she saw the newspaper on the bed. Her father's face looked up at the ceiling, unsuspecting. And the headline about the dead girl loomed eloquent in the shadows.

Hi, I'm Patsy. I'm the tall one.

WHEN SUSAN ARRIVED at Twenty-sixth and California, David Gold was waiting for her in the office of State's Attorney Weathers.

"Dr. Shader," Weathers said. "Glad you could join us."

Abel Weathers distrusted psychics, and he particularly disliked Susan because, four years ago, she had embarrassed him by proving that his prime suspect in a major homicide was innocent. Her psychic gift had been involved, and Weathers, never a man to enjoy admitting he was wrong, had held it against her. Since that time David

Gold had made it his business to act as a buffer between the two. Weathers was always on the lookout for a mistake on Susan's part and enjoyed needling her with skeptical comments about her "gift."

"I don't have to tell you two where we're sitting," Weathers began. "The press is all over me. The story is national now. I've got tabloid reporters up my ass. They're filling up all the downtown hotels, for Christ's sake. Not to mention the bars. If I don't catch a killer soon, the bartenders will be the only people who vote for me." Weathers's flair for scatological humor had not changed, Susan observed. He had an astonishingly dirty mouth, even in official meetings.

"Dave, suppose you summarize," he said. "What have we got that we can run with?"

David Gold looked too tall for his chair. He shifted uncomfortably as he glanced at his notes.

"Three homicides, same MO," he said. "Female athletes, university students. Two basketball players, one volleyball player. Two sophomores, one junior. No break-ins; they let the killer in. Death caused by strangulation. Enucleation of the eyeballs postmortem, followed by some sort of ritual at the bathroom mirror that leaves blood in the sink. No fingerprints."

Weathers was toying idly with the pen in the polished marble stand on his desktop. Susan had never seen him write with it, but he often tapped it or played with it when he was thinking.

"Always the gouged-out eyes," Weathers said. "What a scumbag."

"No matter what else is working against us," Susan said, "the gouged-out eyes are a clue. So are the female athletes."

"We also have a fiber that was found on the bedspread," Gold said. "It almost slipped by because it was so short—less than a centimeter—but Geri Vogel, the ME's specialist, has gone back over the first two scenes and matched it. It's an unusual fiber in color and chemical composition. She thinks it's going to lead us somewhere. But she hasn't got it pinned down yet."

"Thank God for small favors," Weathers said.

"We found saliva in the sink again this time," Gold added. "Type A. Same as the first two scenes. It could be helpful later on."

"Did you check the victim's toothbrush?" Susan asked.

"Yes," Gold said. "The results aren't in yet."

"I've heard of perpetrators using victims' toothbrushes," Susan said. "As a matter of fact, some of them will make themselves at home in all kinds of symbolic ways. Taking the victims' medication, putting on their skin cream, even using their sanitary napkins. It can be compulsive."

Weathers was shaking his head. "Christ, where do these nuts stop?"

"Every crime acts out an anxiety that has multiple roots," Susan said. "Just like a symptom, it can't help alluding to those roots. It reenacts them. That's our great advantage. The act itself tells a story, psychologically speaking. The killer may be clever enough to murder other people, but he is not clever enough to avoid telling that story."

Weathers looked at her.

"Tell me about the eyes," he said. His show of respect for Susan's psychological expertise was unwilling.

"The girls are dead before he gouges out their eyes," Susan said. "That's clear from the bleeding patterns. He strangles them quickly. Then he performs a ritual with the eyes in front of the vanity mirror. A logical assumption would be that he goes through a pantomime of looking through the eyes of the dead woman. Looking at himself, that is. The severed eyes bleed into the sink. Then he leaves, taking the eyeballs with him." She sat back. "As for the saliva, he may drool or spit as part of the ritual. Or," she added a bit uncomfortably, "he may put one or both of the eyeballs in his mouth."

"A wonderful human being." Gold shrugged. "What would the profilers say?"

Susan said, "The scene indicates what profilers call an

organized killer. This means that the victim was selected to be killed rather than raped or robbed. The killing didn't happen as a sudden impulse. If it had, the scene would be messier. Here we have the realization of a fantasy, very detailed and neat.

"The position of the victim in the bathtub is pretty classic," she went on. "Many organized killers place their victims in a particular posture. Also, they often take a remembrance from each crime, which we see here with the eyes. Usually it turns out that the fantasy preceded the crimes and led up to them. I wouldn't be surprised if this killer gouged the eyes out of dolls or mannequins or animals before proceeding to human beings."

She looked at Weathers. "Our scenes would indicate the killer known as the power/control-oriented type. The killer feels the specific need to put the victim in a passive posture. Often there are other signs of controlling behavior, such as ligature and torture. We don't see that here. On the other hand, I think the absence of the eyes speaks pretty eloquently of control over the victim. The killer is actually appropriating part of the victim's body."

"What about background?" Weathers asked.

"We're probably looking for a white man," Susan said. "Late twenties or thirties. Intelligent, but working a job well below his intellectual capacity. Possibly an only child, possibly not. Profilers have done statistical studies of serial killers in prison and have learned some interesting things. The serial killer almost always comes from a dysfunctional family in which the father was absent or abusive or indifferent. In fifty percent of cases there was a history of criminality in the family. In fifty percent of cases there was alcohol abuse in the family. Forty percent were sexually abused as children. In most cases their sexual interests were solitary in nature, such as pornography, masturbation, fetishism, voyeurism. That gives us a lot to think about."

"But only after we catch the son of a bitch," Weathers threw in.

"You're right," Susan said. "So much of the population fits into those categories that they hardly work as clues. However, in assessing possible suspects you can run those factors through the FBI's computers, and your own."

"Is he nuts?" Gold asked.

Susan shrugged. "Organized killers are sociopaths. They may fall into several categories of mental illness, or not be mentally ill at all in the clinical sense. But they do have certain characteristics in common. For instance, they are self-centered. They view the world as a hostile place, unjust toward them. They view authority as unjust, incompetent. They seek a power they have felt denied all their lives. They have trouble distinguishing between fantasy and reality. This is not mental illness. It is a sort of regression, a failure to grow up through ordinary reality testing."

She looked at Gold. "Unfortunately, despite their regressed emotional age, they can be very competent socially. We see a lot of them picking up victims in bars or on college campuses—the Ted Bundy scenario. In this case our man talked his way into the victims' apartments and killed them without causing a disturbance, despite the fact that other students were living right next door. He's probably very friendly, very charming.

"The organized killer will often get off on his own track record. He may keep newspaper clippings about the crimes, or taunt the police. He often refines his technique, choosing his victims with more care and leaving fewer clues. Sometimes," she added with a glance at Weathers, "he will move away from his initial hunting area out of prudence."

"Go west, young man." Gold scowled.

Weathers was looking at Susan. "You said each crime tells a specific story," he said.

"Strangulation itself is a strongly sexual act," Susan said. "But the ritual with the eyes is an important clue. Most serial killers feel compelled to damage the victim's sexual organs in some way. This man may have regressed from the genital organs to a symbolic sexual organ, the eye. It may be that he avoids the sexual organs because he is so afraid of touching them."

Weathers was rolling his eyes.

"With all due respect, Doctor," he said, "this dude is no faggot. He's killed three times. He's got plenty of guts."

Susan had winced at his use of the word *faggot*.

"The two concepts aren't incompatible," Susan said. "It's a mistake to think that killers are brave people, or even reckless. The dominant emotion under their anger is fear. The more you study serial killers or mass murderers, the more you see signs of deep-seated fears, which the killer continues to respect even in his violent rituals. That's the essence of the borderline personality, after all. Sociopathy grows out of fears that can't be controlled." She glanced at the small notebook she had brought with her. "Personally, I'm betting that our man is a hypochondriac."

"Why?" Gold asked.

"The gouging out of the eyes is a pretty obvious ceremonial aimed to protect against damage to his own body," Susan said. "His genitals, of course, but also any symbolically detachable, vulnerable part of the body. Or, indeed, any part that is visible outside his clothes. The eyes, the skin, the hands, and so forth. He's probably impotent. That's almost universal."

She turned a page. "We're probably dealing with an individual who owns a lot of visual pornography. Magazines, videotapes, and so on. Undoubtedly the pornography will be violent. Bondage, torture, leather. I would also suggest that crimes like exhibitionism and window peeping are in his past," she said. "The eyes play so important a role in his pathology that something visual has probably gotten him into trouble with the law. Most serial killers work their way up from relatively minor crimes. You might find rape or attempted rape on his yellow sheet, too."

She furrowed her brow.

"But the key clue, in my opinion, is the fact that the girls are athletes," she said. "Here he's actually giving us a glimpse into his sexual past. We could be looking for a man who has an older sister. Possibly a sister who died."

Weathers was toying with the pen set on his desktop. He kept pulling the pen out of the holder and sticking it back in, making a clicking sound.

"Why died?" asked Gold.

"He's acting out a hostile impulse toward her, but he has to use a substitute," Susan said. "The real sister, if there was one, was someone he venerated, someone he idealized. When he was small he attributed strength to her. Power. Domination."

She looked at Weathers. "His anger, his frustration, had to remain unconscious. As he got older and began to experience sexual impulses he couldn't control, he needed to let off the steam. This probably took the form of exhibitionism or window peeping or both. But over time the coefficient of cruelty entered in. He can't keep his aggressive impulses separate from his sexual ones. This is where the rape or attempted rape comes in. And finally, murder."

"I think we've had enough of the psychoanalytic clinic for one day," said Weathers with obvious irritation. "What did your second sight tell you at the scene?"

"Only what I told David," Susan said. "She's been involved with a man. Someone older, someone she respects and admires a great deal. A professor, possibly. I think the love was unrequited, but I'm not sure. It's certainly something to be followed up."

Gold nodded to Weathers. "I'm doing it," he said.

"And that's all?" Weathers said, looking disappointed.

"I couldn't find anything unusual at the scene," Susan said. "Patsy seems to have been a normal girl. I could be wrong, but my guess is that the killer chose her for her athletic ability, maybe her height, stalked her for a while, and then came to her apartment. She may have known him very casually, perhaps just to say hello to. That's what disarmed her sufficiently for her to let him in."

Weathers sighed. "How do we stop this asshole?"

Gold joined his hands in his lap. "First comes public

information. We concentrate on female college students. The guy only hunts in that group. I've been talking to the campus police at Northwestern, Loyola, the University of Chicago, and the smaller campuses. They're all willing to help in any way they can."

He glanced at Susan. "Meanwhile, if Susan is right, we're looking for a man who has left traces with the law-enforcement agencies in the past. We look for peepers, exhibitionists, rapists. We make the rounds. It may not be enough, but we may be able to hang in until he makes a false move."

Susan returned Gold's look. "I might suggest that you use plainclothes policewomen to pose as university students," she said. "Athletes, of course. Work through the women's athletic coaches."

"That was suggested last night by one of our guys." Gold nodded. "We're working on it."

Weathers sighed. "Okay. I've got to talk to the press. I'm gonna tell them we've got some pretty good clues. But we can't talk about it because we need to leave the killer something to tell us when he confesses. I want to buy some time. But I want you two to know something. My gut tells me it won't be enough. This fucker is smart. I feel that."

He looked at Susan as he stood up. "No matter how many stories he tells," he said, not bothering to conceal his sarcasm.

He ushered Gold and Susan out of the office with little herding motions. Weathers always made a great show of impatience. It increased his sense of his own importance.

In the elevator David Gold seemed even taller than usual as he looked down at Susan.

"Sorry about that," he said.

Susan smiled. "I don't mind. Knowing how hostile he is keeps me honest."

Gold frowned. "If you can stand working that way, more power to you. Personally, I would tweak his nose.

And it would probably get me in a lot of trouble. You can't do anything around here without his help."

Susan was watching the numbers count down as the ground floor approached. The image seemed uncomfortably symbolic, perhaps of time running out.

She had a healthy cynicism about Abel Weathers and the politics of law enforcement. But she had to agree with Weathers about one thing. Her own instincts told her the killer was clever. The usual precautions would probably not be enough. He would kill again, and soon.

5

AN HOUR AFTER her conference with Gold and Weathers, Susan met with the parents of Patsy Morgenstern in an empty office down the hall from David Gold's.

The mother was an overweight woman in her forties who might have appeared jolly had it not been for the fragile, worried look in her eyes. Susan had seen it in the photograph in Patsy's apartment, and it was more palpable now that grief had overcome the face.

The father was leaning forward to listen to Susan, but the entire posture of his large body seemed bent toward his wife, as though to protect her. He did not let go of her hand throughout the interview.

"I know how upset you both are," Susan said, "and the last thing I want to do is to make things worse for you. But we all feel that if we learn everything we can about Patsy, we may find some small clue that will lead us to her killer."

"I just don't understand it," Mrs. Morgenstern said.

"Patsy was a happy, normal girl. Normal in every way. There was nothing in her life that could have led to something like this. We send our daughters to the university to get an education. Not to be murdered." Tears flowed silently down her cheeks.

Her husband squeezed her hand and looked at Susan. "We'll do anything we can to help."

"I understand that Detective Gold has asked you about Patsy's friends and associations at the university," Susan said, "so I don't have to go through all that again. I know you're tired and anxious to get home. What I'd like to ask is what you can tell me about Patsy's romantic life. Her boyfriends, dates, and so forth."

"She had dates, like any other girl," Mrs. Morgenstern said. "She was a lovely, normal girl. I just don't understand it."

Susan could easily see that the mother's overriding concern was to paint a picture of Patsy as normal. It was unlikely that she would get anything helpful from her.

"Mr. Morgenstern, did Patsy ever confide in you about the boyfriends she met at school? Did she ask your advice, for instance?"

He shook his head. "She was pretty private about that kind of thing. She never brought it up in college or in high school. She was a little sensitive. About her size. Her height. But she had lots of friends. Her social life was very active." He glanced at his wife as though in search of confirmation.

"She had a normal social life," Mrs. Morgenstern asserted. "Normal in every way. There was nothing . . . Nothing!"

Susan sensed some embarrassment about sex to go along with Mrs. Morgenstern's maternal protectiveness. Obviously she was a rigid, insecure woman. Sex must have been a painful issue for her. If it was for her daughter as well, she would not have reacted well to this. Susan began to feel Patsy's dilemma. A tall girl, perhaps with few dates in high school, she could not confide her feelings to her mother because of the mother's morbid protectiveness where sex was concerned.

Susan felt frustrated. She wished she could get Mr. Morgenstern alone. On the other hand, it was doubtful that Patsy had ever confided much to her father. Few girls do, at her age.

"Psychologists often say that a girl takes her mother's courtship as a model," Susan hazarded. "Do you mind my asking how you two met?"

"We were high school sweethearts," Mr. Morgenstern said. "Down in Champaign, where we both grew up. My father sold cars down there until he retired. Deanna's dad was a real estate and insurance man. Our families knew each other. We got married just before I started college."

"And Patsy was your first child?" Susan asked.

The mother nodded, avoiding Susan's eyes. Mr. Morgenstern shifted in his chair.

"Was Patsy more or less similar to your other two children?" Susan asked.

"Smarter, I would say." Mr. Morgenstern turned to his wife. "Don't you think, Deanie? Patsy was a very smart girl."

His wife's eyes welled with tears at the sound of the word *was*.

"Oh, my God," she said.

Susan came forward to touch her hand. "This is a terrible time," she said. "Don't be ashamed to let your feelings show. Nothing could be more painful than to lose your firstborn child."

Mrs. Morgenstern nodded. Again Susan noticed a shrouded sidelong glance at Mr. Morgenstern.

"Her high grades helped her to get that big scholarship," he said. "Otherwise they wouldn't have paid for the whole thing. She had a 3.6 average in high school. She was in the National Honor Society."

Susan nodded. She knew from Gold that Patsy's grades had been falling steadily at the university since her freshman year. She was down to a 2.4 average. Susan suspected the low grades were an unconscious expression of her unhappiness.

She turned to Mr. Morgenstern.

"How did she feel about being an athlete?" she asked. "Did her academic ambitions ever conflict with her athletic responsibilities?"

He shook his head. "She was very disciplined. She budgeted her time very well. She had plenty of time for studies as well as practices and games. Of course, that didn't leave her an awful lot of time for the family. But we understood. She had a lot of potential, and she worked hard to fulfill it."

Again Susan had the strong sense of an official version of Patsy's life. But the strong signals she had received from touching Patsy's possessions in the apartment told another story.

"How about her dating life?" she pursued. "Did athletics limit that at all in high school?"

Patsy's father leaned forward. "She never had a steady boyfriend," he said. "The kids used to do a lot of things in groups. You know—movies, outings, parties. She was fairly active in that, but there was never a particular boy . . ."

Susan could see that the topic was unnerving Mrs. Morgenstern.

"I'm sorry if this upsets you," she said. "Was high school a difficult time for Patsy?"

"I wouldn't call it difficult per se," her father began.

"I don't see why a girl has to go steady with every boy who comes along," Mrs. Morgenstern interrupted. "Patsy had a lot of responsibilities. But she was a happy, normal girl. She had all the social life she needed."

"Did she ever express any regret that she lacked a steady boyfriend?" Susan asked.

"Never. Why does every girl have to have a steady boyfriend, anyway? More often than not it just leads to trouble." Mrs. Morgenstern spoke with sudden passion. Her husband turned his handsome face away.

"Patsy wanted to make something of herself," her mother

concluded. "She didn't need boyfriends. She had no regrets. She was a happy, normal girl. Normal in every way!"

Susan sat back. There was no point in pursuing this. Later she might get the father alone. For the moment the best thing was to let them get on with their grieving.

She excused herself and went down the corridor to the Medical Examiner's Office, where David Gold was sipping coffee from a Styrofoam cup and gazing out the window.

"Did you get much?" he asked.

"Very little. They're not very communicative. Especially the mother. But I gathered that Patsy was not very popular in high school. She was self-conscious about her height. No real boyfriends."

"Anything else?"

Susan nodded. "I suspect Patsy was conceived before her parents were married. She was the oldest of three children. The parents got married right after high school. The mother seems quite worried about sex."

Gold put down his coffee cup. "So, not much help."

"No. Not much help."

"Well, I guess there's no point in telling them about this," he said, touching the file folder on the desktop.

"What is it?" Susan asked.

"She had semen in her. ME says she had sex within six hours of her murder."

Susan looked at him for a long moment.

"Does it match the saliva you found in the sink?" she asked.

"We won't get the DNA for a while," he said. "But the ME tells me it looks like yes. Same blood group."

He stood with his arms folded, looking both pleased and disgusted.

6

SNOW HAD BEGUN to fall in the morning, a typical Chicago snow, dusting the dead lawns and swirling along the streets and walks without sticking. In another city those streets would have been black and shiny with melted snow, but here the wind chill was sufficient to keep the pavement dry.

Students were bundled up against the wind, so much so that it was sometimes difficult to tell the girls from the boys. But Susan could not help noticing that girls were walking between classes in groups of five or six. Few girls were to be seen alone. The university's security people were taking the situation seriously. They did not want the killer to find his next victim here.

Stephanie Mertz, Patsy Morgenstern's roommate, had returned to their apartment with the police to remove some of her things, and she was living temporarily in a dorm for graduate students. Her own parents had come up to spend a long weekend with her, and she was receiving counseling from a psychologist at the Student Health Center.

Susan met Stephanie at the Student Union and sat with her on a couch in an empty lounge. Stephanie was a small, pretty girl with green eyes and freckles. She looked confident, but her pallor and the frightened expression in her eyes betrayed the effect of what had happened.

"You're very nice to make time for me," Susan said. "How are you feeling?"

"Pretty good," the girl said. "Better than I was a couple of days ago. I'm still freaked out, I guess. But I can concentrate on my classes, at least."

"That's good," Susan said. "It will take some time. A person doesn't get over a friend's murder easily. You can expect to feel some grief, and even some guilt, for quite a while."

Susan said no more, but she knew she had put it mildly. It is no rare thing for unexpected scarring to set in with a survivor like Stephanie, particularly if she is female and the death of her friend is a sexual crime. Disturbances of the sexual function, such as frigidity, could appear months or even years after the loss and be quite resistant to treatment. In Stephanie's favor was the fact that she was young and healthy. But murder is a trauma of extraordinary emotional significance. Few survivors escape it unscathed.

"I've spoken to Patsy's parents," Susan said. "They were too upset to be of much help. I didn't get the impression that Patsy confided much in them about her life here."

"Her mother, yeah," Stephanie said. "Patsy complained about her all the time. She's neurotic, a worrier. Hovering all the time. She drove Patsy crazy."

"Mothers can be that way." Susan smiled.

"Patsy wouldn't even let me visit her downstate," Stephanie said. "She said the house was like a pressure cooker. With Patsy away at school, her mother was all over her younger sister, Casey. She doesn't give her a moment's peace."

"I take it, then, that Patsy was glad to have left home for college," Susan said.

"She was only sorry she didn't get farther away. She used to say she wished she had gone back east to college, or out west somewhere like UCLA. But her parents couldn't afford it. I remember the first thing she ever said to me, when I met her freshman year, was: *Are your parents as horrible as mine?* It was sort of sad."

"Parents can be a problem," Susan said. "It would be nice if they helped to take pressure off their children, but sometimes they put it on as well."

"Well, they sure put it on Patsy." Stephanie was warming up to Susan. "Her mother was a freak about sex. Always saying that boys were after only one thing—stuff like that. And trying to keep Patsy from wearing attractive clothes, showing off her legs or whatever. Patsy couldn't show her feelings around her parents. She had to keep it all in. She told me she didn't even begin to live until she got here to school."

"Did things go better for her here, in terms of men and dates?" Susan asked.

Stephanie shifted her weight slightly. "Sort of. But not as much as she would have liked. Most of her friends were other athletes. Basketball players, things like that. But they weren't really the kind of people she wanted to meet. She already knew athletes, from high school. She thought they were stupid. Stupid and immature."

Stephanie hesitated. Susan said nothing.

"She really wanted to meet different kinds of people," Stephanie said. "But she had trouble. See, she had this reflex, this way of behaving. Like 'one of the boys.' She was always good-humored. Never down. That sort of thing. It made her a lot of friends, but it also kept the men from really taking her seriously. She saw herself doing it, but she couldn't stop herself. Inside, she was terribly lonely."

"I saw her clothes in the closet in your room," Susan said. "I take it she didn't dress very attractively."

Stephanie nodded. "A lot of the girls here wear baggy clothes. But you're right—Patsy overdid the dressing down. I used to point out to her that she had good-looking legs. A good figure, in fact. But she said she couldn't wear dresses, they made her look too tall."

"I take it, then, that Patsy didn't have a steady boyfriend here at the university," Susan said.

Stephanie shook her head. "There was a basketball player freshman year, Bobby Fallon. But it was never a serious thing. Patsy only went out with him when she needed a date. They broke up at the end of the year, anyway. He's living with some girl now."

"So it wasn't much of a loss to Patsy," Susan offered.

"Not really."

Susan gathered from this answer that the loss was a

blow to Patsy's self-esteem, if nothing else. "What did she do for dates after Bobby?" she asked.

Stephanie shrugged. "Well, it wasn't so easy then. She went through some low times. We all did, at one time or another."

"That's part of college life, too."

"Unless you're very lucky."

Susan leaned forward.

"Stephanie, was there ever a man—a student, perhaps, or in fact anyone—who showed an unwanted sexual interest in Patsy?"

Stephanie laughed. "Any sexual interest would have been welcomed." Then she shook her head. "No. Nothing like that."

"The other two victims," Susan said, "I understand from Patsy's coach that she might have known them slightly. Did you know them?"

"No."

"Did Patsy ever mention any sort of unwelcome sexual advances made to any female athletes she knew?"

The girl shook her head.

"Phone calls? Notes? Pranks?" Susan pursued. "Anything at all."

"No. Nothing like that. I never heard her mention anything of the sort."

There was a silence. Susan knew she had to dig deeper, but she sensed that grief and friendship were making Stephanie protective of Patsy.

"Was there someone Patsy admired but wasn't successful with?" she asked. "Someone she had a crush on? Someone *she* pursued?"

Stephanie looked away.

"Please understand," Susan explained, "that I'm not trying to embarrass Patsy in any way, or to cast the wrong light on her life. Young girls fall in love when they leave home. It's the normal pattern. Quite often that first love leads to a broken heart. It's part of growing up."

Stephanie was still silent. Her resistance was obvious.

"Stephanie, three girls are dead. The police are doing everything they can, but time is running short. I need to know all I can about Patsy. Anything that might give us a clue to what happened—even in the most roundabout way—could help to save the lives of other girls."

Stephanie hesitated for a long moment. Then she sighed. "Yes, there was someone," she said. "The only reason I didn't tell you was that I wasn't supposed to know about it myself. Patsy kept it well hidden. She never told me about him. It was her private thing. The only reason I knew about it was because I opened her desk drawer one day to get some typing paper and saw a letter she had written him. I don't know if she ever sent it. It was a love letter."

"Who is he?" Susan asked.

Stephanie looked pained. She seemed aware of the irony of betraying the secret of a girl who was no longer alive to care about it.

"His name is Ron Giordano. He's a professor here." She seemed relieved.

"What department is he in?" Susan asked.

"Anthropology. Patsy took Intro from him." Stephanie managed a slight smile. "She made me come to his class one day so I could see what he looked like. He's a hunk."

"She never confided in you about her relationship with him?"

Stephanie shook her head. "She stopped talking about him after that semester. But I knew she went to see him in his office. I had the feeling she was, you know, carrying a torch for him. When I found that letter in her desk, I knew I was right."

"Did you meet him yourself?" Susan asked.

"No." Stephanie smiled. "I tried to fit Anthro into my schedule, but he wasn't teaching that course anymore."

"Thank you, Stephanie," Susan said. "You've been a great help." She held out a hand. The girl shook it.

"I guess it must be pretty exciting being a psychiatrist," Stephanie said. "Meeting all different kinds of people, and all. Especially working with the police."

"Yes, it is. It's very interesting work."

"I was thinking of switching to a psych major," Stephanie said. "Would I have to become a medical doctor to do what you do?"

"Some of it, yes," Susan said. "But a doctorate in psychology would equip you to do a great deal of important work."

She smiled. "But first things first. Stick with your counselor here at the Health Service. That will teach you something about therapy even as it helps you through this time. How is it going, by the way?"

"Okay, I guess." The girl fidgeted as she spoke. "The doctor keeps telling me things I already know. Like it's not my fault. Like it's not going to happen to me. Stuff like that. It gets boring."

"Is your counselor a man or a woman?"

"Woman. Doctor Bauer."

"Be patient with her," Susan said. "She's trying to plant some important seeds for you to remember when and if you have any scarring or anxiety from this. I think it's safe to predict that there will be ripples. She's trying to prepare you."

"Oh." Stephanie seemed half-convinced. But her youth as well as her fear were working against the therapy, at least in the short run. She wanted to put the trauma behind her.

"Will you promise me?" Susan asked.

"Okay."

After leaving Stephanie, Susan went to the bank of pay phones adjacent to the cafeteria and called Gold. He was on the street, she was told, and would not be back until five or later.

"I'll call back."

She looked at her watch. It was three-thirty. A good time to catch a college professor in his office.

She hung up the phone and went to a map of the campus. The Anthropology Department was only a hundred yards from where she was standing.

7

RON GIORDANO HAD a small office on the third floor of the Anthropology Building. It was stuffed with books and journals. There was a small coffee stand where an upside-down stack of Styrofoam cups and a large box of Equal testified to the heavy consumption of coffee that took place here.

Giordano had been standing in his office doorway chatting with a colleague when Susan came down the corridor. He was a big man, over six feet tall, wearing faded jeans and a V-neck sweater. When Susan introduced herself, he did not seem particularly surprised to see her.

"I figured I would be hearing from someone sooner or later," he said.

Susan looked around her.

"This place doesn't look big enough for you." She smiled.

"It isn't, really," he said. "But when you work at a university, you get used to being cramped."

Something in his tone made Susan ask, "Intellectually, you mean? Or just physically?"

"You're very perceptive, Doctor. Yes, sometimes there is an intellectual cramping. The university life isn't all it's cracked up to be."

A small photograph of a younger Ron Giordano in football gear was hung behind the door. It seemed to hide there, asserting its existence but loath to attract undue attention.

The picture rang a bell. Susan had already noticed that the man who now sat behind the desk looked familiar.

"I just realized who you are," she said.

Ron Giordano had been a backup quarterback with the Chicago Bears, and then an assistant coach, seven or eight years ago. Susan had seen him play when she watched Bears games with Nick.

"I watched you play," she added.

"Good for you." He smiled, clasping his hands behind his head. "You must have been glued to your TV. I didn't get many minutes."

"How does the university life feel after a football career?" Susan asked.

"In some ways, not so different. You have to be nice to people. You have to show your stuff, but you can't let people perceive you as a threat. There are a lot of politics. Getting promoted is a struggle."

"I know." Susan had had many patients from academia, and all had complained bitterly about the politics of tenure and promotion. To some extent her patients had peeled the scales from her own eyes. She had always thought of academia as a pleasant place, devoted to intellectual pursuits and more or less free from the fierce competition and backbiting of the business world. One of her patients, a tenured English professor from Northwestern, had joked to her that "the intrigue is all the more vicious because the financial stakes are so small. We academics will betray our best friends for a guaranteed salary of thirty thousand a year, or a grant for ten thousand."

"What made you become a professor?" she asked.

"In the first place, a disk problem and a cracked vertebra," he said. "No more football. In the second place, my memory of an anthropology professor back at Ohio State who used to hold us on the edge of our seats with stories of the Nambukwara and Margaret Mead. And finally, a scholarship for graduate work at Johns Hopkins, which got me my doctorate." He smiled. "I thought all I really wanted to do with my life was play football. Now I'm doing something I love much more than passing and running."

"Tell me about Patsy Morgenstern."

His smile faded.

"Patsy was my student," he said. "Introduction to Anthropology, two years ago. Her freshman year. I gave her a B."

He looked steadily at Susan.

"Is that all?" she asked.

"What else would there be?"

"Professor Giordano . . ."

"Ron."

"Ron, then. I'm here in my capacity as a consultant to the Homicide Division, which is investigating the deaths of Patsy and the two other girls. If you like, I can have Detective Gold speak to you before we go any further."

"I know who you are," he said. "I read the papers."

"Oh."

"You're good at your work," he said. "I respect that."

His compliment did not distract Susan from the job at hand.

"As you can imagine," she said, "we're trying to learn everything we can about Patsy, as we did with the previous victims. There are a lot of details to cover. Some of them official, some of them personal. It's impossible to know which ones may turn out to be crucial."

"I understand. I'm sorry if I seemed evasive. Patsy's death came as a shock to me. I'm still trying to deal with it."

"Perhaps it will help if you tell me what you can remember about her."

He nodded. There was a silence as he rocked a bit in his swivel chair, his tawny eyes resting on Susan.

"Patsy was the all-American type," he said, "or tried to be. She was very tall, and very embarrassed about it. I still remember the first time I met her, when she came in to ask about a paper topic. *That's right, I'm the tall one.* It was her standing joke, her way of introducing herself to people. She did it with a smile, lots of good-fellowship and all. But you didn't need to know her very well to realize that it was a real problem."

"She was self-conscious about her height?"

"That's an understatement." Giordano leaned forward. "She came from a tall family. Her father is six-five in his stocking feet. Her brother is six-seven. Patsy was brought up to lie about her height, just as many women lie about their age. When she was five-ten she told people she was five-eight. When she hit six feet in her teens, she hid the fact as though it were a skeleton in the closet. She ended up at six-two, and by that time her height was the bane of her existence."

"How did you learn all this?" Susan asked.

He laughed. "It wasn't hard. I was barely in her confidence before she told me the 'gory details,' as she called them. It was something she was dying to get off her chest. I think it was the official introduction to her private life, for friends."

Susan had the sense that he was minimizing his own relationship with Patsy by casting himself as one of many people who reached that level of her confidence.

"But the tallness was only one element of a larger whole," he went on. "She had been conditioned from an early age to think of herself as an athlete. She was taller than most boys, and had natural athletic ability. By the time she started junior high she was having serious problems with the opposite sex. Too tall. And already she had slipped into the role of 'one of the boys.' It was a poor defense, but she was deep into it before she quite realized what was happening."

He picked up a pencil from the desktop and twirled it in his fingers, looking at Susan. "She had no dates in high school," he said. "Not one. No fix-ups, no boyfriends, no junior prom or senior prom or homecoming. Nothing at all. She hung out with a crowd of girls who were in the same predicament. She was known as the jolliest of the lot, the least self-conscious. But that was garbage. She was completely miserable." He sighed. "She had problems with her mother. That added to the pressure. She wasn't happy at home."

"It sounds like she vented a lot in this office," Susan hazarded.

"Here and out on the track." He nodded. "We used to

run together. I run a lot, to stay in shape. She liked to join me when her courses and her practices allowed it. We would run together, and then have coffee over at the gym or the Union."

He saw the look in Susan's eyes and smiled.

"Sure, she had a crush on me," he said. "That was obvious from the outset. In fact, she used to joke about it. 'This is your number-one groupie,' she would say when she left me a phone message. At first I was taken in by her humor. Then, more and more, I realized how low her self-esteem was."

"Height in a young girl can be as bad a curse as parental divorce or abandonment," Susan said.

He nodded. "I knew a lot of female athletes back in high school and college, but I wasn't perceptive enough at the time to see what they were going through. A male athlete at least has the carrot of professional sports to shoot for. It's not the same for women. After their college careers, they can only look forward to college coaching or high school PE. It's not the same reward. And they've sacrificed just as much as the men."

"You said she had no dates in high school," Susan said. "What about college?"

He raised an eyebrow. "I thought you'd get around to that. To my knowledge she dated a couple of athletes on and off. But the relationships didn't go anywhere. Patsy was a very lonely girl."

Susan was looking at him. "Did you ever speculate about the murders?"

"Sure, I speculated. I didn't know the other girls, but I naturally wondered whether it had something to do with the university. Maybe the killer knew them somehow, maybe he had a thing for female athletes. That kind of thing. But my speculations have led nowhere."

Susan sensed he was hiding something. She got a strong feeling of guilt from him, of responsibility.

"Did Patsy ever ask you to sleep with her?" she asked.

He darkened. "That's a hell of a question."

"Just between us," Susan said. "And believe me, I'm not trying to embarrass you or to throw mud on her memory. I just want to understand her."

A scream came from outside the building. Susan and Giordano rose in one motion and met at the window. A male student had playfully picked up a girl, his girlfriend no doubt, and was whirling her in the air, the movement of their bodies sending eddies of snowflakes skyward.

Susan let out her breath and returned to her seat as Giordano watched her.

"It's hard not to be on edge," she said.

He nodded absently. She could see he was thinking over her question.

"Yes," he said. "She did ask me. It happened her second year here. By then she was one of what I called the old guard, the students who knew me pretty well. She came over to my place one night, looking pretty upset. She had broken up with Bobby, the basketball player she had been dating. She tried to minimize it, but I saw a desperation in her that I had never seen before. I gave her a soft drink and listened to her for a while. Then she came right out and asked me. Would I go to bed with her."

Susan was looking at him steadily. "And what did you say?"

"I said no, of course not." He looked offended.

"How did she take it?"

"She told me she was a virgin. She said she couldn't stand being a virgin any longer, it was killing her. I was the first man she had ever met, she said, whom she would like to lose her virginity with. It made me very sad to hear that."

"Weren't you flattered?" Susan asked.

He shook his head. "Not at all. I left my hero phase behind me a long time ago. All I could feel that night was her terrible loneliness."

He shrugged. "She wasn't the first, you know. There had been others. Lonely, sad girls who couldn't seem to make it in the sexual meat market of college. Very often they turn to a favorite professor. It makes our job more difficult. You want to create an alliance with your students, a bond of trust. But they often want it to be more. Because of their age, and for other reasons."

"I know what you mean," Susan said.

"Of course." He laughed. "Why didn't I think of that? What is the word for it, in psychiatry?"

"Transference," Susan said. "We learn in our training that patients will fall in love with us. It's predictable, and not unhealthy. We try to use it to our advantage. Often, though, it backfires. More than one patient has dropped out of therapy when the psychiatrist refuses to get personally involved." She frowned. "And sometimes the psychiatrist isn't strong enough to resist the seduction."

"Now you know where I'm coming from," he concluded.

"Yes, I do."

Yet Susan still felt that aura of guilt about him. She guessed that his hard-won maturity of outlook had come in part from an indiscretion, no doubt committed when he was starting out in academia. He had resisted Patsy Morgenstern's invitation; perhaps another girl, years before, had caught him at a weak moment.

"Did you ever find out what happened?" Susan asked.

"What do you mean?"

"Patsy Morgenstern was not a virgin when she was murdered," she said. "The medical examiner determined that. Did you know the circumstances?"

He shook his head. Susan was convinced this was the core of his pain and his resistance.

"Did you suspect she slept with someone, on the rebound as it were, after your refusal?"

He stood up. "I may have suspected a lot of things," he said. "But Patsy was never the same to me after that episode. She didn't confide in me anymore, not really. I was just a friend."

Susan smiled. "Almost like a former lover."

He nodded. "Yes, I see what you mean. After all, there was love in the offer she made me. It still gets me when I

think about it. A girl offering something so precious . . ."
His eyes had misted.

"Mr. Giordano . . ."

"Ron."

Susan smiled. "Ron. I can see this is difficult for you.
I'm looking for a clue, no matter how small, to who might
have killed her. If what happened between you and Patsy
offers a hidden link to the things we don't know, I need to
pursue that."

"I understand." He remained on his feet, but his demeanor was gentler. "To be completely honest, I did suspect
that after that evening at my place she lost her virginity with
someone. She didn't come back to my office for several
months. Then one day she showed up at the track. We ran a
few laps together, for old times' sake. She didn't say much.
Neither did I. I knew something was on her mind. Then she
told me she was sorry for what had happened, sorry she'd
put me in that position. I told her there was nothing to be
sorry for. Something in her manner made me strongly suspect that she had done with someone else what she wanted
to do with me. I worried, of course, that it was not the right
person. That the experience had made things worse for
Patsy instead of better." He sighed. "I never found out. We
weren't very close anymore, as I said."

"I appreciate your candor," Susan said.

As she stood up she saw that her skirt was wrinkled. She
smoothed it as best she could. It had been a long day, she
realized. She needed a change of clothes.

"The sad thing," Giordano said, "was that Patsy was really
quite attractive. She had long legs, pretty good-looking ones,
and a nice face. A nice smile. She could have attracted all the
men she wanted, if she had had more confidence."

Susan realized that he was looking at her own legs as he
spoke. She felt his appreciation.

"Her roommate told me the same thing," she said. "She
said she couldn't convince Patsy to dress more attractively."

"It isn't easy being a woman, is it?" he asked. "Even for
a shrink?"

"Even for a shrink." Susan gave him a tight smile.

"Let me walk you down."

He left his office door open as he walked Susan down the corridor to the stairs. The wintry landscape shone through the tall windows, the light already beginning to fade.

"Cold out there," he said. He took Susan's coat and held it for her.

"I never look forward to going outside." She slipped her arms into the coat, feeling the warmth of his hands on her shoulders. "I grew up in a milder climate. I still haven't gotten completely used to Chicago."

"No one ever gets completely used to Chicago," he said. "Not even the natives."

"You've been very helpful," Susan said. "I appreciate it."

"I'm finding this difficult," he said. "Patsy had so much to contribute. She was a fine person."

"That's the terrible thing about murder," Susan said. "It removes valuable people from the world. It impoverishes the rest of us."

He was looking at her closely.

"If I remember anything else," he said, "shall I call you?"

"Of course."

He watched her hurry down the steps, her briefcase slapping against her hip as she gathered the coat around her. A gust of wind blew her hair across her cheek. In that instant she looked like a schoolgirl, skipping along the pavement on strong young legs. Smiling, he let the door close.

Susan had frozen fingers and tingling calves by the time she reached her car. Her hand shook as she turned the key in the lock. The inside of the windshield was coated with ice.

"Come on, come on," she murmured as the engine sprang into life and the heater turned on with a blast.

She held her hands inside her sleeves to keep them warm. As she did so she pondered her interview with Ron Giordano. She didn't doubt his word. He had genuinely liked Patsy Morgenstern. His guilty conscience arose from

the fact that she had asked him for help and he had been unable to give it.

Susan did not believe he had lied about his physical relationship with Patsy. Had he been lying, she would have
seen signs of it.

On the contrary, his sincerity was his most salient quality.
It increased his already considerable attractiveness. Patsy
must have found it irresistible when she crossed his path as
an impressionable freshman two years ago. Susan herself
found it hard to resist.

With this thought in her mind, Susan drove out of the
university. The car slipped suddenly on a bit of ice that she
had not seen, and she slowed down, resolving to proceed
more cautiously.

DAVID GOLD WAS even more of a morning person than
Susan. He was in the habit of falling asleep almost before
his daughters did and waking up at five A.M. or even earlier. Many of his colleagues, hearing of his early hours,
wondered if he was a runner. But Gold was as unathletic as
he could be. His idea of exercise was watching a Bulls
game without putting his feet up.

When they worked a case together, Susan and Gold
would often meet for coffee at six or six-thirty. Gold didn't
go on duty until seven forty-five, and Susan's first patient
was usually at eight. They met at a favorite café a couple
of blocks from Susan's office building, a place run by an
Italian immigrant who believed in strong coffee. Every
cup served in the place was espresso, imported in bulk

from the owner's province. Susan enjoyed the tingling rush of the caffeine, and Gold savored the Italian pastries baked fresh daily on the premises.

The morning after Susan's interview with Ron Giordano, she met with Gold and gave him her impressions of Giordano and his relationship with Patsy Morgenstern.

"So you're telling me he's on the level," Gold concluded, twisting his mug and looking at her.

"I'm pretty convinced of it," Susan said. "He seems a straight shooter to me, very sincere about his work, dedicated to his students."

"You don't think he might have slept with her maybe once or twice?" Gold asked. "It sounds to me like he admired her."

"I really think he was telling the truth."

Gold nodded. "Well, that's one good reason why the semen we found in her wasn't his," he said. "We found blood type A. Giordano is O, according to his medical file at the university."

"Where does that leave us?" Susan asked.

Gold sighed. "We concentrated on male students at the university yesterday," he said. "At all the local colleges, in fact. My guys are up to their elbows in paper. You'd be surprised how many weirdos get into college. With scholarships, yet."

"I know," Susan said. "I've treated a lot of them. It's a difficult age. It brings out all kinds of pathology, even in people who are destined to be normal when they're finished growing up."

"Well, some of these dudes will never be normal for my money."

He sipped his coffee. "Speaking of things not being what they seem," he said. "The ME's people have been working up Patsy's blood. It turns out she was on steroids."

Susan raised an eyebrow. "Really?"

Gold nodded. "There's no doubt about it. The girl from the CCME gave me quite a lecture about it. Apparently they use two processes. The first is a screening assay that shows up the metabolites for a number of drug classes. They take a urine sample and mix it with antibodies for the various drugs, along with compounds of the drugs themselves that are tagged with chemical enzymes. Then they measure the absorption of light that passes through the processed sample to see how much, if any, of the enzyme-tagged drug remains, a tip-off that the antibodies have bound to the drug metabolite present in the sample. In a clean sample, the antibodies and the traces of the compounds themselves bind. In a sample containing metabolites of drugs—the drug by-products after being broken down by the body's metabolism—the metabolites compete with the tagged compounds for antibodies to bind with."

"Stop," Susan protested. "You're making my head spin. Do you know what time of the morning it is, by any chance?"

But Gold would not stop. He had a passion for facts and enjoyed reciting them, even in the morning.

"Then they get even more rigorous," he said. "They take the samples that seem positive and put them through a chromatography and mass spectrometry run. They use a beam of electrons to break up the compound, producing ions of different masses. Each compound has its own mass spectrum. They can identify a drug compound in as low a concentration as one part per billion. Remember the Canadian runner Ben Johnson? The guy who had his Olympic gold medal taken away? That's how they got him. Chromatography and mass spectrometry."

"And this process showed steroids in Patsy Morgenstern?" Susan asked.

"No doubt about it," Gold said. "I guess she thought she needed a little help, with that blown-out knee and all the heavy competition at the varsity level. Or her coach thought she did."

"Someone is going to get embarrassed in this," Susan suggested.

"Not really." Gold shrugged. "I'm Homicide. I don't

care about athletes taking steroids. But I do like to know things that aren't readily apparent."

Susan nodded. Like Gold, she had found that a thorough examination of the life of any person—normal or abnormal—reveals, almost within minutes, secrets unknown to that person's friends and family. All people lead secret lives. Being human involves breaking at least some of the rules society pays lip service to. A homicide detective like Gold found these things out by examining bodies and crime scenes. Susan found them out by listening to the confessions of her patients.

Over the years she had learned to feel compassion for people's private peccadilloes. Society demands such rigid conformity that many of its members can only assert their individuality through the secret transgressions of their sexual and emotional lives.

The only problem is that murderers take that secret life and translate it into violence. Until she met David Gold, Susan had led a sheltered life, even as a psychiatrist. Few of her patients had ever committed a crime, much less a murder. Thanks to Gold and Homicide, she had spent countless hours with killers who seemed hardly different from other people until one found out what they had done.

Gold had motioned to the waitress, pointing at his empty plate. With a smile she took another cream puff from the case by the register and brought it to him.

"Don't you ever gain weight?" Susan asked, guessing that the pastry contained at least two thousand calories.

Gold shook his head. "Good genes, I guess," he said. "Or maybe my ancestors spent so many generations starving in those shtetls that I get to eat all I want."

Susan smiled. She felt sorry for David's wife. Poor Carol Gold, who gained weight very easily and had to do hours of aerobics to keep her weight down, had to watch her husband gobble down all the junk food and desserts he wanted without ever gaining a pound. Even Gold's daughters, lovers of baked goods and candy, could not keep up with him.

"When is Michael coming in?" Gold asked.

"Tuesday."

"The girls are all excited. They're gonna want him to come over. Can you manage that?"

"I don't see why not."

Gold's daughters, Josie and Alissa, were good friends of Michael's and made a great fuss over him when he visited. They insisted on having him for at least one overnight each time. Susan had developed the ritual of taking him over and having dinner with David and Carol at their little house in Franklin Park. It was a charming place, messy but all the more homey for that. Carol was a delightful, warm mother. The Golds were not very serious about their Jewishness, but they did keep the major holidays for the sake of the girls, and intended for them to have their bat mitzvahs when they were old enough.

"I don't care that much if they believe in God," Gold said. "I just want them to feel that things have a meaning, that there is a difference between right and wrong. Good and evil. That's hard to come by these days."

Michael had once asked Susan whether he might become Jewish when he got older. Even as she gave him the predictable answer about his freedom to do whatever he wished, she couldn't help reflecting that David Gold's Jewishness had always fascinated her. She had once asked him what it felt like to be a Jew. He had laughed.

"Have you ever been in a faraway place, like a foreign country, and run into an American when you least expected it?" he had asked. "Well, that's what it's like for any Jew to run into another Jew. You've got something in common. Everything in common, in fact. Sometimes you're not very glad to see him, you wish you could be left alone. But it's a bond. And in this world, a bond with a stranger is a rare thing."

Susan looked at Gold now. He had put down his pastry and was regarding her intently.

"Yesterday in Weathers's office," he said. "You were holding something back. What was it?"

Susan smiled. Gold knew her better than anyone. It was hard to keep things from him.

"To be honest, I felt something different at the Morgenstern scene," Susan said. "It was as though . . ."

"As though what?"

Susan furrowed her brow. "The scene was staged. You and I know that. Staged to re-create a fantasy, no doubt. But I felt it was staged for us as well. I can't say just how. But something about it was less natural than other scenes, even serial murder scenes. I felt confused."

"Maybe it's part of his MO," Gold said. "You said yourself that organized killers refine their technique, taunt the police."

"Yes. Perhaps that was it."

"Well, don't worry about it. We'll get him. He's killed three girls from the same university. Somewhere on that campus there are people who have seen him, people who can make the connection. When you think about it, he hasn't been smart. The victims are too close together. In age, in type, even in alma mater. I think the guy is nearby."

"I hope you're right."

Susan did not want to say any more. Gold's reasoning was sound. So was his assessment of the crime scenes. The killer was very sick, perhaps to the point of becoming careless. And, to judge by appearances, he was very close at hand.

Susan kept her misgivings to herself. She did not want to tell Gold that the evil she'd felt at Patsy Morgenstern's apartment was different from what she normally felt at a murder scene. And now, with hindsight, she could see that the previous two scenes had seemed different as well.

Different how?

She still could not answer that question.

9

"SHE PROBABLY ASKED FOR IT."

Timothy Kuehn rustled his newspaper menacingly. His wife was sitting across the kitchen table from him. An item about the murder was on the third page of the *Sun-Times*. Tim always read the *Sun-Times* because he hated holding the *Tribune*. The tabloid format was much easier for him. In any case, his father had read the *Sun-Times,* as did almost everyone he knew at work. It was a working-man's paper.

He was waiting for his wife's reaction. Her silence spoke volumes.

"Three coeds." He grunted. "Girls run around too much these days anyway."

"What about Emily?" his wife asked. "Does she run around too much?"

The mention of his daughter's name pushed a button, as it always did.

"What are you trying to do?" he asked, lowering the paper. "Piss me off?"

Dorothy looked down at her half-eaten supper.

"Must you use language like that?"

He closed the paper with deliberation. His eyes narrowed as he stared at her.

"Don't bring my daughter up to me," he said.

An angry impulse made her attack when she should have retreated.

"Her life hasn't been a bed of roses, you know."

He slammed down the newspaper. His face had turned

71

red. His lips were trembling. She knew she had made a mistake.

"Nice talking to you." He was standing up, pushing the kitchen chair back violently.

"Where are you going?" she asked. "Don't leave."

"I'm going where I don't have to listen to shit." He spoke the offensive word with pleasure.

He grabbed his coat from the hook by the door.

"Tim!" she cried.

The door was open. She knew she wouldn't be able to talk him out of leaving. In fact, the quarrel was just his excuse to leave.

"See you later." Now his voice sounded more resigned than angry. He was acknowledging the problem between them. On another day this might almost have been an overture. But before she could say another word, he was gone. The car door slammed, and the engine burst into life while Dorothy stood at the table, feeling the brief rush of frigid air swirling around her legs.

The car backed out and tore up the little street with a roar from the aged muffler.

She sat down at the table for a long moment, glancing around the kitchen, which smelled strongly of the pork she had cooked. The silence was oppressive. Since Emily had left, they rarely ate in the dining room anymore. The little kitchen was an arena perfectly sized for their endlessly reiterated conflict. Tonight it felt more cramped, more stale than ever.

She sat for a few more minutes, pushing nervously at the napkin. She glanced at the little pictures of Emily above the calendar. Her daughter would not come home this year, as she had last year. The scene Tim had created on her last visit had driven her away for good. With that the family had ceased to exist in any serious way. And family had always meant everything to Dorothy.

She got up with a sigh and began doing the dishes. At least she had a dishwasher now, she mused, looking with gratitude at the new Kenmore. All her life she had done dishes by hand, resisting the idea of a dishwasher even when Tim had made enough to afford it. But when the new neighbors moved in and Mrs. Costello showed her what a godsend her KitchenAid was, Dorothy took the plunge. Now she could not imagine doing dishes by hand.

She placed the leftover pork in a bowl and rinsed the pan. As she was putting it into the dishwasher, she heard a sharp noise outside, and a small cry of distress. Wiping her hands hurriedly, she went to the door through which her husband had left and looked out the glass pane.

A man was lying on the icy concrete of the drive. He wore a long wool coat, and there was a white cane alongside him. Obviously, he had slipped on the ice.

Dorothy opened the door a few inches and called out, "Are you all right?"

The man was struggling to sit up, breathing heavily. He did not answer.

"Are you all right?"

Realizing he was blind, Dorothy tiptoed across the ice to help him up. He seemed shaken but good-humored.

"My own fault," he said. "I wasn't paying attention."

She helped him to his feet. He was a small man, not more than five feet five or six. She handed him the cane.

"That darned ice," she said. "I put salt down twice today. When is this weather ever going to warm up?"

He moved his head this way and that, as blind people do. His hands were hidden by wool gloves with leather palms.

"Thank you kindly. I'm fine. None the worse for wear."

A stack of cards or handbills was on the ice at his feet. Dorothy saw that it was getting wet.

"You dropped your papers." She retrieved the cards and made an effort to stack them neatly. "Here you go."

"Thank you." He was looking at right angles to her, a faint smile on his lips. He wore dark glasses. "Are you Mrs. Kuehn?"

"Yes."

"Wonderful. So I found my way to you after all. I'm Mr.

Calhoun. I just wanted to drop off an announcement. Your nice neighbor, Mrs. Costello, told me you might be home."

"Thank you." Dorothy was getting cold already, but she had no intention of inviting him in. One had to be careful of strangers, even in this neighborhood. Besides, Tim had long ago told her he would not countenance solicitors in his house. Even the pastor's visits maddened him. He could be very unpleasant to telephone solicitors and door-to-door salesmen.

The blind man peeled off a flyer and held it out in her direction. The legend, WINTER CARNIVAL, looked up at her in the gathering darkness. "Pay us a visit if you have the time. All proceeds go to charity."

Dorothy looked up at the sky, which was now dropping something that looked like freezing rain. "Isn't it terrible for you to be out delivering those in this weather?"

"Oh, no." He smiled. "I never mind the weather. I go out in all kinds of weather. Can't stand staying at home."

"Well, you're braver than I am," she said. "This rain chills my bones."

"Yes, it's not friendly weather," he said. "I used to live in Buffalo. I thought that was bad in the winter. Snow piled up to the windows. But this wind is worse. Sometimes it will blow you right off the sidewalk." He was holding himself with dignity, his cane over his arm. A little man, she thought, with a self-respect proportionate to the battle he had to fight in life. She wondered whether he had been blind from birth.

The flyer in her hand was already moist from the rain.

"Well," she said, "I'd better be getting in. Thanks for stopping by."

"My pleasure, Mrs. Kuehn. Be sure and come see us, now. Lots of prizes. Do you have children?"

"A daughter. But she's away at school."

"College girl?" he asked. "Or private school?"

"College," Dorothy lied.

"Well, I imagine that keeps her busy. Bye-bye, now." He moved off along the walk. His cane whispered against the icy concrete. She was touched by the image of his slow, firm progress.

She went back inside and poured herself a drink. Leaving the flyer on the counter, she quickly finished rinsing the dishes. She put the soap into the Kenmore but waited to turn it on. She wanted to finish the little glass of whiskey.

All her life Dorothy had been a teetotaler. But since Emily had left and Tim had begun drinking so heavily, it seemed that alcohol was a full partner in whatever destiny was overtaking her marriage. She had first tried it out just to see what Tim saw in it. Then, perversely, she had continued to drink, always when he was out, perhaps to get back at him. She knew he would be drunk when he returned. He would fall into bed without speaking to her. An emotion on the borderline between rebellion and hopelessness possessed her as she reflected that whiskey would be on her breath, too, as they both fell asleep.

The glass was finished. She had drunk it more quickly than last night, she mused. She put it into the Kenmore and turned the dishwasher on. Then she headed toward the back of the bungalow. She would change clothes before returning to the living room to watch television.

She would be alone all evening. Tim would stay at the tavern until at least eleven with his drinking buddies, mostly unemployed men in middle age. Assuming, that is, that he really spent all these evenings at the tavern, and only with men. This latter worry had begun to prey on her mind of late.

She took off her blouse and threw it in the hamper. Her skirt she folded and put back in the drawer. She grimaced as she caught a glimpse of herself in the mirror. She was so overweight, so out of shape. It seemed a lifetime ago that she had admired her firm breasts and shapely legs in the mirror of her parents' house.

She opened the closet to get her nightgown. Ah, that tiny closet! And this outmoded bungalow. She wished she and Tim could move farther west, to Hickory Hills perhaps, where they had those nice new houses with two thousand square feet. This place was like living in a trailer.

She slipped the nightgown over her head, turning back toward the bed. When her head came through she saw the man.

He was smiling at her. He looked very different. Almost unrecognizable, in fact. She wondered why. Then she realized it was his eyes. He had taken off the dark glasses. The eyes were tiny, black. Like little pieces of coal, shiny but impenetrable. It made their stare the more unnerving.

"Dorothy," he said.

"How did you get in here?" She was too startled to be scared. The man was shaking his head gently from side to side. His smile was wistful, almost sympathetic.

Dorothy's nostrils twitched at the presence of a sudden odor. It was a sweetish, pungent smell, reminiscent of her long-forgotten chemistry experiments in high school.

"Dorothy. Kuehn," he said. "That's with an *h,* isn't it?"

Dorothy stared at him, her mouth open.

"I hope they spell it right. You're going to be famous."

"Famous? Me?" She put a diffident hand to her breast.

"Of course," he said, coming forward with dainty steps. "A famous person. You've waited all your life for this."

He had her around the waist, almost like a dance partner. It felt a bit absurd, for she was much taller than he. She thought of his slow, steady progress through the snow. The smell was stronger now. Nausea rose inside her.

"And everyone will wonder, *Why Mrs. Kuehn?*" he said. "What did Dorothy do to deserve this honor?"

Like a playful child he had darted behind her and was holding both her arms. She was being pushed toward the floor. She was astonished by his strength. She would have cried out, but the quick hand closing over her throat prevented it.

"You're Number Four!" he exclaimed. "You'll be in all the papers, Dorothy!"

Her breath was cut off now, and she felt a sharp pressure in the middle of her back. The room was going dark. She thought of the blind man's dark glasses, and the hard little black eyes. An image of herself bloomed before her mind, a blind woman adventuring across frozen wastelands with a white cane. Who would show her the way? Where was she headed?

Then the blackness turned red, and she lost consciousness.

10

"THIS IS A SCANDAL," said Jaime's father, turning off the television as he moved toward the dining room.

"Somehow I didn't expect it to go any further." Her mother was putting plates of roast beef on the table as Jaime brought in large bowls of mashed potatoes and peas. The dinner was more copious than usual because Jaime was home tonight.

"Things always go further," he said. "It's the nature of them."

They all sat down. The parents were in the same seats they had occupied since Jaime was a little girl. Facing each other, with Jaime between.

"Well . . ." Jaime was inclined to disagree with him, but she feared her father was right in this case.

They were not strangers to violence, though this quiet home seemed to belie the fact. There had been a time, before Jaime's birth, when this house had been attacked. Her father had made headlines by insisting on remaining here.

"But this time it wasn't a young girl," Jaime said.

"Yes. That is interesting." Her father looked at her over his coffee cup. "What do you make of it?"

He spoke to her as familiarly as if she was his wife. He

always adopted this tone when he asked her opinions on things.

"I guess the bastard is branching out," Jaime said. "Don't they usually?" She spoke with deliberate flippancy, to hide her own nervousness.

"I really don't know," he said, wincing only slightly at her language. "I'm not much on serial killings. The kind I know are different." He reached for a roll. As always, he wore his vest and tie at the dinner table. His formality was a relic of his own childhood, as well as a reflection of his careful personality.

"Actually," Jaime said, "maybe it's not as different as it looks. My sociology professor says that serial killers have a lot in common with hate crimes. The impulse is the same. The victim is chosen because something about him or her creates unbearable tension inside the killer. Like an insult to his identity."

Her father's eyes had narrowed. "Has this professor ever lived on Grand Boulevard?"

"He knows what he's talking about, Dad." Jaime looked impatient. She was surprised at her own calm. Even the fork in her hand was not shaking.

"Well, whatever the truth is, this makes four women dead," he said. "Four is too many. I don't know what's wrong with the police in this city."

Despite her tension Jaime smiled. She liked it when her father sounded as confused and resentful as everybody else. He spent so much of his life trying to be wise that it was nice to see him let down his hair. She enjoyed watching him take out the garbage, swear at a stain on his tie, throw popcorn at the TV screen when the Cubs lost again. Sometimes she wished his public life allowed him more of this.

"I'm sure they're trying as hard as they can," her mother said. "Look at the publicity, for heaven's sake. This couldn't be worse."

Today's headline had been the biggest Jaime had ever seen on a *Tribune*. REIGN OF TERROR DEEPENS. The fact that the woman was older than the three college girls only seemed to fuel the fire.

"It will be worse when it's five," her father said. "And it won't be long. Not the way it's going."

His wife sighed. "You know, everything doesn't have to be viewed from the dark side. Maybe they'll catch him. I'm sure they're moving heaven and earth."

The father did not respond to this. His eyes were on Jaime.

"How's Reta?" he asked, referring to her roommate.

Jaime grimaced.

"Dad, we're fine. Don't worry about us. Just forget it."

"Why don't you move home for a while? Reta won't miss you. She's got the dog."

"Dad . . ."

"I'm serious." Sensing her resistance, he began to dig in his heels.

Her mother sat watching them, saying nothing. This was not the first time she had seen them take up positions on opposite sides. When Jaime was a teenager the dinner table had sometimes felt like a battleground.

"Well, it's a good time to take extra precautions anyway," she hazarded.

"I've spent my whole life taking extra precautions," Jaime reminded her.

"That's true," said Mother, looking at her husband.

"Yes, and sometimes it's not enough," the father insisted. They all knew what he meant. He carried an encyclopedia of violence in his memory. It was impossible to argue with him when he began quoting from it.

"I'll be fine." Jaime heard the tremor in her own voice. "May I be excused?"

She went into her room to get her coat. She paused to look at herself in the mirror. Her face looked so frightened that she could not understand why her parents had not commented on it.

"Come on," she whispered aloud to herself. "Come on!"

At first she had been relieved by the face in the newspaper. The pattern was broken. That had to be good news.

But then recognition had coiled in her like the memory of a misdeed, and she had returned to the kitchen to look again. This time there was no doubt. Her hands shook so badly that she had to drop the newspaper like a hot potato. Luckily for her, her mother had been in another part of the house.

She threw on her coat and returned to the kitchen to say good-bye.

"Take care, sweetie. Have a good week." Her mother kissed her cheek.

"You, too."

Jaime kissed her father a bit too hastily. Alerted, he grasped her hand and smiled.

"Don't listen to me," he said. "I know I'm always the voice of doom."

Jaime nodded. "I know that, Dad."

"But be careful." He could not let her go without a final paternal warning. She was reminded of his many speeches to her when she was dating in high school. He would often have a sidelong gleam of self-criticism in his eyes, as though to say, "I know I'm overprotective, I know I'm ridiculous. But listen to me anyway. You cannot be too careful. No girl can—but least of all you." It was this idea, *least of all you,* that maddened her. She could not stand the burden of being more at risk than other girls. What had she done to deserve it?

"Don't worry about it. Have a good day. I'll call you." She waited patiently for him to let her go. He did so, but as she turned to leave he gave her a last searching look.

PART TWO

11

MICHAEL ARRIVED ON Tuesday, half-asleep after his long journey. Susan gave him supper and put him to bed. When he woke up, Carolyn was waiting, eager to ply him with presents she had bought over the past few months and to ask him how things were in California.

Susan felt a pang as she realized that her son looked older. It had been two months since his last visit. He was taller and slimmer, and he moved differently. Most of all his face bore the signs—subtle but massive—of maturation. Susan felt something akin to grief as she hugged him. It was as though a whole beautiful series of Michaels, two months' worth of fascinating little individuals, had been taken away from her.

Carolyn seemed to be having the same reaction. Her normally hard-boiled, funny personality seemed to melt at the sight of Michael.

Carolyn professed a generalized irritation at children, calling them "a pain in the ass" and claiming she never regretted not having had any with her ex-husband. Yet she doted on Michael with a passionate devotion that made Susan smile, and made her suspect that there was deep discontent behind Carolyn's bluff exterior.

"He looks older, don't you think?" she asked Susan.

"Yes, I think so."

"Damn. I hope those outfits I bought will fit him. I looked all over town for those colors."

Susan smiled. "Don't worry about it. If they don't fit

you can take them back. We'll all go. We can shop for something else."

Carolyn's attachment to Michael seemed doubly significant in the light of her relationships with men. Her ex-husband, to hear her describe him, was an expert manipulator who managed to make her feel guilty for everything she thought and did. "I spent nine years trying to please that bum," she once told Susan, "and the harder I tried the more irritated he got. You should have seen the look on his face when I finally walked out. He was flabbergasted. It was so out of character for me to show any gumption."

Yet Carolyn's troubles with men had not ended with her marriage. She had worked her way up to a position of great responsibility in a few short years, and had won awards for a dozen or more of the investigative features she had produced. But she had not found a new romantic interest of any substance. And when she talked about her work, she painted a picture of herself as a woman drawn inexorably to exploitative relationships, a woman who could never be trusted to stand on her own two feet or to avoid being manipulated by others.

Carolyn treated Michael as though he was the one man she could trust. Astonishingly, he seemed to sense this and was quite courtly and protective toward her in his little way. Sometimes Susan would see them holding hands as they watched television or walked along a street, and she would get the unavoidable impression that it was Michael taking care of Carolyn rather than the other way around. Such was the limitless complexity of human relationships, she mused.

SUSAN BARELY HAD time to get Michael settled before she received a call from David Gold asking her to meet him at Abel Weathers's office. The meeting was in progress when she arrived.

"The press is going to kill me for this," Weathers was saying. "Three coeds is a crime spree. Three coeds and a housewife is a holocaust." It was typical of Weathers to personalize all crime in the city as his own cross to bear.

David Gold once suggested that Weathers would have been happy to eliminate the citizenry entirely for the sake of his own peace of mind. Another detective had disagreed, saying that without the citizenry Weathers would not have an audience for his news conferences.

Gold was sitting quietly in his chair, looking out the window. He knew, as did everyone in Homicide, that this fourth victim was a public relations disaster. Coming so quickly on the heels of the third murder, the death of Dorothy Kuehn was perfectly calculated to spread terror throughout the city. Demands for aggressive action by the authorities were already all over the media. Abel Weathers's face was on every TV screen, photogenic with its deep tan and piercing eyes. He firmly denied that there was reason for panic, insisting that definite leads were being followed up. Reporters' skeptical faces were prominently shown by the news cameramen.

Weathers hated to look bad on television. His mood was dark and irritable.

"What do your guys think?" he asked Gold.

"The feeling is that the killer is branching out." Gold placed his hands on the arms of the chair. "The MO is the same, there's little doubt we're dealing with the same man. Same signature in the method of strangulation. Same eye gouging. Somehow he got her to let him in. Her husband was out drinking with friends. The neighbors saw nothing." Gold shrugged. "What can I say?"

"But why a middle-aged housewife from the South Side?" Weathers asked. "What the hell does she have to do with three female athletes?"

"That's what we can't figure," Gold said. "Unless he's simply widening his hunt pattern. Many serial killers start with one type of victim and get less and less choosy as they go on. Bundy, for instance. He started very neatly, and ended up trying to waste a whole sorority house in a night."

"What about Kuehn?" Weathers asked. "Is there anything unusual about her at all?"

Gold looked at his notes. "She had problems with her

husband," he said. "He's a drinker, and he's been getting worse, according to a couple of the neighbors I talked to. There was some shouting now and then, but no physical abuse. Nobody saw bruises."

"Was the husband accounted for?"

"Sure. That was the first thing we checked. He was drinking at his local watering spot with his usual buddies. He's pretty shook up about things now. Blames himself."

"So, just another all-American family," Weathers said.

"Yes and no." Gold opened the folder he had brought. "I had a long phone conversation with Dorothy Kuehn's daughter this afternoon. Her name is Emily. She's living with a man in Sedona, Arizona. He's an artist, a sculptor. She herself is a craftsperson, a sort of artisan."

He sighed. "She was evasive about her family, but she finally came clean. It turns out she had a problem with her father. He was possessive of her when she was a girl, always following her around, checking up on her, throwing her boyfriends out of the house. Things like that. The mother was a marshmallow, just sitting on the sidelines and doing nothing to help. The daughter ended up getting pregnant and having an abortion. The family is Catholic. When the father discovered what had happened, he threw the girl out. She was only seventeen at the time. She went to California, where a school friend of hers had moved, and got a job. Later she finished a GED and then worked her way through junior college in San Jose."

He closed the file.

"Based on what I could gather from the neighbors, the loss of Emily was the last straw for Dorothy's marriage. Her husband became an outright drunk. The neighbors told my guys that he would storm out of the house early in the evening and come home after midnight, driving pretty badly. Sometimes he would knock over garbage cans. That kind of thing."

He touched the file folder without opening it. "The ME found alcohol in Dorothy's blood. Her neighbors all said she was a teetotaler. Looks like she was beginning to drink."

Weathers was looking at his watch.

"Very interesting," he said, "but it doesn't give us a killer. The husband is clean, so now what?"

Gold shook his head. "What can I tell you? We have no connection to the coeds or the killer. This comes completely out of left field."

Susan sat forward. "There's something I think we should consider," she said.

Weathers regarded her in silence.

"Perhaps the very unlikelihood of Dorothy Kuehn as a victim is a clue," Susan said. "She was the fourth victim in order of time. But she might not have been the fourth in order of choice."

Gold was sitting with his hands clasped behind his neck. "What do you mean?"

"Suppose," Susan said, "that the killer knew Dorothy Kuehn in the past. Suppose he had the image of Dorothy Kuehn in his mind long before he targeted the three college girls. Suppose the image of Dorothy was the oldest, psychologically speaking. It could be that he worked his way up to her—back to her, I should say—by killing the other three. Perhaps she was his original choice."

There was a silence. Gold rubbed his chin ruminatively.

"This theory would accomplish one thing," Susan said. "It would explain the apparent divergence between Dorothy Kuehn and the other victims. The three college girls were tune-ups, so to speak, which finally emboldened the killer to go after his original target."

"Very clever," Weathers said. "The only problem with that is the killer didn't pick three girls who looked like frumpy housewives. He picked athletes."

"Suppose that when the killer knew Dorothy Kuehn, she wasn't a housewife," Susan said. "Suppose she was young, attractive, and perhaps athletic. Like the first three victims."

Gold's eyes had opened wider. "I see what you mean."

"I think we should investigate Dorothy Kuehn's past," Susan said, "with specific attention to the time in her life when she might have appeared, or been perceived, as similar to the three dead coeds. Probably between ages fifteen and twenty-one. Was she an athlete? A cheerleader? Things like that."

Gold said, "It's a stretch."

"But everything serial killers do is a stretch," Susan reminded him. "They choose victims for the most far-fetched, fanciful reasons. The victims remind them of things that happened long ago, even things that were forgotten long ago. We should at least check it out."

Weathers was scowling.

"What if you're wrong?" he asked. "What if the bastard is simply branching out?"

"I agree that that is possible," Susan said. "But serial killers tend to be very rigid in their behavior, especially in the early stages. I find it odd that after three murders so stereotyped in the victim choice and MO, he would deviate. The pattern is just establishing itself. Most serial killers would attack five or six more girls—all athletes, perhaps—before changing anything."

"Why athletes, by the way?" Gold asked.

"There is a certain kind of male who finds athletic females attractive," Susan said. "Adolescent boys almost always fantasize about girls who are strong, active. It can mean several things. An older girl, for instance. Someone who was bigger and stronger than the male when he was young. Our two taller victims particularly suggest this. I wouldn't be surprised if the killer is himself not very tall. These girls were probably taller than he, and were perhaps chosen for that reason."

"Big sister," Weathers observed with a crooked smile. "We always come back to Freud."

"Whatever you may think of Freud," Susan said calmly, "big sisters have a powerful sexual effect on little brothers. In dreams and fantasies they almost always stand for the mothers. So this is something we should consider."

Gold was looking at Susan. "Dorothy Kuehn had a brother," he said. "Younger than her." He opened the file and turned a page. "Four years younger. According to the family, he's long gone. But it wouldn't hurt to look for him."

Weathers was looking at Susan. "You know," he said with a twisted grin, "you ought to stick to evidence once in a while, and cut the Freudian crap. Some killers kill because they like to kill. Not because they had a thing for their sister."

Susan did not react.

Weathers looked at his watch again. "I don't have time for any more of this," he said. "I have to give the press something they can sell, and it can't make us look like assholes. Got any ideas?"

Gold said, "Why don't you tell them the murder of Dorothy Kuehn represents a major break in the case, and we can't divulge details until we run it down? That will buy us some time."

"Not much time," Weathers said. "I'll try it, though."

He turned to Susan. "With all due respect, Doctor, our ass is in a sling. We need more than Freud right now."

"Unfortunately for us," Gold intervened in Susan's defense, "Freud may be all we have."

Weathers was touching the long-stemmed pen on his desk set again. He twirled it in its base, muttering, "Witch doctors." Then he pulled it out and shoved it back in again.

Susan was watching him. "May I use your pen?" she asked.

Weathers smiled. "Forget your own? Isn't that a Freudian slip?" he asked. "Be my guest."

He removed it from the base and held it out to her. She took a small notebook from her purse and jotted something down. Still holding the pen in her hand, she looked at Weathers.

"Does she still swim?" she asked.

"What?" Weathers asked. "Who?"

Susan studied his face, which was turning red.

"Never mind," she said, leaning forward to push the pen back into its base.

"Does who swim?" Weathers pursued.

Susan stood up, looking at Gold. "Shall we go?"

"Yeah." Gold was on his feet. To Weathers he said, "I'll check you later. We'll see about this brother."

Weathers, looking at Susan, did not reply.

Gold and Susan left the office. Weathers sat back behind his desk. He drummed his fingers on the desktop. He looked at his watch. He was already late for his next appointment, but he did not move.

When the room had been silent for a full minute, he opened his wallet and flipped through the plastic card holders until he found a faded snapshot. It showed an adolescent girl in a swimsuit, waving to someone from a diving board. She had bright, playful eyes and a beautiful figure. She could not have been more than seventeen when the picture was taken.

Weathers pursed his lips as he looked at the picture. He took a long breath and replaced it in the wallet.

"Bitch," he said aloud.

12

THE BOY LAY in the small bed under the window, listening to the city's muted sounds mingle with those from inside the apartment.

Beyond the closed door his mother was moving about the living room. Music played, so softly that it was barely a murmur. Pages turned as she read through her papers. A cup was put down gently on a tabletop. All this was eclipsed by the rumble of a truck on the street below, then the slow rise of a siren haunting the city night. A second siren, far away, echoed the first. Then the outer sounds died down, and once again the sweet, slow music whispered beyond the door.

He looked at the old armchair that used to scare him when the lights were out. In a way it still scared him, but he kept his eyes on it, reminding himself he was bigger now.

There were file cabinets against the wall, next to the dresser whose middle drawer was kept empty for his clothes. In a corner were a couple of large cardboard boxes that had been here the first time he came and still had not been put away. His mother apologized for them, but he had come to see them as part of the furniture.

On the wall were his favorite things, the pictures. The bigger one showed his mother with her class at medical school. When he was smaller she used to pick him up and point herself out, laughing at how young and ugly she looked. He did not think she looked ugly.

Alongside this picture hung, in a much smaller frame, the old photograph of his mother's parents. They were posed stiffly, the mother seated in a chair and the father standing beside her. They looked like they lived a very long time ago. The mother's eyes were sad. The father's eyes were hooded and a bit suspicious of the camera. But in them there was a sidelong glance at his wife, which held a secret feeling.

To the right of this picture hung the best of all, the picture of Mother as a girl with her father. They were sitting on top of a picnic table at a state park. Both had their feet on the bench part of the table. They were separated by two or three feet and did not seem to have noticed the photographer until the last second. The father was wearing blue jeans and a wool shirt. He rested his chin on his joined hands and looked into the camera with easy eyes, too full of his languid camping mood to be suspicious.

Mother was holding an ice cream sandwich. She wore shorts and a white T-shirt with a name lettered on it, *Camp Pathfinder*. The word *Ontario* was lost in a furl of the fabric.

The boy loved this photo. The father and daughter were calm and waiting for nothing. The sun sent light and shadow through the tree limbs all around, which were soft and out of focus. A knot in the wood of the tabletop shone beside the little girl's thigh. A bird was sitting on a branch, its beak open, perhaps to sing. The father held a cigarette cupped in his hand, but no smoke came from it.

The ice cream sandwich in Mother's hand had not been touched. The wrapper was gone, she was holding the sandwich itself in fingers that would soon have chocolate stuck to them. And soon a bite would be taken from the ice cream, quick before it melts, and another and another until it was gone. But not yet. The sandwich was new and cold in the shady air.

The boy could come here a thousand times and lie on this bed with the city humming outside, and the sandwich would always be as new as the light in the tree limbs, and the bird would have its beak open to speak, and the little girl and her father would glance curiously out of the picture, together in their camping afternoon, too calm even to smile. It was as though time had slowed down, through a sort of spell. It was so slow that ice cream could not melt or faces turn away. This was the magic of the picture.

A finger knocked quietly at the door.

"Can I say good night?"

"Yes."

She came to sit on the edge of the bed. Her weight pushed the edge of the mattress down, drawing him toward her.

"Did you have a nice day today?" she asked.

"I fed the pigeons," he said. "Carolyn helped me. We took bread."

"That sounds like fun. Did the pigeons come up close to you?"

"They walk funny."

She smiled, running a cool hand across his brow. "Yes, they do."

"Busy."

"Yes. And cooing."

"I drew a picture."

"I know. It's on the refrigerator. I pasted it up just now. I like it very much. It's my favorite picture."

He glanced past her shoulder to the photograph on the wall.

"Mom."

"Yes, honey."

"Do you miss your mother and father?"

She took his hand. She glanced at the picture herself.

"Sometimes," she said. "They died a very long time ago. You know that. But yes, sometimes I miss them."

"Do you remember the afternoon in the picture?" he asked. "With the ice cream?"

She laughed. "You always ask me that. No, I don't remember. Not the park, and not the T-shirt, and not even the ice cream sandwich. I've forgotten."

"Mom, do you wish they were back alive?"

"My parents? Certainly I do."

"What would you do if they were back alive?" he asked. There was insistence in his voice, and perhaps anxiety.

"The first thing I would do," she said, "would be to introduce them to you. They would be so proud of you. Then I would tell them all about you, and about the things that have happened all these years, to you and to me. And they would have a thousand questions, and you and I would answer them all."

"Would you tell them about Daddy and Elaine?"

"Of course I would."

He held her hand as he thought about his father and Elaine. He liked them both, but not as much as his mother. Somehow his visits here, to this odd apartment with its nooks and crannies, and this room that never got finished— somehow all this was more like home than his own house back in California. He guessed it was because his mother was so quiet. Quiet and slow. Nothing ever seemed to hurry her or make a noise in her. And because she was so quiet, time seemed to slow down when he was with her. He didn't have to be ready for anything in advance. This was a nice feeling.

"Shall I tell you a story?" she asked.

"About the birds and the crumbs."

She looked puzzled. "The birds and the crumbs?"

"That's what you told me the last night I was here," he said. "About the crumbs in the forest."

She laughed. "Oh! What a good memory you have. I had forgotten all about that. Was I telling you about Hansel and Gretel?"

He nodded.

"Do you want to hear it again now?"

"Yes."

She looked away, as though trying to remember.

"Well, the parents were so poor that they had decided to send the children into the forest where they would never find their way back," she said. "The father didn't really want to do this, but the stepmother made him do it. Do you remember that?"

He nodded. "Why didn't the stepmother want them to come back?" he asked.

"Because she and the father were so poor," Susan repeated. "And maybe because she didn't love the children as much as the father did."

As she spoke she recalled that Michael was a child of divorce, living with his father and stepmother. No wonder he asked for this story, she thought.

"The first time the children left a trail of little stones and found their way back home. But the second time they left a trail of bread crumbs. And that was their mistake. Do you remember why?"

"Because of the birds."

"That's right. Hansel took a loaf of bread with him and dropped little pieces to make a trail home. But while he and Gretel were in the forest, the birds ate up all the bread crumbs. So when they tried to find their way home, there was no trail."

The story made Susan uncomfortable. Its glib description of parental abandonment was unsettling. So was its evocation of dangers far beyond the powers of small children. She could not help remembering that it was her own work as a law-enforcement consultant that had cost her custody of Michael five years ago. One of her cases had unexpectedly put him at risk, and she had been forced to send him to live with Nick in California for his own safety. Though the fault was not her own, she still felt responsible. This fact never ceased to color her feelings about her son when he came to visit.

The phone rang in the other room. "I'll be right back," she said.

She went into the living room and picked up the receiver. "Hello?"

"This is Gold. Listen. I found Dorothy Kuehn's brother. We've got him downtown. I thought you might want to sit in on some of the interrogation."

"Is he a suspect?"

"Not exactly. He's in voluntarily. But I have hopes. This guy is not entirely kosher."

Susan looked at her watch.

"I was just saying good night to Michael. I'll be down in about half an hour."

Susan returned to the bedroom. Her son was groggy with sleep.

"I'll finish the story tomorrow," she said. "Have a good rest, honey. I love you."

She bent to kiss him. He ran a finger along the inside of her hand, a gesture that was peculiar to him. He gave her a tired smile.

"Good night, Mama."

His eyes were closing fast as she slipped through the door. She left it ajar, so that the light from the living room sent a shaft along the floor and across the ceiling.

A HALF HOUR later Susan was at Area Six Headquarters.

She looked through the one-way mirror into the interrogation room. Two bored-looking detectives were sitting on gunmetal desk chairs across a table from a thirtyish man in jeans and a work shirt. Despite his attire he looked somehow intellectual, even effete. He wore metal-rimmed glasses, his blondish hair was rather long, and his hands, though rough from physical work, were aristocratic, the fingers slim and sensitive.

"He's a loner," Gold was saying. "For the last four years he's worked steady as a mill hand in northern Indiana. But since he graduated from high school he's drifted from job to job, mostly in mills and factories. He spent a few years in California—we're checking on that now. He came back here six years ago. He lives in a little apartment in Gary."

Gold turned over a page of the file. "No convictions here or out west," he said. "He seems to be gay. There were a few gay porno magazines in his apartment, and some pictures of a guy who must have been his lover out in California. No sign of a regular partner here."

He looked at Susan. "But, he has no alibi for any of the crimes. He's almost never at home at night. His landlady told me that. Probably he's out cruising for dates. But he could be up to anything. Egan and Petty are talking to him about the dead girls. He's not saying anything yet. But I have hopes."

"What about his sister?" Susan asked.

"Not much," Gold replied. "He says they came from a repressed family, very strict, Catholic. Apparently his mother wanted him to go into the priesthood, and he himself was interested as a boy. Then he came out of the closet and left home. He had a few letters from Dorothy over the years but never saw the family, not even for funerals. However, he did come back to this part of the country."

As Susan watched, the young man took out a cigarette. One of the detectives lit it for him. The young man darted a look into the detective's face as he drew from the flame.

"What's this?" she asked Gold.

"One of the jackets on his coatrack."

Gold had brought it for Susan. She touched the jacket. It was old, almost threadbare, like a high school letter jacket. She felt in the pockets. A handkerchief, a ticket stub from a movie theater.

"What do you think?" Gold asked.

Susan's eyes half-closed. She pressed the ticket in her fingers. She felt a sudden, very unpleasant impulse, a sort of throb of shame. It always made her uncomfortable to invade the private world of another human being. With Dorothy Kuehn's brother it felt worse than usual.

"What's his name?" Susan asked.

"Henry."

"Could I speak to him?" she asked.

"Wait a minute." Gold left the tiny room. A moment later he appeared in the interrogation room. He spoke briefly to one of the officers, then to the young man, who shrugged.

Susan stood up. The door opened. Gold stood back. "He's all yours."

Susan went around to the door of the interrogation room and knocked timidly. One of the officers opened the door.

"Henry, this is Dr. Shader. She wants to ask you a couple of questions."

Both officers left the room, and Susan was alone with the young man.

"How do you do?" She held out a hand. The young man shook it without enthusiasm. Close up, he was rougher looking than through the one-way mirror. His eyes were suspicious. She saw a tattoo on his upper arm.

"My name is Susan Shader, and I'm helping in the investigation of your sister's death. May I sit down?"

The young man nodded assent.

Susan pulled back the metal chair. "I wonder if you could shed any light on what happened," she said, "based on your knowledge of the neighborhood your sister lived in, and her social contacts. According to what I hear, she lived only a few miles from the area where you both grew up. Tell me, was she still friendly with the friends and relatives you both knew as children?"

The young man looked around him as though Susan were not even there. The posture of his body was eloquent in its expression of contempt for the police and for her.

There was a pack of Marlboros on the tabletop, apparently left by the officers. He tapped one out for himself and lit it with a green plastic lighter that lay beside the pack.

"Could I have one?" Susan asked. She had not smoked

in five years. The red color of the design on the Marlboro pack brought back memories.

The young man studied her face in silence. Then he tapped out a second cigarette, placed it between his lips, and lit it from the burning ash of the first one. He handed it to Susan. She noticed that the filter tip bore a tiny piece of tobacco, moist with his saliva.

She took a drag of the cigarette, smiling slightly. He was watching her with amusement.

"Establish confidence," he said. "Nothing like a shared cigarette."

The unaccustomed smoke hit Susan's lungs with a shock. She had to suppress the impulse to cough. A thousand mornings came back to her, with their mingled aromas of coffee and cigarettes, and the odd tingly throb of nicotine after a night's abstinence.

"Did you ever notice," she asked, "that Marlboros in the soft pack taste quite different from Marlboros in the box?"

He shook his head. "I smoke Kools," he said.

Susan's face lit up. "Kools. I smoked Kools when I was seventeen years old, in high school. That's a strong cigarette."

At this the young man softened a bit. He dragged on his cigarette and tapped the ash into the cheap metal ashtray on the table.

"I'm sorry you're being put through this," she said.

"No big deal." Underneath his sullen manner she could feel his sensitivity. If he was gay, as Gold said, he was probably no stranger to police stations.

"Let me ask you something," she said. "If you were in our shoes, where would you look? Who would you suspect?"

He thought for a moment. "That's easy. Her husband."

"Her husband? Why?"

"He hated her. More than anyone who ever knew her."

"Why?" Susan asked.

"Because she was so popular," he said. "She was everybody's darling, the most-likely-to, cheerleader, all that shit. Tim was a jerk, a nothing. The only reason she married him was to piss off our parents. She succeeded in that. But Tim never forgave her for it. He hated her like the plague."

"Yet he stayed with her," Susan said. She was looking at her cigarette. She could feel the power of the addiction reaching out to her from the past. She resolved not to take another puff.

He shrugged. "Human nature."

She nodded, impressed by his insight. Many of the most destructive relationships, she had found, are also the most resistant to breaking up. People cling ferociously to the things that hurt them.

"What about her daughter, Emily?" Susan asked.

He softened. "I felt sorry for Emily. She came to see me out in California when she ran away. She figured I was the misfit, she could trust me. She's all right. Not like her mother."

"What I meant to ask was, what was Emily's relationship with her father?"

"He was all over her. Possessive, jealous, chasing her boyfriends out of the house. That kind of thing. He never gave her a minute's peace. That's why she ended up getting pregnant, I imagine."

"You're a psychologist." Susan smiled.

He said nothing.

"Do you think Emily was reenacting what happened to her mother?" Susan asked.

"Psychologist yourself," he said. "You're probably right. She just wanted to get back at them, even if it hurt her."

Susan nodded. "And you?" The ash on her cigarette was getting longer and longer. She watched it in fascination.

"Me what?"

"Did you get back at them?"

"My parents?" He seemed surprised and offended.

"Yes. Did you get back at them? Did it hurt you?"

He shook his head. "Doctor, you've got a lot to learn about being gay. A person doesn't come out to hurt his parents. He does it to be who he is. I can see that medical science hasn't advanced much since I was a kid. You still think we're freaks, don't you?"

"I'm sorry for the way I posed the question," Susan

said. "It was clumsy of me. I meant to ask whether your coming out gave you any additional satisfaction because you knew your parents would oppose it."

He looked away. Susan could see that he was far more intelligent than his career in the mills would suggest. Yet, according to Gold's files, he had never found a long-term sexual partner. Apparently he still cruised bars in search of strangers. This was not the lifestyle of a healthy gay man who respected himself. It bore all the earmarks of self-punishment with an unconscious desire to get back at a hated set of parents.

"Satisfaction?" he asked. "I guess I could plead guilty to that."

Susan swung her hand over the ashtray and watched the ash fall off. Her old knowledge of the arcana of smoking had come back; she knew just how long the ash would hold out.

"Well, this may suprise you," she said, "but your brother-in-law was accounted for. He's not the killer."

"Too bad." He seemed disappointed. "Are you sure he didn't hire somebody?"

"It's doubtful," Susan said. "The police will look into every possibility, though."

She smiled. "Will you miss your sister?"

He ground out his cigarette in the ashtray. "Can't say as I will. I hadn't spoken to her in ten years. I wasn't planning to be in touch." He shrugged. "She wasn't much, you know. Getting murdered was probably the closest she got to doing anything important in her life."

"Did she have potential?" Susan asked. "I mean, potential that she never fulfilled?"

He furrowed his brow. "I used to think so. Now I don't. People are what they make of themselves."

Susan stood up. "Thank you for your help," she said.

"No problem. Hope you find your man." He accepted Susan's outstretched hand. This time his handshake was warmer.

Gold was waiting when Susan returned to the observation room.

"Well?"

Susan shook her head.

"Forget him," she said. "He had nothing to do with it."

Gold looked at her. "You sure?"

"As sure as I can be about these things," Susan said. "He is harmless. Women occupy no place in his fantasies. He's carrying a torch for the lover in California, who left him for someone else. He's in a lot of pain, but he's no killer."

"What tipped you off?" Gold asked.

"Pretty much everything." Susan did not say so, but she had known from the minute the cigarette, moist with Henry's saliva, touched her lips, that he was innocent.

Gold grimaced. "So I guess we keep looking. I knew he was too good to be true."

Susan nodded. "I'm sorry, David." She used his first name affectionately. She knew how hard he had been hoping Dorothy Kuehn's brother was the killer. That would have ended the string of murders.

Gold looked at his watch. "Look how late it is. I'd better let you get home to your son."

"Okay." She turned to leave.

"And watch yourself," Gold said. "There's a goddamned killer out there."

Frustration made him break his habit of never swearing.

"I'll watch myself," Susan assured him.

SUSAN SPENT THE next six days with Michael. It had taken her over a month to clear her schedule for this brief time. She had juggled her office patients, rescheduled supervisions, and got another psychiatrist to take over her hospital rounds for the week.

Officially, she was "out of town." In reality she stayed home with Michael most of the time, enjoying an interval of easy domesticity that allowed her to pretend that Michael lived with her all the time. They took walks in Lincoln Park, made lunch in the apartment, shopped in the neighborhood, and talked.

To go with the changes in Michael's body, Susan saw changes in his manner of speech. He was more colloquial now, and when he talked about his schoolmates there was a streetwise edge in his voice that bespoke the pressures of life in public school.

"How is Angela?" she asked as they stood on the El platform one afternoon.

"All right, I guess," Michael said. "She bugs me."

Angela Kim was a girl in Michael's class who had followed him everywhere last fall. Michael had complained about her silent persistence but had secretly felt flattered to have an admirer.

"Does she still send you notes?"

"No. She's friends with Alison Fischer now." He brightened as he changed the subject. "I like Meredith Kruse. She's cool. We watched *Fly Away Home* at her house on pay-per-view."

"Was it good?" Susan asked.

"Sort of. Her mother made brownies."

Elaine had packed some video games in Michael's suitcase, and he played them with an aplomb that made him seem much older to Susan. Nearly everything he said and did confirmed the changes time had wrought in him. He had learned things, felt things of which she knew nothing. In her absence he had asked questions and got answers from others; he had experienced fears and been comforted by a voice that was not hers.

But just when she was feeling the ache of this separation, Michael would turn from the TV or the book he was reading and remind her of the things they had in common.

"Mom, can we rent *Mr. Peabody and the Mermaid* again?"

"If the store still has it. I think they probably do."

"Remember when the man was smoking five cigarettes all at once?" he asked, reminding her of the night last summer when he had laughed until tears came down his face.

"Yes." She smiled. "It was funny, wasn't it?"

Alerted to her moods by his intuition, Michael was quick to reestablish his bond with her through shared memories or private jokes that distracted her from the chasm of time and space that separated them. She could not help reflecting that it was Michael who comforted her over the very situation that must also be leaving its mark on him. No wonder Carolyn depended on him the way she did. Inside his delicate body he was a strong person, and a manly one.

The only exception to Susan's self-imposed exile from work was David Gold, who telephoned every night to bring her up to date on things, and to speak to Michael. It was Gold who invited her at week's end to join him at the Cook County Medical Examiner's Office for a meeting with Geri Vogel, the hair and fiber expert with whom they had worked often.

She arrived ahead of schedule at 2121 West Harrison and found Geri in her office on the third floor.

"Susan, it's been a while," Geri said. "How have you been? How's Michael?"

Geri was herself a divorced woman and a mother. She had met Michael two years ago and always inquired after him.

"He's fine," Susan said. "I'll tell him you said hi."

Gold came in looking harried and impatient.

"I understand you have something important for us," he said.

"It may make your job a lot easier," Geri said. "Let me show you."

She produced a fiber display board on which were placed a swatch of dark green fabric and several individual fibers.

"On the left you see fabric exemplars found at the scenes of the four murders," she said. "Obviously, they match. The comparison microscope leaves no doubt of that."

She stood back to let Gold study the display.

"I checked it out under the polarized-light microscope and fluorescent microscope," Geri said. "The fabric is very fine, but it's lobed almost like a carpet fiber. It's a polymer designed for strength, but very fine so as not to irritate the skin."

Gold held out the board to Susan. She could make nothing out of the tiny fabrics displayed, except that they were greenish in color.

"The dye has faded," Geri said. "When it was new it was probably darker and greener than what you see. I don't think there is any significant wear, though. This would indicate that the garment in question either sat in a warehouse for a long time or was bought and kept on a shelf without being used or laundered."

She motioned to the display board. "The other significant thing is how short all four exemplars are," she said. "None of them is more than two centimeters. From this one would deduce that they are not threads loosened from somewhere but shreds left on the surface of the fabric when it was manufactured."

"In other words," Gold said, "a brand-new garment that was being worn for the first time."

"Or if not the first time," Geri said, "it probably hadn't been washed yet."

"What sort of garment are we talking about?" Gold asked.

"That I'm not sure of," Geri said. "But it's not your everyday retail garment. For one thing the lobal cross section is wrong. This is some sort of industrial or uniform fiber. For another thing, chemical analysis of the dye shows that it is hypoallergenic."

"That should help us," Gold observed.

"I think it's going to." Geri leaned back in her swivel chair. "Hypoallergenic fiber narrows the field. I've been on my modem with the NCIC computers since yesterday, feeding them the dye specifications and the cross section. I could be wrong, but I think this is going to lead us to a very rare fiber."

"I'd like Susan to have a look at the source materials, if that's possible," Gold said.

Geri stood up and led them to an examining table under the tall windows. There were photographs from all four crime scenes.

"The first victim, Cheryl Glaser, was found with the fiber on the floor next to her body," Geri said. "The second, Jennifer Haas, had the fiber in her hair. That would make sense, since the killer strangled both girls. He had to be above them."

She pointed to a photograph of a carpet with a woman's underwear lying on it.

"That's the Patsy Morgenstern scene," she said. "The fiber was found on the underside of her panties. My theory is that the transfer was made while the killer was strangling her. She ended up lying on the fiber."

She turned to Susan. "For a while the Dorothy Kuehn scene had me stumped," she said. "We went through that bedroom with a fine-tooth comb, but I couldn't find it. Then yesterday I went back over the fibers taken from her face and hair. The fiber was found right in her ear, actually trapped by the cilia. A very unusual location, given the length of her hair. But there's no mistake. This is the fiber."

Geri excused herself. When the door had closed Susan studied the fibers visually, then touched them gently with the tips of two fingers. She recalled the confused signals she had received at the Patsy Morgenstern crime scene. She had felt a pervasive evil and violence, but not the specific sexual essence that she expected at the scene of a serial killer's work.

Gold was silent. Susan picked up the photograph of Patsy Morgenstern, the victim she felt closest to. She placed her hand over the image of Patsy's eyeless face.

"The picture of her with her family," she said. "The picture with eyes."

Gold leaned forward. "What?"

"The picture of her with eyes . . ."

"What are you getting, Susan?"

"Eyes. Eyes in a picture." Susan grimaced. "Not like

the crime scene. Something different. I see the eyes very clearly, they stand out."

A coldness ran suddenly into her stomach, turning to nausea.

"I can't quite see . . ." Her head bent forward toward the photograph. "Glasses with eyeballs on them. Remember? At game stores, novelty stores, a pair of glasses with eyes painted on them, on the lenses. No, that's not it, not quite it . . ."

"Take your time," Gold said. "No hurry."

"Campaign buttons," she said. "Eyes closed, eyes opened. Flashers. Flashing buttons. No. Wait."

She sat upright. "I know what it is. Extra eyes. There are eyes on top of the eyes. It's in the photograph. He pastes extra eyes on top of the eyes in the picture. Or he . . . he cuts them out. He cuts out the eyes and puts in other eyes. That's why they stand out so much."

"Who? Who did this?"

"He has a photograph of Patsy. He knows her." She paused. "He's been with her. Slept with her."

Images were crowding each other in Susan's mind. She saw the photograph of Patsy's family. She saw the VCR in Patsy's apartment where the erotic videotapes had been shown. She saw Mrs. Morgenstern talking while her husband looked away. She saw Ron Giordano leaning back in his chair, looking at her.

A headache was crawling along her temples and into her eyes. She sensed that she didn't have much time.

"He's got the shirt on," she said. "He's looking at her. The photograph . . . He keeps it, he looks at it . . . Ouch!"

She held her head with both hands. The photograph slipped from her lap onto the floor. "Oh," she moaned.

"Headache?" Gold asked.

"It's all confused," Susan said. "She wanted him to have it. The picture. But she didn't know. He saw them all, she didn't know that. She couldn't tell. He saw them all."

The throbbing in her head crashed over the images, destroying them.

"David, I'm finished."

She sat back, drained. She felt Gold's hands on her temples, rubbing gently.

"Take it easy. Relax. You did well."

"I couldn't catch it all," she said. "There was too much all at once. Oh, David . . ."

"Sssh. Just rest."

No one knew her gift better than Gold. He understood the price she paid for insight, and the often enigmatic nature of the visions that came to her. They were colored by interference from all kinds of sources. Her own memories, the thoughts of others, tangential material floating in the universe of consciousness. He had learned not to expect too much precision. He had also learned that the clues she provided often led to additional mysteries. Second sight was a door into the unknown.

A small tremor shook her body. She seemed childlike as he looked down at her. He found himself regretting that her work for him forced her to see such terrible things. Sometimes he could feel her sharing the agony of murder victims as she relived what had happened to them. He was glad he himself had no psychic gift. It was better to remain in the dark than to know certain things.

"You okay?" he asked softly.

She didn't answer.

14

"IN 1936," Susan said, her hands on the lectern, "a renowned psychic from southern France named Marie-Céleste Legrandin was given a battery of tests by a group of scientists. She was asked to identify photographs inside envelopes. She was shown a series of locked boxes and asked to say what was inside each. She was shown blank pieces of paper that had been in contact with other pieces of paper bearing various numbers, images, and words. The experiment was strictly controlled using every known scientific criterion.

"Mlle. Legrandin was able to pick out only 18 percent of the target objects. The scientists concluded that her second sight was either fraudulent or not proven, because her record of success was not significantly higher than that of pure chance. The test was touted as proof that parapsychology is fake.

"One half hour after the test, Mlle. Legrandin correctly predicted the kidnapping of the Lindbergh baby. She also predicted the death of Germany's President Hindenburg and the burning of the *Normandie* in New York Harbor. And she predicted the crash of an airliner that was scheduled to take off from Orly Airport the following day.

"Four of the scientists who had conducted the test on her were killed in that plane crash."

Susan looked out at her audience. It was composed of psychiatrists, psychologists, and behavioral scientists who were attending a convention at the Drake Hotel called "Psychology and Probability." Susan had been asked to speak on probability as it affected the controversy over parapsychology.

"What point am I making?" Susan asked. "The traditional scientific method does not test the *reality* of phenomena so much as their *repeatability* and replicability. The method doesn't ask, 'Is this thing real?' Instead it asks, 'Can this thing be repeated on demand?'

"Psychic phenomena *are* real," Susan said. "But they are intermittent. They can't be called up on demand. They can also be mistaken. The scientific method in its classic form has no tolerance for error. Nor does it have a tolerance for intermittence. It craves constancy, repeatability. But not everything in the world is repeatable. Chance is part of reality. And error is an authentic part of experience, even of scientific observation, as modern physics has learned."

Susan smiled at her audience.

"Let me give you an example of what I mean. When a scientist sees a phenomenon such as a tornado, he realizes he cannot re-create it in the laboratory. So he devises instruments to measure wind speed, atmospheric pressure, and so on, and tries to place these instruments where another tornado might occur. He prepares himself for the recurrence of the phenomenon. But does he doubt the existence of the first tornado he saw? Does he contemptuously assert that it never took place? Does he accuse all those who saw it of being fakes? Not at all. He trusts his senses enough to prepare for a recurrence of what he saw.

"That is the difference between ordinary phenomena and psychic phenomena—the attitude of the scientific observer."

Susan glanced at her notes.

"Perhaps the scientific method as we know it is not the correct instrument for a measuring of psychic phenomena. We who practice psychology and psychiatry have found all too often that our most important insights are debunked by critics who unfairly hold us hostage to the scientist's craving for precise replicability. When we cannot show that an identical symptom will always result from identical childhood experiences or identical adult stresses, we are accused of being fakers. We of all people should understand and sympathize with the struggles of parapsychologists to be taken seriously. In the end, we are in the same predicament as they."

Susan looked at her audience. She saw the same assortment of expressions she was used to from other lectures she had given. Many faces were closed in obvious contempt. Others were skeptical but attentive. A few, true believers, had the wide-eyed look of disciples.

Susan had long since learned to address herself to the skeptics and hope for the best.

AFTER HER LECTURE Susan took Michael to the movies downtown. There was a revival of *Pinocchio* at a theater on Randolph Street. Michael was on the edge of his seat throughout the movie, holding Susan's hand and barely touching the popcorn she had bought.

Afterward they walked to her office at 30 North Michigan. The building was silent since it was the weekend. They rode up in the elevator together, and Susan stood Michael on her desk so he could look out at the lake while she went through her mail.

"It's pretty," he said.

"I know it is."

The lake was frozen near the shore, and eddies of snow were blowing this way and that in the park. Michael stood with his hands at his sides, enjoying the view.

"Mom." He turned to look at her. He had hazel eyes, like her own. But their color seemed to be changing as he grew older. Something of Nick was asserting itself in the depths of the irises.

"Yes, sweetie?"

"When I grow up, maybe I could have an office right here."

She smiled. "And what will you do in your office?"

"I'll be a psychiatrist. Like you."

"Are you sure you want to listen to other people's problems all day long?"

"I wouldn't mind. We could go out to lunch when we weren't working."

"You and me?"

"Yes. And to the movies."

"That would be nice," she said.

"Maybe *Pinocchio* would be playing sometimes."

So he had really liked the film, she mused.

"*Pinocchio* is a famous movie. I'm sure it will be revived many times."

"Do people's noses really get bigger when they lie?" the boy asked.

Susan smiled. "No, they don't, honey. It was a sort of . . ." The word *metaphor* came to her, but she didn't want to confuse him with it. "The fact is that when people lie you can usually tell by their faces. The movie just showed that in a more dramatic way."

"And the boys who were turned into donkeys . . . ," he said.

Susan laughed. "That was just the story. Boys don't ever get turned into donkeys, no matter how naughty they are."

Sleepy. Dopey.

Something made Susan pause. She was thinking of the peculiar brutality of so many of the Disney movies. She recalled their disturbing images from her own childhood. The terror of Bambi's parents when Man entered the forest; the Sorcerer's Apprentice frantically trying to sweep out the tides of water—or was it flames?—with his broom. Alice in Wonderland, growing into a giantess after drinking the magic potion, or shrinking to the size of a mouse as the Red Queen hurled threats at her. Critics had blamed Disney for being sadistic and perverse. But it was actually the world of fairy tales that was full of menace and obsession. Disney simply presented stories that were part of his society's folklore. And folktales were stories that acted out children's fears.

She came out of her reverie to see Michael looking at her.

"Can you tell when I lie?" he asked.

She came to put her arms around him.

"Let me see," she said. "Answer this question for me. Do you love me?"

He looked into her face. "Yes."

"In my opinion," she said, "you're not lying. Am I right?"

"Oh, Mom." He smiled, embarrassed.

She patted him on his hips and turned back to her mail. There were three packages on the table. Two were books sent by publishers of professional works, one as a courtesy and one for possible review by Susan. The third was a copy of a collection of essays by analysts on Freud's six famous case histories. One of the essays was by Susan herself.

"What is that book, Mama?" Michael asked.

"Well, it's a book that contains a small part written by me," she said. "Here, look."

She found her essay's title in the table of contents and turned to its opening page. "See my name?" she asked. It was at the top of the page, SUSAN M. SHADER. The essay was entitled "Proximity and Bodily Organs in Compulsion Neurosis." It was about certain themes Freud articulated in what had come to be called the Rat Man analysis.

Susan's eye was caught by one of the paragraphs near the top of the page.

Freud lays stress on the fact that the eye is the erotogenic zone most remote from the sexual object. However, in obsessional neurotics it often behaves as though it were the closest. "Eye contact" in neurotics is an expression that can almost be taken literally.

The words were Susan's own, but they looked strange to her. It was as though something peeked out from between the lines, calling to her in an indecipherable language. She tried briefly to catch it, but gave up. She was mentally tired after the events of recent days, and she found it difficult to sort out her impressions.

Michael was looking at the book. "Can I hold it?" he asked.

"Of course you can, sweetie. You can hold it all the way home if you like."

They took a cab home and made a pizza. After dinner Susan put Michael in his bath and straightened up the living room. He had left the book on the coffee table, and she picked it up.

A phrase from her essay, "the zone most remote from the sexual object," came back to her. She pondered it as she listened to the little splashes Michael was making in the tub.

Only in the real world is vision a relationship with something distant, she reflected. In mental illness, a look is as intimate as an embrace, and sometimes more disturbing. This is also perhaps the secret behind the behavior of voyeurs and exhibitionists. No wonder, come to think of it, that most pornography is visual, photographic.

Something else came to her. Carrying the book in her hand, she went to the phone and dialed David Gold's home number.

"Gold here." His voice sounded tired.

"David, this is Susan. I was just wondering. Have you investigated all the university people who were close to the female athletes?"

"You mean like coaches?"

"Yes. And Buildings and Grounds people. Anyone who might have been in a position to watch the girls practice or play."

"Yeah, we talked to them," Gold said. "It didn't help. Why?"

"I just realized I've been getting some images having to do with the girls and their practices. Something sexual. Someone watching. Maybe not a coach."

There was a silence. Then, "Wait a minute," Gold said. She heard him making a call on the other line.

"What else are you getting on this?" he asked.

"Remember when I was looking at the fibers?" Susan said. "I kept seeing photographs with something done to the eyes. Extra eyes added on, eyes removed—whatever. It occurs to me that someone might have secretly taken pictures of the girls, for sexual purposes. Girls working out, running, practicing."

"Uh-huh. Someone who was on the scene, you mean."

"Yes. Someone in a position to see them whenever he wanted. And to take a picture without being noticed."

There was a brief pause. Gold was probably writing something down.

"Let me get back to you tomorrow," he said. "I have a couple of calls I can make."

Susan hung up and went into Michael's room to help him get ready for bed. The book remained on the table by the phone. She did not think about it again until the next morning.

By that time Gold had already acted on her tip.

15

GOLD WAS ON the phone at six-thirty. He knew Susan would be awake.

"Could you make a quick trip with me before your first patient?" he asked.

"Does it have anything to do with what we talked about last night?"

"You'll find out."

He picked Susan up twenty minutes later in his unmarked car. It was one of those preternaturally dark Chicago mornings that give one the impression of a total eclipse of the sun, or perhaps something even more sinister.

"Have a look in the bag," Gold said. There was a gym bag on the seat next to Susan. She opened it to find a handful of athletic items, including shorts, socks, and a gray cotton workout shirt bearing the logo ILLINOIS.

"Whose are these?" Susan asked.

"You mean you don't know?"

"Patsy's?" she asked.

Gold nodded. "I want you to have a look at the locker room where she kept her stuff. If that doesn't help, we'll check out the gym."

The sky seemed crouched over the earth like a foul-breathed predator as they made their way to the Circle Campus. Gold parked in the No Parking zone next to the gym and led the way to the locker room. There was not a soul around. It was too early.

WOMEN, said the sign outside. Gold didn't even look around him as he led Susan inside. She was carrying Patsy

Morgenstern's gym bag. Memory stirred inside her as the once-familiar smell of perspiration and mildew reached her.

They were halfway down the first row of lockers when she stopped.

"Two rows over," she said: "1334."

Gold smiled. "I see you haven't lost your touch."

Susan's second sight had given her the locker number without difficulty. The gym bag filled with items that had once touched Patsy Morgenstern's skin gave out powerful, unambiguous signals.

The locker was against the wall, approximately in the center of the room's length. Susan had a brief flash of girls changing clothes and calling out jokes to each other, some of them dirty, most of them innocent. Patsy was a source of the good humor, despite the pain in her knee.

There was a combination lock hanging from the handle.

"That's not her lock," Gold said. The locker had been reassigned.

Susan had felt a small weight in the bottom of the gym bag. She reached inside and touched the combination lock that Patsy had used.

"Fourteen left, two revolutions right to 18, left to 26," she said.

"I won't bother to try it," Gold joked.

But something more important had struck Susan. She touched her brow, dropped the gym bag, and took a step backward, away from the wall.

"It's right there," she told Gold. "Behind the wall."

"What is?" Gold did not look surprised.

Susan lowered her voice. "That's where he is. That's where . . ."

She felt a rush of fear. Seeing her pallor, Gold put a hand on her arm.

"Don't worry," he said. "I've got him already. What were you going to say?"

"That's where he watches," Susan said, her voice still small. "There's a hole in the wall." The extrasensory equivalent of a foul, powerful smell hit her as she looked at the locker, and she grimaced.

"Okay," Gold said. "You gave me what I needed. We've already got him downtown."

"Who?"

"Come on. I'll show you."

SUSAN CALLED HER answering service to reschedule her eight o'clock patient. She drove to Area Six Headquarters with Gold. He took her to the viewing window behind the interrogation room where she had met Dorothy Kuehn's brother. Two detectives were sitting at a table, flipping lazily through pages of notes. A somewhat overweight man in his thirties, with curly brown hair and mild eyes, was sitting with them. He wore khaki pants and a work shirt. He did not seem nervous. He had rather the air of a person who is being subjected to an indignity and who endures it with composure. Like a hospital patient preparing to undergo a painful test.

"Who is he?" she asked.

"His name is Kyle Stewart," Gold said. "He's the maintenance man at the gym. He cleans out the girls' locker rooms, the gym floor, the bleachers, and so on. He's been there about eight years. He lives in a basement apartment in an old building a few blocks from the campus. We got a court order to search it this morning. It was a gold mine."

He showed Susan a stack of pictures taken by the police photographer.

"In the first place, every corner of his apartment is full of kinky and violent pornography," he said. "Just about every variety you could think of. But that's not the best part. He seems to have been stealing stuff from the female athletes' lockers, probably for years. He has a collection of support bras, panties, even discarded athletic shoes. T-shirts, halters, whatever the girls might have left in their lockers and not missed. Tampons, too."

Gold looked at Susan.

"You called it, Susan. The guy is a photographer. We

found a Pentax with a zoom lens. He's got hundreds of pictures of the girls working out. Girls in practice, girls lifting weights, girls running laps—you name it. And there are pictures of the girls in the locker room. He took them through a hole in the wall from a little cubbyhole on the other side."

Gold pushed some photographs in evidence bags across to Susan. They were of girls changing clothes in the locker room. All were taken from the same vantage point. The camera caught them in medium close-up, usually at chest level. There were many photographs of girls with their breasts exposed as they changed clothes. Most often the girls' faces were cut off at the chin, but sometimes the eyes were visible. Susan caught her breath as she recognized the face of Patsy Morgenstern.

"I see," she said. Again she looked through the glass at the suspect. He had placed one hand on the tabletop and was nodding as he listened to a question from one of the detectives. He seemed to be concentrating, as though trying to remember something.

"You haven't seen it all," Gold was saying as he produced a second evidence bag. "This is the knockout."

Susan opened the bag. She saw several close-up photos of girls' faces. Some were taken with the secret camera, others were magazine photographs of models. In all cases the eyes of the girl in the image had been painstakingly removed and replaced by other eyes. The effect was frightening. The photographs gave the impression of a grotesque mutilation.

"Just what your second sight was trying to tell you," Gold said. "Extra eyes. But the original eyes he took out."

He tapped the pile of photographs. "Kind of reminds you of the killer's MO, doesn't it?" he asked.

Susan nodded. Her skin crawled from the sight of the pictures, but her mind was racing. This man behind the one-way mirror, speaking so calmly with the police, must be the killer.

"I think the guy is going to crack before tonight," Gold

said. "It turns out he's been in trouble before. Child molestation, exhibitionism, Peeping Tom. Stuff like that."

"Nothing violent?" Susan asked.

"Not until now," Gold said. "Actually, he's pretty popular with the girls. A harmless sort of guy, helpful with little things. Knowledgeable about injuries, apparently, and very sympathetic. These scholarship athletes worry a lot about injuries."

Gold looked at his notes. "Stewart is a vet. He did a tour in the Marines. They gave him a medical discharge for allergies. No bad behavior while in the service. When he got out he found the job at Illinois right away. The personnel people at the university told me they were very satisfied with his work. He managed to keep his trouble with Vice a secret. First there were two arrests for exhibitionism, both involving teenage girls. One dropped and one conviction. Then he was arrested for window peeping, again involving a young girl. Last year he was accused of fondling a little girl on an El train over in Skokie. He pleaded guilty. You'll notice that all these crimes were committed far from the South Side.

"He was on our list of suspects in sexual crimes. Frankly, he fit the profile of a character who will eventually work his way up to something serious."

Susan looked through the glass at the big, rather soft man, who was gazing expressionlessly at his interrogators. On the one hand he had the look of a person who has dealt with the police before. He seemed relaxed, he knew the routine. On the other hand there was something cornered and tragic about his body, and the thick hands that were now clasped on the tabletop.

It was hard to imagine that quiet-looking man as a killer. But the evidence found in Stewart's apartment did not lie. And if he was the killer, the crime spree was over. A perpetrator from close to home was certainly preferable to a serial killer who might murder a dozen or more women before being caught. That didn't make the girls' deaths any less terrible, but it brought hope for those who were still alive. Alive and living in constant fear.

"I can see the connection to the athletes," she said. "But what about the fourth victim? Dorothy Kuehn lived a world away from the first three victims. If this is your man, what put him on to her?"

"Remember your theory that the killer knew Dorothy long before he ever knew the three coeds?" Gold asked.

Susan nodded.

"Stewart's parents live on the South Side," Gold said. "Not one mile from the Kuehn woman and her husband. Stewart grew up there."

Susan was astonished by this news. It was perfectly calculated to erase all doubts about Kyle Stewart.

"Congratulations, Susan," Gold said. "You led us right to him."

As Gold's words echoed in her ears, Susan noticed for the first time that the suspect's work shirt was an unusual and rather sickening shade of green.

16

"IT STARTS IN a library. A huge, dark library, with lots of stacks filled with thousands of very old books. I'm looking for a book. I can see the cover of it and the title right in front of my eyes, but every time the dream ends I can never remember it."

Susan sat quietly, looking into her patient's eyes.

"There is a feeling of urgency," the patient continued, "as though I have to finish in a hurry. I keep running my hand along the spines of the books, and I can see my hand getting filthy from all the dust. The stacks are endless. I rush down the little flights of stairs between the floors, then along more stacks. My legs don't seem to work properly. It's as though I'm running underwater."

The patient looked away, then back at Susan.

"It gets worse and worse. I'm having trouble breathing. There is a sense of . . . disaster. Disaster and embarrassment, as though I've failed to do a job I was supposed to do, and everyone is going to hate me."

There was a pause.

"That's when I see you," the patient said. "You're standing at the top of one of the little staircases. You're wearing a skirt and jacket, like you always wear in the office here. But you're barefoot. No shoes. I call out to you, 'Where is the book? I can't find it. There's no time!' My words are muffled, the way words sometimes are in dreams. I can't make myself understood, no matter how I shout."

The patient looked away again, embarrassed.

"But you don't seem bothered at all. You beckon me forward to you. I come closer. You put both your hands on my shoulders, and you push me down on my knees. Now I see that you're not wearing a suit after all. You're only wearing a bra and panties, and one of those garter belts with long straps. Your hands are soft, but their force is irresistible. You pull my face to your"—the patient sighed uncomfortably—"to your crotch. Your body is undulating, very slowly."

Again there was a pause.

"I can feel that the others are coming, that they're going to blame me. Time has run out. But I can't stop. My hands slide up between your thighs, I touch your panties. They start to come down. You curl one of your legs around my neck. You lean back against the books. You smile. I feel myself beginning to tremble . . . I can't stop."

She sighed. "That's where the dream ends."

There was a long silence. Susan watched her patient dispassionately.

At length she asked, "Was there anything different this time?"

The patient looked away evasively, then turned her eyes back to Susan.

"Yes. It was as though . . . I think the people looking for me were my son and daughter. I think—it was a family gathering. Something like that. They needed me. In the kitchen, whatever."

"Nothing else?"

The woman was breathing shallowly. She gave Susan a guilty glance.

"No. Nothing else."

Susan looked at the clock on her desk. "We're out of time," she said. "See you on Thursday?"

"Yes. Good-bye."

"Good-bye."

The patient got up to leave. She was a school principal from Evanston, the wife of a university professor. She had been seeing Susan on and off for nearly a year. Her fantasies about Susan were nothing new. Nor was her habit of reciting them in dramatic detail. She came from a strict religious upbringing, as had her husband. Their sexual relationship had never been truly functional, despite her conception of the two children. She was struggling to come to terms with the fact that her husband had never satisfied her.

Her fantasies about Susan were a disguise for her true feelings, which were not homosexual at all. What she really wanted was to get out of her marriage. She hoped Susan would give her the courage to ask for a divorce. The dreams always showed Susan providing sexual satisfaction in exchange for rebellion against those who were pursuing the dreamer. Today's new detail—that the son and daughter were the shadowy pursuers—only made it more obvious. It was a dream about obligation, and about revolt.

The part about being barefoot came from a pornographic book the patient had read as a young teenager. It was herself she saw as barefoot. The context was violently heterosexual. She displaced the detail onto Susan in order to disguise her own impulse.

Recently the treatment had bogged down, with Susan gently trying to put the patient in touch with her rebellious instincts, and the patient clinging stubbornly to the transference fantasies about Susan herself. The religious connection was strong, grounded in a great deal of guilt. One of these days the patient would realize that the dusty old book she sought in the library was the Bible.

SUSAN GOT HOME to find the media camped outside the apartment building. One of the investigative reporters at the *Sun-Times* had found out that the arrest of Kyle Stewart was based on a suggestion by Susan. The newspapers were itching to report that the reign of terror was over. The fact that a psychic was involved in the case only added sensation.

Abel Weathers had given a brief news conference in the afternoon to announce that a "suspect" was in custody and that further information would be forthcoming. The press had little difficulty gleaning from the smug expression on Weathers's face that he felt Stewart was the man. When asked about Susan's role in the case, he became vague. He called the investigation a "team effort" and refused to single out any individual for praise.

Susan had to come in through the alley. Carolyn was upstairs with Michael. The answering machine was blinking furiously. Susan cursed herself for not having changed her phone number.

"Jesus Christ," Carolyn exclaimed. "Everybody in the business is after you. *People* magazine, *60 Minutes*, *20/20*, Larry King—forget it. You'll be giving interviews when you're dead."

Michael looked very small and innocent sitting next to Carolyn in front of the TV. A gigantic cheeseburger sat on a plate in front of him, along with a mound of french fries made from scratch by Carolyn. The apartment smelled pleasantly of cooking.

The sight of Michael gave Susan a delicious sense of

home, but the blinking answering machine and her memory of the vehicles outside made her feel as though she were in a besieged fortress.

"Mom, we saw you on TV," Michael said.

"Really?"

Carolyn nodded. "File footage from the Gabriel case. Channel 7 shared it with everybody."

"Oh." Susan remembered the footage. It was not very flattering to her. But at least it gave a rather blurred idea of her face. People would have difficulty recognizing her based on those few seconds of videotape.

There wasn't time to talk to Michael at any length. Susan put him to bed and then spent an hour chatting with Carolyn about the media firestorm surrounding the Stewart arrest.

"Is it really over?" Carolyn asked. Her face left no doubt she was speaking as a woman and not as a journalist.

"We're hoping it is," Susan replied. "The evidence is strong. But I won't feel reassured until David has finished investigating."

"Is the guy a real scumbag?" Carolyn asked.

"No." Susan looked pensive. "That's just the thing. He seemed rather soft. Harmless." She shrugged. "Of course, many killers give that impression. They often look sensitive, even vulnerable."

She could not hide her own uncertainty. When she had gone to look in on Kyle Stewart's interrogation she had hoped to feel a confirmation of his guilt in her gut. It had not happened. Yet he had everything a perpetrator was supposed to have—motive, opportunity, means.

"How soon will we know?" Carolyn asked. "Off the record, of course."

"Soon," Susan said. "There's so much evidence. . . . David won't play with it long without coming to a conclusion."

LATE THAT NIGHT Susan slipped quietly into the spare bedroom to look at Michael. He was lying on his stomach with his head turned to the side. His thick, dark hair was matted from his sleep, and his freckled cheek looked tender and sweet against the pillow.

She came to his side and listened to his breathing. It was always difficult to control the intensity of her love when he was here. His arrivals made her feel suddenly famished, as though she had been denying how much she missed him. It took considerable effort to avoid smothering him.

Her fondest hope for Michael from the time of his birth was that he would simply be normal. Her own childhood had been painfully tainted by her second sight, an unwanted gift that set her apart from her schoolmates. She was thankful that she saw no sign that he had inherited her dubious gift. But she had come to realize that he was, in other ways, an unusual child. She had more than her maternal pride as evidence of this. Ever since preschool his teachers had exclaimed about his intelligence, his creativity, and—this astonished Susan—his leadership abilities. Though a quiet boy, he possessed a tact and intuition that made all those around him feel better about themselves and more willing to cooperate with one another.

"It's one thing to be gifted and bright," his first-grade teacher had told Susan. "Michael has all that. But we need leaders in our world, people with a sense of morality, people with humanitarian abilities. Where is the next Martin Luther King, Jr., going to come from? Unfortunately we don't test for that in our schools, we don't value it and try to nurture it. When I see a boy like Michael, I see that potential. I hope his teachers will help him develop it. You should be very proud of him."

Susan often heard those words echoing in her mind when she watched Michael interact with the people in her own world. He was a true diplomat. Adults and children alike were quick to warm up to him and even to depend on him.

She looked down at him now and dared to gently stroke his hair. Something darkened at the back of her mind as she contemplated his vulnerability. She paused, her hand extended toward him. Then she realized what it was. Three young girls had been slaughtered. Each of those girls had a mother who must have felt the same pride that Susan felt for Michael, the same hopes for a future full of possibilities.

Those three mothers were devastated now.

Susan suppressed a shiver. The world was a dangerous place. Innocence was no guarantee of survival. Nothing was a guarantee of anything. She bent to brush Michael's face with her lips. He stirred slightly, then was quiet.

She tiptoed out of the room, leaving the door ajar the way he liked it. As she did so she remembered the feeling she had got at the Morgenstern crime scene. It was a profound sense of evil, so powerful that she still felt the nausea it had left her with.

It was hard to reconcile that evil with the mild face of Kyle Stewart in the interrogation room. But Susan hoped with all her heart that Gold had found the right man. Anything to end it, she thought.

THE NEXT DAY Susan took Michael downtown to David Gold's office. She wanted to get him out of the apartment. Besides, he never came to town without asking to visit Gold at work.

Gold was waiting in the doorway and swept Michael up in his arms. "How's my man?" he asked, kissing Michael's cheek.

The boy said nothing. He was always shy with Gold at first. Gold bounced him slightly and said, "You're a big boy. Soon you'll be picking me up. Come on inside. I've got something for you."

The something turned out to be an ice cream bar from the freezer down the hall. Michael sat in Gold's swivel chair eating it. His little eyes studied the cluttered room admiringly.

When he wasn't dreaming of being a psychiatrist, Michael planned to become a police detective. He never tired of holding Gold's shield. Gold would not let him see his gun and told him that a gun was by far the least important part of a detective's work. He doted on Michael as the son he had never had. Conversely, Gold was the closest thing to a male role model that Susan could offer Michael on his visits, and she was grateful that he took an interest in the boy. As a matter of fact, they had several character traits in common, such as a sensitivity that was easily wounded by the ugliness of the world and a profound sense of tact.

"Hold the fort for me a minute, will you, partner?" Gold said to the boy now. "I want to talk to your mother."

He took Susan aside and said, "Everything is falling into place. The results came back this morning from the FBI's serology unit. The three main blood group tests all showed the same thing. Our man is a secretor."

Susan nodded. From her years with Gold she had become well versed in blood serum testing. The blood group tests he was talking about were the ABO, Rhesus, and Lewis tests.

"How about the isoenzyme and hemoglobin variants?" she asked.

"Perfect. All four scenes. The killer's saliva was found in the bathroom sinks. We got Stewart's saliva from his toothbrush and the glass in his bathroom. The match is solid."

"And the semen in Patsy Morgenstern?" Susan asked.

"About ninety percent sure. I want to see the DNA on that."

"Who is doing it?" Susan asked.

"The feds." Gold's words did not surprise Susan. The FBI's excellent DNA laboratory only accepted assignments concerning violent crimes in which there was a specific suspect, or crimes that appeared to be part of a series. The "Coed Murders" now fit both categories.

"I've been checking out Stewart's past," Gold went on. "The sports connection goes way back. It seems that he was asthmatic as a boy, so he couldn't go out for sports himself. But he was an avid spectator at all the school games. And he was always hanging around the gym, watching the girls."

"That's normal enough, at that age," Susan put in. "But perhaps not normal in his case."

"I talked to one of his teachers today. She says he was a loner, a nerd. He was overweight back then, more so than now. He was a fairly bright kid, but obsessive about unimportant details. He would write ten first drafts of a paper. He never got anything done. That kind of thing. The kids made fun of him."

"Did he ever have any therapy?" Susan asked.

Gold shook his head. "His parents were strict Lutherans. They didn't believe in medical science, much less psychiatry. There is a note in his academic record from the guidance counselor advising the kid to see the school psychologist. But the parents wouldn't allow it."

"Does he have any siblings?" Susan asked.

"There was a sister, but she died of diabetes when the boy was six."

"Older or younger?" Susan asked.

Gold turned a page of the file. "Older. Two years older."

Susan asked, "Did she wear glasses?"

Gold looked down at the file, then shrugged. "I didn't check that."

"You'll probably find she did," Susan said. "A severe brittle juvenile diabetes can affect the eyes. I suspect that the eye MO harks back to the sister's death."

"He never got into trouble as a kid," Gold said, "except for one thing. He was accused of fondling a girl at school. She was three years younger, a fifth-grader. They threatened to suspend him, but nothing came of it. The girl's parents didn't want to make a stink. His parents were brought in for a conference, and that was it." He looked at his notes. "His teacher told me that Stewart told her he would gladly go to jail if she wouldn't tell his parents about it. He was that afraid of them."

Susan shook her head in wonderment.

"He's a profiler's dream," she said. "A sister dies when he's young. His parents are strict, rigid. He develops asthma. He's an underachiever. He's a loner. He shows symptoms of an obsessional neurosis when he's a young teenager. He's already fixated on girls in athletic situations. He never overcomes this phase of sexual development. In the end, by a sort of natural selection, he finds his niche as a janitor in a college gym, where he can watch girls doing athletic things all the time. For another man, this might have been the solution to all his problems. He might have lived quietly this way forever."

"But Stewart didn't," Gold said.

"The sexual and personal stresses of adult life must have overwhelmed what was left of his mental health," Susan said. "It's a classic case of what happens when childhood emotional problems go untreated. And when an insecure personality is trapped in a very rigid family. It's too bad."

"Too bad for the four victims," Gold added, as though correcting her.

He was right, Susan realized. The sufferings of a mentally ill perpetrator were hardly to be compared with the deaths of his victims. But someday society was going to have to come to terms with the fact that its young people's mental health was a genuine public health concern. The only realistic way to prevent violent crime is to take a genuine interest in the psychological conditions that create criminals. It is not fair to leave young people to their own devices in stressful social situations and then expect the police and courts to clean up the messes they make as grown-ups.

Gold was looking at his watch. "Geri Vogel is supposed to be here," he said. "I took her over to Stewart's place last night. She's got news for us."

At that moment Geri, looking businesslike and energetic in her wool suit, came down the corridor carrying her briefcase. "We meet again," she said to Susan.

"There's a friend of yours here," Susan said, pointing to Michael.

Geri greeted Michael and chatted with him for a moment before joining Susan and Gold in the next room.

"Your son is getting handsomer," she told Susan.

"Thank you. I think so."

Gold took Michael down the hall to visit with two female detectives who were friends of his. When he returned Geri was already opening her briefcase. She seemed excited.

"Arresting Stewart was the missing link," she said. "All my troubles evaporated this morning. I compared the fibers from Stewart's work shirt with those found at the four scenes. They match perfectly. The comparison microscope leaves no doubt of that."

She opened her briefcase and took out a portable display board.

"As I told you the other day, it's a weird fiber. The polymer seems to be designed for strength, yet the fiber is quite fine. I got the retailer's name from Stewart's shirt, and they put me on to the manufacturer."

She handed the display to Gold.

"It's a hypoallergenic synthetic which was developed specifically for work clothes," she said. "It was created for a catalog house that sells clothes, shoes, and accessories of all kinds to businesses and factories. Everything from hard hats to rubber gloves."

Geri pointed to the fabric sample on the board.

"This particular fiber is called Airfree 12, and comes in only two colors, a tan and a dark green. The dye for the dark green is called Forest Green. The dye itself is hypoallergenic, needless to say. And, as you can see from the swatch of fabric, it's not exactly elegant to look at."

She was right. The fabric had an institutional, unattractive look. Susan recognized it easily as the color Kyle Stewart had been wearing in the interrogation room.

"According to his medical history, Stewart is allergic to most natural fabrics. He's suffered from allergies most of his life. It seems to be connected to the asthma he had as a child. There isn't a single item in his apartment that isn't hypoallergenic. He uses special sheets to cover the couch and chair, and the bed itself is hypoallergenic, as are the pillows."

She referred to a notepad from her briefcase. "The clothes he found through the catalog years ago. They don't make that fabric anymore. But Stewart had bought a dozen or more work shirts."

Gold nodded. "We found a pile of unused ones on the top shelf in his closet. Obviously, he was gradually using them up."

Geri nodded. "The dye has faded," she said. "That's clear from the microscopic examination. It's a very easy fabric to pin down, because they only manufactured it in these colors for two years, and it was only sold through the one catalog house."

Gold looked at Susan. "There's your connection to the fourth victim," he said. "How and when he knew Dorothy Kuehn doesn't matter all that much. He was at the scene of her murder. The fabric proves it."

He turned to Geri. "Have you done a statistical breakdown of this yet?"

"I'm working on it," Geri said. "The catalog house is going to overnight me an inventory of all the orders made for the work shirt during the two years it was available. They told me over the phone that it was a poor seller because of the color. We're probably looking at a hundred thousand to one that the fabric could have been at any one of the murder scenes. For it to have been at all four scenes, and in Stewart's apartment, maybe 30 or 40 million to one. This is a rare fabric. Then, of course, you have to add in things like the fact that Stewart knew the coeds. That narrows it down even more."

"Not to mention the eye MO, and all those kinky pictures we found at his place," Gold said. "This is a gold mine. We could take it to a jury tomorrow." He winked at Susan. "Unless, that is, we planted it all. In our obsession to win."

"No more Simpson jokes," Susan said.

When Geri had left Gold closed the door.

"I want to show you something else we found among

Stewart's effects," he said. "It's top secret. Weathers wants me to keep it under wraps, no matter what."

He handed Susan a small snapshot. The picture was of very poor quality and badly wrinkled. It showed the face of a girl.

"It was taken with an old Polaroid that Stewart kept in his closet," Gold said. "Not the same camera that the shots of the girls in the locker rooms were taken with."

Susan looked more closely at the picture.

"My God," she said.

"It's Patsy Morgenstern, the third victim," Gold said. "Stewart had it hidden in a little box, a sort of hope chest, behind his kitchen wall."

Susan studied the photograph. Despite its smallness and the bad lighting under which it was snapped, it was eloquent in the expression it caught in Patsy's eyes. She was gazing straight into the lens, something tender and intense in her expression.

"Look at her shoulders," Gold said.

The girl's shoulders were bare. Her long hair was undone and tumbled down her back.

"What does your second sight tell you?" Gold asked.

Susan felt the margins of the photograph, trying to catch a signal. Something was there, very powerfully, but it would not reveal itself to her.

"Nothing."

"Well, I'll tell you what *my* ESP tells me," Gold said. "They had an affair. It might have been a one-night stand. It might have been more. She let him take that picture when they were together. As a keepsake. Look at the look in her eyes, for Christ's sake. They were lovers."

Susan nodded. It was difficult to avoid Gold's conclusion. Patsy's face bore the tender, soft look of a woman who has given herself to a man. In this case, to the man behind the camera.

"Remember what Giordano told you," Gold said. "She was a virgin. She couldn't take it anymore, she wanted somebody to sleep with her. Giordano refused. Later he suspected she had found someone else to do what she wanted. Well, ten to one Stewart was that man."

Susan continued to run her fingers along the border of the photograph. Maddeningly, the signal she was trying to catch would not clarify itself.

"Suppose she got to know Stewart at the gym," Gold said. "He was a nice guy, right? Supportive. Understanding of athletes' problems. Suppose Stewart expressed some admiration for her. In a tactful way, a nonthreatening way. So when she got desperate enough, she thought of him. They got together, and one thing led to another. Maybe he took the picture that same night. Maybe they were together several times. Who knows?"

He shrugged. "Naturally she didn't tell any of her friends about it. What girl would want to admit she slept with the janitor?"

He sat back in his chair. "Stewart probably told her he wanted something to remember her by. And Christ—maybe he meant it. There's no law against a pervert having an occasional righteous love experience. It happens all the time."

Susan handed him the photograph.

"Have you ever thought of going into psychiatry?" She smiled. "You've got a knack."

"Forget it. From what I've seen of the human mind, give me Walt Disney."

There was a silence. Susan was haunted by the idea of an innocent young girl, oversized and self-conscious, having a brief affair with a sympathetic workingman. The man who would eventually murder her.

"What about the other girls?" she asked. "Do you think he might have had affairs with any of them?"

"We're checking that. But it isn't easy. They wouldn't be inclined to tell their friends about a thing like that. As for Stewart, I couldn't find anything in his stuff to finger any of the other girls. He might have tried, of course. But my gut feeling is that he succeeded with Patsy Morgenstern. And that in itself is a hell of a connection."

He frowned. "The only thing that bothers me is why he

would murder her. He was her lover. She had given him what he wanted. He must have liked her. Maybe he even loved her." He shrugged. "Maybe she threw him out after the one time. Wouldn't see him anymore."

"Even if they remained friendly," Susan said, "it wouldn't be really contradictory for him to end up killing her. The murders were in a separate compartment of his mind from the innocent relationship with Patsy. Remember, she was his third victim. After killing the two other girls, he was out of control. He killed Patsy as he had killed the others, because his sexual instinct had found a new path and he couldn't turn back. It was probably horribly painful for him. But it was too late."

She sighed. "On the other hand, it also wouldn't have been terribly contradictory if he had gone on seeing Patsy and never harmed her. The thing about the human mind is that all sorts of currents can coexist in it. Remember the women who had long-term relationships with Ted Bundy? Most murderers have had normal love affairs alongside their violent crimes."

"Well," Gold said, "if we're right about the semen in her tubes, Stewart was with her as a lover only a few hours before he killed her. That's how long it took for Jekyll to turn into Hyde."

Susan nodded.

"It's just too bad," Gold concluded. "A crapshoot. And she was the loser."

Susan knew what he meant. If Stewart's relationship with Patsy had somehow relieved the sexual and emotional tension he was under, Patsy herself would still be alive.

Instead, Patsy was dead. But she had provided the clues that led to Stewart's arrest.

17

JAIME LAY ON her bed, wearing cutoffs and a faded Chicago Bulls T-shirt several sizes too large for her. These were her at-home garments, worn almost threadbare, but always preferred to the bathrobes her mother had given her over the years, which gathered dust in the closet.

Her senses still tingled from Geoff's caresses. She had left him when she heard the news and come straight home.

The old portable TV on the wicker stand was turned on, the volume low. She had watched the story three times, switching from channel to channel.

The faces of reporters alternated with that of State's Attorney Weathers and an overexposed snapshot of the man, Kyle Stewart, who they said was the killer. The snapshot was so distorted that it was impossible to guess the man's age. He was white, and overweight—that was all she could tell.

They kept showing the face of a woman Jaime did not recognize, a psychic who had apparently had something to do with finding the killer. There was file footage of her leaving the stand in a courtroom, the scene of a trial in which she had testified some years ago. She was a small woman with a pretty figure and calm brown eyes.

One of the reporters from Channel 9 was interviewing women on the street, asking them how they felt now that the killer had been apprehended. Another reporter was on the Circle Campus buttonholing coeds, who smiled self-effacingly as they expressed their relief. The whole thing had a rather pathetic air, Jaime noticed. Perhaps it was the tremendous disproportion between the savagery of the killings and the clumsiness of the interviews.

She sat forward, her hands on her knees, then lay back again. A large black-and-white photograph of her father with Robert Kennedy and Martin Luther King, Jr., hung in a thin black frame behind her bedroom door. It was visible only when the door was closed. She did not want others to see it. She looked at it only when she was alone.

The photograph dated from long before Jaime's birth, when her father was still married to his first wife. He looked much younger in the photograph, but his eyes were the same. Smiling, welcoming, but with something guarded underneath. Her father had always treated politicians with the same courtliness as he did his constituents. He had a talent for making people feel good about themselves. This meant he had to hide his own suspicion. The only people who ever knew of it were his closest advisers, and of course his wife and daughter.

Kennedy wore his usual hard-as-nails face, his smile pulled back from his large teeth as though it hurt him. King seemed very serious, even pained, his dewy eyes not quite focusing on the camera. It always hurt Jaime to see that gentle face. King was the same age as her father. Looking back, she could see that most of a normal life had been denied him. All his accomplishments took place when he was a very young man. He had died at thirty-nine.

On the dresser, in full view for visitors to the room, was a far less formal photo of her father. He was on his knees on the living room floor of their old house, his reading glasses being pulled down his nose by an eighteen-month-old Jaime in corduroy pants and a bright orange T-shirt. She looked gleeful and excited. He bore an expression of good-natured shock as his glasses were appropriated by the child. He was wearing dress shoes and silk trousers, but his shirt was pulled half-out, and his tie was awry, apparently from his horseplay with his small daughter.

She had looked at this picture many times over the years. She was charmed by its energy, and by its depiction of a bond between herself and her father that no longer existed. Years of growth and responsibility had long since eclipsed that simple fatherly tolerance of her childish wildness. The picture seemed to distill a time of profound carelessness, of insouciance, that was not even a memory now.

A key sounded in the apartment door. It opened and closed. Then the tap-tap-tap of the dog's feet on the kitchen floor, and the muted whine of her pleasure as Reta opened the cupboard to get her food.

Jaime lay a moment longer, savoring the peculiar amalgam of her lingering anxiety and her body's pleasure. She wished she could call Geoff and go right back out to meet him again. Making love before and after Kyle Stewart were two very different things.

She got up and padded to the door. Reta was already settling onto the living room couch with a bag of Mrs. Fields cookies. Her greatest weakness.

"Hi," Jaime said.

"Hi, stranger." Reta had barely seen Jaime for the past week. Midterms had her busy at the library during the day, and she spent most evenings with her boyfriend. "What's the good word?"

Jaime shrugged. "Not much new."

"Want a cookie?"

"No, thanks." Jaime had long ago given up cookies, a concession to her pride in her figure and her desire to keep it slim. She was a connoisseur of granola bars and nonfat yogurt, though she rarely thought of food at all.

"I got enough for two." Reta was not really offering. She merely meant that she intended to eat enough for two, as she always did.

The dog—a German shepherd named Duchess—came to Jaime's side and leaned against her. Jaime scratched her behind the ears affectionately.

Reta was holding a huge peanut butter cookie. "They caught that guy. Did you hear?"

Jaime came into the room. "Yes."

"Motherfucker." Reta leaned forward thoughtfully.

"You said it." Jaime stood with her weight on one leg, looking out the window at the frozen lake. The view was beautiful. Her parents had admired it when they helped her pick out the place. The lake seemed endless as the Arctic under the white sky.

"Now I can come home from my four o'clock without an armed guard." Reta was exaggerating. But she had in fact made use of the student escort service since winter began and darkness fell before the end of her last class. The University of Chicago was a dangerous campus at the best of times, so the campus security people were well-prepared for this crisis.

Reta had joked with Jaime about the guys who walked her home. Most were complete nerds, and the one who seemed interesting turned out to be a married exchange student.

"I'm glad it's over," Jaime said.

"Me, too. Now I can get back to worrying about those twenty pounds." Reta bit into her cookie.

"Well . . ."

"You going out tonight?" Reta was not prying. She knew that Jaime had a lover, and that it was a hush-hush relationship. Reta's occasional allusions to it were purely functional. She just wanted to know where Jaime was going to be.

"No, I've got to work." Jaime looked at her watch. "I'm way behind. I'll never be ready for that PSA test."

"Yes, you will." Reta had little patience for Jaime's protests about her unpreparedness. Jaime's 3.7 GPA testified to her inability to fail at anything having to do with worldly responsibility. Jaime had an abnormal sense of duty. Her overachievement was as incurable as Reta's overeating. Reta knew this and felt sorry for her. It was a result of her naturally scrupulous personality, and having a famous father to live up to. As often as Reta had envied Jaime's perfect figure, she had also suspected that Jaime would never be truly happy in love. She carried too much

moral baggage. She would never be able to really let herself go.

"Check you later." Jaime returned to the bedroom and
turned on her desk lamp. The hated PSA textbook awaited
her. She took a last look at the TV before turning it off. It
was over. The murderer had been caught. There was no
reason for further agonizing. Or was there?

For a brief instant she pondered the familiarity of the
emotion inside her. It was relief mingled with a deeper and
permanent dread. A dread that always made her feel guilty,
as though the misfortune that had fallen on others, and
somehow left her intact, was her fault. She had known this
feeling since she was a little girl.

The killer was behind bars. Jaime was free. But she had
one thing in common with him, a bond impossible to deny.

They had both known the victims. All four of them.

18

ON SATURDAY MORNING Susan dropped Michael off at the
Golds' house, where he was to spend the night. Gold had
insisted that Susan stay at home over the weekend and do
as little as possible. She needed some rest.

When she got home Susan went along with David's
plan to the extent of turning off the phone, not checking in
with her answering service, and taking a long, hot bath.
But she felt hemmed in by the invisible siege being laid to
her home by the local and national press. As the day wore
on she became more and more restless.

At last she put on jeans and a Bears sweater and slipped
out the back way. A revival of *Double Indemnity* was

playing at an Old Town theater. Susan ate a box of pop-corn as she delighted in Barbara Stanwyck's portrait of evil and Fred MacMurray's stylish characterization of a man done in by his own lust.

After the movie Susan felt at sixes and sevens. She window-shopped for a few minutes, then on an impulse went to the Old Town Ale House, where she treated herself to a solitary Glenfiddich. An old Billie Holiday recording of "These Foolish Things" was playing, and it brought back memories of medical school, where one of Susan's fellow students had introduced her to classic jazz.

When the record ended she paid for her drink and walked down Wells Street, unsure what to do next. She strolled several blocks, oblivious to the cold. Her senses seemed to be straining toward an invisible signal. This was a familiar feeling, and an uncomfortable one. Psychic overwork often left her prey to wandering extrasensory signals and impulses, almost like a sleeper who cannot shake off dream images when he wakes.

Suddenly she hailed a yellow cab and told the driver to take her to East Ontario Street. He asked what address, and she admitted she wasn't sure.

"You know," the driver observed, "this city is going straight to hell. Have you seen the papers? They're killin' everybody."

"Yes," Susan said. "It's not a happy time."

He eyed her in his rearview mirror.

"They say people are committing suicide because the sun don't shine."

Susan nodded. "That's one reason, apparently."

There was a pause. He drummed his fingers on the wheel. Old apartment buildings went by outside the dirty windows of the cab.

"Have you told her how you feel?" Susan asked absently.

"Told who?" The cabbie looked embarrassed.

Susan came to herself with a shock.

"Oh. Nothing. I'm sorry," she said. "I was thinking of something else. My mind has been wandering all day."

"It's funny you should mention," the driver said. "My wife took off for a week with her relatives. Said she was fed up. I told her if she couldn't take the heat, she should get out of the oven. You know how it is. A man's nerves are shot by the end of the day. You go home and she's sitting there in front of the TV, and you drink a beer, and the next thing you know you're at each other's throats. Just like lighting a stick of dynamite with a tiny little match."

"Yes. It's called having a short fuse." Susan smiled.

"Right. Only I think her fuse is even a little bit shorter than mine. If you know what I mean."

"How did you meet?" Susan asked.

"When I was in the service. A buddy of mine was her brother. Fairly nice fellow. Quiet as a mouse. You'd never know from him that she could be such a wildcat. You can never tell about people."

"It's such a pretty name," Susan said.

"What name?"

Miranda. The name had fascinated her since she first read *The Tempest* in high school. It was so lyrical, and it seemed to speak of an ocean surface glinting with the light of the moon.

The driver suddenly put on the brakes and looked over his shoulder at her. "What did you say?"

Susan opened her eyes. "What's the matter? Why are we stopping?"

He was staring at her suspiciously. "What name did you say?"

"Did I say something?" Susan reddened. "Never mind. Don't pay any attention to me."

"You know," he said, "you look familiar. Haven't I seen your picture in the papers?"

She said nothing. She shrank into herself, as though to hide from his scrutiny.

"Hey. You're not that lady, are you? That doc who fingered the guy that killed those girls? The psychic?"

"No, I'm not. Why don't we finish our ride?" she asked.

Still suspicious, he drove her the rest of the way and

asked where she wanted to get out. She pointed to a side-walk just east of Michigan Avenue.

"Watch yourself," he advised significantly as she paid him.

She got out of the cab but stood leaning on the open door, unable to tear herself away.

"Call her," she said at last. "She's waiting for your call."

"Sure. I'll do that." He drove away shaking his head.

Susan found herself standing before Hatsuhana, the Japanese restaurant where she had once entertained some psychiatrists from New York who were in town for a conference. The voice that had been calling to her since she left the movie theater was louder now. She went inside, smiled as the sushi chefs shouted out their greetings, and was shown to a small table. She ordered an inside-out California roll and a light beer. She felt pleasantly alone until she noticed heads turning in her direction from several nearby tables. She knew her picture was all over the papers. She had thought she would not be recognizable in her jeans and sweater. No such luck, apparently.

She ate her meal quickly and ducked out of the restaurant. Despite the chilly weather, she walked all the way up Michigan Avenue to the Sun-Times Building. She stood on the bridge looking down at the river, with no idea what to do next. Then the voice called her again. She hailed another cab and had herself driven to Trader Vic's.

She was beginning to realize how deeply tired she was, and how ill-advised this outing was. She should be at home in bed, watching television or reading. But something would not let her rest. She sat down at a table in the bar and ordered a brandy. She tried to get up and go home, but the peculiar impulse inside her would not allow it. She kept looking at the clock. Parties of drinkers came and went. The barmaid brought her a second brandy, pointing to a man across the room and saying it was on him. Susan slipped out at the next opportunity.

She found herself sitting in the lobby, watching the clock above the registration desk and trying to make up her mind to leave. She felt as empty of initiative as a person in a bathtub watching the water run out. She could not move.

When the clock's hands marked ten-twenty, Susan suddenly got up. She headed for the Wabash Street entrance, moving quickly.

When she was in the revolving door she saw a familiar face, going in as Susan was going out. The lips curled in a smile, and there was a brief comic pantomime as they whirled around each other in the revolving door, both laughing.

"This is a surprise," said Ron Giordano. "I've been thinking about you all day."

"Really?" she asked. "Why?"

"Oh, because you're big news, I guess." He smiled. "Your face is in all the papers, in case you didn't know." He was wearing slacks and a turtleneck sweater, with a sport jacket as his only protection against the cold.

"I did know—but I haven't looked at them. I don't like that picture."

"Nonsense. It's very attractive. What are you doing down here?"

"Nothing, really," Susan said. "I was just on my way home. How about you?"

"A meeting," he said. "Anthropologists. I was the host. I took them for drinks in Old Town, then we had dinner and came back here."

"Where did you take them for dinner?" she asked.

"Hatsuhana. Japanese place up toward the Water Tower. Do you know it?"

"I've seen it."

"I'll take you there sometime. They have the best Japanese food in the city. Do you like Japanese food?"

"Very much."

"It's settled, then." He looked down at her appraisingly. He was taller than she remembered.

"A lot of people are grateful to you tonight," he added.

"Oh, well . . ."

He glanced over his shoulder at the lobby, which had been full of men in suits only a moment ago but was now completely deserted. A clerk stood at the registration desk, staring at nothing.

"You're right about one thing," Ron Giordano said. "The picture doesn't look quite like you. You seem different. Maybe it's the sweater."

She nodded. "I think I had the idea that I wouldn't be recognized if I was wearing it."

Ron Giordano smiled. "Well, it almost worked. But not quite."

"I guess not."

There was a silence. Susan stood with her coat in her arms, looking like a student in her jeans and sweater. Giordano studied her.

"I kept hoping I'd run into you again," he said. "The city isn't that big. I thought, sooner or later . . ."

"Yes. Paths do tend to cross." Susan avoided his eyes without knowing why.

"Would you like a drink?" he asked.

She looked around her at the suddenly empty lobby. She felt something weaken inside her. It was time to go home. Past time.

"I thought about you all day," he said. "Really."

She nodded. She knew it was true.

"Please?" He was smiling, holding out a hand.

Susan looked at the registration desk, where the sleepy clerk was suppressing a yawn. She already knew which key he would choose.

"All right," she said.

19

THE NEXT MORNING Susan arrived home at eight. She was nervous. She knew Michael would not be coming home until after noon, but she kept worrying that he might have called last night, or that something might have gone wrong at the Golds'.

The apartment was empty and silent. The air seemed stale as the morning sun glazed through the windows. Susan stood motionless in the living room, glancing from one detail to the next. She saw the little hollow in the couch cushion where Michael had sat watching television, and the pile of his books left under the end table. She saw his new jacket, the one she had bought at Marshall Field's, on its hook, and the still-unopened box of Frango mints Carolyn had brought home yesterday.

Susan's senses were dulled and languorous, yet something inside her seemed painfully poised. The apartment looked like a fortress she had abandoned when it was under fire. She wanted to take another long bath in the same tub she had used yesterday, but that seemed an almost perverse luxury. Her clothes felt strange; she wanted to get them off in a hurry.

She hurried into the bedroom, stripping off articles of clothing as she went. The Bears sweater she threw on the bed. She pulled off her jeans with jerky fingers and sat in her bra and panties, feeling cornered. Her own bed, in which Michael had slept with her so often, was untouched. It looked up at her accusingly.

"Come on," she said to the silence. "You're human."

She pulled off the bra and panties, threw them into the hamper, and went into the small bathroom. The reflection of her breasts peeked out at her from the vanity mirror, a brief image of pearly white and pink. Ignoring it, she turned the old porcelain knob and heard the sudden splat and hiss of the shower.

Naked, she got under the water without caring how hot or cold it was. She washed herself clumsily, dropping the soap several times. She shampooed her hair and stood for a long while under the water, feeling the droplets crash against her skin like little punishments.

At last she got out and went into the kitchen, clad in her terry cloth robe, her hair dripping on her shoulders. She picked up the phone and called her answering service.

The first message was from David Gold. The answering service said it was urgent.

Susan called Gold's home number. He answered after one ring.

"This is Susan," she said. "What's up? Is Michael all right?"

"Michael? Sure. He's fine." Gold sounded troubled. "Have you seen the news?" he asked.

"No. What's happening?"

"Brace yourself. Kyle Stewart killed himself in his holding cell early this morning."

Susan's mouth dropped open.

"Killed himself?" she asked. "How?"

"Hanged himself," Gold said. "He got his hands on a nylon cord from somewhere. Probably one of the other inmates. They found him lying on his side with the cord attached to one of the bars."

"On his side?" Susan repeated numbly.

"Stranger things have happened," Gold said. "He had been dead at least an hour when they found him."

There was a silence. Susan thought she heard accusation in it, and she had to pinch herself to remain lucid.

"Weathers is going to give a news conference at eleven," Gold said.

"I'll watch it here before I come for Michael."

"Okay."

Susan puttered around the apartment with the TV on until the news conference began.

Abel Weathers, looking tanned and handsome, excoriated the jail staff for allowing Kyle Stewart to commit suicide. As the staccato pops of news cameras sounded around him, he sought to reassure the public about Stewart's arrest.

"We will continue our thorough investigation of the homicides and of the suspect's suicide," he was saying. "But I feel bound to reassure the public that the evidence against Mr. Stewart was very strong, very powerful. Indeed, the very fact of his suicide suggests that he had the expectation of being convicted for these crimes, and wished to avoid the punishment that surely would have followed a criminal trial."

The muffled sounds of reporters' shouted questions were heard. Weathers looked left and right like a cornered animal.

"I'm not going to get into that now," he replied to one of the questions. "Suffice it to say that what we found is very powerful, very damning. Some excellent police work was done in this case, and that is why we identified the suspect as early as we did."

"Sources have told us that Dr. Shader played a critical role in identifying Stewart as a suspect," shouted a reporter. Susan blushed to hear her name.

"I don't want to comment on that now," Weathers said. "I may comment at a later time." Something about this response seemed ominous to Susan.

As soon as the news conference was over, she called Gold.

"Do you agree with Weathers about Stewart's motive for killing himself?" she asked, fighting the queasy feeling in her stomach.

"Yeah, I agree," Gold said. "The thing is, Stewart was from a neighborhood on the South Side where everybody knew everybody. Some of those neighborhoods are like small towns. He was in the Kiwanis, the Little League, the church—everybody knew him from the time he was a kid. His parents are pillars of the Lutheran community.

"Stewart was himself active in the church, and was known as a helpful guy. He did odd jobs for people in the church, delivered things for elderly people, even did carpentry and home repairs. He was considered a harmless bachelor who was a friend to everybody. There are character witnesses as long as your arm who say he was a great guy."

"What about his convictions for the sex crimes?" Susan asked.

"He managed to hide them. He committed the crimes in areas far from home, and when he was caught he gave his family and friends excuses about why he was out of circulation. He led a double life. I spoke to his mother. She told me he used to be out of town for days at a time, and sometimes he would go out west to visit a friend from the Marines. I got some dates from her, and most of them coincide with the times he was in the jug."

Gold sighed. "But the arrest in the Coed Murders, with his picture on the front pages all over town, blew his cover. I think that was too much for him."

"I see," Susan said.

"It fits the classic pattern, doesn't it?" Gold said. "A harmless guy, a loner, a bachelor—the whole schmear."

"Yes. I guess it does." The sick feeling in Susan's stomach did not seem to respond to the reassuring news that Stewart had been the actual killer.

"I talked to him for quite a while when he was in for interrogation," Gold said. "I found myself liking the guy. He was very sincere, very self-effacing. Not at all like a lowlife. I honestly think he lived two lives. He may not have even remembered the killings. When the seamy side caught up with him, he just couldn't tolerate it. Not only was he a sure bet for death row, but he had lost the support of his community and his family."

Susan recalled the words of Stewart's guidance counselor at school. When caught in a sexual crime as a boy, he had offered to go to prison rather than have his parents find out what he had done.

"So," Gold concluded, "he took the only way out that he could find."

There was a silence.

"Is anything wrong?" Gold asked.

"Not exactly." Susan was remembering the harmless, gentle look of Kyle Stewart through the one-way glass of the interrogation room. He had seemed more like a Peeping Tom than a killer, she had thought. "I'd just like to feel sure about him."

"Think of all those photographs with the eyes removed," Gold said. "It's almost a portrait of the killer's MO. And look at Stewart's contact with the coeds. He knew them all. Not to mention the fibers. When have you seen a stronger case, Susan?"

"I guess you're right." She could not deny his logic.

"Anyway, we're going to stay on it," Gold said. "Weathers told the truth about that. This is multiple homicide, after all. We won't be sure until there aren't any more murders. But my gut feeling is that there won't be."

"I hope not."

Again there was a silence.

"What are you worrying about?" Gold asked. "You're the one who fingered him for us."

"I didn't want him to end up dead in a cell," she said.

"Susan, you're not responsible for the crimes he committed, or for his own despair when we nailed him. You identify too closely with criminals. This isn't your fault. It's Stewart's fault."

Susan sighed. Perhaps he was right.

"I'll see you later, then," she said.

"Good. Get some rest. And stop worrying!"

Gold hung up.

20

MONDAY WAS A long day for Susan. She had four office appointments and a supervision at Northwestern Hospital. At every step of the way, reporters barred her path. She refused to comment on the death of Kyle Stewart or her role in the investigation that had led to his arrest.

Her patients were all aware of her situation and were sympathetic. But their awareness was not a good thing therapeutically. She doggedly brought the subject back to their own troubles, but she sensed the ambivalence her notoriety was creating in them. She cursed the day she ever shared her psychic gift with anyone.

By day's end she was exhausted. Her final stop was at the little market down the street from her apartment building. She bought milk, bread, and breakfast cereal for Michael. Her hands were cold; she realized they had been frozen all day.

She took her few items to the counter, where Mr. Cervantes, the elegant Colombian proprietor, stood beneath the convex mirror that reflected all the corners of the place. His arms were folded across his chest. With his droopy mustache he looked like a bullfighter out of one of the Manet paintings down at the Art Institute.

"Doctor, how are you?" His eyes told her he had heard the news. He would not mention it to her in a million years. His sense of chivalry precluded such an indelicacy.

"Not too bad, Mr. Cervantes. How is your wife?"

"Perfect. Our son is coming to visit next week. She's looking forward to it."

"That's wonderful."

Three years ago Mr. Cervantes's wife had awakened in the middle of the night with a case of pitting edema in her left leg. She was taken to the hospital, where, a day later, the overworked nurses gave her too much anticoagulant medication intravenously. She was bleeding through her pores and complaining of a headache and dizziness. Mr. Cervantes, in a panic, called Susan, who hurried to the hospital and found Mrs. Cervantes inches away from an internal hemorrhage that could have killed her. Susan herself stopped the IV and waited with the patient until her physician could be found.

Ever since that time Mr. Cervantes had said that Susan "saved Clara's life." He sent her a large basket of his choicest fruits every Christmas, and half the time refused to allow her to pay for the groceries she bought at his store.

"Tell her I said hello, will you?"

"She'll be delighted. Did you find everything you need, Doctor?"

"Yes, thanks."

"Just one moment, please." Mr. Cervantes was looking into the convex mirror. He bent slightly to pull something from under the counter and moved quickly toward the back of the store. Susan looked in the mirror and saw a heavyset black girl in a wool coat standing back by the dairy products.

"Can I help you?" Mr. Cervantes's voice was loud and authoritative. The girl murmured something in response, and he came back to Susan.

"I beg your pardon," he said, putting her things in a bag and hitting the keys of the register with quick, fluid hand motions. A confidential glance told her he considered the girl at the back of the store a potential shoplifter. "Have a nice night, now." He smiled as he gave her her change.

"You, too."

The doorbell chimed as Susan went out. Mr. Cervantes stood patiently waiting. The black girl came forward after a moment. Without a word she put a container of yogurt, a small package of cookies, and a single Granny Smith apple on the counter.

"Have you got a spoon?" she asked, not meeting his eyes.

"Certainly." His accented voice rang with suspicion and reproach. His sharp eye had told him she was going to shoplift the cookies. They had been on their way into the large pocket of her wool coat when he had called out to her. Even now her face betrayed disappointment that he had caught her.

"Two sixty-seven," he said. She fiddled lengthily in her purse, pulling out folded dollar bills with some difficulty. She was a very unattractive girl, with a wide nose and thick brows. For the first time it occurred to him that she might be in some sort of trouble, or perhaps on drugs. She didn't seem entirely in control of herself.

She declined the bag he offered her and moved slowly out of the store, shoving the apple and cookies into her pockets and holding the yogurt and spoon in her hand.

Mr. Cervantes stood behind the counter, looking at the rack of *Tribune*s beside the lottery tickets. ACCUSED KILLER SUICIDE, he read. He would have liked to ask Dr. Shader whether she thought the man was really guilty. Time, he supposed, would tell.

OUTSIDE THE STORE, the girl made her way slowly to the corner and turned left. Oblivious to the angry wind rattling street signs and store windows, she walked two blocks to a large apartment building across the street from a playing field and sat down on a bench. The apple bulged in her pocket. She made no move to open the yogurt.

She counted the windows of the tall building, looking slowly upward to the twenty-first floor, then to the right until she found the fifth window from the end. A dim light was on. The curtains were not drawn. No doubt the occupants were enjoying the view of the lake.

She knew that view. She had spent many an evening in that apartment. She used to stand naked before that window, with Marc's arms around her from behind.

"No one can see us," he used to say. "Unless there's some voyeur out on the lake with a telescope."

He seemed to enjoy taking chances. He liked kissing her in public places, even though there was always the possibility that one of his colleagues from school might be in the neighborhood and see him. He would hold her close on the El or in a cab. Often, as a sensual little joke, he would slip his hand inside her coat to her breast when nearby people had their heads turned the other way. "Stop!" she would reproach him; but she didn't really mind. She enjoyed his little reminders that he wanted her.

It had been a whirlwind affair, beginning one night at the University of Chicago library where she worked shelving books. He emerged from the tiny office where he did his research—he was a postdoctoral fellow in history—and struck up a conversation with her. She accepted his offer to join him for coffee, and he confided that he had been watching her for a long time. "You're so beautiful. I can't concentrate on my work when I know you're somewhere in the stacks. But I never miss a night when you're here. I know all your clothes. I wait for certain items to come back. I determine my mood based on what I see in your eyes. Such incredible eyes . . ."

Celeste had never been told she was beautiful. Her appearance had been the bane of her life. Looking in the mirror was torture for her. Applying makeup was always a losing battle. She had not inherited her father's light-skinned, faintly Asian attractiveness. She took after her mother's clumsy, thick-browed relatives.

Celeste was short, with heavy legs and virtually no waist. There was no hint of grace or sensuality in her body. There had been a time, years ago, when she thought her eyes had possibilities, but she could not look at the eyes in the mirror without seeing the wide nose, the heavy cheeks. It was no use.

She had slipped into despair about herself back in high school. A few of the boys had condescended to sleep with her, their caresses completely without tenderness. She had experienced sex as something weightless, almost nonexistent, like the touch of a gnat on the skin of an elephant.

By the middle of her senior year, Celeste's self-esteem was at an all-time low. Yet she ended up applying to college. She had reasonably good grades and a remarkable ability in mathematics. To her amazement she was accepted with a scholarship at the University of Chicago. The offer was too good to refuse.

She did rather well at the university. She studied hard and refused the dates offered by boys whose contemptuous faces revealed what they wanted. For a whole year she remained celibate. Things started to look brighter. She began to think of her life as a clean slate.

Then she met Marc, and everything changed.

Their affair was silent and passionate. He insisted on meeting her four, five times a week. He begged her to do her studying at his apartment, so he could feel her near him as he did his own work. They took long walks, hand in hand, wordless, intimate walks. She sat looking out that window of his, savoring the fact that her eyes were seeing what he himself saw. Soon his arms would slip around her from behind, she would feel the touch of his lips against her neck or her ear, and they would move to the bedroom.

Looking back on it, she had no doubt that he really was in love with her. How could he not be? He seemed to need her so desperately. He savored her, devoured her. More than once she took pity on him when he begged her to stay the night. His bed felt so empty without her, he said.

He learned all about her, of course. She held nothing back. Strangely, the story of her life did not seem so pathetic when it was told to him. He saw her as the heroine of an adventure in which she was wronged, but in which she triumphed in the end. Everything around her—parents, friends, teachers—was, in his eyes, a wasteland without value until it was lit by her own glow. Even her unhappiness had something exalted about it. Or so it seemed to him.

In the end Celeste forgot that she was not beautiful. That was her final leap, and she took it for him.

When he tried to break off the relationship, she was incredulous. She explained patiently that he could not throw her over. It was too late for that. She went through the reasons and was surprised when he resisted them. The day he made her remove her things from his apartment they had a big fight. She punched him and clawed at him and called him a monster. He demanded her key back, and she threw it in his face.

But after a couple of weeks on her own she came to understand that she had been too harsh, too reproachful. She went back to apologize. He didn't answer when she buzzed his intercom. She called from home. His answering machine was a fortress more terrible than the tall building in which he hid from her.

She wrote letters. There was no answer. She took to spying on him from the park across the street. She sat there for hours. One day she saw a young white girl entering the building. The face looked familiar. She thought she had seen her there before. Celeste waited. An hour later the girl emerged on Marc's arm.

Things had gone much too far, and in her next letter Celeste tried to explain that to Marc. She mentioned the girl, generously allowing that she was very pretty. "But she came too late," she wrote. "You belonged to me already. You belong to me now. It's much too late. You've got to understand that."

Tonight Celeste had arrived at this hour because she knew the girl was there. Her name was Camila. She had followed her home one day—a long ride on the El—and looked at the names on her mailbox. Camila Gardiner. Celeste felt sorry for her.

She knew what they were doing up there. She didn't care. The things they might do together were mere flesh. They could not attenuate her prior claim on his soul.

Celeste felt a pang of hunger. She had eaten nothing since she awoke this morning, and these days urgent hungers were part of her life. She opened the yogurt. She ate slowly, looking up at the window.

Her spoon stopped in midair as she saw the silhouette of the girl appear behind the glass. Miniaturized by distance, the shape was nevertheless easily recognizable. Probably she was naked. Another shape appeared. It was Marc. His hands were on her shoulders. He hugged her from behind.

Celeste sat looking up, tears running down her cheeks, the spoon trembling in her hand. It was so hard to fight those silhouettes. So hard to make him understand love when he believed in shadows.

"I beg your pardon."

She started at the sound of the voice. It was a man. He was sitting beside her. For all she knew he might have been there for a long time.

"Are you all right?" he asked. "You seemed . . ."

"What?" She had trouble pulling herself back to the reality of cold and wind after the height she had scaled for Marc.

"You were crying. I don't like to intrude, but you seemed so upset."

He wore thick glasses with horn rims. His hair was cut very short and was a remarkably uniform iron gray. A small white dog was on a leash between his legs. He must live nearby, she thought.

Vapor came from his nostrils in the frigid air. He looked worried. "You're sure you're all right?"

"Yes. I'm fine."

"Well, I hate to see young girls cry," he said, looking away. "It's not fair for things to make you cry at such a young age." He looked around him. "Say, aren't you scared out here all alone? All kinds of weird people could be out here."

He gestured to the building. "Is that where you live?"

Celeste shook her head.

"Oh. I thought maybe your parents were giving you trouble." He smiled. "That's what my daughter used to do when we had a fight. Just go outside the building and sit there until I simmered down. She was stubborn. She always outlasted me. I apologized every time."

He sighed. "But I think it's only natural. Adults have a lot more to apologize for than children do. Children haven't had time to do anything very serious."

He leaned forward. "She died two years ago," he said. "Since then I've apologized a thousand times. But she can't hear anymore. What's the use?"

Celeste sat up. "She died?"

He nodded, not looking at her. "A car accident. She was far away from us at the time. Way down south. She hadn't spoken to me in a year. I didn't even hear about it until nearly a day after it happened. That's the way it goes."

Tears were welling in his eyes, though his expression had not changed. The dog whined faintly. He petted it. She saw age spots on the back of his hand. The fingers were trembling.

"Now all I have is a dog," he said.

"I have to go," she said.

"Do you have parents?" he asked. "How long has it been since you've seen them?"

She smiled at his intuition. It had been a very long time. Her parents didn't even know where she was living now. She had given them up when she left school. She was through with her past.

"Go see them," he said. "You'll never know how much it means, until you have children of your own."

His words struck a chord within her. He must have a sort of second sight, she thought.

"Oh. Well. I have to go."

"Yes, go. I'll stay here and keep your vigil for you."

That was an odd thing for him to say, she reflected. She got up and headed down the block without a backward glance.

The wind was whipping cruelly at her legs. She angled through the park to get away from it. Her El stop was two streets away. Halfway there she turned on her heel. Why should she go home so early? The evening was young. She could not allow herself to be chased away simply because a stranger had spoken to her.

She retraced her steps, staying close to the trees. The wind groaned and cursed in the echo of the tall buildings. She didn't feel the cold; it was only the slapping of the gusts that annoyed her.

"Isn't your name Celeste?"

She stopped in her tracks. The little man was blocking her path. He looked different without his glasses. The dog was nowhere in sight.

She was astonished. She had never seen him before tonight. He could not possibly know her name.

"How did you—"

"Such a pretty name. How can he treat you this way, when you have such a beautiful name?"

His eyes held her paralyzed for a split second too long. She wanted to run, but he had both her hands now and was pulling her into the trees.

"Help!"

He shook his head. "The wind is too loud. They can't hear you, Celeste."

His arm curled around her neck, and he pushed her to the ground with amazing force. Her fall knocked the wind out of her. She noticed a peculiar smell that came from him, reminiscent of sour milk, or ham that had gone bad.

He tightened his grip. Then he paused, bringing his mouth close to her ear.

"Listen to me," he said. "Are you listening?"

Frantic, Celeste nodded.

"You weren't even there, were you?" he asked. "She gave your name, didn't she?"

She couldn't answer, for the grip of his arm was too tight. She didn't know what he was talking about. She tried to nod, hoping to gain time.

"No. You weren't even there. And now you have to die, and your pretty name will be in all the newspapers. *Celeste.*"

She struggled briefly, feeling the life inside her cry out its right to continue. But the arm around her neck pulled harder, and as the blackness rose she forgot everything except the high window and the silhouettes and the moaning wind.

PART THREE

21

PSYCHIC'S ERROR LEADS TO INNOCENT MAN'S DEATH

THAT WAS THE headline used by the *Sun-Times* and disseminated through wire services to a hundred other newspapers.

When the body of Celeste Cawley was found propped against a fountain in Lincoln Park, the eyes gouged out, the real significance of the suicide of Kyle Stewart came through to the city. And the media, sensing the newsworthiness of this revelation, set out to make hay from it.

One of the local reporters, famous for his highly placed sources within the police department, had found out how crucial Susan's second sight had been in the arrest of Kyle Stewart for the crimes. His feature article on the case was 10,000 words long, spread over eight newspaper pages.

It was Dr. Shader who suggested to homicide detectives that the perpetrator was a university employee whose job put him in a position to watch the female athletes as they practiced, showered, and changed clothes. This tip, based on Shader's second sight, led to the arrest of Kyle Stewart, whose maintenance office was located adjacent to the athletes' locker room.

A collection of pornography, combined with photographs of some of the coeds, was found in Stewart's room. This seemed to confirm the psychic's intuition, and Stewart was arrested for multiple murder.

There was no apparent connection between Stewart and the fourth victim, Mrs. Dorothy Kuehn of Oak

161

Lawn. Despite this crucial gap in the chain of evidence, the police placed Stewart, a mild-mannered Marine Corps veteran, in a holding cell at the City Jail. It was there that Stewart, despondent over the damage to his reputation caused by the arrest, took his own life.

The murder of Celeste Cawley, carried out with the same MO as the four previous slayings, might have seemed to a casual eye the result of a copycat with a perverse sense of timing, since Cawley was killed only sixteen hours after Stewart's suicide. However, this reporter has learned that the method of strangulation in the Cawley murder was identical to that employed in the other killings. More damning yet is the fact that crucial trace evidence found at the Cawley scene is identical to that found at the first four scenes. The killer is thus still at large, while Kyle Stewart, a harmless Peeping Tom whose only crime was his collection of kinky photographs, is dead.

Dr. Susan Shader was unavailable for comment. The State's Attorney, asked to respond to the death of an innocent man based on a psychic's intuition, said in a prepared statement, "We have perhaps the finest police force in the nation here in Chicago. If mistakes were made in this case, you can be sure they were not made by Chicago detectives." When asked if this meant the psychic was to be blamed for the two additional deaths, State's Attorney Weathers replied, "You can draw your own conclusions."

The local news stations were slanting the story the same way, and showing over and over again the file footage of Susan leaving the stand after her court testimony some years ago. Susan could not help noticing that she seemed a bit more guilty with each repetition of the footage. Such was the power of film.

A damage control meeting was held at Abel Weathers's office on Tuesday afternoon. All the senior homicide detectives attended, as did the medical examiner, three FBI agents who had been assigned to the case, and representatives of the mayor and governor. Susan was not invited.

It was one of the longest days in Susan's memory. There was no doorman at 30 North Michigan, and a crowd of aggressive reporters and photographers had found their way to the corridor outside Susan's office. She had no choice but to push past them with her head down, hearing cameras click as she went. With their best ambush faces on, the reporters called out questions at her. "How do you feel, Doctor, now that your second sight has caused an innocent man's death?" "Doctor, have you apologized to the family of the innocent man whose death you caused?"

Understandably, two of Susan's patients—a hypochondriacal CEO of a local corporation and the general manager of a sports team, a kindly middle-aged man who suffered from obsessions—did not show up. Whether their absence was the result of Susan's notoriety, their fragile emotional condition, or their desire not to be seen and filmed by the reporters outside the office she did not know.

Amazingly, the three other patients did appear, and Susan held reasonably effective hours with them, the office's good soundproofing keeping out the noise being made by the media.

In the late morning a message was left with Susan's answering service canceling her speech to a convention of forensic experts that had been scheduled for later in the month. She had no illusions about why.

The media siege of the weekend was nothing compared with the mob of reporters clogging the lobby of Susan's apartment building and the street outside. She managed to get upstairs the back way. To her surprise she found Carolyn home.

Her roommate looked chagrined. "Honey," she said, "I know you'll never forgive me for this. I did everything I could, but they went right over my head." Channel 9 had played the story for all it was worth with break-ins throughout the day's programming and a twenty-minute feature at the head of the widely watched noon news. An even longer feature was planned for the nine o'clock news that night.

"I should have quit on the spot," Carolyn said. "The only reason I stayed is because I thought I might be able to help in the weeks to come."

"Forget it." Susan smiled. "It's the nature of the business. I understand that. I let myself in for it when I got involved with cases of this type. It was my own choice. Don't torment yourself about it."

Michael was sitting quietly before the television with Pam, the high school girl who baby-sat for him when he visited. His face left no doubt he was aware of his mother's predicament, but he said nothing about it as Susan bent to hug him.

"Hello, sweetie," she said, holding him close.

"Hello, Mom."

For some reason the sight of his innocence broke down the rampart that had held fast in Susan all day, and she felt a sob coil sharply in her breast. Pam alertly interposed herself, offering to help Michael make popcorn, and Susan hurried into the bedroom to change her clothes.

She was standing in front of the bathroom mirror, staring at her own haunted face, when David Gold's call came. Carolyn knew the code and knocked at the bedroom door to let Susan know who it was.

Susan sat on the bed in her robe as Gold reviewed the day's events.

"Weathers is freaking out," he said. "He was staking his reelection on the Stewart arrest. Now he thinks it's curtains. The only way out for him is to serve you up to the media as the fall guy."

"Well, he's not wrong," Susan said, surprised at her own calm. "I'm the one who gave you Stewart."

"That's bullshit." Gold's profanity was clearly intended as sympathy. "You told us to check out people who were close to the athletes. We did that, and the evidence gave us Stewart. My guys found the pornographic shit in his apartment, and the photographs of the girls, and all the rest. Including the fibers—don't forget that. All you did was con-firm. When I took you into that locker room, that's just what I was after—confirmation. This isn't your collar, Susan. It was a team effort. A team mistake, too."

"You're nice to put it that way," Susan said. "But I think it's safe to say I won't be working cases with you in the future." She sighed. "Perhaps that's for the best."

"Bullshit again," Gold said. "I've got ten perpetrators behind bars because of you. You're the best outside spe-cialist we've ever had in Homicide. Don't let all this media stuff blind you to the realities."

Susan nodded weakly, but she could not find words to say.

"We're still working on trace." Gold was all business again. "So far the ME says no saliva. No semen either. Re-member the fibers Geri Vogel showed us? I'll tell you, that was a damned rare fiber. Put it together with the blood type and in a court of law it would have been more than enough to convict Stewart of the first four crimes. I've been thinking about that all day, and it doesn't make sense to me."

"Not to me, either," Susan said.

"Do me a favor and think about it," Gold said.

"Are you sure you want me to?"

"Of course I'm sure. I want you with me on this. You al-ready know the case. What Weathers doesn't know won't hurt him."

Susan was touched by Gold's confidence in her, but it was not a confidence she shared, at least not at the moment.

Gold heard her reluctance and went on talking to keep her from refusing him.

"You know Cawley was right in your neighborhood when she was attacked, don't you?"

"Yes."

"I'm not sure why, but that itches me somehow," Gold said. "She was the only victim not killed at home. She lived way over on the West Side. She dropped out of the University of Chicago last year. She was working as a shopgirl. What was she doing in Lincoln Park?"

Susan had nothing to offer.

"I'll tell you," Gold said, "I've been in this game long enough to smell a rat. We got so lucky with Stewart—and then the bottom dropped out. His suicide, followed so quickly by Cawley. I've never had so much good luck and so much bad luck all at once. It doesn't seem kosher."

"Yes. I understand."

"Think about that, too, will you?"

"Yes, David." Susan was hunched forward, almost like the victim of a bad stomachache.

"How's my boy?"

"He's fine. Holding up well. Better than I am."

"You going to keep him around?"

"I doubt it. This is too much. I'm going to call Nick. I think Michael should go back to California."

"I'm sorry to hear that." Gold sounded very sad.

"I'm sorry about it, too," Susan said. "I live for my times with him."

"I know. Can I have a word with him?"

Susan sat up and looked through the open door. Michael was in the kitchen with Pam. "Sure. Hang on a minute."

"And, Susan—take it easy. I need you. Keep it together for me, will you?"

"I'll do my best."

She left the receiver on the bed and went to get Michael. He smiled when she said Gold wanted to talk to him. She watched him go into the bedroom and close the door quietly behind him. A man-to-man conversation was in the offing, she suspected.

"Oh," Carolyn was saying. "Bill brought these up while you were on the phone."

Susan turned to see a box of flowers on the kitchen counter. When she opened it the intense smell of fresh roses filled the room.

"Bill said they came earlier," Carolyn said. "He didn't get a chance to bring them up until now."

Susan looked closely at the flowers. The petals seemed amazingly fresh, given the horrible weather. A tiny envelope hid deep between the stems. As Susan fished for it she felt a sharp prick. There were thorns. A drop of blood stood out on her finger; she put it in her mouth to lick it off.

The card inside the envelope bore the name of the florist but no note.

It's a Small World
Flowers for all occasions, delivery anywhere

A smile curled Susan's lips, then faded quickly as her fingers went cold around the card.

22

SUSAN HAD BECOME psychic when she was ten years old.

Her parents were hardworking country people whose truck farm could not support them. Her mother worked part-time as a realtor, her father as a carpenter and small contractor. Many of the toolsheds, garages, and henhouses in the county had been built by him. Sometimes he amused Susan by pointing them out as he took her for drives on Sunday afternoons.

He was a thoughtful man, intellectually restless despite his lack of education. His great passion was the Civil War. He possessed dozens of books about it and corresponded with other students of the war, most of whom were southerners. He also had a vast knowledge about anything concerning the social history of his part of the state. During those long, lazy drives in his battered Ford Fairlane, he would tell Susan stories about the ancestors of her relatives and friends, and the events, both real and legendary, that had occurred here.

He felt connected by his own curiosity to the unspoken past that hid behind the old hills and trees and houses. Later in life Susan would reflect that this intellectual rooting in a past he wished to unearth was a habit of mind she had inherited from her father. In her case it would take the form of a passion for psychological truth.

The night of the fire that killed her parents, Susan and her brother were staying overnight with their cousins. Susan was sitting in the cousins' tree house when the sheriff's car crawled up the long dirt drive, its light blinking like a cyclops. The sheriff got out of the car with a deliberation that made Susan fear he had come to arrest her.

The family gathered around the two orphans with a suffocating firmness. Susan was told over and over again by hovering aunts and uncles, "You have to go on now. You have to carry on, for your little brother. That's what your mom and dad would have wanted." Living became an obligation, a trust. No one asked about Susan's feelings or suggested that she had a right to any feeling other than that of duty.

When Susan realized she was psychic, she did not connect the onset of the gift with the deaths of her parents. It felt like a dormant impulse in her body that had come alive as though on a time signal, much as the stressful yearnings of adolescence appear of their own accord when their time has come.

Listening to the Beatles sing "Norwegian Wood" one afternoon, she touched the picture of John Lennon and knew he would be murdered in New York City.

Writing in her diary, she predicted that a man would kill eight student nurses in Chicago, and that a ninth nurse, hidden under a bed, would identify him to the police. She predicted Richard Nixon's downfall through a thing called Watergate, which had no meaning when it first came to her.

She never told anyone about her gift. It embarrassed and confused her. Images crowded her mind, making concentration difficult at school. Sometimes she was able to identify them as thoughts or fantasies coming from her teacher or fellow students. Sometimes they remained a mystery.

She went through the motions of being a ten-year-old girl. She studied hard in school, but her grades were lower now. She tried to make friends, but her family tragedy frightened the other children, and the faraway look in her eyes put them off. She was hard to talk to. Her teachers thought she was lazy. She spent more and more time at home with her brother, less and less at school activities.

Four years after her parents' deaths she began to sleep around.

Her body was developing early, and boys noticed her. Encouraged by her outcast status at school, they asked her out for long walks in the woods that rimmed the quiet pastures. When she did not resist their advances, they passed her name around among their friends. Sometimes she would sneak out at night to meet a boy. Her aunt and uncle never guessed she was gone.

She predicted the assassination of Martin Luther King, Jr. She predicted the kidnapping of Patty Hearst. She predicted the Tate–La Bianca murders in California, and the Kent State massacre, and the Attica prison riot. The terrible events she saw in the news began to seem like private nightmares that had come true in the real world.

When one of her teachers heard rumors about Susan's promiscuity, she was called in to the school psychologist's office for a conference. She begged the psychologist not to tell her aunt, and her wish was granted.

Just before the beginning of her sophomore year, her aunt became ill. A malignancy was diagnosed, and for the next two years the family was painfully focused on the impending loss. When the end was near Susan and her brother were sent to stay with another aunt and uncle in Baltimore. It was there that Susan's IQ was tested for the first time and she was sent to a special school. She learned of her aunt's death after completing a college-level calculus test one rainy afternoon.

Her experiments with the opposite sex ended with her move to Baltimore. She threw herself into her studies. She read until all hours; her aunt and uncle rarely saw her sleep.

She was a quiet, well-behaved girl who charmed adults with her polite personality and precocious emotional maturity.

One night toward the end of Susan's first year in Baltimore her aunt chanced to see her emerging from the shower. Susan's upper arms were bleeding from cuts she had administered with her uncle's straight razor. Some of the cuts, months old, had scarred over. Others, newer, had begun to bleed on contact with the hot water.

She was sent to a respected Baltimore psychiatrist who explained to her that the deaths of her parents had left a permanent scar, and that the death of her aunt after a long, cruel illness had made the scar deeper. Susan listened in silence, and when the psychiatrist told her there was no real difference between her compulsive studying and her promiscuity, she laughed sarcastically. "That's stupid," she said. She took a long look out the window at the antebellum charm of Charles Street. Then she burst into tears.

During her first months of therapy, her grades dropped again. Then they shot up, and she finished high school a year early. She started at the University of Pennsylvania the following fall and completed a double major in chemistry and mathematics two and a half years later. At age twenty she started medical school. At age twenty-seven she was a resident in psychiatry at Northwestern University Hospital and had completed a training analysis with Berthe Mueller, one of the foremost analyst-teachers in the nation.

Dr. Mueller was the first person Susan told about her second sight. The doctor helped her to understand that in her mental life the second sight had always been considered a gift that came too late to be of use to her. *"If only I had known in advance about the fire, I could have warned my parents!"* This was the cloud under which her clairvoyance had first appeared, and the reason it had always been tainted by shame and foreboding. It was only by learning to accept her own fallibility and vulnerability that she could begin to accept the gift for what it really was.

It was after she had started practicing as a psychiatrist

that Susan began to think of using her psychic gift in a practical way. She did a lot of reading in parapsychology and contributed articles under a pseudonym to some of the scientific journals. She was struck by the parallels between second sight and the unconscious.

She met Nick at a party given by a mutual friend. They were married three months later in San Francisco, where Susan worked in a psychiatric clinic while Nick pursued his career as a civil liberties lawyer. Michael was born; Susan and Nick broke up.

After her return to Chicago she met David Gold at a conference on the psychology of mass murderers. They struck up a conversation at a cocktail party and spent the evening together. He was a kind, introspective man, not at all the stereotype of a detective. Susan felt a pang of regret when he told her he was married. They were friends from that night on.

In a weak moment she told him about her second sight, and he asked her if she would help him on a case. After examining the personal effects of a murder victim on Diversey Parkway, Susan correctly identified an ex-boyfriend as the killer. Her work as a police psychic had begun.

She juggled her three careers—psychiatrist, scholar, and psychic—with increasing confidence as time went on. She learned more about the criminal mind from her work with the police. She began to testify as an expert in criminal cases. The threads of her life seemed to be twining successfully into a vocation that made her feel valuable.

After he had gotten to know her better, David Gold made a joke of asking her if she was quite sure she wasn't Jewish.

"You've got everything a Jewish girl needs except the mother," he said.

Susan understood that he was referring to a feeling of exile, of sadness that emanated from her. She lacked the *shiksa*'s quality of belonging to the mainstream community. She was an outsider. Gold liked her for this.

Susan had a friend as well as a career. The biting Chicago

wind and gray sky began to seem peculiarly comforting. The earth had made a place for her after all in this city full of immigrants.

Then the murder of Cheryl Glaser began the crime spree that led to the arrest and suicide of Kyle Stewart.

THE OFFICE HAD changed. This fact took Susan by surprise, for she had somehow imagined the doctor's space as timeless and safe. The chairs were new. So were the blinds behind which the cityscape loomed.

When she had been here in the old days, there had been a painting between her chair and that of the doctor. It was an abstraction in blacks and browns, earthy and somehow reassuring. It had come to symbolize a formlessness to which she must herself give shape and meaning, like her own life. Often her eyes would stray to it during therapeutic hours, and Dr. Mueller never objected. Once in a while they would talk about it, and its significance for her. The doctor told Susan she had bought it on a trip to Mexico with her husband. It was unsigned. This made it seem even more symbolic, perhaps of a clean slate without intrinsic meaning, which one was free to fill in with one's own eye.

"The painting," Susan said now. "It's gone."

"Yes, it is." The doctor smiled. "Do you miss it?"

Susan shrugged. "It had a meaning for me. But time moves on, I guess."

"Did you feel that time did not apply to this room?" the doctor asked, smiling.

"Every patient feels that, I imagine," Susan said. "This is the one place where one doesn't have to deal with the pressures of the outside world."

"But one is here in order to deal with them. Eventually, anyway," the doctor said.

"But it's the inner pressures first," Susan said. "Isn't it?"

"Yes, I think you're right. The outside world really starts inside us, with our memories, our feelings, the adjustments we made a long time ago."

Susan looked at the place where the painting had been.

"What happened to it?" she asked.

"I gave it away."

"To whom?"

"Someone who admired it. Someone who needed it."

Susan felt a pang of jealousy.

"A patient?"

"Not exactly." Her tone told Susan she could not say any more.

She studied Susan. "Well, you've changed, too," she said.

"How do I look?"

The doctor looked at her. The eyes touched her with their peculiar pressure, cornering her and making her feel naked, but also comforting her. Their relationship of the old days was asserting itself already.

"You look good," the doctor said. "Strong, capable. So many of my patients come in looking defeated. You look like a person who has been standing on her own two feet for a long time."

"In a manner of speaking," Susan said. "Sometimes it doesn't feel like standing."

"I understand." The doctor smiled. "Someone once remarked that the purchase of human feet on the surface of the earth is far less secure than the reputation of gravity would suggest."

"Boats against the current," Susan added, recalling the last line of *The Great Gatsby*, which she used to quote in this room when the burden of memory seemed almost too great to bear.

"Yes, there is that too. The past is part of our gravity. And sometimes its weight makes the present seem difficult to deal with."

There was a silence. Susan felt its pull, just as she felt the magnetism of the doctor's eyes. Therapy is a strange and wonderful thing, she mused. In a way it is even more profound than second sight. Second sight is simply things coming to you. In therapy, things are drawn out of you by a force that penetrates to your deepest self—and at the price of a great resistance. During her training analysis Susan had rarely failed to walk out of this office feeling cleansed. She missed that feeling now that she was on her own.

"How is your little boy?" the doctor asked.

"Not so little anymore." Susan fished in her purse for a picture of Michael. She handed it to the doctor, who put her glasses on. As the familiar eyes squinted behind the glass, Susan noticed the gray hair that had taken over more of her head, the wrinkles that had not been there before.

"He is very handsome," the doctor said. "He looks intelligent."

"He is."

"That is a gift." She handed back the picture. "Is he with you now?"

Susan had kept the doctor abreast of the news about Michael's development. She always sent a long Christmas letter, and once in a while she added a letter in the summer. The doctor never failed to respond, though her own letters were briefer than Susan's. Susan kept them all. She needed the bond of affection and knowledge the letters represented. The doctor knew her better than any other human being and had had a hand in her development. She was like a mother, but even more intimate, because a young woman necessarily keeps some secrets from her mother, while the therapeutic alliance will not let her hide things from her therapist.

"He is," Susan said. "But I've decided to send him back to Nick. Things are too difficult here."

The doctor nodded. "Does this cause some ripples?"

She knew the circumstances behind Susan's custody arrangement with Nick and was well aware of the scars left by Susan's loss of Michael.

"A few, I think." Susan's tone was evasive.

The doctor's silence told Susan she was waiting to hear more. This was Susan's first visit in a very long time. The reason must be serious.

Susan's strength ebbed suddenly, and she dared to voice her self-pity.

"A man is dead because of me," she said. "A girl, too, perhaps. The latest victim."

The doctor looked skeptical. "What makes you feel this?"

"I helped the police find a man who seemed to be the killer of the three college girls and the fourth victim. There was good evidence that he was involved. Right down to some photographs in his apartment that reproduced the killer's MO. Pictures of girls with the eyes removed and replaced with other eyes. He actually knew one of the girls."

Susan clasped her hands nervously. "I had strong feelings. This seemed to be the man. The police agreed with me. Then, suddenly, he committed suicide in jail. The next day another victim was found."

"That sounds like quite a coincidence," said the doctor.

Susan nodded. "That's exactly how it seemed to me. Too sudden. Too perfect."

She gnawed at her lip nervously. "Ever since the beginning of this thing, of these murders, there's been a sort of—interference. I feel drawn into the thing by something urgent in myself, but also by something nameless, coming from outside. The feelings are very strong. I'm beginning to doubt my objectivity."

The doctor was silent.

"And other things," Susan went on. "Being the target of so much hostility. Being suspected even by the people I work with. And now, this man's death, and the girl . . ." She trailed off, consciously waiting for the doctor to help her.

The doctor nodded seriously, indicating that she had heard Susan's plea.

"Your role is not an easy one," she said. "In the interest of justice you have chosen to sit in the hot seat, as it is called. Was that not a risk worth taking? You have helped a lot of people . . ."

"I don't know." Susan felt too miserable to grapple with the truth. "I don't know."

The doctor smiled. It was not a complaisant smile but a rolling-up-the-sleeves smile. Susan recognized it from the old days.

"You face a dilemma," the doctor observed. "Second

sight is never the same as common objectivity. You yourself pointed that out to me a long time ago."

"That's right."

"It comes when it wishes, and not when you call it."

"Yes. And it comes in the form it wishes, not the form I would choose if I had the choice. Often I'm not sure what it is saying."

"Thus it follows that others will always doubt you."

Susan nodded, wanting to bite her fingernails but resisting the temptation.

"And so you doubt yourself," the doctor said. "This is unavoidable. It is hard to be sure where the insights begin and where your own feelings leave off. Particularly the unresolved feelings."

There was a pause. Susan knew that the doctor, having opened the door to a familiar pain, was waiting for her to go through it.

"This is difficult," she hazarded.

The doctor gave her a look of polite expectancy.

"To have to go on dealing with such an old problem," Susan said. "Annoying, too."

"Problems can be annoying as well as frightening." The doctor smiled. "That is perhaps a good sign. Tell me what you are thinking of."

"Michael," Susan said. "He's so vulnerable."

"We are all vulnerable." The doctor nodded. "But there is something else. Isn't there?"

Susan sighed. "Yes."

"Yes?"

"My parents," Susan admitted.

The doctor was silent.

"You know what I mean." Susan looked away. "What happened."

She waited for help. As always, the doctor gave it in the form of a challenge.

"When you say, 'what happened,' are you speaking of a fire and the deaths it caused? Or are you speaking of an event that occurred inside you at that time?"

"What is the difference?" Susan regretted her naive question immediately.

"I believe you know the answer to that."

Susan nodded. "Yes. The fire is over and done with. It happened a long time ago. The other thing goes on happening. It never ends."

"Until . . . ?"

"Until I make it end."

The doctor raised an eyebrow.

"Are you Superman?" she asked. "Are you Wonder Woman?"

Susan laughed weakly. "I know what you're saying. Not, 'until I make it end.' Instead, 'until I let it go.' "

The doctor smiled. "You are still a good student. You remember your lessons." She leaned forward. "And you have learned another thing about your second sight. It came to you right after your parents died. The gift itself is associated with loss, and with guilt. Perhaps you'll never be able to use it without ambivalence. But is this not also true of every gift, every talent?"

There was a pause.

"Few things in life are easy," the doctor went on. "But nothing is more difficult than to be alive when others have died. The sense of responsibility, of unworthiness, can be unbearable. And the identification with the dead, of course."

Susan nodded.

"It is human, too, to be angry with those who have left you." The doctor took the initiative, helping Susan to arm herself for the old struggle. "Unfortunately our mental organism rebels against that anger by turning it on ourselves. We suffer terrible torments for an impulse which, when it first came, was quite natural."

Susan nodded. This was a familiar truth, one she had fought her way to attain with the help of this doctor years ago. She saw a ten-year-old girl left alone in the world, standing on her own two feet when she wanted a mother's arms to carry her. And she saw an adult woman who had chosen a profession in which she would be continually doubted, suspected, vilified by skeptics who did not take her seriously. First as a psychiatrist, then even more profoundly as a psychic. The connection between these two images was the hardest-won insight of her work with Dr. Mueller. It still felt like a prize in her hands.

"So I bring criticism and suspicion down on myself," she said.

"Perhaps because you are challenging the world to abandon you again as it did so long ago."

"And I try to rescue others," Susan said, "as I would have liked to have rescued my parents."

"And as you would have liked to have been rescued yourself."

"By knowing the truth in good time." Susan smiled. The phrase was a sort of private joke between her and the doctor.

"Indeed. But knowing the truth in good time is for fairy tales. In real life we always know the truth only afterward, and through very hard work."

"Sometimes too late," Susan argued.

"That remains to be seen." The doctor's calm phrase had the sound of a checkmate.

There was a new silence, more pregnant than the previous ones because of the meanings that had been planted in the air. The doctor was a connoisseur of silences. Susan, her patient, had become one too.

"Rescue . . . ," she murmured. She thought of Michael, then of herself at his age. Grief coiled within her suddenly, and tears came to her eyes. She saw the box of Kleenex, close at hand, and tried to smile.

"Little girls deserve to be rescued," the doctor offered. "They have done nothing wrong. Have they?"

"I'm sorry." Susan reached for a tissue. "It's my self-pity again."

Now the doctor looked very serious. "I am not so sure that self-pity is a bad thing, if the term is taken in another way. If you could attain to real pity, heartfelt pity, for that little girl who was left alone in the world—if you could do that, would you still punish yourself this way? Perhaps not. After all, you have no desire to punish her, do you?"

"No."

The doctor sat back, gazing at Susan. "Well, then."

Susan took a deep breath. "So what do I do now?"

"You mean about this murder case?" the doctor asked. "Or about everything?"

"Everything starts with the case." Susan spoke decidedly.

The doctor nodded. "Do you remember what Descartes said? The ultimate questions are too complicated to decide now. One must live in the world. That means accepting one's limitations, and accepting some of the world's rules."

"What do you mean?"

"Perhaps the decisions inside you—your sublimations, as we call them—are not so balanced, not so perfect. But those decisions are powerful. They are your commitment to helping. Your commitment to goodness. They have helped others in the past. Use them to help others now. Like Descartes, you will worry about the ultimate questions later. After all, you're a little young to be at peace with yourself."

Susan smiled at this.

"And if your memories act up sometimes and cause you pain, take your self-criticism with a grain of salt. Our mental organism is not built like a Swiss watch." This was an old metaphor, always delivered with humor, for the doctor herself was Swiss. "Much of that inner pain is unnecessary. Try to be as good to yourself as you are to others."

Susan was listening intently. These were truths often repeated in this office, truths whose peculiarity was that they always tried to slip through her fingers. It was hard, hard to grasp them.

"And do not allow your own guilt to discourage you when, in the real world, you fail to find a given truth in good time." The doctor spoke with quiet force. "This is perhaps the most important, because your own discouragement can affect those who need you."

Their time was at an end, Susan knew that. But something

seemed unresolved. She thought of the box of roses she had received after the murder of Celeste Cawley and the suicide of Kyle Stewart.

"I feel as though my own guilt is the final signal meant to confuse me," she said. "But there's more. I feel an intelligence, a presence, doing this to me. I've never felt this way before. In an investigation, or in anything. I've never had so strong a feeling of danger."

"You may be right," the doctor said. "Someone may be using your guilt to confuse you. That someone may be yourself. In any case, you must find out the truth."

"What are you telling me to do?" Susan asked.

The doctor looked at the place on the wall where the picture had once hung, then back to Susan.

"Do your job. Find the killer."

23

CELESTE CAWLEY HAD been two months pregnant at the time of her murder.

The former lover whose Lincoln Park apartment Celeste had been haunting for weeks prior to her death had an ironclad alibi for the time of the killing. He was in bed with Camila Gardiner, the attractive student who had replaced Celeste in his affections. A doorman and two tenants helped confirm this.

The death of Celeste Cawley remained a mystery. She was the only one of the five victims killed outside her home. The manner of her strangulation and the removal of her eyes left no doubt that her killer was the same man who had murdered the previous four victims. Physical evidence pointed clearly to Kyle Stewart as the killer. But Stewart had the ultimate alibi—he was dead at the time the crime was committed.

In her own way Celeste Cawley was as foreign to the case as Dorothy Kuehn had been. She had no connection to the three female athletes who were all students at the Chicago Circle Campus. She lived and worked far from the other victims. She was no longer a student. She was black.

David Gold knew something was wrong with the case, but he did not know what it was. He had spent long hours with the medical examiner, his fellow homicide detectives, and the FBI men who were working the case. Together they had sifted the evidence, putting ever more complex and improbable constructions on the circumstances of the five crimes. The clues always led to the same conclusion. Kyle Stewart, the quiet loner who ogled female athletes and came from a troubled family, was the killer. There was more than enough evidence to bring a conviction in a court of law.

But Stewart was dead, and the killer was still at large.

SUSAN CALLED NICK on Wednesday night to tell him she wanted to send Michael home.

Nick seemed genuinely disappointed.

"Are you sure about this?" he asked. "Michael needs you, you know. You're all he's talked about since Christmas."

These words tugged at Susan's heart. She had to concentrate to keep her hand steady around the phone.

"Thanks, Nick."

"He'll miss you."

Susan said nothing.

"We've been hearing about you," Nick went on. "They're making it tough on you, aren't they?"

"It goes with the territory," Susan said, trying to sound brave. "We had a couple of bad breaks. It happens. I'm just not used to the high stakes involved in all this." She hesitated before adding, "I'm not sure I can take it anymore."

It was only as she said this that she realized how

profoundly the events of recent days had changed her. She had all but made up her mind that her career as a police consultant was over. She was thinking of leaving Chicago and starting over somewhere else, perhaps even in a new career.

"Susan . . ." Nick remonstrated gently. His tone reminded her of a hundred conversations during their courtship and marriage. He had always believed in her and helped her believe in herself. Even when the marriage was collapsing under them, he never lost that touching quality of support and friendship.

"I'm not used to making mistakes that cost people's lives," she said.

"How about doing things that save people's lives?" Nick asked.

She was silent. His point was well taken. Her medical training had prepared her—or should have—for the daunting responsibility that is a doctor's burden. But the specialty of psychiatry, despite its own burdens, had gradually cut her off from the medical practitioner's visceral fear of making a mistake that can cost a patient's life. Her work with the police had reintroduced her to it. She was not sure she possessed the emotional armor to deal with it. The face of Kyle Stewart in the interrogation room, with his look of quiet endurance, haunted her. So did the face of Celeste Cawley, a girl she had never seen in the flesh but whose death was on her own head, or so she felt.

"Maybe we can work something out before the summer," Nick said, trying to cheer her up. "I've been looking at our calendar. We were going to drive up to Aspen, but we can do that any time. Maybe you could take Michael on a vacation somewhere."

"Thank you, Nick. That sounds like a good idea." Susan heard the relief and gratitude in her own voice.

"He's awfully proud of you, you know."

"I know."

Nick was his most kind self. For a brief moment her old need for him bloomed painfully inside her, and she realized once again how much she had lost when their marriage ended. Nick had been a fine husband. He had become an essential part of the emotional ground she walked on.

When their marriage began to fall apart, it had seemed the world was ending. Susan had never seriously considered the possibility that the home she had with Nick could be taken away from her. He knew all her weaknesses, her fears, and her hopes. It seemed incredible that the intimacy they had taken so long to forge could be cut off.

But as the wound of their separation began to heal, Susan was able to look back on the relationship and understand that certain weaknesses had been built into it from the start, like fault lines under a quiet hillside. Weaknesses that had only needed the passage of time and certain unforeseen circumstances to make themselves felt and, ultimately, to doom the marriage.

Her divorce had changed her completely, leaving her feeling like a new person. But she did not regret the time with Nick. It had been an essential part of her heart and of her growth. And it had produced Michael. Every time she talked to Nick she felt this bond, and was strengthened by it.

"I'll call you when I have a flight number," she said.

"Good deal. Hang in there, now." Nick's easygoing slang had not changed. It masked the seriousness of his character.

"I'll do my best."

"And kiss the boy for me."

"Yes."

SUSAN READ TO Michael until his breathing deepened and she saw the mask of sleep on his little face. She closed the book and stood up, preparing to go to bed herself. She doubted she would be able to concentrate on her own book. Or to sleep much, for that matter.

She looked up at the photos on the wall. Her parents were shown together in one frame, she and Quentin in the other. All four faces looked lonely and rather uncomfortable. She had often smiled at the rather too obviously analytic thrust of these photos. The parents were immured in their own space, while she and her brother clung together, a world unto themselves.

She studied the face of her mother. It seemed particularly foreign. Over the years Mother had grown more and more vague in Susan's memory. At the same time the impression of her dark, surrounding warmth had become more powerful. Many were the mornings nowadays that Susan awoke alone and remembered not her husband's arms but those of her mother.

She looked for hints of Michael's physiognomy in the faces of her parents. They must be there, she thought, but she could not see them. The face of Nick rose before her mind's eye, smiling as he had once smiled, and was gone.

She looked at herself in the mirror over the dresser. She had inherited her father's eyebrows, but her eyes were her mother's. Cautious eyes with a hint of sadness, eyes that seemed burdened by what they had seen, or haunted by what they would have liked to see.

Susan wanted to leave, but somehow she could not tear herself away from the photographs. She sensed that they were speaking to her of the problem of origins. How had the distant past sown the seeds for all the events that had brought her to this painful moment? A woman without a husband, soon to be separated once again from the son she loved, and perhaps soon without a profession.

Boats against the current . . .

She tried to forget the recent past. Recent truths, after all, are nothing but reflections of deeper ones. Psychoanalysis had taught her that over and over again.

Suddenly this thought took on a different meaning.

Susan hurried into the living room and dialed David Gold's number.

"Hello?" It was Josie, the older girl.

"Hello, Josie. This is Susan Shader. Is your dad home?"

"Mmm . . . Let me see." A muffled *"Mom!"* could be heard as she called her mother.

Susan tried to think. The idea in her mind was not clear, not easy to grasp, but she felt it all the more powerfully.

"He's on duty. He had to stay late. Mom says if it's an emergency . . ."

"No, honey, it's not. Would you ask him to call me when he gets in?"

"Sure."

Susan hung up. She began to pace the apartment. The nightscape of skyscrapers, from the Hancock Building to the Sears Tower, passed unseen before her eyes.

She was thinking of the three dead college girls, all athletes, and of the fourth victim, Dorothy Kuehn. The case always came back to the same contradiction. Dorothy Kuehn was a departure. Susan had even gone so far as to construct the elaborate theory that Dorothy Kuehn was the first intended victim, and the coeds substitutes. When Kyle Stewart was arrested, and the weight of evidence against him seemed so enormous, Susan and Gold had allowed themselves to be convinced that the flimsy, almost nonexistent connection between Stewart and Dorothy Kuehn was real.

Now it was clear this whole theory was absurd. Stewart was innocent. The connection between the three female athletes, whatever it was, lay far from his sexual obsessions. And now a fourth girl, not an athlete, had been killed. She seemed to have nothing in common with the other victims. Yet she must have had something in common with them, something crucial.

Nothing in common—and everything.

Freud used to say that the great weakness of psychoanalysis was the very fact that it could only analyze after the fact, and never synthesize. An analyst could try to explain why a given patient had developed a given symptom or illness by delving into his or her past. But he could never take a young child and predict what illness might develop. Too many forces were at work, too many inner crossroads. Chance, of course, played a crucial role.

This notion stopped Susan in her tracks.

What if the killer's choice of the coeds, as well as

Dorothy, was made not by similarity but by circumstance? What if chance had played the key role in their deaths as well as Dorothy's?

All along Susan and Gold and everyone else had assumed that the college girls were chosen as members of a category. What if this was not true? What if they were chosen because of who they were *individually*? What if the fourth and fifth victims were chosen for the same reason? A reason that had so far escaped everyone.

Susan got her briefcase from the living room and paged through her notes about the female athletes. All three were about to undertake foreign tours. Tours require passports. To get a passport one had to journey to 230 South Dearborn, where the U.S. Government offices were located. Perhaps the girls had ended up there together by chance.

Susan found a number in her notebook and dialed it.

"Morgenstern residence."

"Mrs. Morgenstern, this is Dr. Shader. We've talked before."

"Oh, yes. Hello, Doctor. What can I do for you?"

"I'm checking over a few details about Patsy and the other two girls from school. Do you by any chance have her passport in the house?"

"Well, I probably do. How does that help?"

"Could you check the date of issue? And, if possible, I'd like the number."

Patsy's mother had the information. Within ten minutes Susan had spoken to the parents of the other dead girls. Their passports were issued on different dates. That meant they could not have been together when they applied for them. But Susan was not discouraged.

Her next call was to the volleyball coach at Illinois.

"Ms. Appleton, I'm working on some details about Patsy Morgenstern. Were there occasions when the team met outside the university for any reason having to do with the upcoming tour?"

"Outside the university? No, not that I can recall. All our meetings took place right here. Unless . . ."

"Yes?"

"Well, we had a banquet at the Radisson last fall."

"Just your team?"

"No, all the teams that were planning tours. That would include lacrosse, basketball, volleyball, and gymnastics."

"All the teams?"

"That's right." The slight pause at the other end of the line told Susan Ms. Appleton might be making a connection.

"Well, I'll keep working on it," Susan said. "Thank you very much."

The conclusion was obvious. All three murdered girls had been at the banquet at the Radisson that day last fall.

But what about Dorothy Kuehn? What about Celeste Cawley?

Susan turned another page of the notebook and found a phone number. She dialed it with a trembling finger.

"Hello?"

"Hello, Mr. Kuehn? This is Susan Shader. Do you remember me? I'm working on your wife's case with Detective Gold and the State's Attorney."

"Oh. Hello, Doctor."

"How are you getting along?" Susan managed a bedside manner. She felt it sincerely, too. Mr. Kuehn had lost a lot when his wife died.

"Not too bad. I heard about your problems on the news. I guess this isn't an easy time for you, either, is it?"

"Not very easy, no. Thank you for your concern. I'd like to ask you a small thing about your wife's activities. Did she come into the Loop very often?"

"Hardly ever. I don't think we see the Loop more than twice a year. Sometimes it seems a million miles away."

"That might help me. Can you think of an occasion last fall when your wife might have come into town for some reason? Lunch with a friend? A meeting of some sort? Business?"

"No, not that I—wait. There is one thing. She had a lunch with some old sorority sisters. They do it every year.

She hadn't been in many years, but this time they convinced her."

"Where was the lunch held?"

"Some hotel on Michigan Avenue. Up toward the Water Tower, I think."

"Can you remember which one?"

"Not offhand, no."

"Do you think you could find out? By contacting the sorority, for instance . . ."

"Wait a moment. It's right here, on the calendar in the kitchen. Last October nineteenth. Sure, here it is. The Radisson. Twelve-thirty P.M. In the Michigan Room. Delta Zeta."

"Thank you very much. That's very helpful."

"I remember that day pretty well. I told her not to go. It was freezing rain. Amazing, at that time of the year. She was a pretty good driver, but that rain was murder."

"Did anything out of the ordinary happen during her lunch, Mr. Kuehn?"

"I don't think so. She said it was boring. Said it wasn't worth the trip."

"How about on the way to or from the hotel?"

"No, not that I can think of."

"Are you sure? Perhaps something very small."

"Well, she said she saw an accident . . ."

"What sort of accident?" Susan asked.

"Oh, a car accident outside the hotel. A fender bender. She gave the police a statement, I think. She mentioned it to me in passing when I got home. I forgot all about it until now."

"Did she tell you anything else about it?"

"Just that there was ice, and that one car skidded into the back of another."

"And that was all she told you about it?"

"Yes. That's all."

"Thank you very much, Mr. Kuehn. I'll be in touch."

"Thank you, Doctor. And good luck."

Susan hung up the phone and looked through her notes. It took her a moment to find the phone number of Stephanie

Mertz, Patsy Morgenstern's roommate. She looked at her watch. Eight-fifteen. A good time to find a college student in.

Stephanie answered the phone on the first ring.

Susan asked her if she remembered the banquet for the volleyball team.

"Sure," Stephanie said. "Patsy was excited about the tour."

"Did Patsy mention anything unusual happening the day of the banquet?"

"Unusual? No, not that I remember."

"Did she witness an accident?"

"Oh. How did you know about that?" Stephanie asked.

"It has come up in the course of the investigation."

"Yes, she said she saw a car accident. A fender bender, she said, outside the hotel."

"Did she tell you anything about the accident?"

"No, I don't think so. It wasn't very important." Stephanie sounded perplexed.

Susan's fingers were crossed. "Was she questioned by the police as a witness?"

"Yes, she was. She came home joking about how cute one of the officers was. She was kind of hoping he might call her."

"Thank you, Stephanie. You've helped me a great deal."

Susan hung up the phone and dialed Area Six Violent Crimes.

"I have an emergency message for David Gold," she said. "Can you put it on his radio?"

"Who is this, please?"

"Dr. Shader. He's expecting my call."

"What is the message?"

"Call me right away. He knows the number."

Susan hung up the phone. She got up, took a step toward the kitchen, then sat back down. She looked around the living room at the old furniture and piles of books. The remnants of her past looked all too familiar.

On an impulse, she took the old pack of Newports from the shelf and threw it into the kitchen wastebasket.

She turned to the phone and sat down to wait.

24

SUSAN MET DAVID GOLD at six-forty the next morning at her office. Since the revamped investigation began, he had been told to have no contact with her. He was placing himself at considerable risk in telling her the latest about the case, not to mention acting on her suggestions.

He looked as fresh and unflappable as ever, his gray suit betraying its age only by the smooth way it fitted itself to his tall body.

"How you doing?" he asked shortly.

"Fine. What's new?"

He frowned, opening a large file folder he had brought with him.

"You hit the nail on the head," he said. "But you and I are the only ones who know it yet. The five victims *were* together. They were all witnesses to a car accident, a fender bender that took place outside the Radisson at two-thirty in the afternoon on October nineteenth."

He held out the top page of the file. "Apparently there was freezing rain. Unusual for that date, but nothing is impossible in this city. A maroon sedan skidded into the back of a Toyota right in the driveway of the hotel. The victims were there, waiting for their own rides, and they saw it happen. The maroon sedan took off, and the police treated it as a hit-and-run. Our five women gave witness statements."

Susan studied the accident report.

"Who is P. Juarez?" she asked.

"The investigating officer," Gold said. "I spoke to him

an hour ago. He doesn't remember the incident all that well. It seemed insignificant at the time. There wasn't much damage to the Toyota. No one got a good look at the license number of the maroon sedan—the closest, as a matter of fact, was Patsy Morgenstern, who saw the number 418, or thought she saw it."

"Was the case ever solved?" Susan asked.

Gold shook his head. "They never found the maroon sedan. After the usual search of the computers, they gave up. The case was closed and forgotten."

"What did Officer Juarez say?" Susan asked. "Did anything stick in his memory about that day?"

"Well, he remembers Patsy Morgenstern. Because of her height. Also she was pretty good-humored, and she seemed interested in him, he said. Juarez is a young guy, good-looking. That's about it."

"I don't understand," Susan said. "Our five victims were together for a fleeting moment, and saw an insignificant accident. How does that add up to murder?"

"That's my problem exactly," Gold said. "We have five of the most spectacular murders in the history of this state, and it turns out they're all linked by a fender bender in front of the Radisson Hotel. It's a case of 'Who cares?' It just doesn't add up."

"Well, it has to add up somehow," Susan said. "This is no coincidence."

Gold was paging slowly through the witness statements.

"There were two men in the maroon sedan," he said. "One at the wheel and the other in the backseat. That arrangement struck two of the witnesses. The man in the backseat was tentatively identified by Cheryl Glaser as a man who had ridden down with her and her friends in the elevator a few minutes before the accident. She couldn't give a good description though. Just said he was short and middle-aged."

Gold closed the file. Not for the first time Susan noticed the almost artistic delicacy of his hands. She had never seen those hands holding a gun.

"I know what the first four victims were doing at the hotel that day," Susan said. "But what about Celeste Cawley?"

Gold shook his head. "I spoke to her parents about it. They never knew anything about it. Her mother told me the Radisson was way out of the girl's alleys. She lived miles from there, and she never went to that area except when she went to Water Tower Place, which she only did during the holidays."

"Well, she was there that day," Susan said.

Gold held up both hands. "You've got me. She was there. She saw the accident. And she's dead. Case closed."

Susan frowned in concentration. "One thing seems sure," she said. "The murders were not the work of a serial killer. We can throw that theory out right now. These women were killed because they were all together at a given time and place. Perhaps they saw something the killer didn't want them to see. Perhaps there was another reason. In any case they were not victims chosen as part of the hunt pattern of a serial killer."

"Know what that means?" Gold asked. "It means the reign of terror might be over. There were five witnesses to the car accident. All five are dead. If we're not looking for a serial killer, the whole thrust of the investigation has to change."

"We have to find out why those witnesses were killed," Susan said.

"Easier said than done," Gold said. "But maybe easier than beating the bushes for a serial freak."

"May I see those statements again?" Susan asked.

He handed over the file. She paged through the statements. It seemed odd to hear the voices of the dead women, however indirectly, as they bore witness to a routine and unimportant event. The blandness of the statements gave no hint of the violence approaching them from the unseen future.

She looked at Gold. "Does this feel right to you?" she asked.

He shook his head slowly. "Nothing ever felt less right to me. Five women killed because of a fender bender? Forget it."

He looked at the file in Susan's hands. "Why don't you take that home with you?" he asked. "See if anything comes up."

Susan knew what he was asking. She was hesitant to use her second sight again on this case. So far it had only got her into trouble. More trouble, in fact, than she had ever been in before.

"The prospect isn't very inviting," she said.

"I know that," Gold said.

"What about you?" Susan asked. "Are you going to tell them about this?"

"I'll have to," he said. "I can sit on it for a few hours. No more."

Susan sighed. "All right."

AFTER GOLD LEFT Susan sat in the armchair beside her desk, facing the empty patient's chair. Her first patient would not be here for half an hour. She might as well start now.

She turned the pages of the police report, reading the witness statements. It was haunting to see the signatures of Patsy Morgenstern and the other girls. Girls on the threshold of their lives, girls with everything to live for. Snuffed out by a killer whose motive Susan could not guess.

The signatures of the four college girls were manifestly different from that of Dorothy Kuehn, the controlled, middle-aged woman. Their signatures were jagged, unformed. Hers was almost too perfect, a model of correct penmanship. It fit what Susan knew of Dorothy Kuehn perfectly. A former sorority girl who lived in straitened circumstances with a husband who drank. A woman out of touch with her feelings, but deeply in touch with appearances.

Susan looked at the handwriting of Patsy Morgenstern. It was overlarge but expressive of timidity in certain features. The *t*'s, for instance, were so short that the cross sometimes did not intersect the top of the letter. The *i*'s were dotted too closely, so that the dot often touched the body of the letter, making it look more like an *l* than an *i*.

It was easy to deduce that Patsy's self-consciousness about her height was affecting her handwriting. Her worry about her sexuality showed as well, in the crowding of certain groups of letters and in a clumsiness in joining certain pairs. On the whole the handwriting tried to be carefree and assertive but only succeeded in looking cramped, troubled.

The signatures of the other girls were full of secrets, too. Cheryl Glaser, the first victim, seemed torn between a rather showy sensuality and something more shrouded. Jennifer Haas, the second victim, showed great intelligence but also a lack of confidence. Were all signatures, then, marked by the conflict of ambivalence about self?

Susan looked at the signature of Celeste Cawley. It was beautiful, the two *C*'s regal in their modeling, the *l*'s lyrical and confident. Interestingly, the first of the *e*'s was Greek while the other two were italic. Here Susan saw an opposite conflict. Superficially the signature was feminine, gentle. But underneath there was anger.

Susan found herself looking more closely. Something did not seem right. She placed two fingers over the signature. She closed her eyes. Her fingers moved slowly over the long-dried ink.

Almost immediately she opened her eyes again. She sat forward, looking down at the page. A feeling, very urgent, had come to her. Again she looked at the two large, pretty *C*'s, the enigma of the different formation of the *e*'s.

Then the answer came to her.

It's a fake.

Susan stood up, holding the sheaf of statements in her hands. She stared out the window for a long moment. The lake reared coldly against the sky, the water frozen near the shore. Flakes of wind-driven snow patted against the windowpanes.

She picked up the phone. She hesitated to leave a message for Gold. She didn't want those around him to know he was in touch with her. But there was no choice. Time, as he had said, was short.

She left the message and worked on her therapy notes until her first patient arrived. The woman was herself a physician, a prominent gynecologist and the wife of a city councilman. For the last seven years, unbeknownst to anyone else, she had been dressing up as a prostitute and streetwalking on South State Street. Ironically, she was not seeing Susan in an attempt to break the habit. Her double life was succeeding remarkably well. Though she was over fifty, she had many satisfied clients as a prostitute. Her reason for seeing Susan was to cure a sudden onset of agoraphobia, which was interfering with both her occupations.

Gold's call interrupted the session, and Susan had to excuse herself and go into another room to talk to him.

"David, do you have samples of Celeste Cawley's handwriting? Her signature?"

"Let me see . . . Yeah. I've got copies of her driver's license, her student ID from her last year at school . . . Yeah, I've got some stuff."

"David, I suspect the signature on the witness statement is a fake. It's Celeste Cawley's name but written by someone else. I don't think Celeste was there that day at all. Someone signed her name in order not to be identified."

"Someone who knew her."

"That's right."

"Why would anyone do that?"

"That's what we'll have to find out."

There was a pause.

"Okay," Gold said. "Can you meet me for lunch?"

Susan looked at her appointment book. "What time?"

"Twelve-thirty. I'll pick you up."

"Can you make it one o'clock?"

"One o'clock. Okay."

* * *

GOLD ARRIVED ON schedule and took Susan to a favorite delicatessen near Fullerton, where she had often had lunch with him before. Her appetite had left her in the lurch because of recent events, so she ordered a small potato salad. Gold smiled with satisfaction when his pastrami sandwich arrived steaming with a huge order of french fries and a fragrant kosher pickle.

Susan was looking at the copies of Celeste Cawley's signature that Gold had put before her. As promised, they included the girl's driver's license, her student ID, and a credit card.

"I was right," she said. "The signature on the witness statement is a phony."

Gold nodded, sipping at his Diet Coke. "She wasn't even there that day," he said decidedly.

"What do you think happened?" Susan asked.

"Somebody else gave her signature. Somebody who didn't want to be there but who was buttonholed by the police as a witness before she could duck out." He took a bite of his sandwich and smiled at Susan as he chewed.

"How do you know all that?" she asked.

"Wait." He waved a hand at someone behind her and stood up. A uniformed officer was approaching them across the slush-stained tile floor. He was a handsome young man with olive skin and dark eyes.

"Pete Juarez," Gold said, "meet Susan Shader."

"Pleased to meet you." The young man shook Susan's hand.

"Sit down, Pete," Gold said. "You hungry?"

"I ate before," Juarez said. "Thanks anyway."

"You remember what we talked about?" Gold asked.

The officer nodded, removing his cap as he sat down. Gold opened a file and pushed some pictures across the table to him. Juarez needed only a moment to study them.

"It's like I told you," he said. "I didn't connect it at the time, because the whole thing didn't make much of an impression on me. But this one"—he pointed to the picture of Celeste Cawley—"is definitely wrong."

"How can you be so sure?" Susan asked.

"The girl who gave me the statement was beautiful," he replied. "Incredibly beautiful. The kind of face you only see on a movie screen or in a fashion magazine. She was really stunning. Her face stuck in my mind."

"And this is not her," Gold said, gesturing to the picture of Celeste Cawley on her driver's license.

"No way," Juarez shook his head. "I've never seen this face. Not that I recall, anyway."

Gold nodded to Susan. Celeste Cawley had not been an attractive girl.

"But the girl you described was black," Gold said.

"Yes. Definitely."

"Do you think you'd know her if you saw her again?"

"Sure. I still see her face. She was that remarkable."

Gold turned to Susan. "I'm going to have Pete look through some portfolios from the big model agencies in town. We might visit some fashion and advertising photographers, too. Chances are the girl he saw is in show business or modeling."

Susan could see that the young officer looked uncomfortable.

"Is anything wrong, Officer Juarez?" she asked.

"To be honest, yeah. If I had been more alert, I might have recognized the first couple of victims from what happened that day at the Radisson. We might have saved some lives." He shrugged. "The simple fact is, I'm just not that great with faces. I concentrate on numbers. License plates, vehicle IDs, that sort of thing. When the pictures of the victims started appearing in the papers, I just didn't make the connection."

Gold said, "Don't worry about it, Pete. It was a stretch anyway." And to Susan, "Pete is not going to tell anyone about this until he hears from me. Are you, Pete?"

Juarez shook his head.

"Officer," Susan asked. "Do you remember anything else about the witnesses that day? Anything at all?"

"Not really. The other three girls seemed to know each

other, but I wasn't sure about that. I did get the impression the black girl was not with them."

He smiled. "One of the girls—the tall one—was very friendly. Sort of fun-loving. *I'm the tall one,* she said. I liked her. I got the impression she wouldn't have minded if I had called her for a date."

"How about the older woman?" Susan asked. "Did anything about her impress you particularly?"

He shook his head. "Just a woman."

"So your main impression from that day was of the beauty of the one girl," Susan said.

"Yeah. It was a powerful impression. It wasn't just her looks. It was her manner. She was—she was a special person. You could feel it. There was something intense about her. It added to her beauty."

"Did she seem in any way uncomfortable, answering your questions?" Gold asked.

"Yes. She seemed nervous. On the other hand, I got the feeling she was used to that. She dealt with it well. I don't know if that makes sense, but that's how she seemed."

"A person who was used to being nervous?" Susan asked.

"Exactly."

A moment later Pete Juarez took his leave. Susan looked at Gold.

"Now what?" she asked.

"Now is easy. Old-fashioned police work. We check out all of Celeste Cawley's friends and associates, past and present. She was a young girl, so it probably won't take very long. Somewhere there is another girl who knew Celeste. Knew her well enough to use her signature. I'm betting it's a contemporary. Someone her own age."

Susan nodded. "Can I help in any way?"

Gold shook his head, bringing the pastrami sandwich back to his lips.

"You sit tight. Wait to hear from me. Let me run with this awhile longer. Then we'll let Weathers in on it, and see what he says."

He motioned to Susan's untouched potato salad. "Come on, woman," he said. "Build up your strength. You're gonna need it before this is over."

Susan picked up her fork and did as she was told.

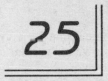

PSYCHIC WAS SEEING PSYCHIATRIST

THAT WAS THE headline Susan saw on the early edition of the *Tribune* the next day when she took Michael for lunch at Water Tower Place. She grimaced as she got on the escalator, holding Michael's hand. One of the aggressive reporters working on the case must have tailed her to Berthe Mueller's office. Naturally her single visit to her onetime training analyst was elevated into a continuing treatment program for mental illness. That was journalism.

Susan picked at her salad while she watched Michael eat his baked potato. This was his favorite restaurant food. He always ordered the potato with everything imaginable piled on top of it, from cheddar cheese to sour cream to bacon bits. He said he liked the way the tinfoil looked wrapped around the potato. He also liked the inordinate size of it. Often he seemed dwarfed by the steaming potato as he sat swinging his little legs back and forth in a restaurant chair. It took him a very long time to eat the potato, but he insisted on finishing all of it, making a sandwich out of the skin at the end. His enthusiasm for the dish had spurred Susan to occasional reflections on its symbolic appearance. There was something womblike and reassuring about a baked potato, bursting forth from its festive, shiny foil, a symbol of plenty and of variety.

When she got back to her office, David Gold was sitting in the waiting room, paging idly through a copy of *The New Yorker*.

"What are you doing here?" she asked.

"Have you got a few minutes?"

She looked at her watch. "All right. Come inside."

Gold seemed visibly excited as he sat down in the chair opposite her desk.

"Listen," he said. "Last October nineteenth, the day of the car accident at the Radisson. That wasn't just any old day."

"What do you mean?" Susan asked.

"It was the day Peter Tomerakian died."

Susan looked surprised. "The investigator?"

"Right. Remember how it went down?"

Susan remembered very well. Peter Tomerakian was a sort of investigative genius, a Ph.D. in mathematics whose brilliant and eccentric work had helped the Justice Department and numerous federal agencies to arrest high-level tax evaders and corporate criminals. Tomerakian had committed suicide last October nineteenth. After his death it had been revealed that he was suffering from lymphatic cancer, and his suicide was attributed to despair over incurable illness.

"There was some controversy, wasn't there?" Susan asked.

"Everything about Tomerakian was controversial." Gold nodded. "He didn't have much respect for traditional methods in police work, much less for the politics of government funding. He went his own way and pretty much thumbed his nose at everybody around him. At the time of his death, he had been working for two and a half years on an international network of stock fraud, money laundering, and drugs. There was a special prosecutor in charge of the investigation, but Tomerakian was the brains behind it. They were only a month or two away from a dozen indictments. Several corporate CEOs and board members would have gone down, not to mention a politician or two. But it never happened. Tomerakian's colleagues were unable to pull together all the work he left behind him. The investigation has been stalled ever since, and now they're talking about taking away the funding."

Susan asked, "How does this affect us?"

Gold crossed a long leg over his knee. "Here's how. Tomerakian believed the mastermind behind the whole business was a man named Haze. Arnold Haze. Have you ever heard the name?"

Susan shook her head.

"All right," Gold said. "This is where it gets interesting. Haze is a sort of legend among law-enforcement people. He's been around for twenty-five years or more, he's been implicated in some of the biggest financial scams ever concocted. And they say he does his own killing. But he's never been in prison, and there aren't a lot of people who even know who he is.

"Nothing is known about the first thirty years of his life," Gold went on. "They've tried every database under the sun, but there is no trace of him as a child or young adult. If there ever was, he found a way to get rid of it."

Gold removed an eight-by-ten glossy photograph from his file and pushed it across the table.

"His first known appearance anywhere was at age thirty or so. His photo turned up in an ongoing surveillance of some mob guys who were making drug deals in Europe. Later they brought in indictments against three of the top mob guys, but Haze was never named in the investigation. Frankly, they didn't know what his connection was."

The photograph showed three men in expensive-looking suits. None was looking at the camera. The two in the foreground had the polished look of bankers or businessmen. The one in the back, his face averted, was shorter, with a fleshy face and small, black eyes like pieces of shiny coal.

"That's him, isn't it?" Susan asked. An odd smell made

her wrinkle her nose. She glanced around her, wondering if the smell came from somewhere in the building.

"Yeah," Gold said. "That's him."

The man in the photograph could have been thirty years old or fifty. He had the kind of pasty, wrinkled physiognomy that did not show age. To judge from the picture, he was short and rather rotund. His hair was sparse, high on the forehead and curly, giving him the look of a Roman tribune.

"After that one episode," Gold was saying, "he dropped out of sight for ten years. Then, in the early eighties, he surfaced as a consultant to Robert Cella, an international conglomerator who had already been under investigation for stock fraud and tax evasion. Haze had created a fake bio and passed himself off as a Vietnam vet, a Harvard Business School graduate, the son of an old Atlanta family. It was an amazing performance. The Treasury and SEC investigators pieced the bio together from a dozen sources. They didn't realize it was all fake until much later.

"Cella was in exile in Paraguay when he died of a drug overdose that was called a suicide by the local authorities. The investigation of his international holdings is still going on; the IRS has an open file on him. But there was and is the suspicion that Haze was behind Cella's death. Haze got his hands on millions of dollars in bonds and other securities that had all belonged to Cella or to companies controlled by Cella."

Susan was looking at the photograph. In the instant it was taken, Haze had tried to look away. His face was caught in half-profile. It was more than obvious that he did not like being photographed. He had probably spent years learning the fine art of sensing the presence of cameras and how to avoid them. His discomfort was palpable.

Sleepy, Grumpy . . .

"A drop of blood that wasn't Cella's was found at the scene of his death," Gold said. "The FBI had it analyzed. They got good results, but they had nothing to compare them with, so they filed it away for future reference. They suspected Haze, but there wasn't a sample of his blood."

Gold was warming to his subject. "After Cella's death Haze played fast and loose in the international securities market and was either a board member or a silent partner in a number of corporations. By now half a dozen agencies were following his trail. There were suspicions he was involved in some arms deals with Iraq and Libya. Also some huge drug deals coming through Panama and Southeast Asia. They never got close to indicting him. During all that time he never set foot on United States soil. Not that anyone could prove, anyway."

Gold looked at Susan.

"Then Peter Tomerakian entered the picture. Peter was a boy wonder. Ph.D. in mathematics from Princeton. Not the sort of guy who would go into law enforcement. But his father had been an FBI man, and Tomerakian romanticized the idea of catching crooks. He became a computer consultant to the FBI, and later a special consultant to the IRS and other agencies. He was a chess champion in his spare time, and a butterfly collector, if you can believe that. Two species of butterflies have his name.

"Tomerakian figured out a way to nail Haze. He created a computerized model of all the corporations in which Haze was a silent partner. It was a sort of fingerprint of the way Haze operated. He worked on it for a couple of years. When the time came to spring the trap, he assembled the files on Haze in several interlocking packages. They were completely safe, because each one was lacking a crucial piece. The answers were in Tomerakian's head. He was pretty paranoid by this time, because he knew the Haze thing involved some people in high places. I think he had a bit of a God complex. He figured this prosecution was going to be the biggest thing since Watergate.

"Then the unexpected happened. Tomerakian died. After his death they found out about the lymphatic cancer. They decided it was suicide. But the hanging looked suspicious, so the FBI went over the scene with a fine-tooth comb.

There were some skin scrapings under Tomerakian's finger-nails. Combine that with the pattern of the asphyxiation, and it didn't look like suicide at all.

"From that point on they called it suicide publicly but treated it as a murder investigation. When they analyzed the scrapings for DNA, they came up identical to the DNA from the Cella murder. That made Haze the prime suspect."

Gold tapped his fingers on the file. "The rest is speculation," he said. "Here's what I think happened. Haze found out Tomerakian was hot on his trail and came here in person to get rid of Tomerakian. He must have felt he couldn't trust anyone else to do the job.

"Tomerakian kept a suite on the sixteenth floor of the Radisson. The place was jammed to the rafters with files and computers. There was a special security system. No one except Tomerakian ever used it.

"Haze must have been confident he wouldn't be identified, because he had kept his face such a dark secret for so long. He killed Tomerakian in the middle of the day. But he was seen in the elevator by five women, and, as luck would have it, he got in a car accident right in front of the hotel and was seen again by the same women. There was no way they wouldn't be able to identify him.

"The fact that Tomerakian managed to scratch Haze while he was being strangled gave us physical evidence to put together with the DNA, plus obvious motive, plus eye-witness proof of opportunity. All that together would be enough to get an extradition and probably to put Haze away. Stock fraud is one thing. Murder is another. Especially murder of a government guy."

Gold sat back and looked at Susan. "So Haze did the logical, the smart thing. He set about killing the witnesses, and he disguised the murders as serial killings."

"But he did one other thing first," Susan said. "He did some research. He found out about Kyle Stewart."

"Why do you say that?" Gold asked.

"Because the murders—the first four, anyway—were

so perfectly orchestrated to frame Stewart," Susan said. "Not only in terms of blood and fiber evidence but, most important, in terms of the MO. The gouged-out eyes."

Gold nodded. "He must have cased the college girls pretty good," he said. "He probably took his time. When he found out Stewart was taking pictures of the girls, he planned the crimes so as to finger Stewart."

"And he fooled us." Susan looked pained.

"For a while," Gold corrected her. "Until one of us figured out the victims weren't chosen by type but because they were linked in another way." He smiled. "That one of us was you."

Susan looked away. "Thanks," she said. "I'm only sorry it took the deaths of Kyle Stewart and Celeste Cawley to bring me to that conclusion."

"Listen, Susan," Gold said with his sternest expression. "I told you when you started in this business that some of our best work comes too late. It's easy for other people to shrug and say, 'Better late than never.' In a cop's line of work it often means an innocent man has spent time in jail, or a perpetrator has found another victim, or a battered wife has been murdered by her husband. The stakes are higher. The potential for tragedy is built into the game."

Susan nodded. "I just—hoped it wouldn't happen to me," she said.

"It had to. Sooner or later." Gold was looking at her steadily. "It's happened to me. And to just about every detective I know."

"Really? It's happened to you?" Susan asked.

He nodded. "I'll tell you about it sometime."

He looked at the file in his hands.

"All right," he said. "Let's look forward, not back. We've got a killer out there. And a new victim already picked out, probably."

"You mean the person who signed Celeste Cawley's name," Susan said.

Gold nodded. "Whoever she is, she isn't very far away,

unless I miss my guess. And neither is Haze. He's too deep into this thing to back out now. He's gonna find her."

"Not before we do," Susan said.

"That's the spirit."

Gold attributed Susan's firmness to mere optimism. He could not know that she was several steps ahead of him.

26

JAIME LAZARUS sat on the stage between her parents. Her mother was holding her hand. Her father, on her left side, was shifting nervously in his chair.

The speaker had reached the end of his introduction.

"Ladies and gentlemen, it is my pleasure to introduce to you the man of whom it has been truly said that he unites in himself the best of our past and the key to our future. A leader of our people when the torch was first passed to him by Martin Luther King, Jr., he has increased his stature ever since. He has widened his vision, deepened his roots, and proved in a thousand ways that he can stand alone against all the voices of division and despair that seek to confuse us and discourage us. He stands alone not for his own sake but for ours. Ladies and gentlemen, it is my privilege to present the Martin Luther King, Jr., Award to the one man to whom it belongs more than to any other. Please welcome the true leader of our people—Aaron James Lazarus."

A standing ovation filled the auditorium. No more than half the faces were black; such was the breadth of Lazarus's appeal. The press was represented in force. So were the local, state, and federal governments. This was an event.

For thirty years Aaron Lazarus had commanded respect for his aggressive leadership, his rigorous insistence on self-determination for the black community, and his steadfast refusal to abandon the ideal of brotherhood taught him by his onetime friend and mentor, Martin Luther King, Jr.

Lazarus got up to make his way to the podium. He looked older now, his hair almost completely gray, his tall body moving more slowly than it once had. But the smile was the same—the lips curled in welcome even as the tawny eyes glinted with a quiet fierceness.

The local journalists smiled as they watched him. He was a familiar figure here in Chicago. Most of them were on a first-name basis with him. They knew his moods, his temper, his famous impatience. But they still found themselves in awe of him.

Lazarus was a unique figure. During the King era he had been considered rather a dull fellow. "Colorless" was a word used tongue-in-cheek to describe him. Educated at Harvard after a boyhood in Alabama, he was thought too intellectual, too scholarly for a social leader. His speeches lacked fire, his personality was too cool and measured for the frantic times.

But after King's death things changed. The movement lost direction as the cities continued to decay and the optimism of the sixties gave way to despair. The hard-line Muslims were too wrapped up in their own politics to be worth anything as leaders. The "black power" brokers melted into nothingness. King's followers, sincere though they were, lacked the fire to direct mass action. It was obvious that the era of hope was ending.

Then something happened. Aaron Lazarus gave a powerful, angry speech before a rally of black students at Georgetown. His message was clear and painful: black people had no one but themselves to blame for their recent misfortunes. White society was not going to lavish further favors upon the black community after the riots of the sixties. It was naive and childish for blacks to stand on the corner waiting for the next Malcolm, the next Martin, to come along and revive a moribund cause. Most of all it was foolish and completely self-destructive to base black pride and initiative upon hatred of whites.

"The white man is not our enemy," Lazarus said. "He is simply trying to survive in a world that has become hostile to him as well as to us. His indifference is merely a sign of his humanity, as is our paralysis. Our only enemy is ourselves. When we have defeated this enemy, we will have no difficulty living in the same society as the white man. He is united with us by his weaknesses as well as his hopes."

The speech got national coverage, for Lazarus's strident harangue of his audience was delivered with an authority that had not been seen in a black leader since the death of Malcolm X.

Later that night someone tried to assassinate Lazarus. A hail of gunfire greeted him as he emerged from his hotel with a group of colleagues. He was seriously wounded— bullets to the chest and hip—and spent over a month in the hospital. He emerged from his convalescence looking older and thinner, and he never walked as quickly again. The traces of his wounds became part of his public persona.

The FBI was slow to find the would-be assassins. Black observers were reminded maddeningly of King's assassination at his motel in Memphis, of Malcolm X riddled with bullets in Harlem. In the end four men were arrested. All were black. Their ties were to black leaders hostile to Lazarus's message of peace, though it was later determined that the attempted assassination was financed in part by right-wing whites.

Now perceived as a hard-nosed peacemaker besieged on all sides by apostles of hate, Lazarus emerged as the only black leader capable of uniting the legacies of King and Malcolm X in a single, powerful message. "We have no time for hate"—that was his slogan. "Hatred is an excuse for inaction," he often repeated. He became a sort of father figure, demanding of his people the same impatience that drove him.

Two more assassination attempts followed. Alerted to the danger he faced, Lazarus escaped injury both times. But the bullets that narrowly missed his body put the finishing glow on his image. He was the man who came back from death, as his name suggested. A man whose enemies were both black and white, a man who could not be defeated morally and so could not be killed.

In the years since, it had been Lazarus who mobilized the black community in the cities, Lazarus who fought tooth and nail for small favors from an indifferent Washington establishment, Lazarus who tirelessly articulated the message that black people must help themselves. Today Lazarus had become to blacks what FDR had once been to the nation—the only credible voice of hope, the only voice that gave courage.

Now, at the podium, Lazarus smiled acknowledgment as the applause slowly abated.

"You humble me," he began, "with an honor that I cannot say I deserve. For I have never felt, in the presence of Martin—and he is certainly present here tonight—that I deserved anything. I felt only that I owed something, to him and to our people.

"Let me accept this award, then, as a token of what I owe rather than as a reward for what I have given. And let me ask you to place your hands around it along with mine, to signify your commitment to what we intend to give together."

In his seat near the center aisle, Arnold Haze sat watching. He nodded in admiration of the speech. Lazarus was clever, even manipulative. He had to be, in order to survive. This room echoed with the violence that had been done to Lazarus and aimed at him. It was one of his weapons, a weapon he used to uplift his people. Like all leaders, he knew how to make the most of what he had.

As Lazarus went on talking, Haze let his eyes rove over

the stage. There were familiar faces. The presenter, Reverend Rowe. The head of the NAACP. The mayor's task force leader. Lazarus's wife, Diane, a stately, gray-haired woman with a kind, tired face.

And there was one unfamiliar face. A black girl, twenty-two years old, dressed in a dark suit, her long hair tied back conservatively, her hands clasped in her lap. She sat beside her mother, her eyes on her father.

Her dull clothes and her lack of makeup did not succeed in obscuring her extraordinary beauty. Indeed, the attempt at self-effacement only dramatized it. She had coffee-colored skin; enormous eyes, whose innocence glinted with a thousand secrets; and a slender body, which perched on her uncomfortable chair with a girlish grace that drew the eye.

Her name, Haze knew, was Jaime. She had not been seen in public since a White House dinner in Lazarus's honor four years ago. She was Lazarus's only child. He had spent a career keeping her out of the public eye. Few photographs of her existed outside Lazarus's own album. Haze had seen them all. They presented a sort of kaleidoscope, speeded up jerkily, from her baby picture to a family portrait from the old Chicago days, to a handful of little-girl pictures from school, and finally, the magnificent nymph that emerged from her adolescence.

Her beauty was a well-kept secret. But she could not be absent tonight. The Martin Luther King, Jr., Award was too important. Not even her protective father could leave her out of this moment.

Haze did not take his eyes off her. Lazarus was into his message now, his voice rasping slightly as he used words he had honed for years.

"Today it is more essential than ever that black Americans abandon their preconceived ideas about white America. The time for resentment has run out when resentment means inaction—which it has *always* meant, *for us*." He paused to let this thought sink in.

"It is time to stop waiting for the scars of slavery to wear away. They will not disappear. They are part of our

identity. It is time to stop waiting for circumstances, social
or historic or economic, to come to our rescue. It is time to
turn our scars into initiative. It is time to act."

Haze was studying the girl's sculptured young face, the
smooth, golden skin, the slender, doelike neck leading to
feminine treasures unseen. The girl's eyes were on her father. It was easy to read her ambivalence about him. He
must have asked a great deal of her over the years, not only
with his voice but through his position. Few things could
be harder than to be the daughter of a great man.

She was looking up at Lazarus with a daughter's familiarity. The ghost of a smile curled her beautiful lips as she
heard the words he had said so many times before. His
shadow warmed her. One could feel that, even from this
distance.

But what about her secret? Surely Lazarus knew nothing
of it. He was absorbed in his own crusade, blinded by his
own limelight. He lived to protect his daughter, not to know
her. He was only a man, after all.

But Haze knew. He knew her secret, and that was why
he was here.

You were there, he said to her in the silence of his gaze.
You were there. And I've found you.

27

THE DAY AFTER her father was given the Martin Luther
King, Jr., Award, Jaime took time out from her studies to
spend an hour in bed with Geoff MacAndrew.

After they made love she found herself crying in Geoff's

arms. When he asked her why, she could not think of a reason. She left the hotel early and hurried home.

Reta had a date and did not come home for dinner. Jaime ate some leftover potato salad and worked on her term paper until the buzzer sounded at seven-thirty.

She padded to the apartment door and pushed the intercom button.

"Yes?"

"Miss Lazarus, there's a Dr. Shader here to see you. She says she's from the police."

Jaime stood with her finger on the button, thinking.

"Working with the police," corrected the doorman in a formal voice.

"I don't understand," Jaime said.

There were confused sounds in the background, followed by a woman's voice. "Miss Lazarus? My name is Susan Shader. I'm working with Detective Gold of the Homicide Division. I wonder if I could have a few minutes of your time?"

Jaime stood back a pace, staring at the intercom as though it were a live thing bent on biting her.

"Miss Lazarus?" the disembodied voice pursued.

For a last instant Jaime hesitated, gritting her teeth. Then she darted forward and pushed the button. "All right. Come on up."

She turned to the phone, seized by the impulse to call Geoff. But she knew he could not help her. She looked this way and that, as though sanctuary awaited her in some corner of the apartment.

It was no use. She stood waiting until a timid knock came at the door. She opened it. A small, pretty woman stood in the hallway, dressed in a gray suit with a leather portfolio in her hand.

"Miss Lazarus? Jaime? I'm Dr. Shader."

"I know. I mean, yes." Jaime stood back to let her visitor in.

Susan entered the apartment sideways, as though embarrassed to violate its space.

"I'm sorry to have showed up this way without calling," she said. "I'm checking on some friends and campus associates of Celeste Cawley. I understand you were once her roommate."

"That's right." Jaime accepted the handshake Susan offered. "We roomed together freshman year."

"Had you been in touch more recently?" Susan asked.

"Not really." Jaime shook her head. "She was pretty busy with her own life. Maybe once a semester she would call, or I would call. Then she dropped out of school."

"Of course you heard about what happened," Susan said.

"Yes, I did." Jaime tried to appear calm. "It came as a shock to me. I had heard about the murders—but Celeste was someone so close to home. I didn't believe it at first."

"I know how hard it can be to have a friend die," Susan said. "Especially when it's someone you've been out of touch with for a while. It doesn't seem real at first."

She glanced at the apartment. "You live in a nice building," she observed. Colorful afghans and throw pillows livened the rather dull furniture. The walls were hung with posters, most of them for exhibitions at the Art Institute of Chicago. It was clearly a student's apartment, but an effort had been made to decorate it tastefully.

"It's more than I can afford," Jaime said. "But my parents insisted. They don't think it's safe enough around here."

"Well, it's good to be extra careful," the doctor said.

"Would you like something to drink?" Jaime asked. "Tea? A soft drink?"

"A Coke would be fine."

"Diet Pepsi?"

"Sure."

Jaime disappeared into the kitchen. Susan made a quick tour of the living room as the sounds of ice and glasses came from the kitchen. She touched the sofa cushions, a row of books on a shelf, a coat and scarf hanging on a hook by the door. She was looking more closely at the books when Jaime came back into the room.

"Here you go."

"Thanks." Susan accepted the glass of soda and took a sip. "I really shouldn't be bothering you at home."

"Oh, it's no trouble."

"I imagine you're deep into spring semester."

"Well, not deep. Midterms aren't until the end of the month."

"What are you majoring in?"

"Political science. I'm doing a minor in European philosophy."

"That must be fun. Have you read much Freud?"

"Some. *Civilization and Its Discontents*. I read *The Future of an Illusion* in my philosophy of religion class."

"Freud is pretty hard on organized religion, isn't he?"

"Well, I'm an atheist—an agnostic, anyway—so I tend to agree with him." Jaime looked at her visitor. "How about you?"

"I'm a psychiatrist—I don't know if I mentioned that," Susan said. "To me Freud is above all a medical subject. I can be interested in what he says about other things without necessarily agreeing with him."

Jaime weighed the diplomacy of this remark.

"Do you practice here in the city?" she asked.

"Yes. My office is on North Michigan."

"Oh." Jaime had the sudden feeling that it would be a great pleasure to walk into an office and sit down to pour one's heart out to this woman. Susan Shader was delicate in appearance, but something very powerful emanated from her. Powerful and feminine.

"How did you start working with the police?"

"One of the homicide detectives asked me to consult on a case a few years ago," Susan said. "One thing led to another."

There was an embarrassed silence as Susan looked at Jaime.

"I gather you've read the papers," she said with a wry smile.

"Afraid so. They're being pretty rough on you, aren't they?"

"I think they feel it's their job," Susan said. "They're worried about innocent people being hurt, just as I am. That's why Detective Gold and I are so concerned to find this killer as soon as humanly possible."

Jaime was studying her cautiously. "Why do you come to me?" she asked. "I haven't been close to Celeste for years."

"We have to check everything. Every person who could possibly give us a clue about Celeste."

Susan noticed a hardcover copy of *To Kill a Mockingbird* in the bookcase.

"Oh, you're lucky," she said. "I've always wondered what the hardcover of this looked like. I have a well-thumbed copy of the old paperback. It's a wonderful book. Do you mind if I look at it?"

Jaime nodded. "It was a gift," she said. "From my father. He's a great admirer of it, too."

Susan opened the cover. There was a bookplate showing a turtle and a hare. The signature, *Jaime Lazarus,* looked relatively recent.

"I always felt this book was one of the deepest meditations about the problem of race separating people," Susan said.

"Actually, I've never been as wild about that aspect of it as I should have been," Jaime said. "Maybe it's because that's my father's province. We live with race every day. It's not romantic. It's not why I read a novel."

"What do you like about it, then?" Susan asked.

"The children," Jaime said. "The way they fantasize about the man in the haunted house. The games they play. The way things are shown through their eyes. My favorite part, I think, is the ending, where the brother and sister are walking through the woods toward home and the man attacks them. It's like a metaphor for life."

"I know what you mean," Susan said. "Childhood is very much like walking through a dark wood. There are a lot of dangers lurking in the shadows. Children are strong, though. They make their way through."

Susan reflected that the two children in Harper Lee's novel had a very special relationship with their widowed father, whose steadiness and tolerance made up for their lack of a mother but whose profession as a lawyer ultimately brought on the danger to their lives. She could not help wondering whether this had an unconscious effect on Jaime, whose father was himself a famous peacemaker with many enemies.

She also thought of Michael, who had lost his home with her because of her own professional activities, and who even now was about to return to California because of the controversy about her. And in her life, as in the Lee novel, an innocent man had died, accused of a crime he did not commit.

She looked again at the bookplate. "You have an interesting signature," she said.

"Really? It's never seemed very interesting to me."

"I'll bet you're a good student. Your handwriting suggests great intelligence."

"Oh." Jaime seemed more on her guard now.

"Your father must be very proud of you," Susan said. "What are your plans after you graduate?"

"Law school," Jaime said. "I hope to practice family law, maybe out west. California."

"You're sure you don't want to help us here in Chicago?" Susan smiled. "The State's Attorney would welcome you with open arms."

"I'm not much on criminal law."

"I can't blame you for that. It's full of frustrations." Susan smiled. "Does your father approve of your plans?"

"He lets me make my own decisions."

"That's nice." Susan glanced around the living room. "I'm a great admirer of your father. I notice you don't keep a picture of him."

"It's in the bedroom. Him and my mother."

"Well, he's a wonderful man, and he's been so good for our country."

"Uh-huh." Jaime was growing more distant by the minute.

Susan sipped at her drink. "Tell me about Celeste," she said.

"Celeste? Well, she was a good roommate. We weren't all that close, but we had good times."

"Did she have a steady boyfriend when you knew her?"

"No. She wasn't very successful with the opposite sex. Not at that time, anyway. She spent most nights around the apartment. I don't think she had a boyfriend at all that year."

"And later?"

"We weren't close enough for her to really tell me."

"She never mentioned anyone in particular when you talked after freshman year?"

Jaime thought for a moment. "Well, there was a guy," she said. "The last time I talked to her she said she had a boyfriend. I sort of got the impression he was older. Maybe . . ."

"Yes?" Susan was smiling, but the attention behind her eyes was intense.

"There might have been something wrong about it," Jaime said. "I mean, like he was married, or trouble, or something. She was just evasive enough that I wondered. But I never found out."

"I see. Would you say that Celeste was a happy person?"

Jaime shook her head. "No, I wouldn't say that."

"I imagine it must have been a bit difficult for her to be your friend."

"Why?" Jaime's tone was protective.

"You are very beautiful," Susan said. "I gather that Celeste was not a very attractive girl."

Jaime ignored the compliment. "She wasn't good-looking," she said. "But she made it worse by not taking better care of herself. She had rings in her ears and nose and everything. A tattoo on her leg. I don't think she really respected herself very much."

"Did you meet her parents?"

"Oh, sure. Freshman year. Several times. They took us out to dinner."

"What was your impression of them?"

"They were—distant. I had the feeling there were problems between them and Celeste that they were trying to keep under wraps when I was around."

"Did Celeste speak of these problems privately to you?"

Jaime grimaced. "She said she hated them. She said they were a couple of bigoted dopes, and she was sorry to be descended from them. She used those words. *I'm sorry to be descended from them.*"

"And she didn't amplify?" Susan asked.

"No, not really. I could see it was a painful subject, so I never tried to draw her out."

"A psychiatrist would say that's a significant choice of words. *Sorry to be descended from them.* Did it strike you that way?"

"What do you mean?"

"Did you ever suspect Celeste was illegitimate?"

Jaime seemed taken aback.

"What gave you that idea?" she asked.

"I asked you first." Susan smiled. "Did you ever suspect that that was the case?"

"To be honest, I did." Jaime curled her legs under her. "She didn't seem to look like either of them. Until you got to know them a little more, and you could see the resemblance to her mother. But they seemed so different . . ."

"Perhaps she never knew," Susan suggested. "Perhaps it was only a suspicion."

Jaime thought back on her roommate's unhappiness, and her fierce but unfocused anger toward her parents. Though she had liked Celeste, it had been a relief to get a new roommate after freshman year. Celeste was too miserable to be around.

"You see a lot, Doctor."

"Oh, well. I'm just speculating. I'm afraid it's the nature of the beast. Don't pay any attention to me." She twisted her glass of Diet Pepsi, looking at the crest of the University of Chicago that was emblazoned on it.

"You said she dropped out of school," she said. "Was she having trouble with her studies?"

"I don't know," Jaime replied. "She might have been. She did pretty well when we were roommates, though. She was smart. And she was stubborn. She would keep at a thing no matter how difficult it was. Like a dog with a bone."

The phone rang. Jaime leaned sideways to answer it, baring her beautiful legs as she stretched.

"Hello? No, fine. Just someone to see me. No, it's nothing to worry about. She's sitting here now."

There was a silence as she listened to the caller. Then she looked at Susan. "Will you hang this up for me if I go into the bedroom? I won't be a minute."

"Of course." Susan took the receiver and watched Jaime leave the room. When she heard the other phone picked up she replaced the receiver but kept her fingers on it for a few seconds, a reflective look on her face.

The copy of *To Kill a Mockingbird* was still on the table. Susan picked it up and took another look at the bookplate, running her fingers gently over the signature. Then she replaced it on the shelf and opened a few more of the books. There were novels, including *The Member of the Wedding* and *The Catcher in the Rye*, and some poetry, including a volume of Emily Dickinson. She let the book fall open in her hands. "I Had no Time to Hate" appeared on the right-hand page.

Jaime's signature on the various bookplates and jackets was remarkably consistent. Always the neat and graceful surface, and the shrouded intensity. It was easy to see she led a sort of double life, very controlled on the surface with slow fires smoldering underneath. One had that impression from looking at her face, too.

"Sorry about that." Jaime was back.

"Not at all. I'm sorry to be in the way."

Jaime flopped back down on the couch. "What's it like to be psychic?" she asked abruptly.

Susan raised an eyebrow. "So you know about that," she said.

"I read the papers," Jaime said.

Susan sighed. "I used to think of it as a mixed blessing. Now it doesn't seem like a blessing at all."

Jaime nodded. "Will it hurt your reputation? As a doctor, I mean. This case . . ."

"It might." Susan looked out the window. "But my reputation isn't as important as catching this killer. If we stop him, I won't care very much what happens to me."

"Well, I'd like to help in any way I can," Jaime said. "I'm just not sure how I can. It's been so long since I even saw Celeste."

"Miss Lazarus . . ."

"Jaime. Call me Jaime."

The doctor smiled. "Jaime, then. I'd like to ask you a question."

"Fire away." The girl leaned back against the couch, a little defensively.

"Why did you sign Celeste's name the day of the car accident at the Radisson?"

There was a silence. Jaime's eyes had opened wide.

"Was it because of the man on the phone just now?" Susan asked.

The girl's eyes opened wider. She was clearly stunned at the extent of Susan's knowledge.

"I don't want to embarrass you," Susan said, "but as you know, the situation is serious. We're trying to save lives. Five people have already been killed."

Jaime made a motion to pick up her glass of soda, but her hand shook and she pulled it back.

"How did you find out?" she asked.

Susan opened her purse and pulled out a folded copy of the witness statement. She handed it to Jaime.

"It was simple enough to determine that the signature

on the statement wasn't Celeste's," she said. "Finding you was the problem."

"How *did* you find me?"

"The officer who took the statements remembered how beautiful you were," Susan said. "When I showed him a picture of Celeste, he knew she wasn't the girl he had interviewed that day. From there it became a question of contacting Celeste's friends and former friends. That's how I found you." This statement was not altogether true. Susan's second sight had helped her narrow the field. She had guessed that the hand that had written Celeste Cawley's name as the policeman stood watching actually wanted to write *Jaime*.

Jaime looked frightened. "What about the . . . man on the phone?" she asked.

"Call it a hunch," Susan said. "You're having an affair with him, aren't you?"

There was a long silence. Jaime looked at Susan through eyes filled with supplication. Then she burst into tears.

Susan saw a box of tissues on the shelf and took it to the girl, feeling very much like a therapist. Jaime wept openly, sobbing into her hands.

Susan said nothing.

"I killed her," Jaime said. "It was because of me."

"Because you signed her name instead of your own?"

Jaime nodded. "I was in the hotel with Geoff. My lover. I couldn't let the police know who I really am. You have to understand. My father is a very visible man. There are people who spend all their time looking for dirt they can use against him. All my life he's kept me protected from that. I couldn't pay him back by . . ." She trailed off, a haunted look in her eyes.

"That's a heavy load for a young girl to bear, isn't it?" Susan asked. "Being responsible not only for herself but for her father as well?"

Jaime looked at her in surprise. It was a look Susan had seen thousands of times in her practice. Patients who lived with their guilt as a constant companion, a sort of second nature, were always shocked when it was explained to them that the guilt was not natural and could be gotten rid of.

"Young women fall in love," Susan said. "They have affairs. You're not the first."

Again the stunned, cleansed look of youth reminded Susan of its own innocence. Then it vanished and Jaime began crying again.

"Tell me," Susan asked. "Did you give Celeste's name because it had been so long since you had seen her?"

"There wasn't time to think," Jaime said. "I had already been talking to the girls, the athletes. They asked me my name. I told them Celeste. Then the police were there, and the girls were listening as I talked to the officer. I couldn't change my name at that point, so I said Celeste again. I just blurted it out, you see. I didn't even think—" Sobs broke her off again.

"That's natural enough," Susan said. "It was just an unimportant accident. So you gave the name of an old roommate. You meant no harm."

"It couldn't have been worse if I had *meant* harm!" the girl cried.

Susan nodded. "I know. Doing harm when we don't mean to is a terrible burden. But perhaps it is more natural for you to blame yourself than to realize how innocent you were." The face of Dr. Berthe Mueller flashed before her mind's eye as she gave this advice, which was so hard for her to accept in her own life.

Jaime threw the tissue on the couch and got another.

"She would be alive if I hadn't—" She shook her head. "Oh, the hell with it. The hell with it!"

"Tell me about the man on the phone," Susan said. "Does he know anything about this?"

"No. Nothing." Jaime shook her head stubbornly.

"You've been living with this alone?" Susan asked.

The girl nodded.

"When did you first realize the accident had been important?" Susan asked.

"When the third girl was killed. Patsy. She was the one who talked to me the most that day. She was so tall, she was embarrassed by her height. I recognized her picture in the paper after she was killed. I started worrying about that day at the hotel . . ."

She looked desperately at Susan. "If I had been quicker, if I had thought it over, I could have warned Celeste," she said. "But it just never occurred to me . . ."

"Of course it didn't," Susan said. "No one can think about things that way. The crimes are strange, Jaime. Even the police have never seen anything like it. You can hardly be held responsible for not seeing to the bottom of a situation so complex."

"If only I hadn't given her name!" Jaime cried.

Susan came to sit beside her on the couch.

"Jaime, you're going to have to learn to realize that you are guilty only of having an affair and being embarrassed about it. You didn't kill anybody. A sick murderer did that."

She paused, looking at the girl. She felt tempted to say, *You're lucky to be alive,* but her years as a therapist told her how wrong a note this would strike.

"You tried to protect your family," she said. "That was asking a great deal of yourself."

At this Jaime seemed to collapse. Tears ran down her face, but she was silent.

"Will you tell my friend Detective Gold what you've told me?" Susan asked.

Jaime looked at her pathetically.

"I'm sure he'll do everything he can to keep your identity out of this," Susan said. "The important thing is not your private life but preventing crimes."

"My father . . ." Jaime's eyes rolled toward the ceiling. She looked like a trapped bird.

"Jaime, if your father knew all about this, he wouldn't

reproach you in the slightest. I feel sure of that. He would only be sorry you've suffered so much in silence."

She squeezed Jaime's hand. "But he won't ever have to know, unless and until you want him to."

Jaime thought for a moment. Then she sighed, a look of surrender in her eyes. "All right," she said.

"May I use your phone?" Susan asked.

"Yes."

Susan picked up the receiver. Before she could dial Gold's number, a knock came at the door.

Jaime started. She looked toward the door.

"Jaime!" The voice sounded urgent but also amused, as though stifling a laugh. "It's . . ." The words were loud, but too muffled to be understandable.

Susan's finger stopped in midair, poised over the push buttons of the phone. She looked at Jaime.

"Do you recognize the voice?"

Jaime shook her head.

"Does your doorman let people up without announcing them?"

Jaime shook her head. "Never."

Susan put down the phone and moved slowly to the door. There was an eyehole. Standing on tiptoe, she looked through it.

A face was visible in the dim hallway. Large horn-rimmed eyeglasses dwarfed the rest of the features. The lenses were tinted, making the eyes hard to see.

Susan recognized them anyway.

Flattening herself against the door, she spoke to Jaime.

"Dial 228-3091," she said. "Detective David Gold. Hurry!"

Looking strangely calm, like a person who has been accustomed to danger all her life, Jaime dialed the number.

Susan held herself against the door as Jaime waited for Homicide to answer. She felt the presence behind her, unmoving.

"Hello," Jaime said into the phone. "My name is . . ."

"Tell them it's from me," Susan interrupted. "Say it's an emergency."

Jaime spoke into the phone, her eyes on Susan. The receiver trembled in her hand, but her voice remained steady.

"He's not there," she said. "They're trying to get him on the radio."

Susan nodded. She heard a tick of metal on metal as the doorknob was tried from the outside. She pushed her body against the door.

A quiet voice came through the thick wood.

"Susan?"

She pushed harder, crushing her elbows and shoulder blades against the door. The knob clicked again, interrogatively.

"Susan? Is that you?"

Time passed. Susan stood with her teeth gritted, staring at the girl on the couch. Was this how it had happened to the others? A friendly, familiar voice outside the door, warm with reassurance, seductive . . .

The tremors had spread through her own limbs now. The feeling of interposing herself between an innocent girl and death was uncanny.

Then Jaime was speaking into the phone again.

"Yes!" she cried. "She's right here. Hurry. Please!"

Jaime looked at Susan.

"He says two minutes. He wants to talk to you."

Susan shook her head. "There's no time. Just tell him to hurry."

She felt more than heard the steps receding down the hall. She kept her eyes on Jaime.

Only later did she recall that at the end there had been a low laugh, at the level of her ear.

28

THANKS TO DAVID GOLD, two Chicago black-and-whites, cruising the always dangerous University of Chicago area, were at Jaime Lazarus's apartment building within seconds of his last words to her on the phone. Backup arrived only a few minutes later.

The officers stayed with Susan and Jaime until Gold himself arrived. The building was sealed and the neighborhood searched thoroughly, but no trace was found of the man Susan had seen through the eyehole of Jaime's door.

"It was him, though." Gold posed his question as a statement.

"I'm sure of it," Susan said. "I would have recognized those eyes anywhere. He spoke to me, too."

In retrospect she was terrified at having seen Arnold Haze at such close quarters. But her fear was tempered by relief, for the faceless enemy she had been fighting all this time had finally shown himself.

She did not tell Gold that there was more than mere vision involved in the feeling she had had when she looked through the eyehole. Ever since the beginning of this case, she had felt as though someone was watching her, second-guessing her, even leading her by the nose. The day the roses arrived after the murder of Celeste Cawley, her suspicion had become a certainty. The roses were meant to rub her nose in Kyle Stewart's death. And to remind her that it was she who had taken the bait that framed Stewart for the murders of the coeds.

"What do we do now?" she asked Gold.

"Take the girl into protective custody, for openers," he said. "And put out an APB on Haze. We might get lucky. Hell, the odds are on our side. So far he's had all the luck."

He watched the female officer who was helping Jaime pack some belongings. Jaime looked very young and vulnerable as she moved around the apartment. For a moment Gold seemed lost in thought. Then he turned to Susan.

"And we can congratulate ourselves on one thing," he said.

"What's that?"

"There's nobody left for him to kill," Gold said. "Think about it."

Susan herself was watching Jaime.

"It's too late," she said. "Is that what you mean?"

"Right," Gold said. "He missed his chance. We're on to him now, and he knows it. We'll launch a nationwide manhunt, maybe get the feds to put him high on their Ten Most Wanted. For multiple murder. There wouldn't be anything for him to gain from trying again on Jaime. Even without her we'd have our case against him. My guess is that he'll head south of the border as quick as he can."

The apartment was now crowded with detectives and uniformed officers, most of them standing around with nothing to do. Jaime, carrying a suitcase in one hand and an overnight bag in the other, came to say good night to Susan.

"Thanks," she said.

"I'm the one who should thank you," Susan said. "You did us a great service tonight."

Gold watched, a ruminative look on his face, as Jaime walked out the door between two detectives.

"Wonders never cease," he said. Then, turning to Susan, "You gonna be all right?"

"Me?" she replied. "Of course. Why not?"

"I almost forgot." He grinned. "You love all this excitement, don't you?"

Susan shook her head at his grim humor.

"Go home and get some rest." Gold patted her cheek affectionately. "We'll talk tomorrow."

JAIME LAZARUS SPENT the night at Police Headquarters, her troubled sleep watched over by two armed guards and a patrolwoman. The next day she was interrogated by detectives who were amazed by the story she told. David Gold heard everything she said and came to the immediate conclusion that the reign of terror caused by the "Coed Killer" was at an end.

The APB was put out nationwide on Arnold Haze. The FBI's director agreed to place him atop the Bureau's Ten Most Wanted List, at least for the time being. Gold doubted, though, that it would result in an arrest. Haze was a smart man who probably had many resources for escape. The real reason for the APB was to let Haze himself know that the authorities were actively pursuing him.

Later in the day Jaime was moved to an apartment in the Loop used for witnesses from the Federal Witness Protection Program and other law-enforcement VIPs, including high-level informers. There she was visited by her parents, whom she told about what had happened to her at the Radisson Hotel, and about her love affair with Geoff MacAndrew.

Two days later a man answering the description of Arnold Haze was spotted at Miami Airport by a member of the security staff. The security man tried to tail him but lost him in the thick crowd of travelers at the busy airport.

The FBI concluded from this that Haze had seized the opportunity to flee. His particulars were circulated through Interpol to police forces around the world.

The public still knew nothing of the real truth behind the "Coed Murders." This created several problems.

In the first place, a high priority was to reassure the public that the string of murders was at an end. However, the perpetrator had not been caught. It was a complex matter to try to explain to a frightened public that the murders would now end because the murderer, though still at large, no longer had a reason to go on killing. This would sound garbled and, worse, humiliating to the authorities.

Nevertheless, the truth could not be withheld much longer, given the explosive nature of the case and the storm of media attention it had already attracted. Some of the mayor's advisers counseled precisely the "hang-out" approach. If a clean breast was not made of the situation now, they reasoned, the public would not believe whatever partial story was put out. And this would destroy the credibility of everyone involved, from the mayor and Abel Weathers to the FBI and the Chicago Police. Improbable though the story might be, it was better to tell it.

This would mean, of course, revealing the connection of the female victims to Peter Tomerakian, whose death had been attributed all this time to suicide. Some of the media would charge cover-up. In the second place, the connection of Jaime Lazarus to the whole business would have to come out. Journalists and crime writers would have a field day. BLACK LEADER'S DAUGHTER CAME WITHIN INCHES OF DEATH. The tabloids would be full of Jaime Lazarus's face for months.

Abel Weathers's publicity consultant was in favor of the "hang-out" approach. His reason was that airing the entire story would help Weathers politically more than it would hurt him. The deaths of the coeds could hardly be blamed on the police or the State's Attorney's Office, given the insane complexity of the whole story. It had been only natural for the authorities to proceed as though the girls' deaths were the work of a serial killer. Finding a path through the labyrinth had taken time.

And in the end the authorities had found the truth. Jaime Lazarus had been saved. This would make a great story. And Abel Weathers's PR man could not resist a great story.

While Weathers and his colleagues were still pondering the issue, the problem was solved for them by a weakness built into their own system of operation. An aggressive reporter with contacts high in the criminal justice community—the same one, in fact, who had pilloried Susan for having caused the death of Kyle Stewart—got his hands on the story and leaked it in a sensational five-part story in the *Sun-Times*.

Now the whole truth was out. Predictably enough, there was some embarrassment. The FBI's failure to handle the Tomerakian situation had resulted in the deaths of five innocent women. It had taken months for the authorities to get to the bottom of the crimes.

However, the public seemed more absorbed in its fascination with the sensational aspect of the case than in the blame attaching to the law-enforcement community. This fascination centered on Susan Shader, the psychic who had managed at the eleventh hour to save Jaime Lazarus from death at the hands of Arnold Haze.

Susan was a celebrity, all the more so because of the fame and beauty of the girl she had saved. Her former tarnished image was forgotten. She was now the brilliant investigator who had single-handedly found the key to the enigma and saved Jaime Lazarus's life—without a second to spare.

Her face and that of Jaime dominated the tabloids both in print and on television. Offers for interviews from the major network news organizations came in at a frightening pace. Susan learned to her amazement that Abel Weathers had made a book deal with a New York publisher. Furthermore, rights to the story as told by Weathers had already been sold to a Hollywood studio.

Susan refused all interviews. When other publishers got around to offering her seven figures for her own memoir of the Coed Murders case, she refused as well. Her only concern was to recover the anonymity she had enjoyed before any of this started.

"That won't be possible," David Gold told her. "You're famous. You're gonna have to learn to live with that."

"You underestimate me," Susan said. "I've spent a lifetime learning how not to be noticed by people. In six months no one will remember me. Then I can get back to my own life."

"Good luck," Gold told her. Despite his skepticism, he had to admit she might get away with it. In her years of work with him she had been involved in sensational cases and managed to keep herself out of the limelight. She might just succeed in fading into obscurity as she wished.

SUSAN TOOK JAIME out to lunch that week. Over steaming bowls of onion soup, they talked about what had happened. It was only now that Jaime told Susan the whole story of her involvement in the case.

"I met Geoff when I was doing a research project for my political science class at the University of Chicago," she said. "It was a group project, and we had to interview people in state and county government. I wasn't the one who got him to do the interview. It was Adele, a friend of mine. But Adele came down with the flu the day before the interview, so I had to go.

"Geoff was very gracious, very informative. He gave me forty-five minutes, though his phone was ringing the whole time. He also steered me to some publications that could help, and to some scholarly works. He remembered his own postgraduate education very well, and was up-to-date on the whole topic.

"He seemed so young." Jaime smiled wistfully. "He was so excited about ideas. So idealistic. Not at all like a politician. He was very gentle, very sensitive. I was in love with him by the end of the interview. He didn't come on to me at all, he was completely professional.

"Afterward, though, I couldn't get him out of my mind. I had never met anyone like him. I guess I have always been attracted by older men. But this was a case of an older man, chronologically, who seemed even younger than me spiritually. I wanted to tap into his excitement about life, as well as his attractiveness.

"To make a long story short, I lost the battle against my own temptation. I called him and asked him to meet me for lunch. We went to a small restaurant in the western part of the Loop, a place none of his political friends would frequent. We talked. I let it get personal. Or made it get personal. He was very kind. At first I thought I was amusing him. Then I saw that it was more."

She sighed. "I practically begged him to take me to a hotel. We spent half the afternoon in bed. It was—amazing. He was slow, tender, helpful . . . I had never felt anything so wonderful in my life.

"After that we were lovers. We met at least once a week, more when I could convince him. He worried a lot about me, about my father. He really respects Dad, he wouldn't hurt his work for anything in the world. I had to keep reassuring him. It wasn't easy.

"He worried about his wife a lot, too. And his children. He has these two sweet little girls. They both look like him, too. I kept telling him I had no designs on him. There was the color thing as well as the age thing. I had no illusions. I told him I was in love with him, and I just wanted to know what it was like to be this much in love. I told him I wanted to be able to remember it for the rest of my life. I meant it.

"But he was worried about me, about what it would do to me when it was over. I kept telling him, I'm young yet. He would smile sadly. 'That's just what worries me,' he said.

"In the end, though, he told me he loved me. It still excites me to say it. He loved me too!"

Susan nodded. She could see how much it had meant to Jaime to take this risk, stepping outside her family to find someone who loved her as a woman. The prize of being loved outweighed the fact that that love could not be permanent.

"Anyway," Jaime went on, "that particular day we met at the Radisson in the Loop. We were very discreet. We came separately. No one saw us. It was a little dangerous, because there was a convention in the hotel. But I insisted. I hadn't seen Geoff in ten days, and I was starving for him. I was limp when I left.

"I rode down in the elevator. Two men got on. Then these three girls, who were laughing. White girls. They were very friendly; we exchanged some joking remarks when the elevator got temporarily stuck between floors. They all looked at me. I could see they were noticing my looks. One of them asked what kind of makeup I use. It's not the first time. I'm pretty, I know that. It's hard to go unnoticed when you look like I do.

"A woman got on. One of the men was doing all the talking. The other one didn't say a word. I happened to glance at him in the mirror in the elevator. He had these two tiny black eyes, like pebbles. You couldn't see into them, but they pierced you like knives. He looked at me, and his stare made me feel shaky. Maybe because I had just been doing something secret.

"We all got out on the ground floor. The girls were waiting for a bus. They introduced themselves to me. They were athletes. They were going on a tour of South America, and they had just been to a banquet. We talked about Illinois and the University of Chicago. Just chitchat. I only caught the name of the tallest girl. She was over six feet tall, and she joked about it. 'I'm Patsy, I'm the tall one.' 'Don't hurt your neck looking up.' Things like that. She was genuinely embarrassed about it, I could see. She was quite pretty, in an unusual way.

"Then this accident happened. A maroon sedan skidded into the back of a little foreign car in front of the hotel. I was close enough to see that the man with the strange eyes was in the backseat of the car that rear-ended the other car. He was swearing and gesticulating. There was another man behind the wheel; I couldn't see his face.

"The sedan sped off, leaving the other car sitting there. The three girls from the elevator were standing right there, and they were like, 'Wow, did you see that?' So I was stuck.

"The police arrived a couple of minutes later. They were

very quick in their work. I hardly had a chance to catch my breath before they were taking my statement. I didn't want to give them my real name because I was worried about Geoff. I wasn't thinking too clearly. I remembered that Celeste and I used to give each other's names sometimes, as a sort of prank, when we lived together. So I gave them her name. I also gave the address of the apartment we had lived in as freshmen. I knew it would lead nowhere.

"Luckily for me, the police didn't ask me for ID. I noticed that the other lady from the elevator was there, too, giving them a statement. I didn't pay much attention to her.

"When the bus came for the girls, I said good-bye to them and wished them luck with their tour. They waved out the bus window, and that's the last I saw of them.

"I pretty much forgot about the incident. But then the murders started. The first two didn't register, because the pictures in the newspapers weren't very good. But the third victim was Patsy. I recognized her name and her photo right away. I was shaken. I had met her, talked to her. Liked her. It seemed incredible, that tall, athletic girl, strangled. It gave me nightmares.

"I went back to the newspapers and looked again at the pictures of the first two victims. I recognized them now as the girls from the Radisson. I wanted to call the police and tell them I had seen the girls together. But I couldn't make up my mind to do it.

"Then the fourth victim died, the woman. At first I didn't remember her. Then I did. Now I was really scared. I started thinking more seriously about calling the police. I figured they needed to know that these killings were not random. There was a common link. I would make the call anonymous, I decided. They didn't really need to know who I was. Just that the victims had been together.

"But before I could call, they arrested that man, that custodian. He knew the three girls. The police seemed sure he was the killer. I guess I assumed he killed them because he knew them. I didn't think too much about the fourth woman.

"Then Stewart committed suicide, and Celeste was murdered. This freaked me out completely. Up until that moment I had thought of it all as something outside myself. Something I had seen. But now I remembered writing down Celeste's name instead of my own. I had fingered her, I had caused her death. When I heard she was pregnant, I thought I was going to die. She and her baby were dead because of me. Because I had tried to protect myself from a scandal.

"Everything was out of hand. Out of control. I didn't know what to do. Then you came to my apartment. You seemed to know so much. It was as though my lies were catching up to me. At first I just wanted to crawl into a hole. Then I began to feel relieved that I didn't have to run anymore. And then—then that knock came at the door. It was like the end of the world."

Susan smiled. "But the world didn't end. Did it?"

Jaime took a deep breath. "My parents have been visiting me," she said.

"Does it help?" Susan asked.

Jaime nodded. "They love me. They don't care about the rest. They only care that I'm safe." She sighed. "I should have known that about them. I should have believed in them more. In us."

Susan smiled. "There's that overactive conscience again. Someday you're going to have to forgive yourself for not having all the answers."

Jaime looked at Susan, a beseeching expression in her eyes.

"Could you help me to do that?" she asked. "If I needed you?"

Susan squeezed her hand. "I think I could," she said. "I doubt that it will ever be necessary. But if a day comes when you think it is, don't hesitate to call. Will you promise me that?"

"Yes." For the first time since they had met, Susan saw Jaime Lazarus smile.

A WEEK LATER things were settling down. Three of the four patients Susan had lost during the Kyle Stewart episode had returned. In a quiet way the medical community was welcoming her back. Invitations had come in for her to deliver lectures at several psychiatric meetings, and a prestigious forensic journal wanted her to contribute an account of the parapsychological implications of her work on the Coed Murders case.

Though life was far from returning to normal, Susan could see a quieter existence on the horizon. Her professional life had been helped more than harmed by her work on the case. It looked as though she would soon be able to get on with her life. That was all she wanted.

She was savoring this relief, and planning for her last days with Michael, when, one windy evening, the doorman buzzed her to announce Aaron Lazarus.

"Who?" Susan asked incredulously.

The doorman, sounding suitably awed, repeated the name. Two minutes later a tall black man with graying hair and penetrating eyes knocked at her door, and she invited Aaron Lazarus to come in.

"My wife wants to thank you as well," he said, "but I wanted to come alone this time."

Susan introduced him to Michael and watched in fascination as the legendary leader bent to shake the hand of the shy little boy. Then she took Lazarus into the kitchen and offered him coffee.

He sat on one of the small chairs, looking surprisingly humble. His dark suit was rumpled, and his collar was loose. He seemed thinner than in his pictures.

"Jaime told us everything," he said. "I suppose you know that."

"Yes."

"Detective Gold explained things to us," he added.

"Your role in it all, I mean. I don't know how to thank you."

"No thanks are necessary," Susan said. "I was just doing my job. I'm the one who needs to thank Jaime. She gave us the final piece of the puzzle."

He gave her a sharp look. "Do you believe the danger is over?" he asked.

"Yes, I do," Susan assured him. "Detective Gold and his colleagues seem very sure of their ground. They know who committed the crimes. He can't gain any advantage by trying to eliminate the witnesses who saw him here in Chicago. It's too late for that. My guess is that he's a long way from here right now, and that he won't be seen in this city again as long as he lives."

Aaron Lazarus's eyes showed that he was measuring Susan's assurances cautiously. As a black man, he was used to promises that were not kept, and to hopes that were raised only to be dashed later. Skepticism was part of his nature.

But now he surprised Susan.

"You know," he said, "I'm just a father."

A tremor shook his tall body, and tears came to his eyes. He put his head in his hands.

Susan went to his side and patted his shoulder.

"I'm sorry," he said.

"It's all right," Susan said. "She's safe. She's going to be fine."

She pondered the strangeness of the moment. There was no man on earth more courageous than Aaron Lazarus. And here he was, fighting back sobs and being comforted by a woman who had never expected to meet him in this life. Surely there was no limit to the complexity of fate.

He pulled a handkerchief from his pocket and wiped his eyes.

"I've spent a lifetime," he said, "fearing that what I do in the world would hurt my daughter. That the people who hate me would take it out on her. There isn't a night that goes by without my sleep being troubled by that fear,

Doctor. And now she came within an inch of dying, because she tried to protect me. She tried not to embarrass me . . ."

Susan sat down opposite him.

"I understand your feelings," she said. "But you must try to put things in perspective. Your daughter was a witness to something that put her at risk. She was just in the wrong place at the wrong time."

Lazarus smiled. His eloquent eyes were bloodshot. She guessed he had slept little in recent days.

"You're being very kind," he said. "But if Jaime hadn't been so worried about protecting me and her mother, the situation might have played itself out very differently." He gave her a probing look. "You know what I mean."

Susan understood. Like his daughter, Aaron Lazarus had a deep sense of responsibility for other people. It could be translated into guilt all too quickly.

"She did nothing wrong, and you did nothing wrong," she said. "Unless it can be considered a crime to have a life to live, and to want to protect those we love."

He nodded. He seemed relieved to have vented what was really on his mind.

"You're a good doctor," he said. "I can see that."

He folded his handkerchief and put it in his pocket. He wore a vest with a gold watch chain. Susan was impressed by his old-school correctness. He sensed this, and smiled at her.

"You know," he said, "when Jaime was very small—about two and a half, I think—we were standing at the curb in our old neighborhood, loading the car for a trip. I had some meetings to attend in other cities, and I was taking the family along. Jaime got away from us for a split second and rushed out past the hood of the car, right into the middle of the street. It wasn't that busy a street, but at that instant it occurred to me that if a car was coming along, there was no way we could react quickly enough to save her. It would be the end."

He looked at Susan. "I knew at that moment what parenthood is all about," he said. "You devote yourself entirely to bringing happiness to a child. But it is precisely that child's capacity for happiness—her hunger for life, her hunger for experience—that puts her at risk. And there's not a goddamned thing you can do about that. The seeds of destruction are built in."

Susan nodded. "I agree. That's every parent's nightmare."

He studied her face. "So you've been through it."

"Yes, I have." She smiled. "And my own sleep is sometimes troubled, just like yours."

"If she had been run over that day," he said musingly, "I would have blamed myself, of course. I was loading the car. I was distracted, I wasn't watching her."

"But you wouldn't have been at fault," Susan said.

He raised an eyebrow to acknowledge the distinction.

"Perhaps not," he said.

He stood up. "Thank you for talking to me, Doctor. And thank you for caring enough to go to Jaime on your own. If you hadn't been so quick, this might have been a car she would not have escaped."

Susan shook his hand. "Life is full of risk, Mr. Lazarus. No one knows that better than you."

"The risk to me is easy to bear," he said. "It's an old friend by now. But the risk to those I love—that's a demon I never have learned to live with."

She walked him through the living room, where Michael still sat in front of the television.

"A beautiful boy," Lazarus murmured to Susan.

"Thank you. I think so."

He picked up his overcoat and stood looking at her.

"You're very small," he observed.

Susan shrugged.

"Well, the smallest are often the most powerful." He allowed her to help him on with the coat.

"Thank you for coming," she said.

He hugged her to him very gently, his embrace surprisingly paternal. Susan found herself responding to it with half-closed eyes.

Then he held her out at arm's length and studied her, a wry smile curling his lips.

"It's a pity you're not one of us," he said. "I could use you."

She pondered his words as he closed the door behind him. That compliment, bestowed by Aaron Lazarus, was a gift she would cherish forever.

29

SUSAN'S LAST DAYS with Michael were bittersweet. She took him to Water Tower Place, to the movies, and to the Museum of Science and Industry. They went to a Bulls game with David Gold, who knew how devoted a fan Michael was and had used his influence to procure the hard-to-get tickets. The opponent was the hated New York Knicks, and the game was sold out.

Michael sat on the edge of his seat, ignoring even his hot dog as he watched Michael Jordan and Scottie Pippen streak down the floor. Jordan had a sore knee and was seen limping now and then, but it did not stop him from scoring almost at will.

Dennis Rodman, the eccentric rebounding specialist, was wearing green hair that night. Michael pointed out to Susan the fact that every ten minutes or so Rodman would receive a pass directly under the basket and lay the ball in. His understanding of the flow of the game seemed to exceed even that of his star teammates.

For most of the first three quarters the Bulls were behind the determined Knicks. Gold kept calling out free advice from his seat next to Michael. "Give it to Harper!"

he cried. Or, again, "Kukoc, don't shoot!" And to Michael, "Kukoc can't shoot tonight. His stroke is way off. Just look at him."

As the Bulls surged ahead to win a ten-point victory, Susan saw Gold put his arm around Michael's shoulder. Their symbiosis was more than obvious. To an uninformed observer they must have looked like father and son.

After the game Gold took Susan and Michael to his favorite restaurant, the Irish Lion on Wabash Street. Gold and Susan drank Bass ale, and Gold ordered mutton pie with soda bread after instructing the waiter ceremoniously about the proper way to prepare Michael's baked potato.

Susan had been here many times with Gold in the past. He seemed as attracted by the atmosphere as he was by the rich food. He sometimes ordered his ale in half yards or even yards, the enormous elongated glasses that had to be held up over one's face like gourds.

"Why are you so crazy about this place?" she once asked.

"Search me," Gold had said. "Maybe because I'm Jewish."

Susan had smiled. "You ought to read *Ulysses*. Mr. Bloom, the hero, is Jewish. And a great connoisseur of Irish food."

"I'll let you read me the good parts," Gold had said. He was not a great reader. He fell asleep every night with a copy of *Sports Illustrated* in his lap. Susan doubted he had read a book in years.

Time was running short. Carolyn took Michael on a major shopping trip to Woodfield Mall and shamelessly plied him with gifts, from stuffed animals to T-shirts and new running shoes. Michael would fly home to California overloaded with booty.

Susan tried to savor the peace of these last few days, but she felt a painful letdown. Michael was about to return to his own life. The next time she saw him he would be an older and bigger Michael, changed once again by the passage of time and by a thousand little events she would never know about.

She took him to the photographer on North Clark Street who regularly took their picture when Michael visited. Michael wore the new sweater that Carolyn had bought him. Susan bought a blouse for the occasion. She superstitiously felt that it was important to wear a new garment that would symbolize future visits with Michael rather than to recall past ones.

The photographer took a series of posed portraits and promised Susan proofs within the week.

"Your boy is getting bigger," he said.

"Yes. He is." She could not hide the regret that went hand in hand with her pride. How different her life would be if Michael were waiting for her every night when she came home from work! If every weekend promised forty-eight beautiful hours with her son.

But that life could not be. The die had been cast, and it was too late to turn back. Michael lived a safe and peaceful life with Nick and Elaine in California. Susan could not offer him the same sort of life here. Recent events had made that clear.

Her ambivalent feelings about herself as a mother reminded her of Aaron Lazarus, with his fierce love for Jaime and his worry about the effect of his professional life on her. Susan and Lazarus had a lot in common.

Susan took Michael to O'Hare on Tuesday morning for the early flight to LAX. Elaine would be waiting at the other end. Susan had made Michael his favorite breakfast of French toast and Canadian bacon. He had eaten it with apparent enjoyment, but he'd seemed preoccupied on the way to the airport.

He held Susan's hand as he sat next to her in the departure lounge. She asked him casual questions about his plans for the coming days, but she felt other questions struggling to pass her lips. Had he really had a good time with her? Did he truly want to come back again? Did he still love her? Questions she could not ask.

When boarding began he turned to look at her.

"Mama, I'll come back soon."

So he suspected what she was thinking, then. His antennae for her feelings were as sharp as ever.

"Will you?" she asked.

"Yes. Will you call me tonight?"

"Of course I'll call you, honey. Why, I'll bet the minute you get home the phone will be ringing. And I'll be on it to tell you how much I miss you."

He nodded.

"Kiss your father for me," she said when it came time for him to board. "Elaine, too. I'll see you soon, sweetheart."

He gave her a long hug, his little arms squeezing her ribs. Susan's eyes misted, but she managed to control herself until after he had disappeared through the door of the jetway with one of the flight attendants.

She could not tear herself away from the departure lounge until the plane had pulled back from the gate. She made her way down the endless O'Hare corridors, avoiding the gaze of passersby who might recognize her from all the recent publicity. She wiped at her tears, but they kept coming. Somehow Michael's departure had crystallized all the pain and loneliness inside her.

She drove to the office, planning to see her regular Tuesday patients until it was time to call the airline and make sure the flight had arrived safely.

Her answering service had a message from Ron Giordano. She called him right away.

"How would you feel about dinner with me tonight?" he asked.

"Dinner?" Susan felt herself blush. The receiver trembled slightly against her ear.

"At that Japanese place we talked about. Hatsuhana. Remember?"

"Oh. Yes. Of course."

"Is it a bad night for you?"

"No," she said. "It's a good night. I'm glad you called."

"Great. I'll look forward to it. I've missed you, Susan."

Susan looked at the clock on her desk. By now Michael was airborne, somewhere over the Great Plains.

"I've missed you, too." Something weakened inside her as she remembered all she knew about Ron Giordano. She would not be alone tonight. She felt an almost pious gratitude that embarrassed her.

"You might consider wearing a disguise," he said. "You're pretty famous around here, you know."

"Don't worry about it. I can shrink into nothing when I put my mind to it." But she was already thinking about what she would wear tonight. She wanted to look pretty.

"I'll pick you up, then. Seven o'clock?"

"Seven. Sounds wonderful." The relief in her voice was palpable.

She hung up and sat through sessions with two patients, eyeing the clock despite herself. She was alone for the lunch hour. She was far too nervous to eat, because of Michael and because of Ron Giordano. She called the airline and was told the flight would arrive on schedule.

Her first afternoon patient, the woman with the double life, rambled inconsequentially about her husband's relatives. Susan tried hard to concentrate on what was being said. But she felt drained of the courage for analytical thought today.

At last, at two o'clock, she was alone. She was about to call the airline one last time when the phone rang. It was Elaine in California. She had convinced the answering service to put her through directly.

"Elaine," Susan said. "How are you? How is Michael?"

There was a brief sound of distress on the other end of the phone. It sufficed to freeze Susan's hand around the receiver.

"Susan, Michael didn't get off the plane. He's not here."

PART FOUR

30

KIDNAPPING IS A federal crime. The FBI's Los Angeles and Chicago offices entered the case within thirty minutes of Susan's frantic call to David Gold. FBI agents arrived at LAX in time to stop the plane from making its return flight.

The attendants who had worked the flight had not seen Michael. His empty seat had been noticed, and the chief flight attendant had radioed ahead to LAX and back to O'Hare to report his absence.

Later that day the passengers who had sat in the surrounding seats were located, two of them still in Los Angeles and a third in Hawaii, where he was starting a monthlong vacation. All of them recalled the empty seat in the middle of row 27. None of them recalled seeing a little boy.

The attendant who had accompanied Michael from the departure lounge down the jetway had not been located. Though Susan recalled her as a tallish, middle-aged woman with auburn hair, she could not pick the face out of the directory of airline employees. She thought she had noticed a name tag on the woman's lapel, but her view had been fleeting. Even under hypnosis she could not remember the name on the tag. The woman's description was being circulated among airline personnel, but so far nothing had come of it.

The flight attendants were still being questioned when David Gold arrived in Los Angeles. The LAPD and FBI agents brought him up to date on the situation. Obviously the boy had been kidnapped. But there seemed no reason to suspect the crew or attendants of anything other than being normally harried airline professionals who had done their jobs in a normal way and had not noticed the little boy who was now missing.

Gold was not satisfied with these secondhand accounts and had a talk with one of the flight attendants. She was a bright, no-nonsense woman named Donna who had twenty-six years' experience and was willing to skip over the usual assurances.

"What do you think of this?" he asked her.

"It was a combination of bad luck on our part and real know-how on the part of the perpetrators," she said. "For instance, the boy was wearing a red-and-white-striped button, which indicates that he is a UM—unaccompanied minor. All our personnel are alert to that. Since the button wasn't issued at the gate, they assumed it came from the ticket counter. So we let it pass without stopping him."

"What about the woman who took him into the jetway?" Gold asked.

"That's where the know-how comes in," Donna said. "She was wearing the uniform of one of our concierges. She had a name tag. No one recognized her, but that's not unusual. She was the key to the abduction."

"What do you think happened?" Gold asked.

"Well, there is a stairway on the way to the jetway," she said. "It leads to operations areas downstairs. I think she took the boy down that stairway. From the basement you can get to the bowels of the airport, which is a whole city. There are alleyways, conveyor belts, baggage carts, even traffic signals. It goes on forever, particularly at O'Hare. She must have had a confederate down there. These people knew what they were doing. They only had a few seconds to work with, and they got the boy."

"What about after the takeoff?" Gold asked. "You noticed he was missing, didn't you?"

"Sure. We searched the bathrooms and overhead bins and radioed to the company to tell them that the passenger on the manifest was not on the plane."

"Why didn't you call the police or the FBI right then?" Gold asked.

Donna was lighting a cigarette. She shook her head, a slight smile on her lips.

"The company doesn't like to call in the law until it has done its own search. Quite frankly, the aim is to avoid embarrassment. In a case like this they would check all the bathrooms and common areas at O'Hare to see if the boy was asleep somewhere or if some sort of mix-up had occurred. And they would ask all the employees what they might have seen. Only after all that was finished would they call the law."

"Why didn't they inform the parents from the air?" Gold asked.

"Same thing." She shrugged. "They wouldn't want to push the panic button until it was absolutely necessary. They would page the parents at the gate of the arrival airport. That's the way it works."

"Kind of rough on the parents, isn't it?" Gold observed, thinking especially of Michael's stepmother, Elaine, who had been alone at the gate when she found out the boy was not on the plane.

Donna nodded. "This kind of thing isn't supposed to happen. And, to give us some credit, Detective, the fact is that it almost never does. We're set up to prevent it—not to deal with it after it happens."

Gold shook her hand. "Thanks for your honesty."

"No problem." Donna blew smoke out of the side of her mouth. "I just hope you get him back."

Gold could only nod.

That evening he met Susan's ex-husband, Nick, who was being questioned by L.A. detectives as well as FBI agents. Nick, an attorney, understood that he was of necessity a suspect and gave full cooperation to the officers despite his obvious worry about his son. He was younger and handsomer than Gold had expected.

Gold also met Elaine. She was a pretty woman with freckled skin and strawberry blond hair who was probably vivacious by nature. One could not tell now, though, for she was clearly drained by her anxiety over Michael.

Gold interviewed Nick alone in the den of his three-bedroom tract home.

"Susan has told me a lot about you. She thinks very highly of you." It was Nick who said these words to Gold.

"Really?" Gold said. "Well, we all think highly of her too. She's a hell of a professional."

"Yes. She always was." Something in Nick's voice suggested that Susan's workaholism had perhaps played a role in the failure of her marriage. Susan had always avoided talking about this part of her past with Gold.

"I'm worried about what this is going to do to her," Gold said. "Michael is everything to her. She's sure to feel that her work with me is behind what's happened."

"Is it?" Nick was watching Gold carefully.

"It may be," Gold admitted. "But we have to follow every possible lead. Can you think of anyone in your own life who could have been involved in this?"

Nick shook his head. "My work is pretty routine. I'm not important enough to make enemies."

"No recent cases that have made you concerned?" Gold pursued.

"Nothing at all."

"What about on the personal level?" Gold asked. "Any old acquaintances who might have it in for you or for Susan?"

Nick shook his head.

"Old girlfriends?" Gold asked.

"No."

"Newer girlfriends?" Gold pursued.

Nick gave him a look. "No girlfriends at all. You're barking up the wrong tree, Lieutenant."

Gold shrugged. "We have to ask everything. Especially in a case like this. You know that, Mr. Swain."

"Sure. I understand. I just want you to be aware that there is nothing on this end that will help you. You don't have to take my word, but don't let anything slow you down."

"I won't," Gold said. "We're already proceeding on the other stuff. Don't worry about that."

Nick nodded. He knew Gold meant Susan and the Coed Murders case.

"How is your wife holding up?" Gold asked.

"As well as can be expected," Nick said. "She's a strong woman. But it's not easy. She's very close to Michael. Waiting for him at that gate at the airport and not seeing him come out—it took a lot out of her. She can't sleep, she can't eat. That sort of thing."

"Has she been crying?"

"We've both been crying, Lieutenant."

Gold nodded in acknowledgment. "I was going to ask how it's affecting you."

Nick sighed. "Michael is a very special boy . . ."

"I know."

"That's right. I forgot. You do know." In these words Gold heard a hint of jealousy. Nick must have often heard Michael speak of Gold. To a small boy the life of a homicide detective must have seemed far more exciting than that of a civil liberties lawyer.

"There are certain people in life," Nick said, "who seem more important somehow. It's as though . . ." He thought for a moment. "I want to say they're touched by God. But that's not quite what I mean. They're different. They seem to have one foot in a higher element than the rest of us. Your heart goes out to them. Michael is such a person. I would feel something special for him even if he wasn't my son."

Gold nodded. He was struggling to contain his own feelings for Michael. He knew what Nick meant. There

was an innocence, even a saintliness about the boy that
made it hard to be dispassionate about him.

"The same goes for Susan," Nick added. And, seeing
the look in Gold's eyes, he added, "Oh, it didn't stop our
marriage from breaking up. But it made it very difficult for
me to let her go. It was the reason I married her in the first
place." He looked at Gold. "You know what I mean."

"No, I don't," Gold said.

"She's psychic, of course. You know that." Again Nick
paused to ponder. "But she's different in other ways. Even
her second sight is connected to a kind of sensitivity. . . .
She's not an ordinary woman."

Gold knew what Nick meant. In that instant he could
see how badly the divorce had scarred him. Perhaps Nick
had never really got over Susan. That was something for
Gold to ponder.

"Anyway, Michael is the center of our world—Elaine's
and mine," Nick concluded. "The idea of him being in
danger, being harmed by someone . . . It's really unbearable." His eyes had misted.

"I know how you feel," Gold said. "And I want you to
know that I think he's safe. We're going to get him back."

Nick brightened. An eager, almost supplicating look
came into his eyes.

"Do you really think so?" he asked.

"Definitely." Gold spoke with conviction, though he
was not sure he was telling the truth.

"Please keep in touch, Lieutenant," Nick said. "I know
you're close to Michael. It would help me and Elaine if . . ."

"If someone with a personal stake were in touch." Gold
nodded. "I understand."

They shook hands. Gold headed for his hotel, certain
now that Nick Swain had nothing to do with his son's
disappearance.

WHILE GOLD WAS in Los Angeles, Susan remained at home,
waiting for a ransom call. Two detectives and an FBI man
were in the apartment, their phones set up in the living

room. A social worker was on hand to keep an eye on Susan and offer assistance as necessary. Susan stayed in the kitchen or in her bedroom.

Carolyn had taken time off from work to remain at home. She was in an anxiety state bordering on panic. She paced the apartment, tears running down her cheeks. She managed to make coffee—terrible coffee—for the officers and to run downstairs now and then to buy doughnuts or sandwiches. She was making an effort to be helpful and responsible, but her emotion made her difficult to be around.

Susan was as still as a statue. Since her interrogation by the FBI men she had barely said a word to anyone. So profound was her silence that the officers would have suspected her of being involved in the boy's disappearance had they not already checked her out thoroughly.

Gold got back from California late Thursday morning, having taken the red-eye so as not to make Susan wait longer than absolutely necessary. They talked in her bedroom. She listened in silence to his news.

"Michael didn't leave O'Hare," Gold said. "On that I'm sure. Everybody saw the empty seat. The stewardesses aren't lying."

Susan nodded, not meeting Gold's eyes.

"We added him to the APB on Haze," Gold said. "But I have to know whether you have any other suspicions."

"Suspicions?" Susan asked.

"How about your patients?" Gold asked. "Anybody who would be capable of a thing like this?"

Susan shook her head. "No."

"You're satisfied about your ex-husband?" he asked. "No concerns there?"

"None at all. Nick loves Michael. He would have no reason."

"I just wanted to hear you say it." Gold nodded.

"How is Nick?" she asked.

"He's okay. He's worried."

"Did you meet Elaine?"

Gold nodded. "She's all right. We left some people with them. They'll handle their end."

He sat back, looking at Susan.

"How about some of the bad guys we've put away in the past?" he asked. "I've been thinking about them myself, on the plane. Anybody with that type of grudge?"

Susan sighed. "I don't think so." The notion did not seem to have occurred to her.

"I'm putting a couple of men on it anyway," Gold said. "Just to make sure."

Susan nodded, obviously without hope.

"Have you had any feelings?" he asked.

She looked down at her hands. They were frozen.

"Haze," she said.

Gold nodded. "That's my take, too. He's got the motive. We'll proceed on that."

Gold could see the effort Susan was making to control herself. It was difficult to look at her face.

"You gonna be okay?" he asked, trying to sound business-like without being unkind.

Susan's response was a small, tense nod.

"Good. I'm going to get to work. I'll be in touch."

Susan's hand came from nowhere to grasp his wrist.

"David . . ."

She didn't say anything more, but he heard her desperation in the sound of his name on her lips.

He squeezed her hand.

"I'll find him."

Susan's eyes seemed to devour him.

"I'll find him," Gold repeated. "This is my town. I'll pick up his trail."

Abruptly she let him go.

Gold left her in the bedroom and closed the door.

"She says she's all right," the social worker told him. "I don't know. She looks like she's hanging by a thread."

Gold shook his head. "She'll be all right," he said. "Don't worry about her. She's a soldier. She won't do anything as long as she thinks there's a chance he's still alive."

Gritting his teeth, Gold left the apartment.

SUSAN FELT A moment's panic at being abandoned by Gold. She realized she had been gambling most of her self-control on her expectation of his return from California.

Still, she did not fall apart. A prideful impulse made her resolve not to crumble in front of all these police and FBI men.

She remembered all she had learned as a therapist about the effects of loss on normal people as well as neurotics. The ego organization succumbs to regression, and the grandiosity of earliest youth can take over. The person who has suffered the loss becomes convinced that it is his or her own fault. No amount of argument or persuasion from the outside can shake this belief, because it is not conscious.

Suicide is always a risk. Survival can be an intolerable burden when the loved one is gone. Susan knew this first-hand because of her parents. The mark left by her own guilt on her developing personality had been permanent.

But Michael was not gone, not dead. Not yet.

Susan recalled Gold's reassuring words and her own weighing of them. The overwhelming probability was that Michael had been abducted by Arnold Haze. Any other construction of the facts would be too remote. If Haze was the abductor, it followed that he had taken Michael in order to pressure the authorities to let Haze himself escape unmolested. There was every probability that he would keep Michael alive as a bargaining chip.

Susan was able to see the wisdom of this logic even as the roiling of her emotions tried to obscure it. "Common sense," she kept repeating to herself. "Wait and see. Don't anticipate."

But the voice inside her was repeating, *You did it to him before, and now you've done it again. Again, again . . .*

She sat looking out her window at the buildings behind.

The city seemed poised around her, waiting. She listened to the beating of her heart. She felt a coldness in her extremities. A peculiar vertigo had taken possession of her, riveting her to the spot while making her feel as though she was about to fly through the walls. Her jaw ached. She must have been grinding her teeth.

Again, again, the voice repeated.

She felt something wet in her hand. She looked down and saw that both her palms were bleeding. She had dug her fingernails through the skin.

It was not until twelve hours later, in the dead of night, that Carolyn convinced her to eat something. She pushed the food into her mouth without tasting it. Then she took a shower and got into bed. Sleep was an impossibility. She looked forward obsessively to David Gold's next call or visit. She felt like a child, entirely dependent on him as she had once been on her mother. There was nothing to think or to feel until he came back.

Her tears still did not come.

31

THAT NIGHT MICHAEL'S picture appeared on the evening news. It was a photograph Susan had never seen before. One of the FBI men explained that they had visited the photographer who took the pictures of her and Michael a few days ago. He had rushed through the developing of this picture.

The portrait showed a smiling Michael who looked palpably older than the boy in any of Susan's other photos.

His face was longer, his cheekbones were changing, and his eyes looked more mature.

The photo looked macabre and alien, projected on the television screen under a graphic, MISSING. Susan could only bear to look at it for an instant.

By evening's end Michael's image had been seen on all the networks and cable stations as well as the local news outlets. Susan herself was a celebrity, so the disappearance of her son was a hot news item.

The photograph was circulated. Chicago police questioned every employee at O'Hare as well as the bus and cab drivers who were at the airport the day of the boy's disappearance. The parking lot employees were questioned. Every hotel and motel in the city was visited. The state police combed the interstate highways for witnesses who might have seen a man and a little boy in a car, at a toll booth, or at a rest area.

Law-enforcement agencies nationwide were alerted to the fact that Arnold Haze and the missing boy were connected. Now that Haze had been promoted to the FBI's Most Wanted list, there could be no doubt that the search had top priority. Police departments from every state were in touch with Chicago, promising all the manpower they could provide.

Luck was not on the side of the authorities. Just as the search was moving into high gear a major snowstorm hit the midsection of the country, brought by frigid Canadian air and a gigantic low-pressure system over the Great Lakes. Over a foot of snow fell, drifting in the high winds. Most of the interstate highways had to be closed Thursday night and Friday. Power failures left thousands of homes and offices without heat.

Traffic in Chicago slowed to a standstill, then almost disappeared as city workers decided to stay home for the duration. David Gold found himself looking out the window at FBI Headquarters and seeing drifts climbing street signs under a strange blue light as afternoon waned.

"Great," he said.

"Dave, you want some coffee?"

Tom Castaneda, the senior FBI agent on Michael's case, had just returned to the office. He carried a Styrofoam cup through which beads of black coffee were oozing by a process of sublimation that Gold had never understood. The sight of it disgusted him.

"No, thanks," Gold said. "I've had enough."

Castaneda sat down behind his desk.

"Any news?" Gold asked.

"Nothing. We're going to be pretty much nowhere until this snow lets up. Just our luck."

Castaneda was a handsome man who would have looked slightly effeminate had it not been for the peculiarly harsh shape of his lips. He was highly educated, with degrees in forensics and sociology to go with his B.A. from the University of Illinois. Eight years ago he had worked with Gold on the Chad Bose multiple murder case and taken a bullet in the chest from the barricaded Bose while Gold looked on. Castaneda's refined manners belied the fact that he was as tough as they came. He was Gold's closest friend in the Bureau.

"Look at that," Gold said. "Even Mother Nature is out to get us."

Castaneda stared out the window for a moment, saying nothing.

"You know," Gold said, "I don't think Haze ever intended to kill the Lazarus girl."

Gold had fallen into the habit of talking in non sequiturs. His mind was in a riot of speculation about various aspects of the case. He blurted out ideas in the midst of conversations on other topics, or out of thin air.

Castaneda was used to it by now. "What do you mean?" he asked.

"I think he was gonna abduct her," Gold said, turning from the window. "Think about it. By that time he had to know we were on to him. We were going to be coming after him for multiple murder. His idea of eliminating witnesses was already old turkey. Jaime would have been more valuable to him as a hostage."

"You may be right." Castaneda nodded, putting his feet on his desktop. "I'm glad he didn't get her. It would have been Lindbergh all over again."

"Anyway," Gold continued, "when he missed his chance with her, he looked for the next best thing. Susan's son was right there."

"Uh-huh."

There was a silence. Gold had been stung by Castaneda's reference to the Lindbergh baby.

"I can't see him just killing the boy," he said. "The situation hasn't changed. Only the hostage has. Michael is worth more to him alive than dead."

"I hope so." Castaneda was maddeningly noncommittal.

"On the other hand, a little boy would slow him down." Gold was trying not to hide from the truth. He had the superstitious feeling that if he articulated all the negative possibilities honestly, they might not come to pass. "And Haze will be easier to spot with a kid in tow than alone."

"Alone we'd never get him," Castaneda said. "He's got so much experience at running. And he knows the law-enforcement community."

"You're right."

Again there was a silence. Gold drummed his fingers on the windowsill.

"I'm betting he hangs on to the kid until he's out of the country," he said.

"Why?" Castaneda seemed interested.

"On the international level his cover is blown," Gold said. "He spent a lot of years keeping out of sight. Now the whole world knows about Tomerakian and about the five dead women. That creates extradition problems. It won't be easy for Haze to find a home."

"So?" Castaneda asked.

"So he won't want to give up anything until he has to," Gold said. "He'll keep the boy alive as a way to make us help him find that safe haven. He'll want to be extradition-proof."

Castaneda nodded. "Maybe."

"Of course, there are countries that don't mind harboring murderers," Gold added. "Your own files show Haze has connections in Libya."

There I go again, he thought. He could not stop playing the devil's advocate, tormenting himself with pessimistic arguments about Michael's chances.

Castaneda said nothing. He knew Gold well enough to see how agitated he was. Many of the things Gold was saying did not require responses. They were just the ruminations of a cop who cared too much about this case, a cop who felt responsible.

The phone rang. It was for Castaneda. Gold tuned him out as he stood staring out the window. Snow was whipping this way and that between the downtown buildings. Yet even in the heart of this storm an experienced Chicagoan could sense spring in the air. It was often said that the city's weather consisted of July, August, and winter. Gray skies and frigid wind were the only things one could depend on. There was truth in this. Spring was a subtle variation on the nasty skies of February and March. There were no such things as fragrant blossoms and balmy Easter weather here.

Susan used to complain about it when she was expecting Michael's visits.

"All he gets in California is sun and pollution," she would say. "I wish I could give him the air I breathed as a little girl in Pennsylvania. Sometimes it was so dewy and fresh that you felt you were drinking it instead of breathing it. Here the air is something you fight."

Gold had sympathized with her. But Chicago was all he knew. He had long since made his peace with the relentless ugliness of the weather here. When Susan spoke of Pennsylvania, she might as well have been describing Tahiti. He could only listen with his imagination.

The memory of her easygoing words made him nervous

again, for he compared it mentally with the tormented look in her eyes the previous morning. If he didn't get Michael back for her, he might never see her old smile again.

He could not help reproaching himself for what had happened to Michael. He felt he should have scented impending trouble when he first learned that Jaime Lazarus had escaped Haze. He knew Haze well enough to know he was a fighter. Haze would not simply turn tail and run after missing his chance with Jaime. He would look for another advantage. Susan's small son was a perfect choice.

A smart cop would have seen this coming. A smart cop would have put Susan and her son into protective custody until there was proof Haze was far away. But David Gold had not thought of this. The sighting of Haze at the Miami Airport had fooled him, as it had everybody else.

This was the logical side of Gold's self-reproach. The less logical side was his memory of having single-handedly brought Susan into the business of law enforcement. It was he who had convinced her to become a police consultant. He clearly recalled how eloquently he had spoken of the drama of police work, the feeling of satisfaction when crimes are solved and perpetrators are put behind bars.

Susan had been impressed. "That must be a good feeling," she told him at the time. "We psychiatrists have to live with constant ambiguity. Very often we can look back on our best work with patients and still wonder if we really helped anybody. Life after therapy is often almost as painful as life without it."

Gold had pressed his advantage, promising Susan concrete results when her psychic instincts were combined with thorough police work. Out of the first six cases she had worked on with him, three had resulted in convictions. After that she was hooked.

Then came the case that cost her custody of her son. Though it was a federal affair in which Gold had not been directly involved, the danger to Michael—then an infant—had been enormous. Susan had had no choice but to give up the boy, for the sake of his own safety.

She had never reproached Gold for this, not even by a hint or a look. But he still felt responsible. And now Michael was gone, perhaps dead, because of the work Susan had done for Gold. It was almost impossible to bear this.

And there was another dimension to Gold's guilt. In a subtle way he had allowed himself to come to depend on Susan. She was smarter than he was, after all. Better educated. And, in some ways, tougher. He trusted her judgment, sometimes more than his own.

Though she was younger than he, and very attractive, he had always found himself drawn by the maternal side of her. This may have had something to do with the fact that she was a physician and a psychiatrist. She was used to being strong for others. This showed through clearly when he saw her with Michael.

In the end Gold had come to feel a secret dependency on Susan. He tried never to show it and affected toward her a paternal, protective attitude, which she responded to. But it was always there, adding a seductive warmth to his friendship with her. And it had lulled him into believing too much in her competence. After she single-handedly rescued Jaime Lazarus, he simply did not think of the possibility of something bad befalling Susan herself. He forgot that she was human.

For all these reasons Gold felt a desperate need to get Michael back unharmed. He suspected there was more to this than merely wishing to undo his own mistake. It seemed like the most important mission of his life.

Castaneda had hung up the phone.

"We've got nothing," he said. "The interstates are drawing a blank on the pictures. Airports and train stations too. Hotels and motor inns are slower, but so far nothing."

Gold turned suddenly from the window.

"You know what?" he said. "I think he's here. I bet the bastard never even left the city."

"What makes you think that?" Castaneda asked.

"He came here to do a job," Gold said. "He killed Tomerakian. When that didn't finish the job, he killed the women, one by one. He's thorough. He's sure of himself. He's not afraid of us. I think he's going to finish the job right here. He's gonna make us escort him right out of the country."

Castaneda was toying with his unlit cigarette.

"He's that arrogant?" he asked.

"Yeah," Gold said. "If arrogant is the right word. Relentless might be a better one."

"It's risky," Castaneda said.

"What is?"

"Hanging around. Trying to make a deal. If it was me I would run like hell."

"You would." Gold had put both hands on Castaneda's desk and was looking into his eyes.

"Yeah. I would get out of this country and not show my face for a long time. All those murder indictments—that's too much."

Gold was leaning forward, his face close to that of his friend. But it was Gold's eyes that looked evasive and worried.

"So you wouldn't need the boy," he said.

Castaneda was holding the coffee cup, still bleeding little drops of dark liquid through the Styrofoam.

"No," he said. "I wouldn't."

Gold turned away.

32

TIME WAS PART of his mother.

For as long as he could remember, the passage of night into day or day into night had been part of his mother's love. The lightening of the morning sky outside the windows was a premonitory sign of her smiling face, soon to appear at his bedroom door. By the same token, the sighing of day toward darkness was the first note in a melody that led to her good-night kiss.

Each hour was part of her protection, from the busy hours of morning play to the gentler, heavier hours of afternoon that sometimes brought his nap and sometimes brought wakefulness. He was old enough to know what an alarm clock was, but he had never needed one. There was no hour that did not know the sound of her voice, her reminders of what time it was, her promises of what they would do today, tonight, tomorrow.

And so, if she was gone now, this must mean that she was coming back. She was the one who made plans in life. This silence must be part of her plan. She would return.

He surveyed the space around him and thought of his own bed. The curtains in the window came back to him, brightly colored and heavy in his room in California, sheer as a white ghost in his mother's apartment in Chicago. The bed, wider in California but cozier in Chicago. Walls, different in each place. Decorative pictures of animals on the yellow wall painted by Elaine. Mysterious photographs on the wall in Mother's apartment.

Funny, he thought, how a person was divided between places. First one, then another, then back again. You could wake up in the morning, or after a nap, and not remember at first where you were. Your body was prepared for either place. In that first moment your cheek would ask the pillow which home this was. Your hand, resting on the sheet, would touch the covers. Were they the light blankets used out west, or the heavier comforter that Mother always brought out for him in Chicago? Which voice would he hear next? Which breakfast would he eat?

But both places were really Mother. Because no matter where you roamed it would be her voice that called you back, reminding you of where you lived. And no matter

how far your dreams took you, it was she who would wake
you up with her gentle "Wake up, sleepyhead."

Sometimes he tried to remember a time from before her
voice. But it was impossible. It seemed he had awakened
to life itself in her voice and her arms. He had never been
without her. And even before he came to the world, she
was planning for him, waiting for him.

"I thought about nothing but you for all those months,"
she told him once. "I kept busy decorating your room and
buying toys and things for your crib. I looked around the
house and imagined you in it. I sat for hours just holding
my tummy and feeling you move. I spoke to you and
asked, 'When are you coming out? I can't wait!' I wanted
to meet you, you see. You were part of me, and I could
hardly wait for you to be part of the world too."

That was his world—a place prepared for him by her.
She had been waiting for him all along. And if he could not
remember what it was like to live inside her body, that did
not matter so much. The world he knew was still her love.

Where was she now? Planning for him. Waiting for
him. How could it be otherwise?

He thought back on the time of the terrible earaches.
They had started one day in the fall when he had played
with her in Lincoln Park and the first frosts were coming.
That afternoon he had had to go to bed and had pulled the
covers around his face, clenching his teeth so as not to cry
too much. She had taken him to the doctor right down the
street. The doctor gave him drops and the pain ebbed.
Later he lay groggy and exhausted in the same bed. She
never left his side.

The earaches kept coming back. The pain was inside. It
seemed to know him better than he knew himself. And he
could never fool her. When the pain was just starting, and
he was still trying to keep it at bay, she would ask, "Is it
starting to hurt?" And she would help him. The sound of
her voice was almost more powerful against the pain than
the drops.

For a while he thought the earaches would never end.

But the doctor talked about the damp weather, the lake air, his young age. He said they would go away, and in the end they did.

And what about this pain? Would it go away too? Was it worse than the earaches? It was inside too, after all.

Why didn't she come? It was dark and he was alone and this was not his home. He kept telling himself that Mama would come. She would hear his voice even before he called out. She would come to get him and take him home. She would put clothes on him so he would not be naked. And this pain would go away as the earaches had gone away. And he would not be alone.

It hurts, it hurts . . .

SUSAN WOKE UP screaming. David Gold heard her first and burst through the door. He held her hands down so she would not hurt herself, and then put his arms around her. She screamed for a long time. The officers in the living room were alarmed. When the sounds began to die down to sobs, they looked at each other and let out low whistles of acknowledgment.

The female officer could not stand it and had to be relieved.

33

TEN DAYS PASSED.

The FBI agents were growing more pessimistic. In cases of child abduction, the lack of a ransom demand within a couple of days of the disappearance nearly always means the child has been killed.

The search had been extended to airports and other points of entry throughout South America. It was known that Arnold Haze had made his home there for years. Perhaps he would get off a plane with the boy. It seemed remote, but it was possible. Haze knew he was holding an important card. He might want to show it.

Some of the media respected Susan's painful situation. Others did not. Reporters and sound trucks were camped outside her apartment building in even greater numbers than during the Kyle Stewart episode. A police detail was on the scene around the clock to keep them out of the building.

The FBI would not allow Susan to go to her office. The security there was less tight, and she was needed at home in the event of a ransom call. Another psychiatrist was covering her patients for the duration of the crisis.

Susan had lost a lot of weight. She must weigh below a hundred pounds by now. Her cheeks were sunken. Her pallor alarmed Carolyn. She tried to eat but could keep very little down. She lay on her bed for hours, staring at the ceiling. Even David Gold had difficulty conversing with her, so haunted was the look in her eyes.

Gold was already thinking of ways to help Susan through her bereavement. And he had his own to think about. He could feel the pull of grief sapping his energy. His own appetite was gone. His eyes had the sunken look of irremediable sorrow in the mirror. He believed Michael was dead. The son he had never had, the only son he wanted.

Abel Weathers came down from his ivory tower long enough to visit Susan. When he left her he seemed drained.

"That was hard," he told Gold.

"I know."

"She looks like a bomb went off inside her."

Gold could only nod. He felt like a family member keeping vigil over a patient with a terminal illness.

"Do you think there's still a chance?" Weathers asked.

Gold looked at him. "What do you think?"

Weathers flushed with anger. "If I ever catch up to that bastard . . ."

He left after shaking Gold's hand. For the first time since Gold had met him, Weathers seemed genuinely touched by the plight of another human being.

The day after Weathers's visit one of the cops on duty called Gold to the front door of the apartment.

"Should I let him in?" he asked, gesturing to a tall figure in the hall.

"Let me handle it."

Gold opened the door. Aaron Lazarus was standing before him, his hat in one hand, the other extended in greeting.

"Susan will be grateful when she hears you came," Gold said. "But I don't think it's best that you see her." Gold was thinking of Jaime Lazarus. Susan had saved Lazarus's daughter at the price of her own son. The sight of Lazarus's face could only remind her of that.

"Who said anything about seeing her?" Lazarus asked, a supercilious look on his face.

"Then why are you here?" Gold asked.

"I can sit, can't I?"

Gold thought it over. Then he smiled.

"We have a lady here who makes the worst coffee in the world," he said. "Are you up for that?"

"Detective, I know all about bad coffee."

Gold stood back to let Lazarus through. "I guess you do at that."

GOLD SPENT COUNTLESS hours with Tom Castaneda and the others, going over every angle of the case. Phone calls came in sporadically from colleagues around the country. Always the news was bad. No progress. Another witness turned out to have seen nothing.

The investigation would soon enter its cosmetic phase. The work would go on, but there would be no more hope of success.

Then the ransom note came.

It arrived in a clumsily wrapped package addressed to

the Chicago PD. The note itself was scrawled on an eight-by-ten-inch piece of notepaper. It was sandwiched between two pieces of dentist's clay.

The package was postmarked Seattle.

The FBI's handwriting experts worked on the note while Michael's dentist was flown in from California. A meeting was held at eight o'clock that evening. Present were Weathers, two of his assistant DAs, three detectives, two FBI agents, and a bite-mark specialist from the ME's office. Also at the conference table was a middle-aged man with silver hair and a deep tan. His name was Dr. Saylor. He was Michael's dentist.

Weathers looked excited. Gold could not tell whether this was because he hoped Michael was alive or because he smelled good publicity in the ransom demand.

"First things first," Weathers said. "Do we have a match?"

Dr. Saylor nodded. "I did some X rays on Michael only last November," he said. "I have a lot of notes on his teeth. Two of the molars are just growing in. This mold was taken from Michael's mouth. I feel sure of it." He seemed shaken as he held the mold in his hands.

"What about the mold itself?" One of the detectives had leaned forward. "Any clue as to where it came from?"

"No luck," said one of the FBI men. "It's a standard dentist's mold. It could have come from any of a hundred dental supply houses. We're running a check on all the local ones, but we don't have much hope."

Gold turned to the ME's assistant. "Does the mold look postmortem to you?" he asked.

The assistant, a pretty young woman whose long auburn hair was tied back in a ponytail, shook her head. "Can't tell," she said. "If the boy was in rigor, it would have been hard to get the mold into his mouth. But rigor lasts only about eight hours. The mold could have been inserted later. Unfortunately, any postmortem changes in the mouth itself would not be reflected in the mold. The material is too hard to take an impression other than the teeth."

"So we have no idea whether he's dead or alive," Weathers said, touching the tips of his fingers together in a steeple shape.

"No, sir. No way to know."

The ransom note was on the overhead projector.

I HAVE THE BOY, it read. THREE MILLION DOLLARS SMALL BILLS UNMARKED. WAIT FOR MY CALL.

"Any ideas?" Weathers asked the others.

Gold said, "My guess is the money demand is just a blind. He wants more than money."

"Is the boy alive?" Weathers pursued.

The FBI men shrugged.

Gold pressed his point. "I think he already has another plan. The whole kidnapping angle is just a way to gain time and to keep us off balance."

"You may be right," Weathers said. "But does it affect the question of the boy? Is a live hostage still useful to him?"

Again the table was silent. No one knew the answer.

"One thing is sure," Weathers said. "He waited ten days just to soften us up. The boy's picture is everywhere. The media are going nuts. The whole city is on the edge of its seat. I'd say Haze has pretty much got the leverage he wanted."

"And another thing," Castaneda threw in. "Haze is holed up pretty good. He's lasted this long without us getting a line on him. He can afford to play it slow. Wherever he is, he feels safe."

Weathers sighed in exasperation.

"So how do we proceed?" he asked. "Like any kidnapping?"

"I think so." It was the senior FBI man who spoke. "When he calls, we negotiate. We ask for proof the boy is still alive. We discuss the ransom, the pickup."

"And we learn what we can," Weathers said. "And pray that it is enough."

"If you want to play it that way," said Castaneda.

"What way?" Weathers asked.

"If you want to seriously try to get the boy back."

There was a silence. Everyone knew it was possible to give up on getting Michael back alive and to concentrate on collaring Haze before he escaped the country. Indeed, this game plan could be adopted in secret, while the press was told everything possible was being done to save the boy.

Weathers now showed a sincerity Gold had never seen in him before.

"Fuck that. We're going to get the boy back," he said.

The agents nodded. David Gold breathed a sigh.

"Now let's proceed to the note," Weathers said.

Castaneda introduced Roy Cunningham, a document and handwriting analyst from Quantico. Cunningham, a handsome agent who looked like a younger and slimmer John Travolta, opened his briefcase. He produced enlarged photographs on a special glossy paper.

"The block printing doesn't tell us much," he said, "but we got lucky with the note itself. Let me show you some exhibits."

He passed the photographs around the table.

"This is a new technique in document analysis pioneered by the Secret Service," he said. "You place your target document onto a metal mesh surface and stretch a special plastic material tightly across the top. Sort of like Saran Wrap. The object is to suck the document and the plastic tight onto the mesh. Then you use a chemical similar to the toner from a copying machine, which clings to the electrostatically charged areas. When you pull the original document away from the superimposed plate, all the latent images on the page become apparent."

"What are latent images?" Gold asked.

"If the document came from a pad or a stack of paper, we're talking about things written on the pages above the subject page," Cunningham said. "Not only can we see what was written but we can determine the sequence in which the pages were written and torn off. In other words, which pages were above which pages. We can also determine which words were rewritten, if any."

He pointed at the photographs making the rounds.

"It so happens that our ransom note was torn off a pad," he said. "We have impressions from three other pages that were on the pad above the page the note was written on. They make interesting reading."

David Gold was handed the photographs. To his eye the writing on the missing pages was indecipherable.

"What does it say?" he asked.

"The page right on top of the ransom note had an address written on it," Cunningham said. "10385 Dearlove Road. That's in a condominium complex up in Glenview, near the air base."

Gold looked closely at the shadowy tracings in the photograph. Gradually the writing came into focus.

"So what's in Glenview?" he asked.

"I'm coming to that." Cunningham pointed to the second photograph. "On the next page we have the following memo: *ORD-LAX 453 3/11 2:25 P.M.*"

"A flight from Chicago to L.A.," Gold said.

"But not the one Michael was to fly on," Castaneda put in.

"What's the deal?" Gold asked. "Was he checking out flights for himself?"

"We're not sure," Cunningham said. "But we're checking out the passenger list from this flight. Something might turn up."

The third page was even harder to read than the first two. Gold squinted at it but could not make out the message.

"You guys have better eyes than I do," he said.

Cunningham smiled. "We computer-enhanced it. We couldn't see it with the naked eye either. But we finally got it. *ATA 733 ORD-MEX $775 × 2.*"

"What's MEX?" Gold asked.

"Mexico City Airport." Cunningham was looking at the

photograph. "It could be that Haze plans to take that flight. You notice that the fare is given for two people."

"Christ," Gold said. "He wrote his travel arrangements on the same pad as the ransom note."

Cunningham nodded. "People don't realize the technology we have now. There is a common perception that if you press hard you can leave an impression on the pages below the one you're writing on. But no one thinks of impressions that are already on the blank page you're writing on. That's our ace in the hole."

"So what are we gonna do about this?" Weathers asked.

"You'll notice that there is no date given for the Mexico City flight," Cunningham said. "We'll check the passenger lists for all recent dates, and of course from now on. Keeping an eye out for children, of course. And we'll try to foresee any clever tricks Haze might pull."

"What about the pad itself?" Weathers asked. "Any chance of finding it?"

"That's a needle in a haystack," Cunningham said. "But we're checking it out. The pad is standard low-budget office supply. I have some men making the rounds."

Weathers was looking around the table. "That's it, then?" The others nodded.

"Thank you," he said. "You guys keep at it. I'll see about raising three million dollars."

The feeling in the room was truly optimistic for the first time since Michael's disappearance. Arnold Haze had left a trail. A faint one, to be sure. But the men around this table made it their profession to follow faint trails.

34

ARNOLD HAZE WAS watching television.

The face of a Channel 7 reporter was on the screen.

"It was confirmed this morning," she said, "that a ransom demand has been made in the sensational kidnapping of the six-year-old son of psychiatrist and psychic Dr. Susan Shader. At a news conference outside his office, State's Attorney Abel Weathers made the announcement personally."

Haze leaned forward, a glass of Pommard in his hand. The cat darted out of his lap but twined itself affectionately around his legs.

The reporter's face disappeared, replaced by that of the State's Attorney. As usual, Weathers wore his stern, tough-on-criminals look, the eyebrows beetled, the eyes boring into the camera almost accusingly.

"No, I can't provide details about the demand at this time," he said in answer to a question. "It might compromise Michael's safe return."

Using the boy's first name, Haze noted. There was no sense in Weathers seeming uncaring when he had an opportunity to seem loving and protective. His PR man must have suggested that.

A scarcely audible question was called out about the dental mold. Sure enough, Haze reflected, the media's sources within the police department had come through. And been well paid for it.

Weathers stonewalled.

"We have received nothing that might give us a clue to

Michael's whereabouts," he replied irritably. "We are pursuing all avenues to secure his safe release. That's all I want to say for now."

"Mr. State's Attorney," asked another reporter, closer to the microphones, "is there any truth to the rumor that Michael has been taken by the murderer in the Coed Murders case? As a reprisal for Dr. Shader's involvement in the case?"

"No truth," Weathers said.

He was lying. The signs were obvious. One of them was the little flutter of the eyelids as Weathers kept his gaze rigidly on the camera. His ego, knowing his statement was a lie, tried to be somewhere else. Another was the faint tremor of the skin around his ears. Had Weathers's shoulders been visible, a slight shift of the body to the left or right would have been seen. Finally, of course, there was the choice of words. Too dramatic, too stagy. Liars always chose their words for effect, without realizing that this was precisely what gave them away.

Haze had spent years as an interrogator. During that time he had learned a lot of tricks from his colleagues, but even more from his readings in psychology and psychophysiology. There was a vast but disorganized literature on lying and its effects on the body. Though the physical evidence of lying was not admissible in a court of law, the criteria were clearly established and could be demonstrated without error.

Freud's groundbreaking early article "Psychoanalysis and the Ascertaining of Truth in Courts of Law" had stated many of the major themes. It was Freud who realized early on that all human beings are liars, at least where the embarrassing facts of their inner life are concerned. They try hard to hide the truth, but it escapes in a thousand little signs, as subtle as they are eloquent. A specialist can quantify them, but anyone can sense their presence.

Haze sometimes turned on the television just to watch the parade of liars. Politicians, corporate executives, evangelists—they all spoke in the liar's special language.

And lawyers! The Simpson attorneys had put on a better show than the witnesses they were interrogating.

Weathers was lying. He knew there was a connection between the kidnapping and the murder spree. He just didn't want to talk about it.

"Mr. State's Attorney," asked another reporter, "we know that it was Dr. Shader who personally saved Jaime Lazarus from the Coed Killer. Isn't it true that after the rescue of Miss Lazarus there were no significant security measures taken to protect either the doctor or her son?"

"That is not true," Weathers said. "All appropriate security measures were taken. The Chicago Police Department is in no way to blame for Michael's abduction. I might add, though, that we all take this as a personal attack on every member of this law-enforcement team. We will not rest until Michael has been returned safe to his mother, and his abductors brought to justice."

"Are there definite leads to the kidnapper?" several reporters shouted at once.

"Yes, there are," Weathers said. "We expect a prompt resolution to the case."

"Do you think the boy is still alive?" someone asked.

"I most certainly do," Weathers said.

One of the more aggressive reporters decided to press the point.

"Would you tell us if you didn't?"

Anger clouded Weathers's handsome face.

"We're going to bring Michael back to his mother," he said. "I don't have anything more to say."

Haze used his remote control to mute the sound as Weathers's face disappeared from the screen, replaced by the portrait photo of Michael that had been making the rounds for the last week.

Things were about where Haze wanted them to be. The police were playing his game by his rules. He had kept silent for ten days to soften them up. Obviously it had worked. The boy's abduction was national news. The whole country was on the edge of its seat, waiting with its classic mixture of anxiety and sadism for the news that he had been found dead.

They would deal. They had no choice. Susan Shader, a heroine ten days ago for her brilliant police work, was now a celebrated victim whose anguish went to the heart of every parent in America. It was Lindbergh all over again.

"Come on, pussy," Haze said, clucking his tongue. The cat leaped silently into his lap. He put a hand under her forepaws and lifted her up. Her beautiful, jewel-like eyes were close to his face.

"They can't catch us, can they?" he asked, nuzzling the cat against his cheek. "We'll fool them all."

Without knowing precisely why, he thought of the psychic as the cat purred. There was an old myth to the effect that cats were psychic.

"Can you read my mind, puss-puss?" he asked affectionately. "What am I thinking? What am I thinking at this very moment?"

The cat licked his nose with a rough tongue. He tried to kiss her nose, but she pulled back.

"Don't you know?" he asked. "Come on. Don't play hard to get."

She gave him a sharp look and bounded from his grasp. He laughed and raised his glass to his lips. As he did so he turned to look over his shoulder. The door to the bedroom was ajar. He saw the small shape under the blanket.

"Nasty cat," he said to the animal. "You're too smart for your own good."

35

CARDS AND LETTERS were arriving from all over the nation. They expressed a peculiar mixture of evasion and sympathy. Thanks to most people's familiarity with terminal illness, two familiar phrases found their way into nearly all the cards.

Our thoughts are with you.

Our prayers are with you.

Heartfelt though they were, both phrases were appropriate to a situation without hope.

Susan saw some of the cards, but it was Carolyn who took charge of saving them and making plans to answer them. It was a painful task. Obviously they could not be answered for some time. And by the time Susan had leisure to write responses, she would know whether Michael had lived or died.

Susan spent most of her time at the desk in the corner of her bedroom. She read. She worked on her article on schizophrenia. She made notes for a future lecture on the psychic implications of unconscious communication.

Each morning she returned to her desk and looked at her work from the previous day. She did not remember a word of it. When she picked up the book she had been reading, the chapters she had already read looked as fresh as if she had never opened the book before.

Her hands and feet were permanently frozen. No amount of coverings could warm them, not even a hot bath. Slow tremors went through her body as she sat still at her desk. They seemed to start in her stomach and radiate along her spine. A headache had settled itself in her temples and the back of her neck. It had now become so familiar that she did not think to take medication for it. She was grateful for the pain. It proved that she still had some connection to the reality of her flesh.

More and more she found her thoughts straying to the distant past, when as a little girl she had played in the backyard of her parents' house or wandered the meadows and pastures of her little town. Some of the sights and sounds came back to her with startling clarity. She heard the loud buzz of the cicadas in the tree limbs as dusk crept over the lawn. She saw a huge bumblebee loafing through the air over a bed of tulips. She had not thought of those tulips in twenty years.

The purple daisies came back to her, too. And the ancient porcelain sink in the kitchen, where her mother stood washing dishes and looking out the window. There was buttermilk in the refrigerator. The dish towels hung on three stiff rods that swung out from their hinge in the corner. If you weren't careful one of them could poke you in the eye when you ran into the kitchen.

Memorable events from the early years came back as well. There was the time the bird had become trapped in the screened-in porch at the back of the house. Alerted by her mother's shouts, Susan had run in from the backyard and seen the bird flying madly this way and that, striking the screens with the full force of its flight. Bang! Bang! Bang! And her mother frantically waving the broom as she tried to shoo it out through the door. But the bird was too frightened. For a long time it flew back and forth, smashing itself against the screens until they were sure it would break its neck.

She could not recall how it had ended. Had the bird escaped? But she did recall the time the neighborhood boys found the gigantic spider under her window. It had spun its web across the top of the bush and all along the bottom of the window frame. It was a huge, ugly thing, and the boys, out of a misguided sense of chivalry toward Susan, decided to kill it. They stuck pins through it, one after another, the points bringing red drops of blood speckled with gray liquid, while the spider's long legs clenched and shuddered under the torture. Susan hung back, not daring to stop her friends. Finally the beast died, perplexed no doubt in its final throes by this unexpected fate. The boys shouted in triumph as they ground it under a stone.

Susan put her hands over her eyes and took a deep breath. She knew she was losing her grip on herself. Depersonalizing, derealizing—call it what one liked. She was coming unglued. She tried to alter the train of her thoughts, but they had an initiative all their own. She thought of the many patients she had seen in disturbed wards over the years. For the first time she was experiencing something akin to their helplessness. Thoughts, memories, feelings crashed on her like waves. She had no control over them.

CAROLYN WAS ALARMED by the look in Susan's eyes.

"Is she going to be all right?" she asked Gold.

"Let's wait and see what happens," he said. "She'll pull through one way or another. It depends on what she has to get over."

Carolyn shook her head. "I've seen a lot of victims in my work, but they're always on videotape. This is different. This is unbearable."

"Don't worry about it," Gold said, touching her arm. He had never liked Carolyn much. She was too aggressive in her manner and too emotional. She tended to bray her feelings as though she wanted the whole city to rush to her rescue. He knew how self-destructive she was in her relationships with men. This only made him more impatient with her. But now he saw the intensity of her grief over Michael, and her love for Susan. They made Carolyn seem truly human at last.

"How about you?" he asked. "How are you holding up?"

"Don't worry about me," she said. "I'll be all right."

Carolyn was forcing herself to be strong and businesslike in this terrible situation. Her coffee was disgusting, her jerky movements and constant tears were irritating, but she was staying at her post. He had to respect her for that.

"Good for you," he said. "Hang in there."

"By the way," she said, "the package of proofs came in from the photographer. The one who took those portraits of Susan with Michael before . . . before . . ."

She gave Gold a stricken look. "What shall I do?" she asked. "Shall I tell her, at least? I mean, it might upset her, but she should at least know they're here."

"Let me tell her," Gold said, "when I think the time is right."

At that moment one of the detectives came in with a man Gold had not seen before. He was in his thirties, but he seemed younger. He had dark, fine hair, thinning a little atop a narrow brow, and clear blue eyes that surveyed the apartment curiously. He wore jeans and a very old sweater, and carried a threadbare leather jacket over his arm.

Gold moved toward the detective, intending to ask who this was. Before he got there the stranger's eyes had focused on him, and Gold already knew.

"You must be Quentin."

The eyes expressed acknowledgment. So this was the brother of whom Susan had spoken, albeit rarely and laconically, all these years. Gold was amazed by Quentin's appearance. There was no superficial resemblance to Susan, none at all. Quentin was much taller and darker, very different in bone structure and coloring. He looked as though he came from another family entirely, even another country. Yet the look in his eyes and the posture of his body left no doubt that he was Susan's brother.

"You must be Detective Gold."

Gold felt an odd satisfaction. So Susan had mentioned him to her brother. His own existence was known to this complete stranger, whose nomadic movements kept him thousands of miles from his sister most of the time.

"Glad to meet you." Gold shook a male hand that seemed strong despite its narrow bones.

"Is my sister here?"

Gold did not have time to reply. The door had opened behind him, and Susan was standing there.

"Quentin."

With a sound Gold had never heard her make before, she moved forward to her brother. Without embracing they went into the bedroom together.

Feeling an involuntary pang of jealousy, Gold watched the door close behind them. Then he turned back to the other cops.

36

"NOW, THE WOODCUTTER was very poor," Arnold Haze said. "This you must understand right away. He was so poor that it was no longer possible to feed all the mouths in the family. He would never even have considered the stepmother's suggestion if he had not been desperate."

Michael was sitting at the table, a bowl of cereal before him. The bottle of milk was on the table in case he wanted more. The cereal box bore a picture of Michael Jordan.

"It was the stepmother's idea to get rid of the two children," Haze said. "She explained to the woodcutter that if they didn't get rid of the children, the whole family would starve. The woodcutter loved the children very much, not only for themselves but because they reminded him so much of his first wife. He spent many a sleepless night worrying about what to do. But he finally agreed with the stepmother that there was no choice. The children had to die."

Haze was looking out the window ruminatively. There was nothing to see but the nondescript windows on the old buildings across the alley. He drummed two of his fingers on the table. The boy toyed with a spoonful of his cereal, waiting for the story to continue.

"At last the fateful day came," Haze said. "The woodcutter took the children deep into the forest and told them he would come back for them later. He had no intention of coming back. He intended for the children to die there, either of starvation or at the hands of the wild beasts who lived there. He kissed both children and left them. But what he did not realize was that Hansel had left a trail of pebbles as they came through the forest. He waited with Gretel until the first light of dawn came and followed the trail of pebbles all the way back home."

Haze smiled at the boy. "Can you imagine how the stepmother felt when she saw those two children come back?"

Michael nodded.

"She was upset, and frustrated," Haze said. "And most of all, she had to pretend she was happy to see the children. And when the woodcutter came home from his day's work, he also was shocked and surprised."

"And did he have to pretend too?" Michael asked.

Haze raised an eyebrow in appreciation of the boy's intelligence.

"You're quite right to ask," he said. "The woodcutter was genuinely relieved to see his children alive, for he had not really wanted to kill them in the first place. He was filled with joy as he hugged them and played with them.

"But in the end, he could not deny that the stepmother's plan was a sound one. He could no longer take care of the children and feed them, so once again he took them deep into the forest and told them he would come back the next day.

"This time Hansel left a trail of bread crumbs to lead him back through the forest. But when he and Gretel woke up the next morning, the birds had eaten the bread crumbs, and there was no trail for them to follow."

The boy was looking at Haze through small, pale eyes. He had asked for this story. Haze was surprised he himself remembered it so well.

"And then what happened?" he asked.

"I'll tell you the rest tonight," Haze said. "Finish your cereal, now."

The boy put a spoonful of cereal in his mouth.

"Sometimes the real world is just like a fairy tale," Haze said. "For instance, you already know the reason why your mother asked me to take care of you for a while. Don't you, Michael?"

The boy nodded. "To keep me safe."

"Yes, to keep you safe. But there's more than that. She asked me to keep you in a safe place *where no one could find you.* And when our time is over and the danger is past, I have to bring you back to her, safe and sound. Does that remind you of Hansel and Gretel?"

The boy thought for a moment. "Yes."

"Right now we're deep in the forest where no one can find us," Haze said. "But I know the trail that will lead us home to your mama. And as soon as she tells me, I'm going to take you back to her."

The boy seemed to ponder. "But the stepmother . . ."

"How bright you are!" Haze said. "You're right. The stepmother didn't really want Hansel and Gretel to come home. She hoped they would die in the forest. But your mother isn't like that. She wants you home more than anything in the world. And just think how her face will light up when she sees you come through the door!"

Michael smiled. It was a small, tactful smile, intended to placate. He knew something was wrong. His mother had always told him never to go anywhere with a stranger. And he wouldn't have, except for the fact that she left him with strangers at the airport anyway. The man had told him it was a secret, and very important. Mother was not there, so Michael had said yes.

Now he was left to his own devices, like the children in the fairy tale. He didn't know what to do. He wanted to believe there was truth in what the man said. The man's reassurances comforted him. He could not quite bring himself to believe that it was all false, that the man only wanted to harm him.

And so he had to reassure the man that he thought everything was all right. This was a new experience for him. The only time he had ever had to reassure an adult about anything was when Daddy asked him if he understood why he and Mama had separated.

"We both loved you, and we both wanted to be with you all the time," Daddy had said. "But we didn't think it was best for us all to live together anymore. So we separated. And we still love you just as much as ever. Do you understand?"

Michael had not understood. But he had realized that it was important to the adults that he say he understood. They thought they were reassuring him, but it was he who had to reassure them by making believe.

And that was what he had to do now.

The man stood up and moved behind Michael. He put both hands on Michael's shoulders. The strange smell came. Michael wrinkled his nose.

"In a few minutes I'm going to go out for a little while," the man said. "Do you remember our promise?"

Michael nodded. "I'll be very quiet, and I won't answer the door."

"That's a good boy. Silence is golden. Your mommy will be proud when I tell her how quiet you can be."

The hands held on for another moment, squeezing ever so slightly at his collarbones. Then they let go.

37

AT THE SIX o'clock meeting in Weathers's office, Agent Cunningham brought bad news about the ransom note.

"It turns out the latent images on the note are a dead end," he said. "We found out where it came from."

"The pad itself?" Gold asked. "I thought it belonged to our man. Like a motel notepad."

Cunningham shook his head. "It's the wrong size for that. Too big. This is an eight-by-ten pad. It doesn't have any kind of logo on it, but we figured we should run it down anyway. The handwriting on the upper pages was longhand, as you saw. The ransom note is in caps. There was always the chance that our thinking was wrong. So, since we were checking out everything anyway, we decided to canvass all the travel agents and reservation desks around town. We got lucky this morning. Or maybe I should say unlucky."

He looked at his notes.

"The pad on which the ransom note was written belongs to a little travel agency on Milwaukee Avenue, on the North Side. They're too new—and maybe too poor—to have pads with their company name on them, so they bought this one at a stationery store down the street."

"Did you talk to the agents?" Weathers asked.

"Sure did. Two middle-aged ladies and a sixteen-year-old girl who is the daughter of one of the ladies. They identified the pad by size and paper type. The interesting thing, though, is that none of their pads was missing."

There was a silence.

"Do they remember making those notes about the L.A. and Mexico City flights?" one of the detectives asked.

"The girl does. She wrote them down when she was checking some flight times and prices for a customer."

"What customer?"

Cunningham's lips made a crooked smile.

"A lady from the neighborhood. She was thinking of taking her spinster sister on a vacation to Mexico."

A collective sigh greeted this news.

"And remember the mysterious address up in Glenview? The Dearlove Road address?" Cunningham added. "That's where the teenage girl's boyfriend lives. She was just doodling when she wrote it down. She remembers doing it."

"And the other two notes are in her handwriting," Gold said, more as a statement than as a question.

"Yeah. We checked that."

Weathers was fuming. "I assume you're not telling me that these ladies and this girl are kidnappers. So what the fuck happened?"

"The girl only works three afternoons a week," Cunningham said. "Her desk is right in the front of the place, near the door to the street. I think what happened was Haze went in there and saw the two agents on their phones. He stood by the empty desk in the front and saw the pad lying on it. He either stole a few pages of the pad or, if he had a little extra chutzpah, he leaned over and wrote the note right there while nobody was looking. The two ladies were busy and didn't pay any attention to him."

Weathers sighed. "Jesus Christ."

Cunningham shrugged. "He probably just took a walk around that neighborhood, dropping into one business after another until he found a pad with no one around."

"I'll bet he's also smart enough to know all about document examination," Gold said. "He knew we would get impressions of the previous pages from the pad. He just wanted to play with us."

"What about the handwriting?" Weathers asked.

"Disguised."

"Fuck."

"Just to be safe," Cunningham said, "we're checking the hotels and motels in that neighborhood. Apartment managers, too. You never know."

Those present nodded. But from what they had just heard they knew the search of the neighborhood would turn up nothing. Or if there was a trail, it would be a dead end. The quarry was too clever for simple mistakes.

38

ARNOLD HAZE ran his hand between the boy's thighs.

"Does it tickle?"

"Yes." The boy wriggled. The soap fell out of Haze's hand.

"Look what you made me do!" Haze plunged his hand under the water. His fingers brushed against the boy's toes as he felt for the soap.

"I'll bet you're almost old enough to take your own bath without anyone helping," Haze said.

"I can take my own bath."

"Good for you."

Haze found the soap.

"This may tickle for one more moment, but then no more."

He ran the soap between the small buttocks, feeling the genitals for a brief instant, slippery and tight.

"Good boy."

He rinsed his hands and sat back. The boy sat down in

the water. A rubber dragon, bought by Haze, floated under the tap.

"What is your teacher's name?" Haze asked.

"Mrs. Ocher."

"That's a nice name. Is she nice?"

"Yes. She's nice." The boy reached for the dragon, then thought better and sat looking at it. His arms and legs were very slender, Haze noticed. He must be growing fast, his bones outreaching his appetite.

"But not as nice as your mom."

Michael thought for a moment. "Maybe . . ."

"She's nice in another way. Is that what you mean?"

Michael nodded. He had noticed that the man often supplied answers when he himself had trouble articulating them.

"Tell me about Elaine," Haze said.

"Mmm. She's nice, too. She's very smiley."

"She smiles a lot?"

"And laughs."

"It's nice when people laugh, isn't it? Does Elaine laugh with your dad?"

"Uh-huh." Now the boy reached for the dragon. It slipped through his fingers and bobbed just out of reach.

"Tell me," Haze asked, sitting back. "Does your mommy ever read your mind?"

Now the boy caught the dragon. He gave it a squeeze, and a faint spluttering sound came out.

"Read my mind?" he repeated.

"Yes. Does she read your mind?"

"Yes."

"Can you remember a time when she read your mind?"

"Yes. I wanted popcorn. She said, 'I'll bet you want popcorn.' And another time I didn't want to go to school, and she said it. 'I'll bet you wish you could stay home today.' " A small smile curled the boy's lips.

Haze nodded. He recalled the Rat Man analysis, in which the patient told Freud that one of his earliest memories was his belief that his parents could read his thoughts.

In his case it was part of an infantile neurosis, but the belief was probably universal. Perhaps the boy did not even know what true second sight was.

"Does she ever know things that surprise other people?" he pursued. "Things that other people don't know?"

The boy was silent, thinking.

"Can she tell the future?" Haze asked.

"No. I don't think so."

So she kept it a secret from the boy. Well, that made sense. Being a shrink, she wouldn't want to intimidate him.

Sleepy. Grumpy.

Haze paused, his eyes half-closed. He seemed to be trying to remember something. Then he looked at the boy.

"Tell me," he asked. "Which is better—being with your dad in California or with your mom here?"

"Mmm . . . I like them both."

"How are they different?"

"There it's warmer. I go to school without a jacket. And shopping. It's kind of dry. Here it's wet all the time. The sun doesn't come out."

"Where would you like to live when you grow up?"

"Chicago."

Haze smiled. It was easy to see where the boy felt more at home.

"And tell me, Michael—what would you like to be when you grow up?"

"A policeman. Like Uncle David."

"Uncle David? I thought your uncle's name was Quentin."

"He's not my real uncle."

"Which one? David or Quentin?"

"Quentin is my real uncle. David is a policeman. A detective."

"Detective. That's a nice word. It sounds important."

"Or a psychiatrist."

"Psychiatrist?"

"I'd like to be a psychiatrist too."

"Ah." Again Haze smiled. "What does a psychiatrist do?"

"He listens to people. And if they're sad he makes them happy. That's what my mama does."

"Of course. She is a very fine psychiatrist, your mother. Will you have an office like she does?"

"Thirty North Michigan." The boy nodded.

"In the same building?" Haze asked.

"Then we'll have lunch together."

"Well, that's a good idea. Lunch with your mother. That would be a lot of fun. What is your favorite thing to eat for lunch?"

"At home or in a restaurant?"

"In a restaurant."

"A baked potato."

"A baked potato! With sour cream?"

"And bacon bits, and melted cheese."

"That sounds wonderful," Haze said. "But can a little boy like you eat a whole baked potato with all the trimmings?"

"Yes, I can." The boy sounded offended.

Haze pulled out the stopper. The water began ebbing fast. *Bashful . . .*

"No hair wash tonight," he said. "Your hair is still pretty clean."

The boy nodded.

"Stand up now."

Tenderly Haze patted the little body dry with the towel. He admired the frail shoulder blades, the slender back. This was a beautiful child.

Sleepy. Grumpy.

Haze felt his hand tremble. Something was upsetting him, though he could not tell what. The sight of the boy's nudity, his vulnerability, was sending an alarm signal through him.

Sleepy. Grumpy. Which dwarf are you today?

Suddenly the answer came to him.

When Haze was just this boy's age—perhaps a bit younger—his mother would make fun of his penis when she bathed him. She called it Sleepy when it was flaccid,

Grumpy when her caresses made it hard. And on those occasions when he tried to turn away, she would pull him back and tickle him, saying, "Are you Bashful today? Shall I call you Bashful?" Haze's mother, too, had been a mind reader in her way.

The memory made his heart beat faster. The boy, sensing something, was looking at him. Haze studied the candid little face. There was little doubt that this sweet child had been spared everything that Haze had gone through in those "formative" years.

"And one last question," he said. "Of all the things in the world, what do you like best?"

The boy seemed lost in thought as Haze dried his legs. There was a dreamy, almost visionary look in his little eyes. Not for the first time Haze reflected that he was a special person, sure to grow up into a remarkable individual. Knowing him this way made one long to know the mother who had borne him.

"Being with Mama," the boy said at last.

An odd, composite look came over Haze's face. The boy did not see it.

"Being with your mother? Why?"

There was a pause.

"I don't know," said the boy.

"That's all right. Some things we don't have to know. We only have to feel them. I'm quite sure that her favorite thing is being with you, too."

The boy stepped over the edge of the tub and stood naked before Haze.

"Do you like being with my mother, too?" he asked.

Haze smiled.

"There's nothing I like more," he said. "But I'm not lucky like you. I don't get to see her very often. Almost never, in fact."

"Oh."

He watched the boy pull up his underpants. The tiny penis disappeared behind the cotton with a little bounce.

"And now to bed. Off you go."

The boy went toward the bedroom, where the pajamas lay folded. His bare legs moved with delicate grace.

Sleepy. Grumpy.

Arnold Haze licked his lips, his eyes glued to the little boy. With difficulty he suppressed the impulse surging inside him. The effort left him almost breathless.

"Not yet," he murmured. "Control yourself. Not until the end."

39

SUSAN WAS LYING with her head in Quentin's lap. Quentin was stroking her hair in silence.

The movement of his hand was like a magnet, pulling at her pain and soothing it. It was the first thing since Michael's disappearance that had had something like a tranquilizing influence on her nerves. For this brief moment she was able to close her eyes and let her thoughts wander, without feeling the panic inside her grow tighter and tighter.

She smiled to think of their past together. When they were small the positions had been reversed. It was always Quentin who lay with his head in her lap. As a boy he was excitable and sometimes violent. Impatient with the frustrations of homework, he always had low grades. He was sensitive to the tiniest slight from a schoolmate and got into a lot of fights, most of which he lost because of his small size. Many was the time Susan had dried his tears and calmed him down in the quiet of her bedroom. He never went to their aunt for comfort.

Susan knew that their parents' deaths had hit Quentin

very hard, but she never understood the precise nature of his wound. He would not let her know. She knew he was less introspective than she was. Her entire career in psychiatry had the significance of an attempt at self-knowledge. Quentin had no such recourse. He was a different kind of person.

In later years he came into his own intellectually and completed several advanced degrees in technological subjects. He worked as a consultant to various laboratories and computer firms. The work suited him because it allowed him to avoid staying in one place more than a few weeks or months. He would telephone Susan from Seattle or Virginia or Edmonton, never volunteering what he was doing there or how long he intended to stay. Susan herself sometimes journeyed back to Pennsylvania to see her surviving relatives. But the slightest hint of a family obligation was enough to make Quentin run for cover. He had never been back, and she was sure he never would.

After Michael's birth, which Quentin came from Houston to be present for, he stayed away for nearly four years. On occasional phone calls he would hear her news, but about himself he was so evasive that she finally stopped asking him even the most basic questions about his doings.

She sent him photos of Michael, which he seemed grateful for. Every few months a parcel would arrive for Michael containing a present from Quentin. The gifts reflected Quentin's own interests more than those of a small boy— sophisticated computer games, metal sculptures illustrating the laws of physics—but Michael prized them all the more.

Susan worried about Quentin's solitary existence. He never spoke of women. She sensed he lacked the patience for a long-term relationship. He rarely had anything good to say about the people he encountered in his work. Susan knew he was lonely. But she could never be sure he was unhappy. She suspected he had the sort of mild character disorder that allowed him to enjoy his alienation from the world.

Quentin had never warmed up to Nick. That may have been one reason he stayed away. When Susan got her divorce, Quentin seemed relieved. She hesitated to attribute this to outright jealousy, but the fact was that Quentin had depended on her for almost everything throughout his youth and remained, in his unpredictable way, somewhat possessive of her.

Today the tables were turned. It was Susan who nestled in the protection of Quentin's warmth, hoping it would hold the world at bay as long as possible. She kept her eyes closed. The slow movement of his hand was hypnotic.

"He still a Bulls fan?" he asked.

"Michael? Yes." Susan nodded. "And Atlanta. The Braves."

"Atlanta? That's something new, isn't it?"

"He loves Greg Maddux. He has his picture in his bedroom in California."

"I was in Atlanta just last month. I could have got him some stuff." He was silent for a moment. "Oh, well. I'm going back. I'll do it then."

A brief shudder went through Susan and was gone. Only in this situation, with Quentin, could she dare to pretend that things were normal, that Michael was safe somewhere and still had a future. Since the kidnapping she had not allowed herself a moment of denial, because she knew that if she did so the return to reality would be too agonizing to bear. She had to keep contemplating the worst at every moment.

"I can get Maddux's autograph on a baseball," he added. "The guys I work for have season tickets."

She found his hand and squeezed it. Fanciful though it might be, his evocation of a future with Michael gave her precious comfort.

"Quentin," she said suddenly.

"Yes?"

"Do you remember the picture of me and Daddy at the campground? The one where I'm holding the ice cream sandwich?"

There was a silence.

"Governor Dodge State Park. Yes."

"Michael loves that picture. The ice cream sandwich fascinates him. He likes the fact that it never melts. He talked about it so much that I had a negative made from the print and sent him a copy. He says it's his favorite picture of me."

"Ah."

"Quentin, do you remember that day? Michael always asks me, and I can never remember. It's a blank to me."

She sensed she was crossing a line. Quentin did not like to think about the time before their parents' deaths. Susan herself had difficulty thinking about it for more than a moment at a time. It had assumed an almost prehistoric aspect, like a world that had never really existed because it had lasted for so short a time. Believing in it meant that you had to believe in what came after. And that was very painful.

"Not offhand," he said. "No."

"Oh. I just wondered."

She was almost relieved he had been unable to remember. She regretted having brought it up.

Another silence came. She could feel Quentin thinking things over.

"You getting any feelings?" he asked.

Quentin considered his sister's extrasensory insights as dependable as money in the bank. He had been a firsthand observer of them as a boy and had rarely known them to be wrong. There were times when he would let her know his thoughts without bothering to say them out loud. He was that sure of her gift, and of her love.

When they were children, he had seemed a virtual extension of her self. There was scarcely an emotion inside her that did not have its echo in him. In those days she did not even try to imagine a life in which he would not be at her side, feeling with her, knowing her, depending on her. It was not until years after they separated that she began to realize how much she missed him. By then it was too late.

Adult life had made its claims on her, and forced him into an existence that shut her out.

In answer to his question she shook her head. "Nothing," she said. "I'm too afraid."

He nodded in silence. There was nothing further to say.

She heard the traffic outside, and a distant siren.

"Christ, it's cold in this town." He let his hand come to rest against her temple. "How do you stand it?"

She said nothing. The question did not need an answer.

The siren died away very slowly. Before it disappeared another one was coming from the north to take its place.

"You're okay with the rest of this, though," he said.

Again the brief shudder shook her. She knew what he was asking. If the worst came, would she survive it?

"Yes," she said.

"Good girl."

Good girl. That wasn't Quentin's expression. He had never used it before. It came from their mother. Those were the words she used to use when she was proud of something Susan had done and wanted to praise her.

She allowed herself a small smile. So he had dared to reach into the past for her after all, if only in one lost phrase of love.

A knock came at the door. It was David Gold. He was carrying a shopping bag that looked like it had come from a women's clothing store.

"Susan, can I have a word with you?" he asked.

Quentin got up and left the room. Gold sat down on the edge of the bed. Susan looked fearfully at the bag.

"What have you got there?" she asked.

"Weathers would have my ass if he knew I took this," Gold said. "But we're not getting anywhere. I need you."

He removed two evidence bags from the larger bag. The first contained the ransom note.

"Go on, touch it," he said. "They dusted it long ago. There's nothing."

Susan ran her fingers over the scrawled message. But already she was looking at the other bag.

"The dentist's mold?" she asked.

Gold nodded. He removed the mold and held it out for her to touch.

Susan steeled herself. This mold had been inside her son's mouth. If he was dead, a single touch of her finger to the clay would tell her so.

She reached out for it. Her hand stopped in midair.

"Go on," Gold said. "You're all I've got. There isn't much time."

Closing her eyes, she let her hand touch the mold. The ransom note fell to the floor. She took the mold to her breast and held it tight. Tears flowed down her cheeks. A sound came from her throat, a sort of rhythmic moaning.

"Take your time." It was Gold's favorite phrase when she was using her second sight.

But there was no time. Her terror twined itself around the mad hurry inside her. She squeezed the mold tighter and tighter against her breast. Then she let out a sharp cry and fell back against the pillow.

Gold had not moved.

"What?" he asked.

"He's alive." She began to weep like a child.

Gold patted her hand tentatively. He wanted to comfort her but also to get more from her.

"Where, Susan?"

She shook her head. She smiled through her tears.

"I don't know. I can't . . . I don't know."

"Try. Please."

She held the mold in both her hands. She closed her eyes. Her brow furrowed. Again the peculiar moaning sounded in her throat. Her fingers tensed around the clay. Then she let it go.

"Nothing," she said. "There's nothing, David."

His disappointment was obvious.

"I'm trying too hard," she said. "I'm too close to it. It's never been this way before. I can't let go enough."

He sighed. "You sure?"

She paused, as though on the track of something. Then she gave up.

"I'm sure. It's a blank."

Gold nodded. He understood. Like all specialists, psychics are least effective when members of their families are involved. If it were Carol or one of his girls who had been abducted, Gold would have taken himself off the case immediately. He could not ask Susan to do the impossible.

"All right," he said. "Don't worry. I'll take it from here."

He packed the things away and stood up to leave.

"Where did you get that bag?" she asked him.

"Carol's closet."

She nodded. He moved toward the door. Her voice stopped him.

"The note," she said. "It was Haze who wrote it."

Gold nodded. "Okay. Thanks."

He started to say something else. Then he thought better of it. He left quietly. Susan turned on her side.

Chiropractic. The word was in her hand where the mold had been. Not *Chiropractor* but *Chiropractic.* It was strange, like a word never heard before.

And something else. Something else. Hurry!

The name of a thing. The name of a bird. The name of a—

Eagle. Yes. No? Not clear, not there anymore. Still . . .

Eagle.

Chiropractic.

The knob was turning. Quentin was coming back.

She turned to meet his eyes, as she had done long ago.

40

THE BOY WAS alone in the apartment.

Something had awakened him. A noise from the street, perhaps, or from somewhere else in the building.

His eyes were open, but he felt groggy. This was not the first time he had felt this way. Every time the man went out, it seemed, Michael slept until he came back. A strange, heavy sleep.

He got up and went into the living room. He was too little to know the telltale signs of a furnished apartment. The threadbare rugs, the indentations in the old couch cushions, the scorched lampshades. However, the old-style porcelain plumbing fixtures were familiar to him from his mother's Lincoln Park apartment. So were the radiators and the countless coats of whitewash on the walls. The smell of old buildings was here, of course, though when the man came home his own strange smell eclipsed it.

There were few signs of occupancy here, other than the milk and fruit in the refrigerator, the newspaper sitting on the counter, and the coloring books and crayons littering the living room rug. There was no telephone.

The boy looked longingly at the old TV. The man had forbidden him to watch it when he was alone. He did not dare to turn it on.

In California the TV was the hearth around which the family gathered in the evenings. Elaine was a great lover of movies and was always either renting them or recording them for herself and Michael. It was she who had shown him *Gone With the Wind* and *All This and Heaven Too* and the scary one, *Night of the Hunter*, in which the mad preacher pursued the little children through the countryside. She always put her hands over her eyes during the scary parts, but Michael did not believe she was actually afraid.

Daddy usually worked during the movies, but he stayed in the room. The sound of the TV didn't seem to bother him. He would always put away his work when snack time came. He insisted on making the popcorn himself, shaking paprika and Parmesan cheese into the bag before serving it. "I am the chief of popcorn," he would say. "You"— meaning Michael—"are the chief of soda pop. And you"— turning to Elaine—"are the chief of provocation." Elaine invariably curled her lip at this, but Daddy wouldn't stop saying it.

When he was in Chicago, Michael could watch anything he wanted. His mother took him down to the video store and let him choose the movie. Like his father, she usually did some work during the movie. But she let Michael make the popcorn. "You do it better than I do," she said.

Elaine often scratched his back while they watched television. But his favorite thing was to lie with his head in his mother's lap. She would stroke his hair, her fingers very gentle and peaceful. The image on the screen would be turned on its side because he was not upright, but he didn't care. His mother's touch was hypnotic, and his closeness to her made the movie itself hypnotic, in a strange and special way.

Now that he lacked television, there was nothing to do in the evenings but color some more pictures, or read the books he had already read. He could ask for more books, he supposed; but something made him keep silent.

Today the man had promised Michael he would make him a baked potato with all the trimmings. "Because you've been such a good boy. And because I don't want your mother to think I haven't been treating you right." He wrote down all the ingredients before he left.

The boy moved slowly around the apartment. He crawled under the kitchen table, hid inside the empty closet, went back and forth between the bedroom and the living room. He pretended he was playing hide and seek with Sean and Lydia, his next-door neighbors in California. They were noisy children who always fought with each other. Back home he often got tired of them. But now he repeated the game they had played so often, pretending that in another minute one or the other of them would leap out at him from a hiding place.

"Here I come, ready or not," he called out.

As he searched he repeated the phrases he had heard Sean's mother say when she came outside to look for them.

"Where in the world have they got to?"

"Sean, I'm going to kill you. Lydie!"

The words echoed in the empty apartment. A truck rumbled through a street or alley outside. A distant siren got louder, then died away. The springs of the foldout sofa creaked as he climbed across it.

He pushed the kitchen chair to the sink and climbed up. His sleepiness made him dizzy, and he had to brace himself against the wall. The water was dripping as usual. It made a rusty stain by the drain hole. Balancing himself on his knees, Michael opened the cupboard. There were a few plastic glasses that didn't match, and some chipped plates. In the back was a large plastic tumbler that bore a picture of Scottie Pippen. Michael wanted to have a drink out of it, but he was afraid the man would punish him if he found out he had been looking in the cupboards.

He hesitated for a long moment, then took out the tumbler. He intended to drink some milk out of it. There was a bag of cookies on the counter, left there by the man yesterday. Michael would eat the cookies and drink from the tumbler while reading his book on the living room couch.

Footsteps sounded in the hall. Michael hurriedly put the tumbler back. A jingle of keys told him he was in trouble.

He closed the cupboard door and turned to jump down to the floor.

He caught a glimpse of the view from the window over the sink. Rooftops and windows and, in the distance, a skyline that included the Sears Tower. He recognized it because his mother had pointed it out when they went to the top of the John Hancock Building.

Across the alley were windows in the brick facade of an old building. *AAA Loans* and *Chara Dentistry* and an odd word, *Chiropractic*. They wheeled past his eyes as he squirmed to get down from the counter. The key was turning in the lock now.

He was moving the chair back toward the table when the man came in.

"What are you doing up? I thought you were going to take a nice long nap. Are you all right?"

The small black eyes swept the kitchen. "What have you been up to?"

Michael was silent.

"Have you been looking in the cupboards?"

The man crossed to the counter with his grocery bag. "I got the potatoes," he said. "And all the trimmings. I hope bacon bits are good enough. I'm not much of a bacon chef."

He held up a narrow, shiny box. "And I got the tinfoil," he added proudly. "So your potato will look just like in a restaurant."

As he put the things on the counter he looked at the boy. "What were you looking for?" he asked.

Michael was standing by the table. He seemed embarrassed.

"Have you been naughty?" the man asked.

Michael shook his head. "There's a cup," he said. "It says Scottie Pippen."

The man raised an eyebrow and opened the cupboard door.

"Ah," he said. "So there is. Did you want to have a drink out of it?"

Michael nodded.

"I should have known that boys will be boys." The man smiled. "I can't leave a red-blooded fellow like you here all alone all day without your doing a little exploring. Well, I'll just wash it out to make sure it's clean. Would you like some milk?"

"Yes."

"How about a cookie to go with it?"

"Yes."

"What's a cookie without milk, or vice versa?" the man asked. "Do you know what that means, by the way? *Vice versa?*"

The boy shook his head.

"Well, it means the other way around." Haze put the potatoes into an old chipped bowl and opened the refrigerator to put away the sour cream and cheddar cheese. "For instance, if Hansel laughed at Gretel . . ."

He looked out the window. Nothing but the alley and the cityscape in the distance. The boy already knew this was Chicago. There was no phone. No other apartments on this floor. Haze had won him over psychologically, as far as that went. The boy was his ally in keeping their whereabouts a secret.

The windows across the alley. The dentist. The chiropractor. Would any of that give the boy ideas? Haze didn't think so. It was the outside world, too remote to be included in his six-year-old plans. At the moment those plans could hardly go beyond carrying out Haze's wishes, trying to please Haze.

"If Hansel laughed at Gretel, and Gretel laughed at Hansel, you could say that Hansel laughed at Gretel and *vice versa*. Do you see what I mean?"

The boy thought it over. His little legs dangled from the chair, the feet swinging back and forth.

"Now you try," Haze said.

"Mmm . . . If Susan got mad at Bob, and vice versa, then they would be mad at each other."

"Who are Susan and Bob?"

"On *Sesame Street*."

"What an intelligent boy you are. You're quite right. They would be mad at each other. When I tell your mother about all the smart things you've said, she's going to be very proud. Why, she may not even believe me!"

Haze glanced through the window again. *Eagle. Chara. Chiropractic.* There was no phone book here, and no phone. Nevertheless, one must take every precaution, assume the worst. He should have killed the boy that first day.

He would do it tomorrow.

41

WHEN CAROLYN CAME with the morning coffee, she found Quentin in the room alone.

"Where's Susan?" she asked.

Quentin smiled. "She couldn't take it anymore. She went down to her office to check the mail and get a book she wanted."

"Did she tell the detectives?"

He shook his head. "They wouldn't have let her go. She just ducked out when no one was looking."

"Oh." Carolyn looked worried. "What about the phone? What if someone calls about the ransom?"

"She'll be back in an hour," Quentin said. "Besides, they're not going to call."

Carolyn's face fell. "I guess you're right." She looked at the cup of coffee in her hand. "Want this?"

"No, thanks." Quentin knew how Carolyn's coffee tasted. He had got into the habit of running down to the 7-Eleven when he wanted coffee.

"Is she all right?" Carolyn asked.

Quentin gave her a look that told her not to ask such questions. They all knew what the situation was.

Sighing, Carolyn went back to the kitchen. Let Susan have her little vacation, then, she thought. An hour would be soon enough to start waiting again.

She left for the station without telling the FBI men about Susan's departure. They were bored with their own vigil and paid little attention to the grieving mother behind the bedroom door anyway.

It wasn't until that afternoon that they realized Susan had run away. Quentin refused to explain her departure.

She had a head start of nearly eighteen hours.

42

THE BELL RANG at two-forty in the outer office. M. F. Eagler stopped what he was doing.

He looked at his watch. There was no appointment for this hour. He discouraged walk-in trade. Better safe than sorry.

He closed the door to the examining room and moved quickly into the outer office. A small woman with curly hair was smiling at him.

"Dr. Eagler?"

"Yes. How may I help you?"

"Well, I'm not sure you can." She fiddled in her purse. "I can't seem to find that note. Oh, never mind." She smiled. "You're the chiropractor?"

"Yes, that's me." He gave her a wary look.

"I was supposed to meet my neighbor here," she said. "They told me he was a patient of yours. Mr. Cahill."

The doctor raised an eyebrow. "Well, that's odd. I don't have a patient named Cahill. Are you sure you have the right person?"

"Well, not absolutely sure." She looked at her purse without opening it. "You see, he's not very precise sometimes. He gets a little confused now and then . . ."

The doctor stood watching her, his courtly expression masking obvious impatience.

"He had this terrible pain," she said. "He said he was going to do something about it right away, today. He could hardly stand up. . . . Are you sure he didn't call you?" She looked past him at the secretary's desk. "Perhaps your secretary talked to him."

"Mrs. Thornton is not in today," he said. "But I would have known about your friend in any case. I'm afraid he hasn't called me. There must be some mistake."

She sighed helplessly.

"I just don't understand it. He was in so much pain. . . . You see, I was supposed to drive him home."

With an odd look the doctor asked, "When did the pain start?"

She sighed. "Well, he's had a bad back for years. Since before his wife died. But it never really laid him up. He just had to sleep on a hard board. And he has one of those special chairs. Orthopedic."

"Has he seen a specialist before?" M. F. Eagler spoke in an unctuous voice, leaning toward her.

"He may have, but he didn't tell me. He got your name from a neighbor lady. . . . He told me he was going to call you. I don't see how I could have got the name wrong . . ."

"As I say, there must be a mistake. Now, if you'll excuse me, I have a patient . . ."

There was something helpless about her. She seemed confused herself. He moved to open the door for her.

"Ouch!" She tripped and fell forward. He managed to catch her before she hit the floor.

"Are you all right?" She was remarkably light. She could not weigh very much. As a matter of fact, she seemed undernourished.

"Oh, fine, thank you. My feet just got tangled up. I'm terribly sorry."

She had taken both his hands and was struggling to her feet. "I don't know what's the matter with me. I've been dropping things all day, and now this . . ."

Her hands were fine and small. In that instant he noticed an odd, intent look in her eyes. Had she lied about the reason for her visit?

He tried to seem helpful and understanding. Perhaps she just needed a little courage to say what was on her mind.

"You're quite sure you're all right?" he asked.

"Yes, thank you."

There was a silence. She held on to his hands a moment too long.

"Well, then, if there's nothing I can do for you . . ." He made his voice as inviting as possible.

"Do you think . . . Could you help him?" There was supplication in her manner.

"That's what I'm here for, ma'am. To help people. I can always help."

"Let me think it over," she said.

"That's right. You think it over." He held the door open. "You're sure you're going to be all right?"

"Yes. Thank you, Doctor."

He locked the door and returned to the inner office. He was sure she had been feeling him out. But she seemed slightly crazy. No sense in blurting things out, he thought. Better safe than sorry.

SUSAN STOOD ON the landing, thinking. She went down the stairs and out the front door. The street was busy enough. Brick apartment buildings extended as far as the eye could see, with storefront businesses on most of the ground floors. This was one of those Chicago streets that went on for miles with hardly a sight to catch the eye.

Dr. M. F. Eagler was an abortionist. That truth had been in his eyes from the moment she entered the office. But it had taken the touch of his hands to make her sure.

An abortionist . . . Quite an anachronism, she mused. She had heard about neighborhood abortionists who still existed despite the readily available and far safer abortion clinics. Women from various subcultures, Catholic for the most part, felt too exposed in the clinics, and they patronized the old-style abortionists to hide their shame. Despite the many efforts at education by the state, the practice persisted.

Susan felt dissatisfied. She had not found out what she came for. Dr. Eagler had something to hide, but it was not her son. He had not recognized her. He was probably too wrapped up in his seedy profession to take notice of people outside it. And he was not involved in any way with Arnold Haze.

Susan stood looking up and down the street. It did not offer her a clue. She turned back to the building and went in the front door. Something told her she should not leave yet.

She made her way up the stairs and along the corridor past Dr. Eagler's office. The signs on the other office doors indicated a building less than half occupied. The businesses were down-at-heels—a loan company that seemed closed, a jeweler, a dentist whose waiting room was empty.

She paused by a window over a radiator in the hall. There was nothing to see through it except the alley and the apartment buildings beyond. Sad old buildings with wooden back stairs and fire escapes. Dirty windows to kitchens and bedrooms, and beaded glass panes over bathrooms. Ice covered the crumpled concrete in the alley, for the sun could not penetrate it at this season. A grim view.

She let her eyes wander over the windows. The view from them must be just as depressing as the one she was looking at now.

She stood for a moment, thinking. Then she turned and

walked quickly back out of the building and down the sidewalk to the alley.

Stepping gingerly to avoid both the ice and the garbage that littered the alley, she made her way behind the building. At last she found what she was looking for. A flaked gold sign painted on a frosted window, long since attacked by the weather and rather dim, but still readable.

Eagle
Chiropractic

The *r* was faded, she noticed. *Eagler* now looked like *Eagle*.

She stood for a long moment studying the sign, her hands in her pockets.

Then she turned around.

43

DAVID GOLD sat looking at Quentin.

Quentin seemed very calm. He still held the paperback book he had been reading. The implication was that as soon as Gold had finished, Quentin could get back to more important things.

"Quentin, where did she go?"

Gold was fighting to rein in his own anxiety. Michael was already in the hands of Arnold Haze. If Susan went up against Haze alone, she might become his second hostage. Her intrusion might trigger a double homicide. Then everything would be lost.

"She didn't say," Quentin said.

"Look, Quentin. I know Susan. She wouldn't go off without telling someone where she could be found. She's been working with me for years. She always plays it safe. Now, tell me. Where did she go?"

Quentin said nothing.

"What did she find out?" Gold probed. "Was it the mold I brought? The ransom note?"

Quentin dangled the book between his knees. With his high forehead and narrow face, he could have been a college professor. The look in his eyes was exquisitely bland.

"Quentin, I'm the one who brought that stuff. I wanted her to see it. I hoped she would feel something. Don't hang me up, now. Tell me what she found. Tell me what she felt."

Quentin thought for a moment.

"She doesn't trust you," he said.

Gold was shocked. "She told you that?"

"Not you personally," Quentin said. "Your colleagues. She doesn't trust them to be careful enough with the boy's life. She wanted a head start."

Gold ran a hand through his hair. God save me from civilians, he thought.

"Look, Quentin. Nobody's going in anywhere with guns blazing. For Christ's sake, we want to get Michael back as much as you do. But this guy Haze is an animal. You can't go up against someone like that alone. Not you, not Susan—not anybody. Just let the professionals do their work, okay? We got this far as a team, didn't we?"

Quentin looked up suspiciously. "I wouldn't say that. Susan got you this far."

Gold sighed.

"Maybe she did. Maybe she was smarter. I'll grant you that. But she's a psychic, not a SWAT team. You don't understand what we're dealing with."

Quentin was silent. He felt he knew precisely what was at stake. The police were concerned above all to arrest a killer. They wanted the public to be safe from Arnold Haze, but they also wanted their collar. In the end they would sacrifice Michael to that cause. Quentin knew this because Susan knew it. And Susan knew it because she could read the minds of the "professionals" outside this room as easily as they themselves could see the glitter of cocaine in the eyes of a street thug.

Quentin's belief in his sister was absolute. He knew her powers and her love. She would bring Michael back alive. That could not be said of the police, no matter how David Gold tried to argue the contrary.

"She said she wanted a head start." Quentin stuck to his guns.

"How long a head start?" Gold asked. "Just tell me that."

Quentin thought for a moment. "No."

Gold stood up angrily.

"Jesus Christ, Quentin. There's a time and a place for loyalty. We're fighting the clock. Susan has had her head start. Okay? You gave it to her. She's way ahead of us. Just tell me where to go. Tell me how to help her. Please."

Quentin was studying Gold's face.

"You care a lot about this, don't you?" he asked.

Gold sighed his exasperation.

"She's talked about you often," Quentin said. "She trusts you."

"Quentin—" Gold held up both hands in surrender. "What do you want me to say? That I care? Of course I care. That little boy means as much to me as my own daughters."

"And about her?" Quentin asked.

Gold searched for words, then gave up.

"I don't want her to get killed trying to save him," he said. "What more can I say?"

"You would let one die to save the other," Quentin said. "You'll go for the best odds."

Gold turned red. There was truth in Quentin's words.

Quentin curled his lip in acknowledgment. "I won't tell you," he said.

44

MICHAEL WAS CRYING.

"I want my mother."

Arnold Haze sat across the small kitchen table from the boy. He drummed two fingers on the old Formica surface impatiently.

"Michael," he said. "We've discussed this over and over again. Your mother has something very important to do, something very secret. That's why she asked me to take care of you. In a couple of days she will call, and it will all be over. You just have to be patient."

The boy was looking at Haze, tears coming down his cheeks.

"I want my mama," he said.

Haze saw the rebellion in the small eyes. The boy had played along until now, but he was at the end of his courage.

"Michael, think a moment. This time is very important to your mother. She's counting on you. How do you think she would feel if she knew you weren't doing your part to help her? What would she think?"

The boy said nothing. He sniffled and wiped at his eyes.

"Now, I want you to come with me," Haze said. "I'm going to give you a pill to help you relax. It's a pill your mother gave me just for this purpose. Once you've had a little sleep, you'll feel differently."

The boy did not move. He had the helpless air of very small children when they know they are out of their element. He no longer trusted Haze. But he had no means of escape, no weapons with which to fight back. He could only cry out his rebellion through his own tears.

"No," he said. "I want my mama."

Haze got up. "Michael, that's enough," he said. "You're coming with me."

This was the end. He could no longer cope with the boy's desperation. He would have to make it the rest of the way without him.

He started around the table. "I'm going to have to tell your mother what a fuss you're making. She's not going to be pleased."

The boy got up from his chair and hid behind it. Haze pulled it away with one hand.

"Let's go into the bedroom now," he said.

The boy retreated to the couch. As Haze approached, he curled up against the cushions in a fetal position. Perhaps he knows, Haze thought.

A knock sounded at the door. Haze turned to look.

"Mama!" the boy cried. "Mama!"

He leaped up from the couch. Catching him around the neck, Haze pulled him roughly against his chest and put a hand over his mouth. The little hands tugged at his fingers.

Again the knock sounded.

"Who is it?" Haze called.

There was no answer. A third knock, more urgent, came at the door.

"Wait a moment."

Haze pulled the boy into the bedroom. He managed with some difficulty to replace the gag he had used when they first arrived, and to bind the small wrists with a cord. He pushed the boy into the closet and closed the door.

When he returned to the living room, he found Susan standing there.

"Where is he?" she asked. "I heard him. Where is he?"

"How did you get in?"

Haze thought of the Luger he kept in his coat. It was in the kitchen. He had been too preoccupied by the boy's tantrum to take proper precautions.

Susan was coming closer. She looked very small, very intense.

"Where is he?" The command in her voice was powerful.

Haze stood aside, pointing to the bedroom.

"In there."

Her maternal instincts were stronger than her caution. She walked right past Haze, hardly even looking at him.

He hit her just below the ear with a sharp chopping blow. She crumpled to the floor six inches from the door behind which her son lay hidden.

SUSAN CAME BACK to consciousness slowly. The pain in her head and neck glowed red behind her eyes, blinding her at first to her surroundings.

Then she saw the room around her. It was a nondescript bedroom, apparently in a furnished apartment. An old landscape above the dresser was all she could clearly see from where she lay. She was tied hand and foot. She was naked.

There was no sign of Michael.

She felt wounds under her hair as she moved her head on the pillow. Moving her eyes was intensely painful.

She surveyed her body dispassionately. She knew she had a concussion, because she had been knocked unconscious. She could not see or palpate her scalp, so she could not know whether there were depressed areas. Her eyes seemed to be focusing normally, which was a good sign. Her neck felt rigid, but there did not seem to be any paralysis or weakness in her extremities. Her condition could be a lot worse, she concluded.

There was no sound in the room. Routine building noises murmured behind the walls. Outside the window the remote sounds of traffic were audible. Other than that there was nothing.

Susan stirred slightly. Her body was stiff. She wondered how long she had been here.

She gathered her wits and opened her mouth.

"Hello?" she called.

Something moved beyond the door.

"Hello?"

She heard small padding steps. Then the door opened. Arnold Haze came into the room.

"You're back among the living." He smiled. "I was getting worried."

Susan looked at him. "Where is my son?"

"Do you want something to drink?" he asked. "How about an aspirin? That was a nasty knock you took. I'm sorry."

"Where is my son?" Susan was surprised at the strength of her own voice.

"Safe. That's all I can tell you for now."

Haze stood at the foot of the bed. "Your coming here was not convenient. The situation with your boy was simpler before you came. I think you can appreciate that."

Susan took a deep breath. As she did so she smelled Haze for the first time. She had been smelling that odor of chloroform and rotting fruit for over a month.

"What's that smell?" she asked. "Diabetes?"

Haze shook his head. "Why should I tell you things that will help you catch me later on? Let's forget the smell. All right?"

Susan nodded.

"I'd like to go to the bathroom," she said.

He sat down on the edge of the bed and regarded her.

"Your photographs in the press don't do you justice," he said. "You're very lovely. Quite stunning, in your way."

Susan looked into his eyes. They were like tiny beads or pebbles, so dark that she could not tell where the irises left off and the pupils began. The eyeballs themselves were small, so that they seemed to float in the occipital orbits rather than to fill them completely.

At first glance they looked dead and without expression, but after a moment she realized they communicated a sharp watchfulness. He was studying her, a little smile playing around his lips. The skin of his face was loose, sallow. Combined with the unpleasant smell, it all would have given the impression of putrefaction and decay had it not been for the intense life in the eyes.

"It's a mysterious sort of beauty," he added. "Not right on the surface."

He crossed his arms over his chest.

"Tell me," he said. "Did you get the roses?"

Susan nodded. "I thought it was you."

He smiled. "You and I go back a long way," he said. "It's wonderful to meet you at last."

She studied his face. "Did you know I was involved from the outset?"

He thought for a moment. "You mean the eye motif?"

She was silent.

"The gouging?" he asked. "Is that what you mean?"

Susan nodded.

"Like second sight. Is that what you mean? Take out the eyes, and what is left is second sight? Yes, it occurred to me. A grace note. But not until after I saw Stewart's photographs. It did bring a sort of unity to the campaign. Indeed, I saw you coming, Doctor."

"I thought so," she said. "I felt it."

Susan shuddered. It hurt to think that Haze had planned his mutilation of those innocent girls just to taunt her about her second sight. On the other hand, he might be lying. He looked like a man who would tell the truth as seldom as possible.

He looked more closely at her. "I can feel your gift," he said. "Right through your skin." He nodded. "Quite remarkable."

"I need to go to the bathroom," Susan repeated.

"Tell me," he asked. "How old were you when it came to you—the gift? Were you very small?"

"I'm not shy," Susan said. "I'll urinate in the sheets. There's no point in playing games with me."

He smiled. "Point taken," he said. "Wait here."

He left the room and returned with a bedpan. He placed it under her and went away while she used it. He knocked before he came back in.

"All set?"

She nodded, looking away as he removed the bedpan.

"I'm sorry," he said. "I'm a little preoccupied. You must forgive me if I seem absentminded." He saw the pain in her face and repeated, "Are you sure you wouldn't like an aspirin?"

She shook her head.

He took the bedpan away. She heard sounds in the next room. Water running, a cupboard being opened. When he returned he was eating something out of a paper bag.

"Personally," he said between mouthfuls, "I can't stand aspirin on an empty stomach. Ibuprofen is a little better, but even then the heartburn is unbearable."

Susan was looking up at him.

"How did you manage to abduct Michael at the airport?" she asked.

He stopped chewing long enough to smile. "That was an achievement. I'd love to tell you how it was done, just for my own narcissism. But let's leave it as a professional secret. Tell me—how did you find me here?"

Susan smiled weakly. "Call that a professional secret, too."

Haze nodded appreciatively. "I can see I'm not dealing with just anyone. I render homage to your ability. It may yet be of help to both of us."

There was a silence. Victim and captor were thinking about each other, and about the circumstances that had brought them together.

"Tell me," Haze said. "Were you the first one to see the connection to Peter Tomerakian?"

Susan shook her head. "I guessed that the victims were connected in some way. It was David Gold who found out about Tomerakian and put it all together."

Haze nodded. "How close were you to the Cawley connection when I eliminated her? The false signature, I mean?"

Susan gritted her teeth. "We were far behind. We thought Stewart was the killer."

Haze shook his head. "I should have known. The police are so slow. I was quite upset by that business. I thought my neck was in a noose. It was silly of me to worry as much as I did."

He looked at Susan.

"Of course, I can't blame you for being taken in. Stewart was a fall guy made in heaven. He had motive, opportunity—and he knew the girls. Extraordinary. It was almost as though fate itself were giving me my marching orders."

He smiled at Susan.

"How did you reconcile Kuehn with the others?" he asked. "I've wondered about that."

Susan sighed. "Stewart lived near Dorothy's family when he was a boy. For a while we thought that was the connection. That was our mistake."

"Ah. Raveling your own web." Haze seemed pleased.

"And how did you go about finding Miss Lazarus?" he asked.

"By checking Celeste Cawley's close friends and former roommates," Susan said.

"Just as I did." Haze nodded. "Of course, you didn't have a face to work from."

Susan said nothing. She did not want to let him know that her second sight had played a role in locating Jaime. Something told her that a mention of her gift would provoke him.

"By the way," he asked, "did you guess my intention that night at Miss Lazarus's apartment?"

"What do you mean?"

"I wasn't going to harm her. I needed a hostage."

Susan shook her head. "No. I didn't see that."

"You should have. At that point it was obvious that a hostage was my best bet. Particularly the daughter of the great Aaron Lazarus. The police hold all the cards when all you've left behind is a trail of corpses. A hostage is different. For a hostage they'll deal."

Susan was watching him intently.

"Don't tell me." He smiled. "I know what you're thinking. The son of a famous psychic approximately equals the daughter of a famous civil rights leader."

Susan said nothing.

"Well, that's exactly my point," Haze explained. "When you stopped me at Jaime's door, I reviewed my options, and of course I thought of your son. By now you were a heroine, very high-profile. The exotic nature of your profession only increased your prestige. I knew that your little boy could be the next Lindbergh baby if I handled it right."

He smiled proudly. "There is always another card to play. I've found that out."

He went away for a moment. Susan heard the refrigerator door being opened in the next room. When he returned he had the paper bag in his hand. He was chewing on something as he sat down on the edge of the bed. She wondered if he was trying to make her hungry. Starvation was perhaps part of his plan to intimidate her. She only hoped he was not starving Michael too.

"But now you're here," he said. "That complicates matters."

He placed his hand on Susan's thigh. Her skin crawled. He moved his hand up toward her hip. She suppressed the tremor in her limbs.

"Don't worry," he said. "I was never one for the fair sex." He smiled. "Which is one explanation for the fact that none of the victims was molested. Not the only one, of course."

Susan felt peculiar sensations emanating from the skin he had touched. Her own anxiety made it difficult to sort them out. He was lying, of course, in some of the things he said. But which things?

"Where is my son?" she asked.

Haze shrugged. "Not here. Not anymore. You can understand that." There was reproach in his voice.

"I need proof." It was difficult to drive a bargain when she was tied up naked, but she felt she had to make a show of resistance.

"What kind of proof?"

"I need to see him."

"You've already seen him once."

"I need to see him again."

"You mean you doubt my word?"

"You know what I mean." Small tremors shook Susan's limbs, but she held fast.

Haze smiled. "You're a devoted mother, I can see that. Tell me, was it painful for you to be pilloried in the press when your son was in a position to know about it?"

Susan thought for a moment. "Yes. I didn't want him to feel tainted by it."

"Tainted, yes." Haze nodded. "Children tend to take on the blame even for the sins of the fathers. Is there a term in psychiatry for that?"

"Not that I know of."

"There should be." Haze looked down at her. "I've been observing him during his visit with me. He is a very sensitive child. He feels responsible for the pain you're enduring due to his absence. Of course, he won't tell me that aloud, but I can see it."

These words hurt Susan terribly. Her thoughts about Michael's sequestration had never extended to the idea that he might feel guilty about being a prisoner. Yet she knew that Haze's insight was correct. It only made her longing for her son the more unbearable.

"Let me see him," she said. "Please."

Haze seemed lost in thought for a moment. Again he ate something from the bag, chewing slowly.

"So tell me," he asked, "how old were you when the gift came? Were you very small?"

"I want my son!" Her words came out as a shriek.

He stopped chewing and looked at her.

"You want your son?" he asked. His words were distorted by the food in his mouth. She wondered if he was trying to disgust her by talking with his mouth full.

She nodded, struggling to control herself. "Yes."

"How much do you want him?" Haze asked.

Susan did not answer. The games were starting, she realized. It was important that she fight him by retaining a remnant of dignity, no matter what he did to her. The appearance of composure might be her only hope.

Haze was watching her, a smile on his face. He was guessing her thoughts, measuring her resistance.

He finished chewing and swallowed. He turned away briefly and put something else from the bag in his mouth. Then he leaned slowly forward until his face was directly above hers.

His eyes twinkled. In that instant he reminded her of the cat that had swallowed the canary.

Suddenly he grabbed Susan's jaw between his thumb and fingers and squeezed her mouth open. His face came closer. She saw his tongue hang out, and on it a thing that made nausea crash inside her like an earthquake.

Before she could scream it dropped into her mouth.

She gagged. Her eyes were open wide. Her body went rigid.

"Swallow it!" Haze snarled. "Swallow it, do you hear? Swallow it or I'll kill you now!"

Susan passed out.

46

DAVID GOLD sat watching Tom Castaneda doodle on his legal pad with an ancient red ballpoint pen. The cap had been deformed by repeated chewing, Gold noticed. An artifact of Castaneda's long struggle to give up cigarettes. Several opened packs of chewing gum, strewn over the desktop, bore witness to the same thing.

"It was my fault," Gold said.

"What?" Castaneda looked up.

"Playing it solo. Showing her that stuff without telling you or the other guys."

"You mean the mold, and the ransom note?"

Gold nodded.

Castaneda shrugged. "You thought you had a better chance that way. I can see that."

There was veiled disapproval in his tone. It is anathema for any law-enforcement officer to pursue a line of evidence without informing his colleagues. Cooperation is the essence of police work, especially where issues of life and death are at stake.

"I never figured on the brother springing her," Gold said. "And holding out on me. Christ, he's a stubborn bastard." He felt himself slipping into profanity from accumulated frustration. He could not stop himself.

"Maybe some good will come out of it," Castaneda said, sliding one of the packages of gum across the blotter like a hockey puck. "Maybe she'll find out what we couldn't."

"If she tells us," Gold said. "If she lives that long."

He shook his head. "I should have known, when she told me the boy was alive. I should have realized she was getting more than just that. I took her at her word. Stupid. I know her better than anyone else around here."

"Don't torture yourself," Castaneda said without conviction.

"I'm too close to this case," Gold said. "I should have taken myself off. The kid is like a son to me. I'm off my game."

Castaneda said nothing. The truth of Gold's self-reproach was too obvious to deny. He was not himself lately. Castaneda had never seen his colleague so emotional.

The phone rang. "Yeah," said Castaneda into the receiver. After a moment he held it out to Gold. "It's for you."

Gold took the phone. It was one of the detectives in Susan's apartment. They had been talking to Quentin in Gold's absence.

"Anything new?" Gold asked.

"He won't budge." The detective sounded tired.

"I'm coming back over in a few minutes," Gold said. "I'll see what I can do. Did you find her car yet?"

He turned red as he listened to the reply. Castaneda, watching him, raised an eyebrow.

"You didn't?" Gold said into the phone. "Why the hell not?"

He listened for a moment, then shouted, "Well, do it now, for Christ's sake!"

He slammed down the phone and looked at Castaneda. "They didn't put out an APB on her car," he said.

Castaneda gave him a neutral look. "Didn't you tell them to?"

Gold grimaced. "I thought I did. I must have forgotten. And they didn't think of it for themselves. Goddamn it. No wonder the politicians say we don't do our jobs."

Gold swept out of the office without another word. Castaneda slowly removed a stick of Doublemint from the package and fiddled with the wrapper.

"Too close to the case," he murmured, watching the dust swirl in the vacuum left by David Gold's anger.

47

SUSAN AWOKE TO a splitting headache.

She was disoriented. In all her life she had only experienced unconsciousness a handful of times. Now, at the hands of Arnold Haze, she had experienced it twice in two days. First through concussion and then through shock.

Her joints were stiff. Her body ached. Cramplike pains went through her stomach in slow waves. She realized she was dehydrated.

Haze came in bearing a large tumbler of water with a straw.

"You must be thirsty," he said. "Drink this."

She drank greedily. The rush of liquid made the cramps in her stomach worse, but she felt something like strength returning to her.

"This is your son's favorite glass," Haze said.

Susan looked at the tumbler. The face of Scottie Pippen smiled at her.

"Perhaps I'll let him take it home as a souvenir," Haze said.

Now Susan became aware of her hunger. It came to her as a throb of confusion in her mind. The room seemed to recede slightly. She was weaker than she had realized.

Haze put the tumbler aside and looked down at her.

"Where were we?" he asked. "Oh, yes. How old were you when the gift came?"

Susan was silent for a long moment before replying. "Ten."

"Ten!" Haze raised an eyebrow. "So small. It must have seemed very strange."

Susan let her eyes wander past his face to the corners of the room, the ceiling. She had to make an effort to keep the image still.

"A lot of things were strange then," she said. "The second sight was less disturbing than some of the other things."

"Such as?"

"The deaths of my parents. Being an orphan." She thought for a moment. "Then puberty."

He nodded, studying her. She seemed vulnerable and waiflike in her nudity. But he was aware of her depth. He had felt it pursuing him these past weeks. She was someone to be reckoned with.

"Tell me," he asked. "How did this affect your marriage?"

"I don't know what you mean."

"How did your husband cope with the fact that you could see things he couldn't? That you knew so many things. Private things."

Susan smiled sadly. "That wasn't a problem. The flaw in our marriage had nothing to do with second sight."

"Ah." He nodded. "But men in general, though—it must be a two-edged sword. I would imagine it makes them quite uncomfortable. Your gift. On the other hand, it seems to me that a red-blooded man would be excited by it. Turned on by it. Am I right?"

Susan knew where he was going. He was subtle, but her years of psychiatry had given her insight into manipulative behavior.

"To some extent," she replied in a neutral voice.

"Ah!" he exclaimed. "You're very honest. I knew you were a woman of substance. I can see I'll have to be careful around you."

He crossed his arms. As he sat on the edge of the bed, he looked rather like a physician, Susan thought.

"And as a therapist," he pursued. "It must give you an advantage. I imagine you find certain answers more quickly than another psychiatrist would."

She looked up at him. "Sometimes."

"Sometimes?"

"The technique we learn gives us the important answers," she said. "And then there are certain mysteries we never penetrate. The mind isn't as transparent as all that."

"You're modest," he said. "That's a good quality. But you shouldn't push it too far."

He leaned over her. "Tell me. Can you feel what I'm thinking right now? Right this moment?"

His face loomed in front of her, blocking out the room. The tiny eyes were only inches from her own. The smell was overpowering.

He touched her bound hand. A sliver of light appeared inside her mind and began to widen slowly. She kept her eyes on his, sensing that this was the moment to stand up to him. She had seen everything, not only through her second sight but in her medical practice. Few of the horrors the mind could conceive were foreign to her.

The shaft of light widened further. A sunny day, a child. A sandbox with a little red truck in it. The child smiling up as a shadow fell . . .

Revulsion made Susan gasp as she saw what he wanted her to see. She fought to keep her eyes fixed on his, but in the end she looked away.

He was smiling. "Well, you've got me convinced. They say second sight is a fraud, but I believe in you, Doctor."

Susan had not thrown up since the beginning of her pregnancy with Michael. She needed to throw up now. But somehow she held it in.

He got up and stood at the end of the bed.

"Let's talk about the future," he said. "As I say, the son of a famous psychic approximately equals the daughter of a famous civil rights leader. Provided, that is, that the correct spin is put on the story."

Susan was listening carefully. This was the moment she had been waiting for.

He petted her hand paternally. "The desired denouement is obvious," he said. "Your son is restored to you. In return, I go about my business, a free man without fear of extradition or reprisal. Peter Tomerakian's case died with Peter. The murders of the girls are a closed book, a piece of history. Miss Lazarus is safe, and that's the important thing. Such is my plan. The plan most satisfactory to all parties."

Susan nodded, relieved by his reference to Michael.

"Our problem is that I now have both the hostage and his mother," Haze said. "There is no one for me to release your handsome son to. No one for me to send my next ransom note to. A ridiculous predicament, but real nonetheless. Do you see?"

Susan thought for a moment.

"Why don't you let Michael go," she asked, "and keep me instead?"

Haze smiled pityingly. "A mother's brave plea," he said. "That makes a story, doesn't it? But it won't work, Doctor. Right now I have the Lindbergh baby, and that's the best story in town. The police will deal to get the boy back. They'll pay whatever I ask. But you're just a woman. They would happily let me kill you if they thought it would give them a chance to bring me to justice."

Susan saw the wisdom of these words. She could not help clinging to them, for they indicated that Haze still had a stake in keeping Michael alive.

"What will you do, then?" she asked.

"What do you suggest?"

Susan struggled to make her mind work efficiently. She was blinded by her concern for Michael.

"I don't know," she said at last.

"Well, I can deal on the basis that I have both of you,"

Haze offered. "That makes a good story, too. Not quite as strong as the Lindbergh angle, but fairly strong."

Susan was silent.

And he can kill us both, she thought.

"Ah-ah," Haze interrupted her. "I know what you're thinking. No, Doctor. I still need a hostage. I'm not so arrogant as to think that after everything that has happened, I can just walk away. No, I won't make it unless I have something to trade."

He paused, letting her think it over.

"And what good is a small boy," he asked, "without a mother to restore him to?"

His logic was sound. Yet Susan could not see where it was leading.

"Where is my son?" she asked, tears welling in her eyes.

Haze nodded acknowledgment. "See what I mean?" he asked. "This is the story, Susan. You and your boy. Everyone wants to see how it is going to end. I can't let them down."

He smiled. "And he is a beautiful boy. You must be very proud of him. So sweet and thoughtful. More than once in recent days it has been he who lifted my spirits, rather than the reverse."

Susan's tears flowed down her cheeks. She wanted so much to be clever. But her love for Michael crowded rational thought from her mind.

"Where is he?" she gasped. "I want to see him."

"That is impossible," he said. "You ought to know that. But I have brought something along to ease your mind."

He stood up, crossed to the kitchen, and returned. He held out a large piece of paper torn from a drawing pad.

"Can you see all right in this light?" he asked.

Painfully Susan raised her head from the pillow. Haze was displaying a drawing in crayon. It showed a woman holding the hand of a child. A tall building was in the background, and behind it a cityscape. Susan recognized Michael's drawing style immediately. The strokes were childish but filled with an imaginative yearning, as though he wanted very much to be able to evoke things that were not yet within his powers.

The building was her apartment building; the cityscape included the dark John Hancock Building, narrowing toward the two enormous antennas at its top. The woman was Susan, as her short skirt and brown hair made clear. Surprisingly, Michael had managed to capture something about her posture that was strikingly recognizable. A sort of diffidence that softened her competent maternal exterior.

Susan's eyes filled with tears. Her hands twisted in their bonds, eager to touch the paper.

"Look at the signature," Haze said.

The name MICHAEL was written at the bottom of the page. Alongside it were the mysterious words DALEY TO LOBBY DEMS.

"What does it mean?" Susan asked.

"That is the headline of today's *Sun-Times*," Haze said.

Susan understood. The handwriting was clearly Michael's. Haze was proving to her that, for today at least, her son was alive.

"Please," she asked. "Let me touch it."

Haze came to her side. He let her clutch the drawing in a trembling hand.

"So you see," he said. "My own resourcefulness is at your service. I have not sought to make things easier for myself by punishing you. I give you proof that your son is alive."

"Thank you." Her voice was very small.

"And so you must help me," Haze said.

"How?"

He gave her a long, slow look. "I'm going to let you think about that for a while," he said.

Pulling the drawing out of her hand, he took it and left the room.

48

DALEY TO LOBBY DEMS

THE NEWSPAPER SAT unread on the desk in front of David Gold.

He was in the tiny office located between his kitchen and the garage. The desk had come from a garage sale. The wooden swivel chair, whose base was temperamental, had been bought at Goodwill Industries during the first year of his marriage. He had put together the metal bookcases himself.

The only decoration on the walls was the Chicago Symphony's yearly calendar. The color photograph showed the string section. Carol was clearly visible in the foreground, along with a dozen other violists. Gold never turned the page but pasted the new months under this picture one by one.

He had come home to get a half hour's peace, and to think. So far he wasn't doing very well. He could hear his daughters arguing in the kitchen. Josie, the older one, was browbeating Alissa over something at school.

Sometimes he wished the girls didn't go to the same school. They were jealous of each other's friends. As they neared puberty they got more strident in their competition. Gold would often come home after an exhausting day and find himself eating his supper in the midst of an explosive quarrel, with Carol trying unsuccessfully to calm the girls after her own hard day of rehearsals. David suspected that his daughters' frenetic fights were designed as a competi-

331

tion for their busy mother's attention. He did not know how to smooth things over, because his attempts at intervention only made them turn on him with redoubled resentment.

He would just have to wait until they got older, he mused He was only a cop—not a psychologist.

Susan had a way with them. Every time she came over for dinner, or even for a drink, they turned into little angels. They would show her their rooms, their school projects, tell her about their boyfriends, in a perfectly civilized and ladylike way. They even seemed to compete in good behavior, to impress her.

It was a lucky thing that Carol was not the jealous type. She joked with Susan about the sweetness she brought out in the girls. "Can't you take them for the summer or something?" she would ask. Susan would reply tactfully, "Their good behavior would vanish quickly enough if I was the responsible one."

Carol liked Susan. As a Jewish girl from Skokie who had spent most of her life around other Jewish girls, Carol found Susan exotic and fascinating. Like David himself, Carol saw something Jewish in Susan, something sad and exiled and determined. It harmonized oddly with Susan's *shiksa* looks, her Presbyterian background, her country relatives. Often Gold would look at them together and feel as though two different species of Jewish girls had come into his life, one familiar and understandable, the other foreign. Interestingly enough, he had never felt a desire to visit the Holy Land until he met Susan. He found himself joking with her about making a trip there together. Though he could not understand why, the idea intrigued him.

There was something Jewish about Susan's second sight, he felt. He had never told her this, had not even thought it through for himself. It was part of her charm— the gift she did not want to have, the insight she would have shunned had she had the choice.

Once, in a weak moment, she had confessed to him that her gift connected her to spiritual things, though she re-

fused to discuss it in any more detail. This had amazed
Gold, for Susan was as skeptical as anyone he had ever
met. Her faith went against the grain of her own character,
but she made room for it in herself anyway, like a foreign
body she lacked the heart to banish. There was something
Jewish about this too, Gold thought.

The girls were getting louder. Gold stood up to tell them
to be quiet. The phone rang, stopping him in his tracks.

"Gold here."

"Detective Gold? This is Pete Juarez. Remember me?
From Traffic?"

"Pete! Sure. How you doing?"

"Listen. You had an APB on a '93 Toyota, didn't you? I
found it for you."

"Already? Way to go. Where is it?"

"Uptown. Not ten minutes from your office."

"What's the address?"

Gold wrote hastily on a piece of scrap paper as Juarez
gave him the address.

"Want me to pick you up?" Juarez asked.

"I'll meet you there."

Afer pocketing the piece of paper, Gold swept out of the
house without a word to his daughters.

MANY HOURS HAD passed. Susan was weak from hunger,
and her thoughts had been racing all this time. The silence
of the past few hours had seemed nocturnal. There was
light in the cracks around the windows. She guessed it was
morning.

The door opened. Arnold Haze came into the bedroom "Hungry?" he asked.

Susan said nothing. She wondered whether she had only moments to live. She was convinced that if she and Michael were both to die, Haze would kill her first. He would keep Michael alive until he was sure he was of no further use.

Haze stood at the end of the bed, looking down at her. He guessed her thoughts.

"Stop worrying," he said. "Everything is going according to plan. They're negotiating for you now. They're stalling, of course. Trying to get a fix on me. Such childish manipulations. But one has to let them save face."

He studied Susan's naked body.

"Do you need to go to the bathroom?" he asked.

She shook her head. Then she wished she had said yes. Every transaction that took place between herself and Haze implied some sort of alliance, however frail. As such it might increase her chances of staying alive.

"Do I have to lie here like this?" she asked.

"Do you mean naked?" he asked.

She nodded.

"I'm afraid so," he said. "It's a precaution."

"What about Michael?" Susan asked. "Have you got him tied up this way too?" For an instant she recalled her nightmare vision of Michael trapped naked in a strange place. She almost gasped aloud.

"On the contrary," Haze said. "He's fully dressed and playing with a rather expensive collection of video games. In a location far from here, I might add. You see how your arrival upset my arrangements." He smiled. "I should send you a bill when this is all over. Accommodations, breakfast cereal, baked potatoes . . ."

"Did you make him baked potatoes?" Susan could not suppress the thrill of recognition that sounded in her voice.

"I certainly did. Bacon bits, cheddar cheese, sour cream—the entire treatment." Haze smiled. "I worked my fingers to the bone."

Susan could not help feeling comforted by his words. In some small way he had tried to please Michael. There was a grain of humanity in Haze.

"Thank you," she said.

"You're welcome," he said. "Now, let's get back to business. During your sleep I had time to think things over, and I've decided on a course of action. I'm going to let you go and keep the boy."

Susan felt no relief hearing this. It seemed to her that as Haze's prisoner she was in some way connected to Michael. If Haze let her go she would revert to the hellish alienation from her son that she had endured when she did not know where he was.

"Why not let Michael go and keep me?" she volunteered desperately.

Haze shook his head.

"I'm afraid your fatigue and hunger are going to your head. We already discussed that option, don't you remember? A boy in the hand is worth ten adults."

Susan lay back against the bed. "Yes."

"Good. Your release will accomplish several ends at once. For instance, it shows my good faith to the authorities. It proves that I am willing to trade for my freedom. That forces them to take the idea of a deal more seriously. Particularly once the press finds out you have been released unharmed."

Susan looked at him. She could not deny the correctness of this logic.

"Second," Haze went on, "in freeing you I gain for myself an ally on the outside. You will know I have the boy. You already know what my overall plan is—freedom in a safe place in exchange for your son. You will of course be motivated to make this plan a success. You will do whatever is necessary to ensure that the police and FBI keep their promises to me."

Susan did not know what to say to this.

"I can impose conditions to improve the chances of this plan," he added. "For instance, once you are free I will deal

only with you. All arrangements will be made through you
In the end, the boy will be turned over to you personally, in
a safe place and under conditions arranged with you. Do
you follow my drift?"

Susan nodded.

"I can also ascertain whether you are keeping your part
of the bargain," he said. "Do you doubt that?"

She shook her head. The time for underestimating Haze
was long past. If he could kidnap her son under the noses
of a hundred witnesses and a crew of airline personnel, he
could do whatever he wished.

Haze was removing a syringe from a small bag.

"What's that?" Susan asked.

"There's no time like the present," he said, pushing the
syringe into a tiny bottle filled with colorless liquid.

50

DAVID GOLD drove along the east-west streets with no re-
gard for the caked ice under his wheels or the cars parked
in crowded ranks on either side. When he came to a stop
sign, he hit the siren and drove right through. It was one of
those late winter days when the sun beat angrily on the
housetops but could not penetrate to the icy pavement because of the shadows of the roofs. Dirty piles of snow
lined the curbs, relics of the storm.

He screeched to a stop on a narrow street among old
brick apartment buildings. The neighborhood had slipped
badly in the past twenty years or so. Graffiti testified to the
presence of gangs, and flat tires on some of the parked cars
bespoke vandalism and decay.

A police car was squeezed among the parked cars, its light blinking. Pete Juarez was standing alongside it, his breath visible in clouds of steam in the frigid air.

"Pete," Gold said, shaking his hand. "Thanks for calling."

Juarez gestured to the green Toyota, which was double-parked near the corner. Gold recognized the license number, 3X3 Y4F, immediately.

"Door's unlocked," he said. "Not a good idea in this neighborhood. She must have been in a hurry."

Gold had jerked open the door and sat down in the front seat. His long legs were cruelly squeezed by the position of the seat, but he did not change it. For all he knew, the car might be part of a crime scene.

"No keys," he said.

Juarez nodded. He glanced at the rows of parked cars crowding the street.

"Lucky she didn't find a space," he said. "It was easier to find it this way."

The Toyota was frozen solid. Gold's breath was already clouding the inside of the windshield. Still, in this cold there was no telling how long the car had been here.

Gold went back to his own car and got on the radio.

"This is Gold," he told the dispatcher. "I've got the green Toyota. Patch me through to Homicide. We have a probable hostage situation. I'll need teams to go door-to-door."

After he got off the radio he returned to Susan's car. He gave the driver's seat a long look, then the passenger's seat. "Goddamn it," he murmured.

He tried the glove compartment. It was unlocked. Inside there was a can of lock de-icer, the car's manual, and a pair of leather gloves, which he recognized easily.

He was about to get out of the car again when he noticed the ashtray. It was closed. Susan had not smoked in years. To his knowledge no one had ever smoked in this car. He opened the ashtray anyway.

Curled inside was a Post-it note in pencil. Gold pulled it out and looked at it.

1485 Apt. C, it read.

Gold banged his head on the doorframe as he stood back. "Shit." Pete Juarez was watching him in silence. Gold stood rubbing his head and glancing quickly at the sad old buildings lining the street.

"Come with me," he said.

"You called backup, didn't you?"

"We're not waiting for any backup," Gold said, pulling out his gun. "Let's go."

51

"WHAT ARE YOU going to give me?" Susan asked.

"Sodium amytal," Haze said: "0.25 grams. You're fairly small. It should be more than enough."

Susan could not deny he had made a humane choice. Sodium amytal given intravenously or intramuscularly is powerful enough to subdue agitated and combative patients but has no significant side effects. She would wake up a few hours hence with a hangover and perhaps a headache.

Haze came to her side. "Now be a good girl. This won't hurt a bit."

It occurred to Susan that this might be her final experience on earth, this injection at the hands of a criminal who had lulled her with his story of putting her to sleep. The syringe might contain a larger dose of sodium amytal, enough to cause respiratory depression and death. Or, obviously, some other, more immediately lethal drug, like cyanide.

He swabbed her arm with alcohol. His left hand squeezed her triceps.

"That's good," he said. "You've got good veins."

The touch of his fingers sent an alarm signal through her. She realized the danger was coming from another direction.

I was never one for the fair sex.

She thought of Michael. In less than a minute she would be unconscious, completely unable to help her son. And now it occurred to her that Michael was in danger of something perhaps worse than death.

"Wait," she said.

Haze looked down at her, the syringe in his hand.

"Don't do it," she said.

"What do you mean?" he asked.

"Please." Tears welled in her eyes. "Please—spare him. Do me that one favor."

Haze seemed interested. "Whatever do you mean?"

She sighed. "You know what I mean."

Haze hesitated, watching her weep. Then, slowly, he touched a finger to one of her tears. He brought the moistened finger to his lips and sucked it pensively.

"Just supposing that I do know what you mean," he asked, "what are you suggesting?"

"You can have me," she said. "You said you found me attractive."

Haze seemed intrigued by her desperation. He touched his moistened finger to her nipple. The skin crawled under his touch.

"Another quid pro quo?" he asked. "Take me, not him? Is that it?"

Susan nodded, tears flowing down her cheeks.

"A brave mother's plea," he murmured.

"Please!" She was breathing hard. He could see both her disgust and her resolve to overcome it.

"You heard what I said before," he reminded her.

"Nevertheless," she said. And on a desperate impulse she added, "I can—do things, for you."

Haze studied her for a long moment. Then he stood up and put away the syringe.

He returned to her side. Despite her tangled hair, she was beautiful in her nudity. Her small, shapely legs, her flat stomach, the delicate bones and firm little breasts. When he first took her clothes off he had noticed the girlish look of her. But it was alloyed with something very womanly, very maternal.

"Well, now," he said.

He came to her side. She was trembling. He bent to kiss her foot.

"Pretty toes," he said.

He stood up, holding on to both her ankles. He squeezed them slightly. He looked at her legs, pulled wide apart by her bonds.

"The sexy psychic."

He ran a finger up the inside of her thigh. When it found her sex he rubbed gently at her pubic hair.

"Don't you have to go to the bathroom?" he asked. "It's been a long time."

She said nothing. He found her clitoris and stroked it.

"Number one?" he asked. "Just a little?"

He played with the clitoris for a moment. Then he pushed his finger lower. She could feel him getting excited.

"Your little boy came from here," he said, pushing apart the vaginal lips. *"Inter urinas et faeces nascimur."*

He held the finger to his lips, tasting it as if it were wine being offered by a sommelier. Then he applied it to her crotch again, probing. She felt a sharp pain.

He paused, an evaluative smile on his face.

"The mother instead of the son," he said. "Isn't that somewhere in Krafft-Ebing? Or Havelock Ellis?"

He loosened his belt. His trousers came down. The smell of him grew overpowering as more of his skin was bared.

"This is where he came from, isn't it?" he asked, studying her. "The beautiful boy . . ."

His underpants came down. Susan saw a small penis between his legs.

She caught a sharp look in his eyes. Perhaps he had seen her looking at him. In any case, he seemed to reconsider.

"No," he said. "I don't think so."

She could feel his aversion to the female sexual parts. She also suspected he had only been taunting her up to now. In rejecting her he wanted to make her think about what was really in his mind.

"Abandon hope, all ye who enter here." He was about to turn away. Desperate, she tried to think of something to hold him with.

As he bent to pull up his underpants, a voice came to her rescue. It was not her own.

"Sleepy," she said.

Haze looked at her. "What did you say?"

"Sleepy. Grumpy. Which dwarf are you today?" The voice was knowing, mocking. She saw a woman bathing a little boy. The woman was smiling.

"What?" Haze had turned pale.

"Sleepy. Grumpy." The woman reached between the boy's legs. Susan was looking up at Haze. She felt the woman's smile on her own lips.

"Or are you Bashful today? Shall I call you Bashful?"

Now it was Haze's turn to tremble.

"Bitch," he said. "You bitch."

He put his hand between her legs.

"Perhaps I need to teach you a lesson after all," he said.

Susan was aware she had won a victory over him. But he knew it too. He might kill her for that reason alone. And that would leave him a free hand with Michael.

"This is what he will feel," he said, pushing his finger into her. "Just what you're feeling."

The finger pushed deeper.

"Does it hurt?" he asked.

He felt her panic. He smiled. He looked down at his penis, which was erect now.

"All right," he said. "You've got me convinced. But we'll have to turn you over on your tummy, won't we?"

He began to untie her hand. She lay inert, tears welling in her eyes.

"Please . . . ," she said.

Haze shook his head. "Too late, I'm afraid. You shouldn't have provoked me."

The knot came undone. His fingers were trembling in his excitement.

"A pretty girl is like a melody . . ."

He reached for Susan's wrist. "Only one moment more . . ."

In that instant her hand darted forward, the thumb held rigid. Before he could react it plunged into his left eye socket, tearing at the ligaments and displacing the eyeball.

He screamed. His hands both went to his face.

"Bitch . . ."

He leaned back reflexively, his hands over his eyes. Blood was already streaming through his fingers.

"Bitch . . ." In that instant his voice sounded oddly young, like a boy crying after being struck in the face. But he was recovering his physical composure. He slumped forward, keeping his weight over Susan's body.

"Now you've done it," he said. "Now you've done it."

He felt for her throat with a trembling hand. The fingers fluttered over her breasts, leaving a smear of blood in their passage.

Susan thrashed this way and that, her knees bumping against Haze's torso. But she was bound too tightly to do any damage. Hot drops of blood fell on her naked stomach as he moved atop her. He was breathing hard.

"You've killed him now," he said. "Your precious son . . ."

He clawed at her face. Long fingernails scored her cheek. Rage and pain were making him imprecise, but she knew he had the advantage. In another moment he would overpower her.

"Bitch . . ." His hand found her throat and closed around it. He shook her, banging her head against the pillow. He was incredibly strong.

Dazed by the shocks to her head, Susan saw two Hazes hovering ghostlike before her eyes. She felt herself begin to wilt under his power. Like a prey in the grasp of the predator, her body was giving up.

No! She fought her way back to lucidity and remembered her free hand. She found his carotid sinus and pressed hard. Sensing what she was up to, Haze tried to grab her wrist. He was too late.

She had seen it done only once, by an orderly in a state hospital. Steady pressure on the carotid sinus would cause an abortive grand mal seizure. It was a cruel way to immobilize a violent patient. In the old days it was commonly done by orderlies who didn't want to wait for straitjackets. Today it was grounds for imprisonment.

Already Haze's muscles were losing their tone. Susan squeezed harder. He gave her a long look of hatred and frustration, blood flowing from his damaged eye.

Then the seizure hit, throwing him into convulsions. He slumped atop her, his arms jerking spasmodically.

She pushed him off her and reached to untie her other hand. He lay on the floor, his respiration stertorous. There was no need to fear him now.

It took her a long time, it seemed, to loosen the knot. Her own hands were shaking now. She broke a fingernail, but the cord finally came undone.

She undid the knots at her ankles and squirmed off the bed. She tried to stand up, but her legs collapsed under her. She lay on the carpet beside Haze, struggling to get control of her feet. She dared to look at his left eye. The eyeball protruded oddly from the orbit, the black, pebblelike iris visible as blood flowed down his cheek.

Finally she got up and staggered to the door.

She opened it and entered a small kitchen. The old cabinets were buried under a hundred coats of whitewash. Some of them had glass panes behind which empty shelves were visible.

Two doors were in front of her. Both had keys in the locks. She tried the first one. It opened into the hall. She glanced to left and right. There was a staircase and a tiny elevator.

She closed it and tried the other door. It opened to reveal Michael, tied hand and foot on a small bed, a large piece of duct tape over his mouth.

Oblivious to her nudity, Susan rushed to his side.

"It's all right now," she said. "It's all right, sweetie."

She gave him a single frantic hug. Then she fumbled with the knots. She hesitated to rip off the tape, for fear of hurting him.

"I missed you so much," she said. "I missed you so much."

His hands came free. Instantly he wrapped his arms around her neck and hugged her hard.

"Darling," she said. "My sweet Michael."

She had trouble getting him to let go long enough for her to free his feet. His face was pale, tearstained.

"You're all right now," she repeated. "Everything is going to be fine. You're getting out of here, right now."

His legs were free. He nestled in her arms. She felt something strange inside her, like a crack widening in the wall of a dam. It seemed to come from a long time ago, a slow thing that was now speeding up to a climax. Frightened, she pushed it back and held fast to her son.

She was picking delicately at the tape over the boy's mouth as a knock came at the apartment door.

"Police! Open up!"

She staggered to her feet, holding Michael in her arms.

"Susan! Are you in there?"

It was the voice of David Gold, sounding like the conscience of the world announcing its return after a long absence.

Epilogue

"LET HIM GO! Come on, Michael. Come with me."

Josie Gold had Michael by both hands and was pulling him toward her room. Her sister was holding tight to his waist.

"No way. He's staying here."

The girls pulled him this way and that. Michael looked like a rag doll, his face expressing amusement and patience as he waited to see who would be stronger.

"Girls," Carol called out. "Be nice. Michael is your guest."

The hubbub ebbed to bearable proportions as the three children returned to the living room. Carol smiled at Susan.

"You know," she said, "these two may be fighting over him in another way someday. Either one of them would give her eyeteeth to marry him when he grows up."

"Do you really think so?" Susan asked.

"Sure. Haven't you seen the way they look at him?"

Susan had to admit that there was something touchingly romantic about the way the girls doted on Michael. Each in her own way was deeply attached to him. Josie, the more mercurial, seemed to surround him like a possessive mother. Alissa, the shyer, related to him in a more diffident and admiring way. Susan could not predict what sort of man Michael would be when he grew up. Perhaps her own divided personality, which paid tribute both to inner passion and to the duty of control, would leave its mark on him. Nick, too, was a person who needed to feel in control.

And David Gold, Michael's surrogate father, was a man who never allowed his sensitivity full sway; he remained always on guard against chaos and violence. Perhaps even he would mark Michael by his example.

"Well, we'll see," Susan said. She looked at Michael, who was listening dutifully to Josie's instructions about the game they were to play. He had not changed. He was still the same Michael, always the diplomat. Susan thought of the ordeal he had been through, and his reticence in talking about it. "It wasn't so bad," he had told her, with the obvious intention of sparing her feelings. "I missed you. That was all."

The strength of children never ceased to amaze her. Children endure horrors that would drive an adult into insanity and emerge with their little shoulders squared and their minds as open as ever, still hungry for experience.

She heard David Gold's voice from the kitchen.

"Michael! Come here a minute. I want to show you something."

Michael went to the kitchen, the girls trailing behind him. Gold, holding up a spatula, gestured to the platter of meat on the counter. Though summer was still a long way off, today's meal was to be picnic food, with hamburgers and hot dogs, potato salad, baked beans, and lots of ice cream for the children.

Susan smiled. Surprisingly, she felt neither closer to Gold nor further away, despite all they had gone through together. It was Gold who had believed in her when everyone else had given up on her. Gold who had arrived to rescue her when she needed him most. But now the world had reverted to its familiar self, and David was just a man, overworked and not entirely equal to life. That was precisely his charm, Susan reflected.

David handed the spatula to Michael. The murmurs of the girls' voices gave a lazy feel to the darkening afternoon.

The world was indeed showing its sanest face nowadays. The snowstorm had been winter's last gasp, and ice was rapidly melting all over the city. Potholes were crumpling the streets, and drivers were swearing at the city's slowness to fill them, but spring was in the air and Chicagoans were grateful.

Last night Susan and Michael had dined at the home of Aaron Lazarus. Susan had spent a pleasant evening talking with the Lazaruses about the surprising number of people they knew in common, while Michael, clearly under the spell of Jaime's beauty, had been lavishly entertained by her.

The whole truth about Susan's role in the arrest of Arnold Haze was now known, and her notoriety had reached unmanageable proportions. Her face had made the cover of all the national magazines, and a dozen books were being written about the Tomerakian case, the Coed Murders, and the ultimate arrest of Arnold Haze.

"Now you know what it's like to be a hero," Aaron Lazarus told her.

"I'll take anonymity every time," Susan said.

"You and me both. What can be worse than being admired by total strangers?" Lazarus was sincere in what he said, but Susan knew that he viewed the situation differently than she did. Heroism was a life's work to him, and notoriety was one of the weapons he used to make changes in the world. He had long since given up on a truly private life. Susan herself still held out hope for one.

She believed the hubbub would die down after a while. Arnold Haze was under armed guard in the Cook County Jail. Surgery had been performed unsuccessfully on his injured eye. The optic nerve was damaged, and the eye could not be saved.

"He won't be needing it where he's going," David Gold had said. Charges had been filed against Haze for six murders. He would almost certainly get the death penalty, but since few executions were being carried out in Illinois, he would no doubt end up on death row at one of the maximum-security prisons.

Susan would have to testify against Haze. She looked forward to it, not for the ordeal it would undoubtedly present but for the symbolic turning of the final page on the tragic case it represented. And, she hoped, for an end to her tenure in the limelight.

Nick and Elaine were still here in town, waiting to take Michael back to California. Understandably, neither of them had the courage to let Michael fly alone again. Susan and Michael had shown them around the city, with Michael proudly pointing out the sights from the top of the Hancock Building.

Nick had offered to let Michael stay awhile longer, but Susan was eager for him to get back to normal living.

"Why don't you take him for a vacation when things settle down?" Nick suggested. "Go to the Bahamas, or Florida. Or New Orleans. It will be warm down there in a few weeks."

Susan squeezed his hand. "Thanks, Nick," she said. It was typical of Nick to think of her even when he was so eager to take his son home.

Quentin had left town not long after Nick and Elaine arrived. Susan suspected she might not see him again for years. But he had sent a postcard from Atlanta bearing a team picture of the Braves. So he had not forgotten his promise to Michael, she thought.

Ron Giordano had called repeatedly in recent days to see how Susan was doing. Tomorrow night she was to keep her long-postponed dinner date with him.

Yes, things were settling down. Susan doubted she would allow herself to be convinced to work on a case with the police any time soon. She needed to put her practice back together and get back to work on her writing. She wished she could silence her psychic gift for the duration, but she knew that was impossible. The countless voices she heard, the faces she saw, were a permanent part of her world. They offered neither final truth nor peace of mind. They were part of the challenge of living. She was long since used to them.

She looked at Carol Gold. A bright, interesting woman with a sense of humor about her own struggles as well as those of her husband and daughters, Carol had become a close friend.

"So tell me," Susan said. "What are you working on?"

Carol smiled. "Actually, I'm into something good. They're assembling a chamber group to record Mozart's string quintets for a label in Europe. I auditioned for it two weeks ago. It's down to me and two other violists from the CSO."

"Congratulations," Susan said.

"It would mean recording in Belgium," Carol said. "Do you know anything about Belgium?"

"Not a thing."

"Well, I'll get Dave to take me. He needs to widen his horizons anyway."

David Gold's profession did not allow him many trips to see his wife perform on tour with the Chicago Symphony. But he went to all the concerts he could when the orchestra was in town. Though he complained bitterly about Carol's long hours of rehearsal, he was enormously proud of her work. He liked to chaff her by claiming that he could pick out the sound of her viola in the orchestra's recordings.

"What about you?" Carol asked.

"I'm going to take it easy for a while," Susan said. "Or at least try to."

David Gold came into the room.

"Your son is a mean short-order cook," he said. "You know, they say all the best chefs are men."

Michael was behind him in the doorway. Gold had fashioned a makeshift apron for him out of one of his old Chicago PD sweatshirts. AREA SIX VIOLENT CRIMES, read the large black logo. Michael's eyes shone with pride. His smiling face showed no trace of what he had suffered so recently. Susan felt a pang of retrospective anguish as she contemplated him.

David read her thoughts easily.

"Yeah, he's a *mensch*," he said. "I always knew that."

And he winked at Susan, who smiled at the word that was David Gold's highest compliment.

By general consent "the case" was not mentioned during dinner. Susan and Michael returned home at eight. They watched a last rented movie, *The Wind in the Willows*. Susan made Michael popcorn and a pizza, conscious that she was piling on his favorite pleasures as though to deny his departure.

They did not do much talking in the course of the evening, but when Susan came in to kiss him good night Michael wanted to talk. He told her all about his conversations with the Gold girls and their plans for the summer. And he talked about *The Wind in the Willows*. He was eager to read the book. Though it was a little old for him, he was determined to try.

"Mom, is Mr. Toad the same in the book as he was in the movie?" he asked.

"I think so, honey. Pretty much the same," Susan said. "He's good-hearted but very silly. He gets excited about one plan after the other, and always ends up in trouble. Rat and Mole have to bail him out."

"And Mr. Badger."

"Yes. Mr. Badger."

"I like Mr. Badger the best," Michael said. "I like his big house, with all the rooms, under the ground."

"So do I." Susan ran a hand through Michael's hair, reflecting that she herself was drawn to Mr. Badger as the fatherly figure who saves his friends from danger by his wisdom as well as his physical strength. The far-flung tunnels of the badger's warm home, which extend to all the corners of the Wild Wood, are like metaphors for his knowledge of the world, which knows solutions to all practical mysteries and offers safety and comfort at the darkest of times.

All her life Susan had been providing her own safety. The home she once took for granted was only a memory. She wondered if Michael, a child of divorce, had his own sense of exile. She wished he did not have to endure such a thing. But she respected him for enduring it so quietly.

"When Rat and Mole thought they were completely lost," she said, "they found the door to Mr. Badger's house hidden under the snow."

"Yes."

Michael was looking over Susan's shoulder at the picture on the wall, the one that showed Susan as a girl, holding her ice cream sandwich against the background of trees.

"Mom."

"Yes, honey?"

"Do you see the bird in the picture?"

Susan squinted to focus her nearsighted eyes on the photo in the shadows.

"Is there a bird?" she asked.

"Yes. He's in the branches right behind you."

Susan got up to look at the picture. Indeed, just to the left of the ice cream sandwich in her ten-year-old hand, a little bird was visible, perched in the branches of one of the trees behind the picnic table.

"So he is," she said. "You've got better eyes than I do."

There was a silence.

"Mom?" Michael said.

"Yes, sweetie."

"The birds that ate the crumbs when the children were lost in the wood. What kind of birds were they?"

Susan smiled. "I don't know, honey. Just birds."

The thought of Hansel and Gretel, with their vain search for safety, disturbed her. She wondered whether Michael was alluding to his own imprisonment at the hands of Arnold Haze.

Children, alas, are never free to be as innocent as they might be. Childhood is an obstacle course that can only be negotiated through a guile and wariness that do not come naturally to children. And adults, strong and cynical though they try to seem, are themselves still trying to find their way through a dark place without a trail to lead them.

Michael had left Susan a trail, and Susan had followed it. But who would leave those precious clues for Michael? Who would show him the way home?

Fatigue swept over Susan suddenly. With her hand on Michael's shoulder, she closed her eyes. Memory stirred inside her, on the borderline of dreams. She was in the state park with her brother, or rather on the little path that led into the campground from the road to town. Their sneakered feet slid across the floor of dry needles with a swishing sound. The lake was so near that she could almost feel it. She was walking fast, the ice cream in one hand and Quentin's hand in the other.

"Aren't we going to eat it?"

"Not till we get back."

"But it's going to melt!"

"It won't melt. You'll see."

They almost ran the last half mile. Mother was standing over the camp stove, saying something. Susan let go of Quentin's hand and gave him his ice cream sandwich. Then she hurried to the picnic table where her father was reading the paper. All day she had been thinking of eating her ice cream at her father's side. She had not bothered to explain that to Quentin.

"Is that ice cream? Did you get your brother some too?"

"Yes."

Daddy was distracted by something in the newspaper, but he petted her shoulder with his free hand.

Suddenly Mother was coming toward them with the camera.

"Don't you two make a picture. Wait one more second, Sukie. Just let me get this."

"Mom, it's going to melt!"

"No, it won't. Smile, now. Good girl."

Susan's eyes had opened in surprise. This was a memory she had sought countless times in vain to recapture. Now, of its own accord, it had come back to her.

She realized her eyes were misty. The memory was not

easy to bear, for it measured loss as well as history. No wonder Quentin refused to think about the past.

"Good girl."

Startled by the sound of the words, she looked down at Michael.

"What did you say?" she asked.

"Good girl." He smiled. "I said, *Good girl.*"

Susan's eyes opened wide. "Why did you say that?"

The boy shrugged. "I just did."

"No, but why?"

"I don't know." He smiled. "Maybe you looked like a good girl to me."

Susan turned pale. No one in the world knew those words. They came from a time that was gone forever.

Oh, no.

She took Michael's hand. Her fingers were trembling.

"Sweetie," she said. "When you were alone with the man, did you know I was going to come?"

He nodded. "Yes."

"Did you see me?"

"Yes. I saw you."

"I mean . . ." She cursed the ambiguity of her own questions, the frail borderline between second sight and love. "I mean, could you see me coming to find you?"

"Yes. I could see you."

Susan closed her eyes. She tried to think of a question that would evade the truth she didn't want to hear. But it was no use.

"Did you know what I was thinking about?" she asked. "When you were alone?"

There was a silence. She began to hope she had been wrong.

"The bird," Michael said suddenly. "The one in the porch. It couldn't get out. It flew this way and that way, but it kept hitting the screen. Is that it, Mom?"

Tears welled in Susan's eyes. "What bird?" she asked.

"In your house," he said. "You were there, too."

My God. He's got the gift.

She wiped at her eyes. She held Michael close, as though to protect him. She thought of the long years behind her, and the years ahead of him. It didn't seem fair. Her only dream for her son had been a peaceful, ordinary life. By carrying her own burden of secrets, she had hoped to set him free. Now it was too late even for that.

"But, Mom," he said. "It did get out. It flew away."

"Did it?" she asked. "Are you sure?"

"Yes. It flew up all at once, into the trees."

Susan heard an unearthly reassurance in his small voice. Despite herself she clung to it, as to a thing she had waited all her life to hear.

An image crossed her mind suddenly, come from nowhere. A little boy with his hands over his eyes, playing peekaboo. A girl gesturing desperately, but unseen, to warn him. And the boy's eyes, full of laughter and mischief, as though he did not need to see, for he already understood everything.

**If you enjoyed this novel,
try the thrillers of
Philip Luber and Gini Hartzmark.**

GINI HARTZMARK

Don't miss her Kate Milholland novels!

PRINCIPAL DEFENSE

FINAL OPTION

BITTER BUSINESS

FATAL REACTION

ROUGH TRADE

"When it comes to the legal thriller,
Gini Hartzmark's work is top of the line."
—LES ROBERTS

Published by Ivy Books.
Available at your local bookstore.